THE EMMA BOVARY OF BAILRIGG

THE EMMA BOVARY OF BAILRIGG

S. KADISON

*Poison of jealousy laps
the disappointed heart
Doubling its grievance.*
Aeschylus.

PENNILESS PRESS PUBLICATIONS
www.pennilesspress.co.uk/books

Published by
Penniless Press Publications 2017

© S. Kadison 2017

The author asserts his moral right to be identified as the author of the work.

All rights reserved. No part of this publication may be reproduced, stored in a retrieval system or transmitted in any form or by any means, electronic, mechanical, photocopying, recording or otherwise, without the prior permission of the publishers

ISBN 978-0-244-02357-7

Cover: The Lady in Blue –J.B.C Corot

PREVIOUSLY PUBLISHED IN THE
ENTIRELY AVOIDABLE INSANITY SERIES

VOL 1 PONGO

VOL 2 A BIT OF WHAT'S GOOD

VOL 3 THE UNEXPECTED COMFORTS OF CLIFF RICHARD

VOL 4 ICICLES IN AUGUST

VOL 5 BARBED WIRE, BROKEN GLASS AND SAVAGE DOGS

VOL 6 TEN MILES HOME

CONTENTS

TWO TINS OF SARDINES	9
THE MAGIC OF LITERATURE	37
A FALL	62
SOMETHING SIMPLE AND ESSENTIAL	90
BABY BLUES	115
THE EMMA BOVARY OF BAILRIGG	142
A REUNION, A START, A DECLINE	169
SACKED	194
GERONIMO	220
LA VIE EST AILLEURS	248

for Geoffrey Ainsworth,
teacher.

TWO TINS OF SARDINES

Mary was pregnant. He was going to be an uncle. That was something.

"You'll be aunty Sylvia, at fourteen. Not bad, eh?"

His sister was slightly less amenable to his teasing, which was just as it should be. She was shoving her big brother aside a bit to make room for the new Sylvia. He was glad. She had a chance. His mother had shifted her allegiance from the Railway Mission and was now a regular at Lune Street Methodist. He was pleased about that too because Sylvia's social life span around two hubs: her school friends and the church. The Railway Mission was a limited, fundamentalist place. Lune Street was presided over by Tony Winter, a free thinking, questioning, unconventional vicar relaxed about the so-called sexual revolution, who had supported the recent abortion and homosexuality legislation, read Tom Paine, admired Robert Owen and Nye Bevan, was quite happy if his congregation expressed doubts about the existence of god and saw the church as primarily a social institution whose purpose was to be open to all and to offer practical help as well as moral guidance to anyone who asked. Winter wasn't at all convinced he was capable of giving moral guidance. What he loathed in religious people was any hint of moral superiority. He hadn't trained a as vicar because he believed he knew the truth or possessed the moral genius of Christ, but because it was the only way he could see of combining making a living with helping people without getting enmeshed in bureaucracy. There'd been a time when he thought of training as a social worker or a teacher, but he rebelled against becoming a servant of the State. Even at its best, in the NHS or the welfare system as a whole, it was burdened with a need to control and supervise. He admired doctors, nurses, teachers, all the folk who got up in the morning thinking more about how they could help others than put money in their pockets; but he knew he needed leeway. The Methodist Church was democratic. He would be able to run his own church as he wished.

Most churches insisted on attendance as a qualification for membership of the youth club. Winter admitted anyone.

"Why should I let in only the converted," he would say to his elders who objected to the petty vandalism of some of the disaffected kids who came along looking for mischief, "is that what Christ would have done?"

"Christ didn't have to pay for the damage," said Lily Tabener, the fearsome seventy-year-old who had been attending since the age of three and for whom god was a punitive rather than a forgiving presence.

"Oh, don't worry about that. I'll pay. I'm rolling in it. I'm nearly a millionaire."

The liberal policy meant a variety of young folk turned up. The place had a reputation: you could crash in on a Sunday or Wednesday night, buy a drink, play table tennis, meet other kids, have a dance, mess about and have a laugh. Week by week there were bits of damage but little by little the kids themselves made them good. There were lads and lasses who could replace a broken pane or fix a chair, plaster the hole someone had kicked in the wall or rewire the socket smashed by a brick, conjure new curtains, fit new upholstery, paint and varnish. By dint of treating the misdemeanours as trivialities, Winter won the support of almost all the youngsters.

"Winter's okay," even some of those who thought themselves untamed hard-cases, beyond the reach of authority would say. "He's a decent bloke. Leave him alone."

On Friday evenings, Winter ran his argumentative discussion club. It was voluntary but lots of kids turned up because it was something to do and a way of getting together. Winter invited speakers or set the debate off himself with some controversial introduction:

"Why shouldn't couples live together if they want to? What difference does a marriage licence make?"

Or:

"When people work, what they produce should belong to them. That's simple justice."

Andy was relieved to discover Sylvia was turning up for these sessions, had got to know a good circle of young folk from the youth club and was breaking the narrow bounds in which his mother had made her live, fraying the ropes which tied her to his mother's victimhood and nihilism. He wasn't so happy, though, with his mother's reaction to his sister's incipient bid for maturity.

When he arrived home for the Christmas vacation, his mother told him about Mary.

"Oh, that's great news," he said.

"There'll be a lot to be done. It's no picnic looking after a baby," she said as if Mary were facing something as tough as swimming the Atlantic.

He left her in the kitchen and sat in the front room with *The Wild Duck*. Why did she always have to look for the negative? It troubled him. He pulled on his overcoat and went to walk off his disturbance.

That evening Sylvia went out to one of her friend's. There was the usual curfew. Andy worked, alone in the back room, books and papers littering the old dining table in a way he was getting used to, writing an essay on Ibsen whose work he found slightly puzzling. He was struggling to site him in the development of drama but hadn't read enough. Shakespeare and a few other Elizabethans he was familiar with, Osborne, Pinter and the kitchen sink dramas he'd eagerly absorbed from *Play For Today* or *The Wednesday Play*, struck a note he recognised, but how Restoration drama and Sheridan transmogrified into the gloomy ponderousness of the Norwegian he was at a loss to grasp. At eight o'clock, tired of being on his own and in need of a bit of relief, he went through to the front room where his mother was comfortable with her legs beneath her watching the television.

He wondered if he should nip to *The Fleece*. There were sure to be people he knew. Uncle Henry might be there, propping the pillar by the gents as usual, steadily absorbing five pints. If John Rutherford was home from Bristol where he was now doing a PhD he might be rolling a thin, scruffy fag in the snug waiting his turn at the dart board and maybe Duddy would pop in. Alan Madison was a regular and Andy always enjoyed a chat to him. Girls too, which brought his thoughts back to Jane, and soured his mood.

"What time's Syl due back?"

"Nine o'clock," said his mother, looking at the mantelpiece. "I've told 'er, not a minute later. It were near half past when she came in last week. I said to her, I said, "I'm on pins 'ere. Don't you think 'o that? Eh? Don't you?" I said nine o'clock. It's late enough at 'er age....."

He switched off and attended to the idiocy on the screen. At least there'd be news before long.

"I'll just make myself a brew. Fancy one?"

"No. I'm all right till my milky drink. I like a milky drink before I go to bed."

Elsie looked at the clock again as her son left the room. It was odd how she felt less than comfortable in his presence. It had never occurred to her, when her children were little, that she would do anything but dote. Part of her wished Andy was independent and no longer under her roof. It was true he was here for only a few weeks, but he was nearly twenty-two. At his age she was suffering the blackout and rationing. Her brothers were in the forces. Bert was in Egypt; but if it hadn't been for the war she'd have been married. She and Bert had to spend the first nine years of their marriage in her dad's house; but that was because of the shortage, her mother's illness and her dad's dependence. Things were different now. What puzzled her was why her son wanted to study. She understood he was thinking of teaching in a university, but she still couldn't quite see how he could postpone the important things in life. Would he ever marry and produce children? Did he have a girlfriend? It was all worrying.

The hands seemed to stand still. She should have said half past eight, at least then there might have been a chance of her being in by nine; but if she had, she'd have been scalded by anxiety as soon as the big hand touched six. She wished Sylvia would show more reluctance about going out, as she'd done. At thirteen, she wouldn't have dreamed of going out to enjoy herself, leaving her mother at home. Being out of the house for an hour to shop or go to church was bad enough. Her thoughts were always with her mother and the horrible fear, for example, that the house might catch fire and she would be trapped in her bed would clamp her mind and she was tempted to stop singing the hymn, put down the book, and dash home to ensure the flames weren't licking into the sky above her little front-door-on-the-pavement and back-yard house.

Why didn't Sylvia reassure her before she went out? Why didn't she say:

"Don't worry, mum. I'll be home before nine."

Why did she always exceed the curfew by a few minutes, and sometimes as much as half an hour? It felt as if her daughter was deliberately defying her, provoking her. She could almost believe she was sitting looking at her watch saying to herself:

"Nine o'clock. Now she'll be worried."

Her son came back just before the start of the news.

"It's nearly nine. Where is she?" said Elsie.

She got up and pulled aside the heavy, yellow curtains. All she could see was the garden.

"No sign of her."

"It's not nine yet. Sit down."

"It's a minute to. She should be coming down't road. I'll go and see."

"Don't bother," said Andy. "She'll be here."

"That's what you say. 'Owt could 'appen to her."

"She's sensible. She'll keep herself safe."

"I'll go and see."

She went out leaving the doors open so the cold draught filtered around Andy's legs stretched before the gas fire. The news, which he always watched in anticipation of something good was bad as ever. Heath was boasting about taking Britain into the EEC. Andy had the feeling it was a trick. He was enthusiastic for greater co-operation with Europe. He liked to think of himself as European and anything which made it easier to visit or possibly work in France, he was happy about; but Heath was for business. He'd already bared his teeth at the poor. Wasn't he looking at the EEC simply as an opportunity for more money for big business? The events of 1968 were still fresh in Andy's mind and he'd read a brief survey, *French Revolution 1968*, which had spurred his sense that there was a movement which could challenge capitalism. Before he left F.E.D., his view was thoroughly social democratic: good wages and conditions, universal, free public services, robust trade unions; a reformed, liberal capitalism in which the drive to maximum profit would be tempered by institutions whose purpose was to look after people's needs and rights in the workplace which would raise the status and autonomy of employees. He looked back on it now, no more than months later as a Noddy and Big Ears vision.

The undercurrent of Heath's administration was nasty. Bloody Sunday gave the tone. As did the attempts to shackle the unions. In Heath's accent, in his demeanour, was snobbery, that curious self-complacency which was the essence of Toryism. The economic theory was meringue. What it served was an underlying sense of self Andy knew well. The kind of view of himself and others he found in Robert Jones: casting himself as superior, worthy, endowed, entitled and as a consequence looking down his nose at those he considered inferior, unworthy, lacking entitlement. Where did it come from that unpleasant, preening, self-satisfied, everything-for-me-and-nothing-for-you way of being? It *was* a way of being, not merely a set of ideas, which was what made it so terrifying. The girls he knew in Penwortham who refused to have anything to do with lads from the secondary, who chose boyfriends for their money, really did think they were superior. Where did it come from? They were willing, these folk, glibly to consign others to poverty, idleness, alienation, as if they didn't suffer as they would. How odd it was that literature was full of appeals to shared humanity and intelligent denigration of assumptions of election, yet the disease was everywhere. Was it a disease or was it something inherent in the human mind?

His perspective now was that a gentle social democracy superimposed on the vicious capitalism that couldn't see a human being for the pound notes, was a fairy tale. There had to be a radical change.

"Not hide nor hair of her," said his mother, closing the door. "Look at' time."

"It's only a few minutes past."

"She'll be the death o' me, she will. Where can she be till this time? I'll 'ave to go and look for her."

She was out of the room before he could object and back in seconds, pulling on her coat and fastening her scarf around her head in the charming way she always had and which had so pleased him as a boy.

"I'll go," he said, getting up.

"Eh?"

"Take your coat off and sit down. I'll go and find her. Don't worry. Where is she?"

"Elaine Roberts's. Do y'know where she lives?"

"Yeah. Yeah. I know it. I'll be there in no time."

He tied his laces and buttoned his overcoat as his mother explained the route, described the house, explained the route again, gave him instructions how to ring the bell, went to the curtains, wrung her hands, speculated as to what might have happened to Sylvia as if a latter-day Ripper was sure to have abducted her during the half mile walk home and she was now lying in her own blood, in the gutter, her throat gaping from a brutal wound, her tripes sliding down the grid.

"Sit down," he said, "I'll be back in no time."

He closed the inner door behind him, left the storm door ajar and passing between the gateposts turned left, hoping it was the right direction, aware his mother was watching from between the curtains. He hadn't listened to her directions, had no idea where Elaine Roberts lived nor any intention of going in search of Sylvia. She would arrive soon enough. He just needed to wander around a bit till she appeared.

He went briskly, to work off his anxiety. It was odd how impossible it was to remain calm when his mother was rising into panic. Her agitation was extreme. She was pale, her face stretched into a queer grimace as she turned from the window. Her body was tense as a pulled bow-string. She paced. She clenched her fists. She was unable to keep still. She uttered desperate imprecations.

Why did such a small matter elicit such a far-gone reaction? Was there some quirk in her brain? Was it inborn? Was she incapable of measuring the seriousness of an incident and responding accordingly because of some given discrepancy? Or was it rather some conflict laid down by experience? It seemed to Andy, at these moments, she was always fighting down something in herself. As if she wished for what she feared. Sylvia was at her friend's. It was a snail's hour away. She was thirteen and pushing for independence. Of course, she was a few minutes late. He thought back to himself at her age. The curfew wasn't so severe. So long as he was in for nine or so, his mother never bothered. Was it because he was a boy? Did she assume he could take care of himself?

He could, in a way, but he was a skinny, sliver of a boy when his classmates were pushing six feet and twelve stones. John Kenny was six inches taller when they were in the third year, muscular, fast, as strong as many men, while he still had knots-in-cotton biceps and willowy legs. He could look after himself because he knew the situations to avoid, the lads not to antagonize, the touchy, lunatic bullies who would kick your teeth if you looked at them the wrong way. He remembered the times John had rescued him; the evening when he was cycling back from his house in Howick and a bigger lad stood in his way at the Blashaw Lane bus-stop. He had to yank on his brakes and the bully began the usual routine:

"What time d'you go to bed at night lad?"

John, out of some protective instinct, had followed him at two hundred yards and seeing the incident rode up calmly to where the older boy, a cigarette in his fingers was looming over Andy.

"All right, Nana?"

"Yeah."

"Who's your friend?"

Andy laughed.

John straddled his crossbar, his big feet in his polished black boots flat on the pavement. He folded his arms across his broad chest. His yellow, hand-knitted polo-neck clung tight to his weight-developed muscles. The stranger turned away and looked towards Howick for his bus.

"What d'you want to talk to my friend for?" said John.

The tough guy, two inches shorter than John, weaker, less athletic and without that killer instinct which made Andy's friend such a good fighter, if he had to defend himself, was quiet now, trying to pretend he hadn't heard, that he was nothing but an I-mind-my-own-business kid waiting for the bus.

"If you'd touched him I'd have shoved that fag down your throat by now," said John, matter-of-factly.

Though Andy was glad he'd been saved a possible beating, he shrank from the violence.

"See you, tomorrow, Nana," said John.

"Yeah, thanks John."

As Andy stood on the pedals he heard John say:

"If I see you round here again, I'll break your teeth lad."

There were dangers. He'd been saved by John and by other friends. Blackie was strong and more than once had grabbed a lad who was looking for trouble and tossed him into a hedge as if he was as light as a bonfire night guy. There were risks for Sylvia, but serious incidents were rare. He'd never known a girl who'd been assaulted in public. From his mother's behaviour, you'd have thought they lived in a war zone, that Sylvia was a Protestant making her way home alone, late at night, from the Divis Flats. This was Penwortham. Rapes and assaults were rare. The groves and avenues were quiet. There was really little to fear and he knew Sylvia would be careful.

The discrepancy between the real risk and the fear was so great, there must be something else behind it. He walked round the block and round again. Which direction would she come from? He needed to keep an eye on both ends of Woodland Grove so that when she appeared he could warn her. He walked between the grove and Highgate which allowed him time to spot her if she entered their street from the other end.

What was his mother's real fear? Wasn't it Sylvia's independence? Wasn't it that she was his mother's last link? Once she was gone, his mother was alone and he knew she lacked the wherewithal to make a new life for herself. She was fifty. Her dad lived to seventy-eight. His brother, in his eighties, was still walking over Catbells at the weekend. She might live another thirty years, or more. She could find another man. She could yet make something of her life; but he knew she didn't want to. She'd chosen the identity of victim in the belief the world's sympathy must come to her.

In this desperate nihilism, she clung to Sylvia. She was hers. She must stay with her. She must adore and abide by her mother. She must accept the absolute nature of motherhood.

As he thought his way through this sticky morass of out-of-kilter emotions, he wished he could be free of it. He would have liked to leave and never return. Yet he owed a responsibility to his sister. She needed some small gap by which she could escape the tight, gateless enclosure her mother had made for her. He'd always tried to be kind and light-hearted, to show her that her mother's ponderous, stone-heavy, dragging feelings weren't necessary; that her turning her back on life was a bad choice. What could he do for his mother? He could be a good son and that was all. He couldn't be her psychiatrist. He knew there was something wrong which exceeded a son's love. He had to accept that; but he could help Sylvia.

She appeared. He recognised her hurried walk, her slightly hunched shoulders, the clenching of herself against the cold. He hurried to meet her.

"Hello, little sister."

"Hello big brother. What are you doing here?"

"Mum's going frantic. She was coming to look for you. I said I'd get you. Tell her I picked you up from Elaine's. She's in an absolute state."

"Why?"

"Because you're three seconds late and the big bad wolf is going to gobble you up before you get to Woodland Grove."

She laughed.

"What time is it?"

He looked at the watch Mary had bought him for his twenty-first.

"Twenty-five past. She's probably called Interpol by now. Our descriptions will be circulating in every capital in Europe. She'll be convinced we've been kidnapped by Mexican bandits and sold into slavery."

She laughed again.

"I haven't got my watch on. I wasn't thinking about the time."

"No, nor should you when you're enjoying yourself. But just try to avoid sparking up her anxiety. She's beside herself."

"What does she think's going to happen?"

"I know. I know."

Sylvia tried to avoid an anxiety fest, but her mother was quick to call after her and then to follow as she went upstairs:

"I said nine o'clock. I've been on pins, I have. You'll be the death o' me. D'you hear? You'll be the death o' me. I said nine o'clock and you've school tomorrow. Eh? Why can't you get home at nine? I'll have heart failure one of these days, the way you go on...."

"All right. I wasn't watching the clock, that's all."

"Watchin't clock? I don't believe you even look at't clock. And me sittin' 'ere waitin', thinkin' all kinds. All kinds. Anything might have happened...."

The girl closed her door. She was at that age where her room was no longer simply a part of the house but a refuge and an outpost. Like all young people she was making of this little space the new land of autonomy she had to conquer. Her door was no longer merely a door. It was a threshold. This arena of her mother's house was now hers. It was an ambivalent space. Her mother owned it. The house was hers. Yet Sylvia thought of it as inviolable. She was no longer a child whose territory could be entered by her mother at will. She no longer experienced herself as living in her mother's house. She lived in the house, but this part of it was hers. It was hers not through ownership but through need. She had to have a space that was hers. Her mother was no longer absolute. She owned the house but she didn't own its space. There was this room where a new Sylvia was being born and her mother had to stay away. She mustn't trample the shoots in the soft earth. She mustn't take hold of the warm eggs in the newly-built nest and let them fall to the ground and smash. There was an assertion against her mother in the staking out of her room as hers. She was a pioneer. Her bedroom was virgin land. She was growing the most difficult plant: a new selfhood. She needed her mother to recognise it. She needed the closed door to be a barrier that must not be crossed. Her mother had no right of entry. She must ask to be admitted.

The door opened before she'd had time to put down her bag:

"Think on. Nine o'clock if I say nine o'clock. Where've you been anyway? Eh?"

"Elaine's."

"All this time? What, the two of you? Was no one else there?"

"No."

"Eh, yer a close thing and no mistake. I'll say that. I don't know what to believe I don't. I've a good mind to say you'll stay at home. What would yer think o' that, eh?"

"I want to go to bed."

"Aye, and so do I. Bed. I've been on pins, I have. I don't know if I'll get to sleep at all, I don't. I was worried sick, I was….."

Sylvia sat on the bed and let the storm of woe subside. In the end, her mother always ran out of energy. She had to summon so many of her resources to sustain the flow of factitious anguish, the high, major key of her desperate complaint was bound to subside into a minor coda.

"Anyway, did you have a good time?" she said at length.

"It was all right."

"Well, get yourself to bed, or you'll be tired out in't mornin'."

There was some comfort in the warmth of her covers but Sylvia had to think herself beyond her mother, beyond the walls of this house, beyond Penwortham, beyond Preston, beyond Lancashire, beyond England to be free of the weight that oppressed her mind and body. She could have believed concrete had been poured into her skull and her chest. She had to be free. Only by thinking of her escape to America could she relieve the pain that made her want to cry. Once she was there, everything would change. She would live beneath the unceasing sunshine of California, or with the confident, funny people of New York; she would be as carefree as Dick Van Dyck. All difficulties would be resolved with the ease of an episode on *The Waltons* where no moral cess pit couldn't be turned to roses and lavender in half an hour. America was a land where everything was easy, nothing troubled people more than a nettle sting, and people pushed their identity before them like a shopping trolley, full of the products they'd pulled from the shelves of life's global supermarket. That was what she felt an inordinate need to do. She had to take hold of a view of herself, a conception of who she was utterly different and remote from what she had been and what her mother imagined her to be, and force it on the world. It had to be perpetually cheerful, thoroughly irrepressible and founded in a few simple certainties like those which dominated the American life she saw on the television. That was how she could escape.

Elsie put herself to bed in a negative mood. From somewhere in her mind there came a tiny sense of guilt, but she crushed it mercilessly. She was Sylvia's mother. She had to look after her. What would folk say if something happened to her on her way home? No, she was justified. She was absolutely justified. God was with her. Didn't the

Bible say *Honour thy mother and father*? She was a mother. She must be honoured. She must be obeyed. A mother was absolute. Sylvia had no right to disobey her. If she said nine o'clock, it must be nine o'clock.

She was weary. Her feeling had given way like a rotten floor and she was left with flatness, deadness, emptiness. Why was it always like this? Why did every bid for what she thought would make her happy cast her into this desert of meaninglessness? She had no idea she was seeking an impossible control. It had never crept into her thinking that we don't make our own minds: they are made for us by those we relate to. She didn't know that by seizing a false doctrine, the debased idea derived from Judeo-Christian eschatology that our individuality is our own to make, she had deceived herself: she believed she was in possession of the truth; she knew what to do; she knew the way; she knew how to win elevation and pre-eminence; she knew what would bring praise and salvation. She had no inkling that when we seek to make others admire and valorise us, we ensure the opposite. She was unaware that the genius of living is to reject all idea of gaining praise, adulation, promotion, reward, advancement and to do what demands to be done. She was blind to the truth that the people who are most genuinely admired are those who have no need of admiration.

Andy was downstairs thinking about his mother, Ibsen and the news. He would have liked to talk to his mother about the playwright. How odd it was that he couldn't. He would have liked to take her to the theatre. Had she ever been to see a professional production? Not as far as he knew. What a terrible thing it was that culture was as remote from her as the nearest star. She used to watch *The Wednesday Play* or *Play for Today*; if there was a serialisation of Dickens, she would follow it. Timidity prevented her. Partly it was that she was a woman alone. She didn't want to turn up at the *Century Theatre* on her own; but that didn't account for it fully. There were groups, organised trips. It was a lack of confidence in her ability to respond to a culture which seemed handed down. It was *their* culture. It was discussed by people with posh accents and Oxbridge degrees. *They* owned it.

He wished he could wean her from this fear. He was cocky. He'd read Lawrence, the vertical invader, the heretic, and loved his chutzpah. Culture didn't belong to the toffs. He wished he could make his mother attend confidently to Ibsen and Sophocles.

What chance, given her entrapment in anxiety? If he hadn't been here, she would have gone out looking for Sylvia. There would probably have been some hysterical outburst on the street or at Elaine's front door. Yet he couldn't be here, except during vacations. How terrible for Sylvia. He and Mary had lived free from their mother's straitjacketing neurosis while their dad had been at home. Mary for fourteen years, he for eleven; but Sylvia had been caught in the small circle of his mother's constricting worries since a baby. Her fantasy of escape to America troubled him. That glib, empty, everyone's-happy-in-the-USA culture fed through the television like saline solution to the dying was the measure of how grim and defeating the real circumstances of her life were. Television, he said to himself, is the cry of the oppressed creature, the heart of the heartless world, the soul of soulless circumstances. He laughed at his own conceit.

The news was irritating. Part of him wanted never to watch it, never to read a paper. It was too superficial for tolerance. Yet, another part enforced a sense of responsibility. Everyone was responsible. It couldn't be left to politicians or journalists. Social problems had to be solved socially and that meant everyone was implicated. Heath made him livid. The whole Tory assumption that business was the answer made him livid. Business is no good, said Lawrence. Wasn't it obvious business was the problem? If people were motivated by making money, they would never see beyond the most limited self-interest. Andy didn't even accept that enlightened self-interest was entirely morally defensible; what did "enlightened" mean? The moral imperative was to set everyone else's interest as high as your own.

It wasn't the moral question which disturbed him most though: it was the simple wrong-headedness of the belief that we can enhance our lives by acting against others. It was a kind of madness. Heath spoke of the need for "competitiveness", as if life was a matter of always trying to do the next person down. Competition was fine for children's sports days. It was a bit of fun; but the idea that life itself was a game everyone was trying to win by driving others into less fortunate conditions, that no one could make anything, sell anything, exchange anything without thinking of *getting one over*, was risibly foolish. Yet people like Heath seemed to believe that evolution had made us incapable of anything better than accumulating pound notes and bragging about it. Of course, Heath claimed to believe in god, which Andy no longer did, his illusions shattered by Darwin and the existentialists. God, it seemed, sat on high with his ledger adding up how much each of us had in the bank and reserving the places at his right hand for the richest. Christ, it seemed, was the recalcitrant son.

What puzzled Andy was why people at the bottom end voted for Heath. People like Duncan McKay, the driver he recalled from F.E.D. who used to treat him to diatribes about lazy Pakis ruining the country, the need for strong government and the disgrace of trade unionism. He was one of those men it was pointless to argue with. Incapable of objectivity, resistant to evidence, he would have insisted the earth was the centre of the universe if he'd felt he needed to. He wasn't any more capable of political analysis than of explaining Latin grammar. His views were psychopathology parading as politics. Hating Pakistanis was his emotional and psychological problem. Irrational hatred has nothing to do with the person hated. McKay was one of those people who imagine their inner confusions and conflicts, given robust expression, amount to a political philosophy.

Wasn't that why he voted for Heath; out of ignorance and prejudice and crass, benighted arrogance? Such was democracy. People couldn't be forced to think. If they decided to collapse into their own morass of unexamined vicious assumptions, they were free to do so. What was required though, was leadership; people who could think properly and clarify issues so the public would listen. What hummed away within Andy was the feeling that maybe that was a responsibility he might take on in a small way, but at the same time, he blenched from it.

/

Bert Lang suspected his son would be home from university and wondered if he should turn up. What about Christmas? Should he arrive at midday when the odour of roast turkey was drifting warmly from the kitchen, when the whiff of roast potatoes would remind him of what he'd once enjoyed? Should he take gifts? Maybe if he bought something for Elsie she would accept it gracefully. He knew it was hopeless. If he were to arrive, he would be the interloper, no more welcome than Christ himself. The idea made him snort. What should he do on Christmas Day? He'd fathered five children but he wouldn't see any of them; not unless he crashed Woodland Grove like a drunk invading a party at eleven on a Saturday night. His youngest son's mother had cut off all contact. He fully expected never to see the lad. Oddly, he felt it didn't matter much. She was young. She'd find a man. The boy would have a step-father and no doubt a better man than himself.

He stopped short in his thinking. Why was he accusing himself? He was quite willing to do all he could for the child, just as he was eager to be the best father he could to Elsie's children. He was being excluded. He was being denied. Hadn't he always been? Wasn't that why self-accusation came so easily? He'd been denied a father, a mother, brothers and sisters, decency, comfort, security, care. From the day he arrived on the good planet which hosted his wayward species, he'd been at odds. He hadn't chosen to be what he was, it had been forced on him.

Yet in so far as he had chosen, he didn't need to castigate himself: he'd worked, he'd provided, he'd made an effort to be a half-decent husband and father. He could prop up the crumbling legs of his selfhood on these crutches of self-justification; but it was no good. He needed Elsie to welcome him. He needed to able to spend a few calm, happy friendly hours at Woodland Grove on Christmas Day and to leave letting his children know he was thinking of them and they were welcome to visit him.

Some chance. He decided to call on Slick Sticks.

It was simple for him to take some time out during the day. Wickham didn't tug on the leash. His mind was fixed on money. So long as Bert brought houses onto the books and they sold quickly, so long as the fees rolled in like the tide, he wouldn't have cared if his employee spent half his day in bed. Slick Sticks was in the same bedsit in Avenham, with the park endowed by Victorian philanthropists as his back garden, breathing the same air as the middle-classes of Bushell Place whose expensive houses looked out on the boulevard leading from the Harris art college to the stone steps down to the river, the old tram bridge and the view of the meander as the water swerved away towards the Ribble Valley.

At the window were grey, torn, net curtains. By the door, six bell pushes each with the name of the tenant behind transparent plastic. It was nearly midday. Bert assumed he would still be in bed.

The first ring brought the sound of movement. Slick opened the door gingerly, poking his nose into the freshness. When he dragged it wide Bert was shocked by the emaciated, etiolated, unshaven, stooped figure in limp black trousers and a surprisingly white vest.

"That underwear looks smart, Sam," he said. "Is it Daz?"

Slick took the fabric between the thumb and index finger of his right hand, gave a little tug and moving aside to let his friend in said:

"Marks and Sparks best. Pinched it yesterday. I was bloody freezin'"

"You want to get some porridge down you. You're wastin' away."

"Porridge is the Scots' worst tradition. Whiskey is the best. Come through."

The odour of tobacco, stale booze and warm bodies hung in the atmosphere. It was cloying and Bert's instinct was to throw open the windows. On the long, low coffee table by the sofa were piled plates smeared with HP sauce, egg yolk, grease, the congealed remains of baked beans; half empty glasses, mugs and cups clustered together as if to defend themselves against the threat of hot water and washing-up liquid; two ash-trays purloined from pubs overflowed with dog-ends and the dry, grey remnants of burnt tobacco and paper; empty wine, whiskey, vodka and gin bottles stood proud to declare their previous power to tempt; a copy of *The Sporting Life* hung over the near edge, stained with spilt spirits or beer. On the sofa lay a woman of thirty or so, her hair dyed black, her eyes smudged with mascara, her lips deep red with last night's lipstick. She was short and dumpy. Her black skirt barely covered her haunches, her white, lacey blouse revealed her weighty breasts. In her fingers was a burning cigarette. She smiled and Bert saw most of her teeth were missing.

"This is Brenda," said Slick. "Brenda, this is Bert, an old friend of mine. A visitor from the world of respectability you and I have never inhabited."

"Nice to meet you, Brenda," said Bert, refraining from shaking her hand.

"Move your fat arse will you and let the man sit down. He's been working all morning."

"So have I," she said, pulling on her fag, coughing, laughing from the back of her sand and cement throat, "in a manner of speaking."

"You've never done a day's work in your life," said Slick. "You live off your capital."

"A girl's got to make the best of what she's got. What do you say, Bert?"

"Making a living is no easy business," he said, settling himself in the corner as she swung her feet to the floor.

"Brenda's just going," said Slick.

"Charming," she said with a little squirm of displeasure. "Aren't I good enough for your friends?"

"We have to talk business," said Slick. "You'd be bored to death. Bert is an expert on double-entry book-keeping. Numbers. You don't want to have to listen to that, do you?"

"I don't know. I was good at arithmetic at school. We might have something in common."

She smiled. Her one upper front tooth smudged with red, stood like an inverted gravestone before the cavern of her mouth.

"Get your coat on and skedaddle," said Slick. "Fancy a brew, Bert?"

Always ready for a cup of tea, which was not merely a thirst-quencher but redolent of belonging, Bert declined.

"Coffee?"

"No, thanks," said Bert knowing that what Slick would offer wouldn't be a fine blend of aromatic grounds, percolated to perfection and mixed with warmed milk or topped with froth but a stir-in-the-mug, unpalatable Nescafe and a gurgle from last week's bottle whose sourness would have to be concealed by tablespoons of white granulated.

Brenda had put on her red, plastic coat and collected her matching handbag from the bedroom. She tottered over the filthy carpet in black patent heels, her thin, bandy legs in dark nylons.

"Well, nice to meet you, Bert. Maybe we'll have the chance to get to know one another next time."

"Yes, nice to meet you, Brenda. Take it easy."

"Don't ask," said Slick as she pulled the door behind her.

"I wouldn't dream of it," said Bert.

"Dream? Bloody nightmare, more like."

Slick lit a cigarette and poured boiling water into the mug he'd rinsed cursorily.

"Bird of passage?"

"Can't bloody well get rid of her. Truth is, I need the money."

"Is she well off?"

"Her old man made a fortune in cement. Drank himself to death at fifty-five. She inherited half."

"Crikey. Why are you still living here?"

"She's do-lally. It's in the family. Living with her would put me in a coffin in a fortnight. Anyway, to what do I owe this unsolicited visit from the other side," he coughed raucously and perched on the straight-backed chair opposite.

Bert laughed.

"You're right. I should have popped in. Busy keeping Ken Wickham from ending in the bankruptcy court."

"Still working for that smooth git?"

"Pays the bills, and who else can I work for?"

"I thought you'd have enough to retire by now."

"Need to wait for the State pension."

"Sixty-five. Christ, I'll be long gone before then."

Bert wanted to say something about Slick's loss of weight.

"Give up the fags and the booze and you'll live to ninety."

"Who'd want to live to ninety without fags and booze?"

"Everybody."

Bert smiled.

"Yeah, maybe you're right, but it's too late."

"I don't know. You're in remarkably good shape for a man who hasn't eaten a vegetable for thirty years and whose idea of exercise is reaching for his fag packet."

Slick gulped his coffee.

"God, that's bloody horrible."

He lit a fag and enjoyed the first sharp intake of smoke.

"You haven't sacked your cleaner yet."

"Anyway, Santa Claus, where's my Christmas present?"

"I'll be here on Christmas morning with a selection box and Charles Buchan's football annual."

"Chuck in a hundred Number Six and you'll be welcome. What are you doing for Christmas anyway?"

"Beans on toast and the radio. What about you?"

"Not visiting Elsie and the nippers?"

"Well, I'm invited, of course. 'Bert,' she said to me, 'for old time's sake, why don't you come and join us for turkey, pudding and crackers. We'll be as cosy as the Cratchit's. God bless us, everyone." Yes, I'm as welcome as herpes in Elsie's house, Sam. It's just that I prefer spending my time alone in my bungalow thinking about the Cuban missile crisis, my blissful childhood and how good society has been to me."

Slick huffed and coughed.

"So you're goin' anyway."

"I don't know. I don't know what to do."

"They're your kids."

"Yeah, but Andy is a grown man and Sylvia wouldn't recognise me if she passed me on Fishergate."

"What about the other one?"

"Mary? I can't intrude there. Matter of fact, I don't even have her address. Can you believe that? I brought her up for fourteen years and I don't know where she lives."

"Nothing endures, Bert, except misery."

"That's why I come here, Sam. You cheer me up."

"You should barge in if you want to, mate. Take 'em some presents. She won't kick you out."

"No, but there'll be a hell of an atmosphere."

"The lad'll be glad to see you. How's he doin'?"

"Oh, fine," said Bert, leaning forward and nodding, "he's at Lancaster. English, French and Russian he's studying." He gave a little laugh. "Russian, must have a bit of brain, eh Sam?"

"Yeah. Like you. You'd've been a professor if you'd had the chances kids have today."

"You'd've written symphonies."

"I'd've learned to do something properly instead of pretending I can play the drums."

"Well, Ringo Starr pretends too."

"Don't insult me. I can't play like Art Blakey but I'm not as bad as Ringo."

"Anyway, what might have been doesn't do us any good, does it?"

"It can do, Bert. You're fifty. You might live another thirty years. That's enough time for another life. You get on with your lad, don't you?"

"Yeah, he's the one who doesn't turn his back. Elsie has convinced the others I have cloven hoofs."

"There you are. He'll do all right, get married, have a few kids. You'll be a grandad. Make the best of that. Those kids won't have any reason to treat you like an oik at Eton."

Bert laughed. It was odd that Slick could think in such a way; that he could offer him the prospect of a warm, family life as the grandad of Andy's kids when his own existence was remote from accepted family norms. Was there regret within him that he hadn't found his way to a conventional life? Bert had always inwardly accused him of satyriasis. He was an immature character who could no more control his sexual impulses than the tide could choose when to come in. Something had failed. Maybe it was ingrained; perhaps there was some small fault in his brain which prevented the normal pattern of maturation. On the other hand, maybe it had been a choice; perhaps the challenge life had put before him had been too much. Who could work it out?

It was certain Slick didn't understand it. His catastrophic stumble through life was as incomprehensible to him as Sanskrit. It was easy for others to look at him and condemn. It was easy for him. His own life had collapsed, but he didn't live in squalor. He owned his bungalow. He was bringing in good money. He neither smoked nor drank. It was too easy to look at Slick and dismiss him as feckless, foolish, indulgent, selfish, neglectful, irrational, inadequate, unworthy, reprehensible, irresponsible; but would he live like this if he'd been able to find his way to something better?

He was at the centre of his own tragedy and he could gain no purchase. He had no perspective from which he could view himself. Without that distance, it was impossible for him to take hold of his life and improve it. Bert knew the same was true of himself. Within him were two forces: one dragged him down, the other demanded he understand himself. He was fighting for insight but it wouldn't arrive. He was at a loss to understand why he was lonely, why his work was as unsatisfying as candy floss, why he felt himself falling into the abyss of the Bert Lang he'd been as a boy, barefoot, neglected, hungry, cold, dirty and rejected. His abiding feeling was that this was what he deserved. It was his fate. He was guilty and this was his punishment.

"Yeah, maybe you're right. In a few years, I'll be dangling babies on my knee and going round to Andy's for Sunday tea. In the meantime, Christmas is advancing like a charging rhino."

"You could come here."

"Are you getting a turkey?"

"No, but I'll buy two tins of sardines and some mince pies. We can slob in front of the telly all day pretending we're happy and when the queen makes her speech we can stand and salute like good patriots. We could even go to midnight mass to kick things off. *Good Christian men rejoice, with heart and soul and voice..* What a great culture we inhabit Bert. Bishops who believe the universe was made by an old geezer in the sky, aristocrats who believe they're superior by nature. We've so much to be thankful for."

"Brenda joining you?"

"Can't keep her away. She'll be ginned up on Christmas Eve and convalescent on the day itself. Company, Bert. Who wouldn't we admit into our bedroom not to be lonely?"

"Three would be a crowd, Sam."

"Doesn't bother me. I need someone who understands what a conversation is."

"I couldn't intrude on your intimacy. It's only twenty-four hours. It's a day like any other."

"So is the day you're born, your wedding day, the day your kids were born, the day you die. If I were you, I'd go and see them. Take a peace offering for Elsie."

Bert wondered if he could spend the day with some of his Satsangi friends, but Tessa excepted, they had families and Christmas was a time when families withdrew into their own space and shut the door on the rest of the world; when the shared space which had always been his meagre comfort shut down. He had belonged to a family from the time Tom Craxton let him live under his roof to the day Elsie kicked him out. Most of his life he'd been an outsider. Perhaps that was what he should relish. Shut the door, forget Christmas, turn on the radio, grate some Cheddar onto bread and stick in under the grill for lunch. Why not?

He had to make a call at a house in Mellor. It was one of those, big, detached, just-out-of-town places, long and low with whitewashed walls, a dry, leafless clematis clinging away the winter, a detached garage, a Land Rover and a BMW on the drive, a friendly Labrador, a couple in their thirties and three children running through the open-plan kitchen and the wide lounge with the timber ceiling and a roaring coal fire. The woman, neat dark, quick, intelligent and charming made him a cup of tea and brought a plate bearing a wedge of Victoria sponge. He had no difficulty easing the *property* onto the books. The business concluded he wanted to linger. The room was beautifully warm. They were amiable, chatty people. The man ran a printing business. She was a dentist. The children were happy, laughing, spirited. He became aware of the couple's discomfort. They were fidgeting. She cast glances at her husband. He sat very calmly and politely and allowed Bert to spin ever thinner the thread of small talk.

As he drove away he said to himself: "Sod it. They're my children for god's sake. If she's frosty, too bad. I'll turn up at lunch time with a present for each of them and one for Mary they can pass on. Andy will talk to me. It'll be good to catch up. He's a good lad. He always was. I had good children. What the hell did I do to deserve that?"

There was no snow. The sky was grey and though it was chilly, it wasn't one of those bright, cold days which make you glad of the winter; just another of those unexceptional, oppressive, make-the-best of-it mornings there were so many of. He timed his arrival for twelve. His assumption was Elsie would still be cooking. They wouldn't eat till one or two. He'd have time to chat to Andy before the three of them sat down and he had to flee, like a burglar caught with hands in the jewellery drawer. He parked under the leaning rowan tree. The storm door was open, as ever. He liked that. It had always been the way in Talbot Road. The rest of the houses had their front doors firmly closed against the world, but here there was a kind of invitation, a dropping of defensiveness, a welcome.

He gave a quick rap on the glass door and walked in. The front room was empty. He stepped into the back room where Andy and Sylvia were facing one another at each end of the table in the bay.

"Hello folks," he said.

Sylvia looked at him as if was wearing a loincloth and carrying a spear.

"All right, dad?" said Andy.

At that moment, Elsie arrived from the kitchen, bearing the steaming turkey whose fatty odour almost defeated his resilience. Her face tightened as she passed him, saying as she went to place the crisp-skinned bird in the middle of the table:

"We're just about to have our dinner"

She turned, hurried away to the kitchen for roast potatoes, Brussels sprouts, carrots, and gravy.

"There are presents for you here," he said, placing them on the sideboard he'd bought seventeen years earlier. "And one for Mary."

Andy nodded.

"I'll see she gets it," he said.

Elsie swept past, turned once more, came back again, sat down with her back to him and said:

"Serve yourselves children. I'll carve."

He stood speechless for less than a second.

"Well, happy Christmas folks. Enjoy your dinner."

"Happy Christmas, dad," said Andy with a nod and a smile.

Sylvia spooned a roast potato onto her plate, Elsie carved silently.

He left.

Between Christmas and New Year, Andy received a letter from Jane Bentnick. He'd written to her at the start of the holiday and having no reply, sent a note a few days later saying: "If you've broken your arm, try writing with your feet." She had. On a piece of light blue, heavy notepaper she'd managed: "Andy, you bugger."

What was he supposed to make of that?

There was a football match on Hurst Grange Park. Alan Madison, home from university in Newcastle was playing, as were a few other lads he knew. He'd gone for a walk to think his way through his confusions, but it was good to loiter on the touchline. Madison's girlfriend, a small, blonde Geordie whose accent he was pleased to eavesdrop was close by with her baby. Andy had heard Madison had become a father. It seemed somehow appropriate: he had a get-on-with-living-and-deal-with-the-consequences attitude Andy found appealing. It was hard to imagine him being wearily cautious, planning the trajectory of his life like a provincial bank manager agonising over a loan of a thousand pounds to a window cleaner to buy a new van. It was reckless, of course, to get his girlfriend pregnant while they were both students, but it displayed an appetite for life and an absence of self-regarding pusillanimity. It made him think of Shakespeare. He'd been reckless in the same way. It fitted with the love of life which poured from his plays.

A lad he recognised from school passed, wearing wellingtons for the mud, a woolly hat pulled down to his eyes.

"All reet, Nana?"

"All right?"

"Not seen you for a bit. What y'up to?"

"Student."

"Aye. Where's that?"

"Lancaster."

"All reet?"

"Yeah, keeps me out o' trouble."

The lad laughed.

"See y'in a bit."

"Yeah. Take it easy."

What was his name? Ashcroft? Something like that. One of those lads Andy'd known in passing, who had been part of his social landscape but who he'd never spent time or established any liaison with. It was odd that such passing, apparently insignificant acquaintances could provide such reassurance. At school, after all, he'd inhabited a very small house of friendship: Duddy, Wheels, Blackie, John Kenny for a while. Yet at the same time, the lads and lasses he saw every day, who he shared classrooms with, passed on the corridor, said no more than hello to on the playground had a place in his emotional topography. They were always there. He attributed characteristics to them. Ashcroft, or whatever his name was, he'd always thought of as friendly, easy-going but not the kind of lad he wanted a friendship with; not someone who would appreciate his irony and sense of fun; just a good lad he could say hello to, maybe kick a ball around with for ten minutes; but all the same, part of his life.

Almost the same was true of Alan Madison. They barely knew one another but there was a frisson of understanding between them. Andy had admired him as a non-conformist. That they'd refused to make him a prefect at Hutton Grammar he liked. Madison had too much cheek about him, was too willing to make up his own mind and follow his own instincts to be liked by teachers who valued obedience and deference. He was no more put out by not being given a badge than a cat would be by not having a bell round its neck. He and Andy weren't friends, but they would never forget one another. They would always be part of the important background of one another's lives.

The ref blew for half-time. The *Penwortham Hill Rovers* players in their green shirts, muddied shorts, knees and boots, squelched to the touchline for quartered oranges and a swig of water. Madison, his thick, black hair on his shoulders and his wild man's beard covering his face to his cheekbones, spotted Andy as he came to see his wife.

"How you doin'?" he called with a smile.

"Okay, Maddy. How are you?"

"Knackered."

Andy laughed. The second half kicked off. He followed the path through the trees towards Hill Road where the big, detached houses of the upper-middle-classes stood in their grounds and gardens, symbols of their remoteness from the town, its terraces, pavements, factories and the history which had made the wealth which built them. Valley Road was posher still. That it was unmade, a stretch of suspension-shattering pot-holes that filled with water in winter or kicked up grey dust under tyres in summer, spoke of its exclusivity. To the right was a field in which two horses were grazing, serene and indifferent, their necks bent to the rough grass. To the left, the houses stood aloft, raised like whips as if to demand submission of those poor enough to have pass on foot. Andy stepped over and round the puddles. Why didn't the folk who lived here pay to have the road made? They were wealthy enough? It occurred to him their wealth was the problem: they owned a private road. The local authority had neither the right nor the responsibility to bring tarmac; but nor did the residents want to club together to have the work done. They owned the few yards of road in front of their house. Why should they pay for any more? Their money made them mean. Separated from one another by what they prided themselves on, their relationships were competitive, inward, grasping, my-money-is-mine-and-your-is-yours-and-ne'er-the-twain-shall-meet. Maybe also they liked the road to be as rough as a sixteenth century cart-track because it deterred visitors; but to Andy it seemed idiotic.

He walked on, over the old bridge to Broadgate and into Avenham Park. What was he to make of Jane? On the Sunday after their hasty coupling, he'd gone to her room as arranged, looking forward to drifting to the bar, a chat, a few pints and a finding his way further into the territory of her selfhood so different from his own. She was defensive as a provoked cobra. Embarrassed by the stand-off in front of her room-mate, Andy was ready to retreat. She put on her coat. He followed her down the stairs.

"Let's go to your room," she said.

"Okay."

She perched on the bed in her coat, her knees pressed together, her mouth tight.

"Shall I make some coffee?"

"No."

"No, I wouldn't accept an invitation to drink my coffee either. As my mate says, it's either crude oil or cat's piss."

"I've got a problem," she said.

He almost wanted to laugh. He was tempted to say: "Look, if it's an in-growing toe-nail you're talking to the wrong bloke. If you need to know how to conjugate an imperfective I can help you."

He was sitting on his chair, his legs crossed. He knew the declaration was a provocation. In the seconds before he responded he was aware she'd laid a trap; but what was the danger? His feeling was beginning to turn negative and heavy but he retained enough of his light-hearted chutzpah not to be blade-tongued.

"What's that?" he said, cocking his head to the left and smiling.

"I can't say no," she said.

THE MAGIC OF LITERATURE

"You know me, Bert," said Ken Wickham, expanding his chest and putting his arm round the shoulders of his colleague, "I pay my debts."

"You haven't paid so far."

"Cash-flow, Bert." He turned away putting enough distance between them to be able to deliver the sermon. "We're hard-headed business-men you and me. We know the way the world works. That's all it is, Bert. Business. Nothing personal."

"It's personal to me. You've four thousand quid of mine."

"And you'll get it back. All in good time."

"Why don't you flog that ocean-going yacht?"

Wickham laughed, shaking his head and wagging his index finger condescendingly.

"That's my property. I've made my money fair and square. I enjoy the benefits. That's what business is for. We're not in it so we have to live like the plebs. Trust me, Bert. You'll get your money."

Bert would no more have trusted Wickham than a scorpion. The business should have been flourishing but it was tilting towards ship-wreck. Bert had advised his boss to be frugal, stash money away and open another branch. The trick was to be neither too big nor too small. It was easy to trip yourself up by expanding too far too fast, expecting too much, being under-resourced. On the other hand, there was enough work to make two more branches viable. Wickham was convinced he would soon be national.

"Think big, Bert. Another branch. Another two. That's petty stuff. I want Wickham's to have branches in every town in Britain. Ambi-tion. You've got have ambition. I'm talking to venture capitalists. I took one to dinner last week.."

"A few less dinners and a bit more graft might be useful," said Bert.

"You're not a man to mince your words, are you? What you've got to understand is that if you want to be big you've got to look big. I take a bloke with money out on my yacht, he's impressed. I look the part. He thinks he's onto a good thing. Your trouble Bert is you'd take the chap for fish and chips and expect him to throw in twenty grand."

"He could pay for his own fish and chips as far as I'm concerned. It's work that makes an enterprise flourish. The rest is decoration."

The sole cause of the turbulence was Wickham's spending. What he paid himself Bert couldn't find out, but his new suits, expensive shirts, hand-made shoes, lavish holidays, eternal lunches in Lancashire's best restaurants, private schools for his children, an indoor swimming pool as part of the extension to his five-bedroom house, his gold cuff links and Rolex watch, the diamonds which sparkled on his wife's neck were the undeniable testimony to his distance from reality.

Bert wondered if he genuinely was mad. What did madness look like? Was Wickham suffering from a mental illness or was he just bad or foolish? The idea that wouldn't leave Bert was the odd nothing-can-go-wrong mentality which dominated Wickham's thinking. He was like a child who doesn't know that roller-skating on the tarmac can lead to grazed knees and elbows. It was as if some part of his brain which could see only happy outcomes had been switched on and that which could anticipate difficulties turned off. Was that because he had some mental defect? Bert was at a loss to know. He felt if he understood, his boss's behaviour would be less disturbing. If he could give a name to Wickham's oddness, he would have it under some control.

He was carrying the business so completely it enraged him. Wickham was spending the money he made. How could that be right? If he made the money, he should decide what was done with it. Yet because Wickham was nominally the boss, he could do everything in secret. Bert was making himself a meal in his little kitchen, boiling brown rice and slicing peppers, carrots, mushrooms, spring onions and tomatoes. He was thinking how much he could make if he were running the business on his own. Maybe that's what he should do: he had enough capital. He could open an office. He was a genius at bringing houses onto the books. He'd suck in all Wickham's trade in no time.

Once, the idea would have excited him. When he took over the delicatessen and then converted it to *The Minotaur*, the notion of being *your own boss* and running a good business, lifted him. Now, it was no more attractive than the thought of working on a production line. There was something dead at the heart of it. Oh, he knew how to do it all right. He was astute. He could no doubt have put tens of thousands in the bank but why did he need to? He had a place to live, he was comfortable. No, what was missing from his life wasn't money.

Remembering his days in the coffee bar he was struck by his sense of loneliness. Not that there weren't people around: there were the staff, the customers; he was surrounded by people all day. It was rather that he was alone in his enterprise. He'd expected this would be a liberation but it felt like imprisonment. He was running the place by himself, for himself. He recalled the times he took a few notes from the till and treated the staff at the end of the week. It cheered him up. At Christmas he gave them a cash bonus. The impulse to share broke down the walls of his isolation.

That was bad business. Business was getting as much work as possible from your staff for the least cost. When he mentioned to small business folk in the Chamber of Commerce that he handed out unexpected little windfalls to his staff, they shook their heads : word would get around; it was important for employers to stick together; they must form a common front; employees must always be told what they are being paid is the maximum the business can afford.

In the end, Bert had been worn down by the idea of profit. *The Minotaur* did well. He had a handy few thousand in the bank. He could have opened a second café. He could have pushed for a chain; but what was he doing? Accumulating pound notes. Why? The emptiness of business struck him like a virus. He didn't mind the work. Serving people sandwiches, cakes and coffee was as congenial as most other activities; but the motivation stalled him. There was a horrifying abyss at the heart of business. It was the sense of being alone, against all others, concerned only for your daily or weekly takings and annual profit. It gave him a sickened sense of being alienated from his fellow human beings which he desperately needed to escape.

At least Andy wouldn't have to earn his living that way. Maybe he'd be a university lecturer. The idea filled Bert with a sense of purpose and rightness. Yes, to be able to pass on knowledge, that was a real gift; and to work at a distance from money. It wasn't as if students would arrive in the lecture theatres, grubby fivers in their hands.

There was rightful discretion in the exclusion of money. A university was an arena from which money, as the essence of relationships, had been expelled. The indirect nature of the money-link was humanising. He was dragged down by always having to see people as a source of lucre. When he sat in the cosy living-room of a terrace in Mill Hill at tea-time, the kids coming and going as their parents tried to cajole them into stillness and quiet, the couple eager to listen to his offer, they were commission. At the back of his mind as he delivered his slick spiel was the ticking of his inner calculator. How pleasant it would be if he was paid from some more remote source and he could offer a service, if the clients themselves had nothing to pay.

He was relieved by the idea that there was a humanised realm in which his son could earn a living with greater dignity but depressed by the thought it was a realm he'd been denied access to. It required qualifications. He was the leave-school-at-thirteen boy, the on-the-troopship-at-seventeen boy, the de-mobbed-and-get-what-work-you-can young man. Had he been practical he would have earned a living sweating joints, putting on roofs, assembling aircraft, or digging channels for wires under plaster; but all he had was his charm and his ability to convince. He'd been dragged into salesmanship like a thick branch, ripped from an overhanging tree in a storm is dragged downstream and out to sea to bob and toss forever on the heedless waves.

If he could have studied. If he could have qualified. He might have been a teacher. He could have taught English. The idea of himself away from the need to hustle for money was odd. It had been so much of his life it almost felt as if it was his nature, as if it was imprinted in his genes. Yet the picture of life in a school, where money makes no incursion, where the children are guaranteed an education regardless of their parents' wealth, where he could have relaxed into teaching them how to write, how to appreciate Shakespeare or H.G.Wells; the view of himself as a responsible professional fulfilling society's instruction, was foreign to his feeling. It hadn't been a possibility so the sensibility which went with it hadn't arisen. He was struck by the sudden thought that he was what he was through circumstance. Did that mean he could have been almost anything? Surely not. There was the limit of his endowment. Yet it did mean he could have been significantly different. Everybody could. Toss a coin and he could have been a royal or a well-educated son of the middle-classes. It was mere circumstance which made him the bastard son of a wayward girl and an opportunistic squaddie and who could blame or praise themselves for what circumstance had delivered?

He was what he'd been made. There was no remedy for that. He was fifty. It was too late. His life had been ruined by poverty, war and commercialism; but his son had escaped. He hoped he would be a university lecturer. He might write books. He might become a professor. His feeling brightened at the prospect. Imagine that books bearing the name Andrew Lang were on library shelves across the world. His name. Perhaps he would write a book which would be studied for decades or even centuries. That was how things were in that world. A man could write a book about literature in the twentieth century and three hundred years later scholars could still be reading it. His name could be preserved. Him, Bert Lang, the chill-arsed boy from the backstreets of Preston, the cockroaches-and-bare-flagstones boy might have produced a son who would make a lasting contribution to human culture. That was something. It was a diamond in the mud of his existence, a melody in the cacophony of failure, exclusion and misery which had blighted him.

As he sat at the little bar to eat, his thoughts jerked back to Wickham. Was he mad? If he was, maybe the whole society was insane. He was a businessman and business was what society was about. The idea put him off his food. Business. He knew it inside out. He'd worked for ICI and he knew how the honest, diligent work of scientists, serious people who had studied hard to understand physics and chemistry, was suborned to glib salesmanship. The paint he'd sold was good. He had no doubt about that. He wasn't offering customers a product he didn't believe in; but he was serving money rather than knowledge and truth. He was the man with the patter. He was the honey-voiced purveyor who helped ensure the shareholders got their dividends, the executives their fat salaries and ICI a bigger share of the market. Paint. That's all it was. Paint for people's bathrooms, kitchens, living-rooms, window-frames, doors, skirting boards; paint to keep the weather out and to make things look nice. Why did that have to serve the debased intention of money-making? Why couldn't paint be made and delivered to people in a spirit of generosity and helpfulness?

Wickham. Why did he want money? Why had he bought a yacht he couldn't afford? There was some weakness in him, some horrible absence he was trying to fill with money. Was that how the whole of society worked? Was everyone's daily life organised around some ludicrous compensation? Was everyone trying to prove what could never be proven: their essential worth. As if a man could measure his value in pound notes. It was madness.

What Tessa had said to him the previous week came back to him. She called round on Wednesday evening when he was settled with his mug of tea, listening to Radio 3, and inevitably, unfortunately, dispiritingly, they fell to talking about his work and his disenchantment. When he wondered aloud if Wickham was suffering from some mental illness, she said:

"He's not mad, Bert, he's just a businessman."

"Does that explain why he borrows thousands to buy a yacht, takes people out for lavish lunches every week and does no more work than a sloth?"

"Of course it does. That's what businessmen are supposed to do. They aren't supposed to work. That's what the lower orders do. Work is what you do if you don't have money. If you have money someone else does the work."

"Yes, me."

"Wickham is a good capitalist. He knows money is supposed to work for him not he for money. That's what you do. That's because you're an incorrigible pleb, Bert."

"I wish I had the will to work for myself."

"Why not start a co-operative?"

"In estate agency?"

"Why not? The enterprise is irrelevant, it's the relationships that matter."

"I'd never find anyone. All the folk in estate agency are flat-against-the-wall business people. They think Michael Foot is a dangerous Bolshevik."

"Do something else. A vegetarian café. You'd find co-operative minded people who'd do that."

"Yes. Good idea. I could try."

He could try; but the sense of hopelessness pervaded him before he'd done more than run the idea round his mind three times. The attractiveness of a co-operative was as great as the likelihood of establishing one was tiny. It was like trying to quench a forest fire with a watering can, like holding back an avalanche with a wind-break. Sitting alone, enjoying the tasty food, he could allow the happy conception of work with others, effort and benefits shared, and the ruling impulse being social beneficence rather than individual greed to suffuse and soothe his mind; but once move into the public realm, take the first step to realize what was inwardly recognised as a superior way to live, and he would be faced with prejudice, ignorance, sneering, cynicism and viciousness.

In his lounge, the central heating pumping, his mug of tea on the table beside him, he took Bevan's *In Place of Fear* from his shelves. He'd inscribed his name and the date he'd bought it on the fly-leaf. Twenty years ago. Why had he felt he should write his name? Simply in case it was lost? No, there was some identification at work. He was a young man. Mary was still a baby and Andy not yet born. He was living in Tom Craxton's house. The war was behind him. Fascism was defeated. Democracy had triumphed. The dole queues belonged in the thirties. Never again. Poverty, war, fear, insecurity. They were all behind him. His children would never know them. He'd written his name as if adding it to a petition. In place of fear. The future would give confidence to people like him. It had been terrible to live through the poverty of his young years, the rise of Hitler, the need to risk your life to ensure the most basic freedom; but it was done. He was in his father-in-law's little terrace but he would get his own house. They would live well. His children would get an education. Democracy would ensure society's wealth and power were spread widely. He'd signed his name to enrol himself in the great enterprise of raising the people to democratic responsibility.

Bevan would have agreed with Tessa: co-operatives are superior to lucre-mad business. He flicked through and read a paragraph here and there:

The individual who is called on to alienate a painful part of his private income to the tax collector is not made any the more willing because it is going to finance purposes it is not easy for him to con-

demn...The power and prosperity of tax evaders thwarts one of the main aims of Socialism: the establishment of just social relations....

Wickham was a tax evader. He was one of those businessmen whose mentality is no better than the spiv's. Nothing pleased him more than the cash transaction.

"What goes in your back pocket, the taxman doesn't know about," he would say.

Bert despised him for it. Paying your taxes was a fundamental social duty and a test of a person's honesty. Yet it seemed to Bert that was meagre. People like Wickham were no better than shop-lifters or pick-pockets. They were dishonest in their essential relation to their fellow citizens. Wickham might pay for his kids to be educated and for his medical care, but he expected his street to be lit, the roads to be tarmaced, his bins to be emptied, his employees who'd been educated by the State to be able to read and write, parks to be maintained, the police to investigate if his car was stolen.

Bert paused over Bevan's use of *painful*. He genuinely didn't feel pain at paying his taxes. On the contrary, he would gladly have paid more to see the NHS improved or more teachers employed. The thought of paying his taxes so kids could be taught to read, could grow up, like his son, to go to university, to become educated, thoughtful people made him proud. He wanted to be part of that. He wanted to belong to a society where generosity trumped meanness and where the good of all reigned over blind self-interest.

Did that make him a freak? Was Bevan right that paying taxes is inherently painful? He didn't think so. Was Tom Craxton a freak? He would have accepted more tax being taken from his petty wage if it would help someone struggling in sickness. Most of the people he'd grown up amongst would have felt the same. No, it wasn't painful to pay tax unless you were lost in the wilderness of the-world-ends-at-my-front-door-ism. What was tax anyway but a means of shifting money from one place to another; and what was money but a convenience elevated to the level of a virtue? There would be no need for tax if what was produced was in the hands of those who produced it. Hadn't Bevan, after all, elaborated the idea of the NHS out of the Tredegar miners' sickness scheme? Wasn't it only because an arrogant, self-justifying, deludedly entitled minority had their hands on most of the wealth that taxes were necessary at all? Wouldn't people voluntarily, willingly, happily contribute to the common good if the wealth they made together they owned together?

Until we make the cross-over to a spirit of co-operation, the latent energies of democratic participation cannot be fully released...

Bert gave a little laugh. Tessa was right; but it struck him Bevan's formulation worked in reverse: not until the latent energies of democratic participation were released could a cross-over to a spirit of co-operation be made.

Where was democracy? What a feeble thing it was. He went to work every day and there was no more democracy in Wickham's enterprise than in the relation of a medieval lord to a serf. As for ICI, what had the insistence he wear a suit been but a raw expression of control? How could a society think of itself as democratic when people spent their working lives robbed of responsibility, told what to do, subjected to arbitrary rules, when contracts were drawn up by the employers and tilted drastically in their favour.

He set the book aside. How much longer would he live? What chance was there that the dream he'd believed in when he bought the volume would be realised before his demise? What puzzled him was how it had failed. He'd imagined by now he would be living in a society of far greater equality and openness, that people of his class, people from the grim streets, the damp houses, people of threadbare clothes and leaky shoes would have found their confidence. Yet Heath was in power. It was still taken for granted that business was the way to make wealth, that men like Wickham were the custodians of a good society. The idea made him snort with derision.

Still, there was a future. Maybe Mary, Andy and Sylvia would watch the birth of the new world he'd hoped for . He felt the sudden pain in his right thigh which more and more made him wince and stopped him as he walked. He rubbed his muscles and once again resolved he must see the doctor. As he closed the book he realised that in thinking about what might be ahead, he hadn't included his two other children. Were they his? He'd fathered them but he wasn't their father. The idea chilled his innards. How had this happened? How could he have stopped it? He stood up, hoping movement would relieve his pain, but it intensified.

"Christ," he said to himself. "What the hell's causing that?"

Mary Lang was looking forward to giving up work. Ted agreed that until the child started school she should stay at home. She left him with his delusion. She wasn't going to stop at one and by the time the first was of school age she'd have her second to look after, and then her third. Three at least but she felt four was a good number. She'd worked since she was sixteen and she knew what it was about. At school, she'd been attracted by the idea of a career. The old myth of the woman belonging in the home was no more than confetti scattered to the winds. She imagined she would be a mother and a career woman; but the truth about work had slowly closed down on her, like the lid of a coffin in which she was buried alive.

She enjoyed her tasks. Everything that had to be done had something pleasant about it. She was odd in that she had no revulsion from household tasks. Her friends and the women she worked with complained about the washing up or the ironing and wished they could afford to have it all done for them or fantasised some machine which could take over.

"Oh," they would say, "imagine it, sitting back with a glass of wine and a box of chocolates watching the telly instead of having to iron shirts and blouses."

She laughed and joined in, but was acutely aware that the idea of lounging on the sofa, stuffing herself indulgently didn't appeal at all. The idea of being briskly in command of her household was much more congenial. She knew where every item of clothing was. If Ted said:

"Where's my thick, brown and white work shirt?"

she would answer:

"In your second drawer on the right."

She could have found every piece of her underwear within seconds. She knew how many teaspoons where in the cutlery drawer and where every pan, cup, saucer and side plate was kept.

Yet there was no effort in this. She didn't torment herself nor did she think it any kind of achievement. It simply came ordinarily to her and she was glad of it. She didn't for a second think any the worse of her colleagues if they said:

""Where are my sandals?" he said to me. "How should I know. Do I wear 'em, I said." "You'd think he was a baby the way he expects me to look after him."

They were right. A grown man should be able to look after himself; but it was a fact that Ted couldn't keep track of his clothes. His tools he was much more disciplined about. They were his livelihood and he had an intimate relation to them. If he put his favourite hammer down somewhere and couldn't find it, he'd be grumpy and puzzled till it showed itself, as if it's loss were a diminution of his being. She didn't bother to ask herself if his lack of awareness of where his socks and jumpers were came from the way he'd been raised or was a trait he could do nothing about. It wasn't a problem she needed to find an answer to. It was an opportunity. She loved to have everything in order. She adored the smell and feel of newly-ironed clothes. She exulted in her little kitchen being neat and spotless and delighted in being able to lay her hands immediately on the can opener, the slotted spoon or the cheese grater.

The difference between home and work was that in her house the tasks imposed themselves and responding to them was a great fulfilment; in the office, the tasks were part of a system and the system had its politics. She'd come to despise the competition for money and place. Her impulse was to do the work as well as she could. The business of pushing and positioning for promotion struck her as vulgar and cheap. She was comfortable with the idea that she might never go back to work, or at least not for twenty-five years or so. She would stay at home till her youngest was sixteen. Let Ted think what he liked.

"They're all doin' it," said Ted one evening as they began their meal.

"Well, they're all wrong."

"Aye, but why should I miss out?"

"You're not missing out, you're doing what's right."

"And they get more bonus then me."

"What good does it do them? They lower themselves for a few pounds a week. It's disgusting."

"It is, luv, but it's what goes on."

"What goes on is not my business. My conscience is my business."

"Who'd be in trouble if it were found out?"

"All of them."

"They can't sack all of 'em. It's hundreds o' men."

"They're all breaking the law, They can all be sent to prison."

"That wouldn't 'appen. I don't reckon anyway. It's the bonus clerk they'd go after. He's the one set it up and he's making the big money. The blokes are just gettin' a few quid."

Ted was working on a big, *spec* housing site near St Helen's. He was fed up with hammering on skirting boards all day. One house after another, one living room or bedroom after the next; fitting the cheap, low, inadequate trim that kept the cost down and *Terry's* profits up. George Terry was the archetypal working-man-made-good: a bricklayer from Bootle who set up a little building firm when he was twenty-one and moved on from renovating terraces which he re-sold at tight margins, just enough to fund the next project and put a bit aside each time, to house- building on a large scale which had made him, in seventeen years, the biggest in the north-west. His trick was to throw them up fast, make them all the same, divide the labour so that men were focussed on one task all day, and sell them for four times what it cost to build.

The money wasn't bad. For a time, Ted had been able to compensate for the bone-melting boredom by counting the fivers in his pay packet. He was a working man. That's what working men did: lived for pay day, counted the money, went to the pub or the bookies and girded themselves for another week of repetitive, demeaning labour. Little by little the hillock of Friday became a poor compensation for the unbroken, flat expanse of the rest of the week. Monday morning was the worst: getting up at six, pulling on his thick socks and boots, swinging his snap bag over his shoulder, turning up at the still quiet site, hauling his tool bag to the first house, getting down on his knees to hammer the virgin board to the wall. Those initial blows were like the key in the lock of a prison cell. What was he doing here? Why had he reduced his skills to what any bloke could do after a day's training? He was making money. Once the thought had roused him. It was the great incentive. It was what got millions of people out of bed and when he was young, when he was eighteen and looking forward to being time-served, his head was full of bonus rates and how much he could pull in if he worked Saturdays and what kind of car he could buy and where he could go on holiday and how much that suit was in *John Collier* and how, if he grafted, he could earn more than a teacher and maybe as much as a doctor.

He was still as ambitious for money. He wanted a big house. He was going to build it himself. For ten thousand he could have a place worth thirty-five or forty. He wanted more holidays in Austria. It was the good life. He would work hard for it; but this job was almost worse than the days he'd spent in the gents' outfitters, bored, out-of-place and humiliated by measuring inside legs or reaching boxed shirts down from high shelves.

He should work for himself. He'd make a good living. He was skilled and diligent. Word would get round. He was known anyway. The phone was always ringing with offers of foreigners.

Mary was funny about that: little jobs on the side; the woman whose roof was leaking because her lead flashing needed replacing. He climbed up with the roll on his shoulder, stripped back the slates, took up the old stuff and laid the new. No more than an afternoon's effort and the money went straight in his back pocket.

"You should declare it," Mary would say.

"Why should I? She's happy to pay me cash, that's my good luck. Why should I let the taxman get his mitts on it?"

"Because that's what pays for hospitals and schools. I have to pay tax on what I earn. Everybody should. What you're doing is cheating."

He laughed and teased her:

"What's up, luv? Do you think Inland Revenue's going to come knocking in middle o't night and I'll be carted off to Strangeways?"

"That's not the point."

"All't blokes do foreigners for cash. I can't see what's wrong wi' it?"

"What's wrong with it is that those of us who are paid salaries can't wriggle out. It should be one rule for all, not one for us and another for men who swindle the system."

He didn't understand it. He had to pay tax on what he earned at Terry's. That was enough. If he grafted a bit more in the evenings or at weekends, that was his business. People got their jobs done, he got a bit extra. Everyone was happy. Mary, though, wasn't happy with the culture of jobs-on-the-side at all.

"You can' stop it," he said.

"Maybe not, but it doesn't make it right."

"Gives blokes a chance to put a bit in't bank. Why shouldn't they? Doctors do it, seeing private patients."

"I'm not in favour of that either," she said.

He shook his head.

"You've some funny ideas, you Langs."

"It's just a question of fairness and honesty. Somebody needs a job doing they should hire a tradesman in the proper way, above board. They should get an estimate and a receipt and it should all be done properly. That's the way everyone is looked after."

"Aye, well, that's a woman's view, but it's not how blokes see it."

"It's nothing to do with being a woman. It's what my grandad believed and my dad too."

He teased his wife for her principles, but he was glad of them. She was as reliable as gravity. He could trust her absolutely; but he couldn't follow her into that odd territory of let-the-world-do-what-it-likes-I-answer-to-my-own-conscience. He'd been raised to go along with things. The Catholic Church and the Tory Party were the sources of values and behaviour in his parents' house. The Pope and Churchill were to be obeyed and admired. Confession and Hail Marys were the way to eternal salvation, sharp elbows in pursuit of money the path to earthly comfort.

Like all the blokes on the site, he was a member of UCATT. He expected the union to push for better wages and conditions and he would even join a strike if necessary; but he wouldn't vote Labour. He saw no distinction between the self-interest Churchill stood for and that of wanting the union to fight his corner. It was true the blokes stuck together. They'd go on strike for one another's pay if need be; but he couldn't sublimate that to a principle. The blokes wanted money for themselves. What was wrong with that? Why should people be penalised for doing well? That was what Labour stood for. If people got rich, good for them. At the same time, he was dismissive of George Terry's way of running his business: making him a skirting-board slave was the way he got rich. He didn't like it. He had to get out.

Just now a scam was under way: the bonus clerk would fiddle the figures if the blokes agreed to split the extra sixty-forty. He was adding a pound, two pounds, three pounds to virtually everyone's packet and creaming off sixty percent. One of the electricians had calculated he must be making at least a hundred and twenty a week. The average joiner was picking up a bit more than twenty.

"He'll get nabbed before long," said a brickie as they ate their snap.

"I reckon he'll do a runner first," said another.

Ted was tempted but wanted Mary on his side. If she'd agreed, he would have joined in, but to do it entirely alone, with the risk of being sacked and having to go home to face her was too unnerving. When he told her, she was outraged.

"It's only takin' money from the boss," he said. "I thought that's what you socialists were all for."

"Not by theft," she said, straightening the tablecloth, "honestly and democratically."

"He makes his money from our work anyway. Why shouldn't we have a bit of it back?"

"You should, but not by stealing. They harm themselves more than him."

He didn't understand. How did they harm themselves by putting a few quid a week in their pocket? And if they were caught, they could plead ignorance. The bonus clerk would be up for it. All the same, he couldn't creep out on the thin branch alone. On his knees, cutting another mitre, the thought the blokes around him were taking home two or three quid more was another piece of grit in his sock, another flea bite he was scratching all day. He had to get out.

When her brother went back to university Sylvia felt the tightening of the home's atmosphere. While Andy was around, there was space her mother didn't control. He created an island of easy-going, light-heartedness in the middle of her lake of anxiety, heaviness and negativity. He was always reading and she looked at some of the books scattered on the back-room table along with his mess of papers in bafflement. She could neither pronounce nor understand the French. She flicked them open and found pages and pages of dense print in the foreign language. She felt in the presence of something alien. Yet her brother was still as he'd been before this serious study seized him. She'd never imagined, when he was a teenager in skin tight jeans and winkle-pinkers, careless of his homework, always out with his mates, on his bike or the tennis courts, he'd transform into this man who could sit, quiet and intense, reading some impenetrable book for hours.

She wasn't like him and that worried her. She wasn't like Mary either. She didn't have her skills nor her focus. She was herself and she had to make her own way; but alone with her mother she was presented daily with a burden: her mother depended on her company. How could she ever leave her? Mary and Andy had broken away, but her mother clung to her like a falling aviator to a half-open parachute. How could she ever push her away? America. It was only when she let her mind be soaked in dreams of escape she could see any way out.

She came home to an empty house. She had two hours to herself before her mother arrived and began questioning. She watched the television, ate some cereal, sometimes went to a friend's house for an hour.

"Have you been out?" her mother would say before she had her coat off.

"Only to Heather's."

"What d'you go there for?"

"Nothing."

"Nothing?"

"Just to see her?"

"What d'you want to see her about?"

"Not about anything."

"What d'you go for then?"

"I don't know."

"I'd better get t'tea on't go. I'm jiggered. What d'you want to eat?"

"I don't mind."

"I've some meat pie. I'll do some chips. And I've a crumble. Come in't kitchen you can make t' custard."

In the little cold space at the back of the house, the gas cooker against the rear, blue wall, the ancient washing machine with its mangle tucked under the wooden wall cupboards, the stainless-steel sink and drainer beneath which Elsie kept her cleaning materials, the red, ill-fitting lino underfoot, Sylvia listened as her mother began to retell the events of her day, repetitively, compulsively, desperately.

"Well, I said to her, I said, you can't do that it won't kill t'surface bacteria. God love us, that's basic. You've got to kill't surface bacteria first off. I said to her, I said, I showed you that this mornin'. Well, she wasn't for 'avin' it, but I told her. That's my job on't line if someone gets food poisoning. You've to fry't meat off first. That's basic. I told her, I said...."

Sylvia said nothing because she knew she wasn't required to. Her mother wasn't interested in conversation. She would monologue until she was weary, until every little incident had been recounted, retold, looked at from every possible angle, then she would collapse into herself like a house on a sink hole, sit in her corner of the sofa her right leg rocking, rocking as regularly as a baby's cradle, drink her tea before falling asleep, her head back, her mouth open, her breathing slow and rasping.

Her daughter wondered what her brother was doing. What was life like at university? It would be Easter before he was home again, except for one of his come-and-go visits, when he cycled down on a Sunday for example, had lunch with them, made her laugh for an hour and jumped back on his bike.

In the first term at Lancaster, Andy and his mates had got up at half past six one morning a week to go and hand out milk to children at Dallas Road Primary. The pupils were grateful, charming and cheeky.

"I don't like milk," a cocky lad of six or seven said to him.

"Never mind," said Andy, "give it your cat."

"I haven't got a cat."

"Well find a stray. Here, have the carton. It's free. Give it one of your mates if you don't want it."

An Asian girl of ten, tall and dignified, took the carton with a little bow and a quiet thank you.

"My pleasure," said Andy.

He hadn't intended to get involved in political activity. He wanted to learn, to read and above all to write. The scattered, foolish notions of what he might do with his life which had infested his brain as a child and adolescent, the infantile fantasy of playing football for a living, the preposterous, ephemeral identification with pop stars and the temptation to join one of the many three-chord, drum-abusing bands that sprang up like weeds between flagstones; the hopeless belief when he started at F.E.D. that he might find a pleasant, friendly way to make a living without having to change his relaxed approach to life had coalesced into the single desire to write what was in his head.

There was the matter of making a living. Lawrence had been a teacher for more than ten years. He could do the same. Lawrence had earned little from his writing. He made no connection between writing and money. That would have led in the wrong direction: seeking some commercial subject. It was what he *had* to do that mattered. Paying the mortgage from it was almost certainly impossible. He was familiar with the stories of neglected genius, of great works turned down by a hundred publishers, of epochal manuscripts yellowing in drawers for years.

He was working steadily at poems. The couple he'd had accepted by *Continuum* would shift him from private scribbling to an occupant of the public realm. Two small, insignificant poems, but it was impossible to predict what their effect might be. How many people would read them? How long would they endure? There was no reason why in twenty years' time, thirty, forty, a hundred someone might not dig out a dusty copy of the magazine in some disorganised bookshop, read one of the poems, like it, reflect on it, and in some minute way be changed by it. That was the magic of literature. It transcended the ephemeral. Its power to interest and to engage could endure across monumental social changes. Not long ago, he'd read Sophocles for the first time. How strange but marvellous that a boy from the back streets of Preston in the mid-twentieth century could read a play written two thousand years earlier in a thoroughly different culture and find it compelling. *Oedipus Rex* wasn't a housewarmer. It wasn't written with an eye on how much it might put in the bank. It existed at a higher level. All real literature did.

To be part of that, even in a small way, in the tiniest way, was better than any reward of money, status, power. This activity, which had become the central preoccupation of his life, was at odds with the blow-your-bubble-and-wait-for-it-to-burst culture he inhabited. Most of the students around him were pursuing degrees in order to get good jobs, earn well, buy the nice house in the suburbs or the country, drive the look-at-me cars and take holidays in exotic corners; but none of that entered his head. He wanted to be able to write like Lawrence. Some part of him knew he could produce novels, but another part of him was perpetually defeated. He made a beginning, clattering out three pages on his sticking-keys portable. When he re-read it a week later, it disgusted him. He tore it, dropped it in the bin under his sink and went out for a long walk.

Perhaps he should give up. Maybe he was insane. What made him think he was a writer? He strode into Lancaster. What interest did the people he saw in the street have in literature? How many of them had read Lawrence or Chaucer or Skelton? How many of them cared? Was he wasting his time? Was he a deluded fool pursuing some impossible aim that was sure to lead him to disappointment and even despair? He was reluctant to admit to himself that reading what he'd written and being nauseated by it did engender despair. It drove him into isolation and blankness. It was impossible to speak to anyone. He couldn't talk to Rob or Mike or Steve about his writing. It came from a self far removed from the one that drank with them in the bar, joked around in the tea-time kitchen, sat in interminable lectures, lazed with them in one of their rooms in the evening and long into the night as they played guitars and talked about nothing. It was a secret self he was almost ashamed of. Yet it was his most authentic identity and in being unable to connect it to others there was real despair.

He read the reviews pages of the so-called quality press, most of which infuriated him by their glibness, and looked at the TLS in the library. There seemed no correspondence between his intense, delicate, other-realm activity and publishing. The world of publishing struck him as no less hard-headed business than the second-hand car trade. He recalled with acute embarrassment which made his cheeks burn as he passed *The Ring O' Bells* and wondered if he should nip in for a pint, his pathetic, naïve submission of his poems to *Studio Vista* or whatever the outfit was called; the absence of response; his sending them out to *Macmillan* and *Faber* and *Cape* only to receive the bland, dead replies that as an unpublished poet he was of no interest.

When he thought of his writing, his mind turned inward. All the vivid evocation of the life of working-class Eastwood he found in Lawrence came from the capacity to explore minutely inner reactions to external stimuli. What was the relationship between that and the double-entry, bottom-line world of publishing?

He was in a university. He was studying literature. Yet who, among his teachers could help him in his struggle to be a writer? His lecturers could write about literature but could they write the stuff itself. Where was he going to find help?

He walked till he was exhausted, thirsty and hot which helped quell his turmoil. He called in *The Blue Bell* for a drink and sitting alone, watching the pair of girls at the bar chatting and laughing in their untroubled way, he was struck by the idea of his freakishness. Perhaps he should give up, do like everyone else: get a good job, a nice house and forget the impulse to write. He knew he couldn't do it. He would try again. He knew an image would come to him and he would bash out ten paragraphs hoping this time they would rise to the level of what he recognised as literature; and he knew that disappointment would spread through him like a virus attacking an infirm body and that slowly it would transform to self-contempt; that he would be unbale to write again for weeks but that, in the end, another image would come and along with it the high, blue-sky-and-sunshine feeling that he could grab what was hidden in his mind and turn it into something which might compare to *The Blind Man* or *Second Best*.

Jane Bentnick was watching for his return. During the Christmas vacation she'd been to Nancy to see Jean-Claude. They'd reignited the torrid blaze of their sexual liaison. She had sworn undying love. He'd reciprocated. Yet she was sure when she was away, he would take his opportunities. At home in Reigate, she'd resolved to have no more to do with Andy Lang. Who was he? A northerner. A socialist. Oh, he was good-looking, but she could resist that. No, she would ignore him. Let him beg her, she'd shun him.

He didn't beg.

She saw him with Sue Border in Bowland Bar after a lecture and her passionate jealousy that would have driven her to murder churned her insides. She stood by her window smoking. No sign of him. The desire to possess, to control was so mad in her she knew what she was going to do. When she saw him, she would go and knock on his door. He would let her in. She knew that. He was too soft to turn her away. She would tell him to close the curtains. Unceremoniously, she would strip, pull off her ring, put it on his beside cabinet and get under the sheets. He would be helpless.

At last he appeared. She stood still as a stalking tiger. There he was, her prey. There he was slim and easy in his movements. He was wearing his light blue polo neck. Oh, yes that was him. The blue-eyed boy. She knew the jumper set off the light of his eyes. He did it deliberately. Who was he trying to charm? Sue Border? That bitch. She wouldn't have him. She stubbed her long cigarette in the red, tin ashtray. Looking in the mirror she decided a little mascara would help. She picked up her heavy brush and dragged it through her clean, shining hair. A last look through the window: he was at his desk. Well, he would get no work done this afternoon.

She knocked twice: quick, urgent little raps, as if there was some emergency. When he opened she walked in. Oh, the fool. He didn't have the strength to stop her. She closed the door. He stood by the chair, leaning, smiling in pleasant welcome.

"Shut the curtains," she said.

For less than a second she thought he was going to make one of his wry comments, but he turned and before he could face her again, she had already tossed her coat on the armchair at the foot of the bed and was unbuttoning her blouse. He didn't speak. She stared into his eyes as with absolute calm, she took off her jeans, her bra, her socks, her knickers. She was naked and he was clothed. She moved past him, twisted the ring off her finger, placed it silently on the cabinet and got into his bed.

The power of a woman's sexuality. The weakness of a man. Her confidence was complete, not only because she knew her eighteen-year-old body, slim, full, her breasts white and heavy, her thighs thick with life, her face prettier than ninety-nine per cent was as irresistible as gold to a miser, dice to a compulsive gambler, the bottle to an alcoholic, but because she knew how polite he was. His courtesy would have prevented him turning her down.

She watched him impassively as he took off his clothes. There was no doubt he was attractive. Not just his beautiful face, marred though it was by acne, but also his boyish body. He wasn't powerfully masculine, muscular, hirsute. He didn't possess that slightly frightening power a man's body has if it is crudely strong and lacking any feminine traits; but his movements were both masculine and charming and his unpinchable waist, his slender legs and arms and his hairless chest might have been those of a sixteen-year-old, which softened and delighted her.

It was such an easy conquest she was almost contemptuous, but in spite of herself she wondered if she might be falling in love. She got out of bed to douse her cigarette in the sink.

"I'd better be going," she said, shaking her thick hair.

"Why?"

"Your friends will be back soon. I don't want them knowing."

"Knowing what?"

"That we've been to bed together."

"I don't think they'll be either shocked or interested."

"I don't like them knowing everything."

"Everything?"

"What do you tell them?"

"Oh, I tell them we share a passion for stamp-collecting."

"What do you think of my breasts?"

She faced him and put a hand beneath each one to lift them a little.

"I think they're beautiful."

"Do you think they're big enough?"

"For what?"

"Men like big breasts, don't they?"

"They're probably less impressed by them than they think they are."

"Do you think I could be in *Playboy*?"

"I think that would be a very bad idea."

"Why?"

"Because it makes a lot of money."

"What's wrong with making money?"

"It usually involves corruption."

"I don't think they're big enough."

She lifted her cotton, Marks and Spencer, faded pink knickers from the chair and stepped into them.

"You don't have to go. I'll make some coffee."

"No," she said, putting her arms through the straps of her bra, "I have to go."

She was surprised by her desire to stay. Her fierce jealousy had disappeared like wispy clouds in a May breeze. He was hers. It was impossible to hold back her mind. She found her feelings running on to togetherness and she had to fight hard to retain her cynicism. The impulse simply to be kind and soft to him impelled her in the opposite direction. The natural action would be to stay with him. They could eat together. Spend the evening together. Share his bed. In all this there was peril. She was being dragged away from what she should be. She should be Jean-Claude's girl-friend. She loved him. They were fated. She wanted to disdain her fellow students. This was Lancaster. The best people were at Oxbridge or Durham or Bristol. That's where she should have been. It had always been her assumption that being a pupil at Ashford School meant the best universities would be open to her. It had been a shock when her A Levels were below what she expected and she had to scramble for a place through clearing. She'd believed that people from her background would be assured a place in the best institutions. There were people from ordinary schools in the north who had better grades and were getting places at Oxbridge. That wasn't how it was supposed to be. What was the point of private school if it didn't guarantee opportunities denied to the rest?

Lancaster. What kind of place was that? She had no idea where it was. The North was a nebulous area beyond London inhabited by people of lower intelligence who ruined the country by voting Labour. Being ignorant about The North was a status symbol. Lancaster. They might as well have been sending her to darkest Africa.

She was determined to remain aloof. She would have nothing to do with these inferior types. She had a boyfriend. She had her friends from school. She had no need of these lower people.

Yet when she crossed Alexandra Square and saw the students sitting on the steps, talking and laughing, when she sat in a lecture in Lonsdale Theatre among the fifty students doing French and wondered who they all were and was tempted to get to know them; when she first spotted Andy Lang in the foyer of the French Department and felt that curious, irresistible shock of interest and desire which she so wanted not to happen, her stern resolve bent like white-hot iron; her youth was too much for her. She was telling herself her life was settled, she was a mature, experienced woman with a lover who held her like the sun forces the earth's orbit. She had no need of friendship. She had no need of a lover from amongst these lighter people. Yet life surged in her and overthrew these flimsy defences. She couldn't see Andy Lang but she was tormented by the need to know him. Oh, it was so wrong. It was so unfair. Why was she here?

"What's so urgent?" he said.

She was buttoning her blouse against her inordinate wish to get back into bed with him. To be warm beside him. To feel secure. He did make her feel secure. Why was that? To know she was in bed with one of the best-looking boys on campus. To be glad he was intelligent, polite, funny and kind. All that she wanted more than anything as she reached for her coat; but she had to go. She had to let him know she was not easily had. She had to go at once and write to Jean-Claude.

She couldn't help herself though.

"We could go for a drink later," she said before she closed the door.

"We could go for several," he said.

She couldn't have bruised Jean-Claude more had she been pummelling his ribs with knuckle-dusters. With each scribbled sentence, her expressions became more desperate, more importunate. He may think he could make use of distance to sneak from room to room, from bed to bed, but she'd show him she could squeeze his balls. She knew he couldn't let her go. He was glued to her, not just because he wanted exclusive access to her body, but because they were as bad for one another as a bingo hall for a weak-minded woman who believes every new card will be the one that will bring the jackpot and whose children live on egg and chips. They were incapable of leaving one another. He was no more something she could renounce than the cigarette she pulled from the silver packet and lit with her blue *briquet,* bought on the station in Nancy. They were wrapped in barbed wire, like her parents.

Wasn't that what love meant? Wasn't it the desperate clinging of two drowning people who could do nothing but drag each other under? She wasn't supposed to fall for the likes of Andy Lang. His type was to be disdained. They were the undesirables of the spookology of Ashford School. She fought hard against the recognition of what she'd just done and pushed the scream of her missive to a higher volume.

The folded sheets in the pregnant blue envelope, she scrawled the name and address, took stamps from her drawer, pulled on her coat and strode to the post box. What to do now? She could go and knock on Andy's door. No, she needed weed. She headed down the Spine to find the dealer.

A FALL

It was a tiredness more debilitating than she could have imagined. She dragged herself home from the training kitchen, made something to eat and spent the evening asleep on the sofa. There were days when it would lift a little and at the weekends she could find her energy return, briefly; but her old self was gone. Was this ageing? Was it the after-effect of the menopause? Did all women of her age feel like this? Was she going to be as weary, day after day, for the rest of her life?

One Sunday, because it was bright and calm and because walking kept her uncle active in his eighties, she decided to stroll home from Lune Street Methodists, where she'd been turning up regularly for months. Perhaps it would help to make her feel more energetic. Maybe that was the trouble: too much work in that hot kitchen and not enough pleasant exercise in the fresh air. There was something you needed which came from sunlight. That was why Mary and Andy had been given sunlamp treatment when they were young. It was one of those post-war, look-after-the-people-properly measures which Labour had introduced. Free orange juice. That was vitamin C. What was it you got from sunlight?

She was crossing Penwortham Bridge when a sudden sense of being pushed from behind startled her. There might have been a hand in the middle of her back forcing her forward. She dropped to her knees. Fell, supporting herself on her hand in her lilac leather gloves. Cars were passing. What would people think? Why did no one stop? She looked over shoulder. No one. What had driven her down? Could she get up?

The strap of her handbag was broken. Her best bag. She lifted herself gingerly. Her tights were torn at the knees which were bleeding. She tried, feebly, to fit the handle back into the little brass clasp. She would just have to carry it under her arm. Penwortham Hill was ahead of her. Would she make it to the top? She went on, slowly, with small, unnerved steps. She would be late. Would Sylvia worry? Would she come looking for her? What had made her fall? What could it be?

A FALL

Sylvia wasn't in the living-room. Elsie mounted the stairs as if for the last time. She pushed open her daughter's bedroom door. She was at her dressing-table, brushing her hair.

"I've had a fall."

The girl turned to look at her.

"For all't world it felt as if someone were pushin' me in't back. I went right down. Right down. My knees are bleedin'. And folk were passin' and no one stopped. I could've been dyin'there. No one stopped."

She began to sob.

The teenager sat still and looked at her.

"Shall I call an ambulance?" she said.

"Ambulance. You might've come and looked for me," said the mother. "Where did you think I was? Anythin' could've happened to me. Fat lot you care, admirin' yourself in't mirror while I'm on my knees on Penwortham Bridge. And I suppose you've done nowt to get't dinner ready?"

Her daughter, pale and unresponsive, sat silent and immobile.

"You can peel't potatoes while I sort myself out."

In her untidy room, the sheets of the double bed thrown aside, her nightie draped over the footboard, she rolled off her tights and inspected her scraped knees. She had some Dettol. She went to the bathroom, filled the sink, added a capful which made the clear water milky and dabbed her wounds with the dampened, folded face-cloth. She applied *Germolene* and *Elastoplast* from the drawer of her dressing table, hung her best clothes in the wardrobe, pulled on the worn, comfortable skirt she liked to relax in and the blue jumper Andy had bought her for Christmas. Her poor bag. How much had she paid for that? She tried once more, ineffectually, to repair it. She would have to buy another. There was an expense she couldn't afford; but why was she so tired? Why had she fallen? She thought of her father's diabetes. Was that it? No. She wasn't losing weight like he did. Was she dying? She was fifty. She'd always thought she would live into her seventies. Yet maybe not. What would happen to Sylvia? Would Mary take her in? She would. Surely, she would. She was a good lass. She always had been.

She would have to go to the doctor. Her rational mind whose ideas were as clear and sensible as ever, worked in the midst of her emotional turmoil. She would go tomorrow after work. She began at once to rehearse what she would say to him:

"I've no energy, doctor. It's all I can do to get through't day at work. Once I'm home I'm jiggered."

She reflected that "jiggered" might not be the right term to use before a professional. Perhaps "exhausted" would be better.

"Once I'm home I'm exhausted. I can't tell you. I've barely't energy to lift a spoon and I was walking home from church, it was a nice day so I thought I'd walk, well, I was crossin't bridge, when for all't world it might've been a hand pushin' me in't back. I went down. You can see my knees...."

She continued her rehearsal as she went down to the kitchen where Sylvia was standing at the sink pulling the blade of the peeler across the skin of a big King Edward.

"I shall 'ave to go to't doctor's tomorrow," she said. "I don't know what's wrong wi' me, I'm sure I don't. I've too much to do, I know that. You could 'elp me a bit more round't th'ouse for a start. That'd be summat. 'Ere, gimme that. We've not got all day," and she took the peeler and potato from her and with that pained intensity which always distorted her features, her lips pulled back over her teeth, her eyes screwed as if against smoke, her body tense as though she was being tested, as if punishment would arrive out of the air if she didn't peel this vegetable quickly and efficiently enough, she left her daughter standing idle, not knowing what she should help with next, hesitant to touch anything for fear of doing wrong so that she lingered hopelessly for two minutes before withdrawing to the front room where she found a soothing American comedy to watch.

The waiting room was crowded. Beside her a woman of sixty was sneezing and coughing without bringing her hand to her mouth and nose. Elsie was inclined to berate her:

"Dear 'eaven," she would have liked to say, "we don't want yer germs. Don't you know when you sneeze and cough yer germs go everywhere? They're in't th'air for minutes. We're all breathin' 'em. Lord 'elp us we'll all be down wi' it, woman."

She said nothing but she wondered if she should speak to Doctor Fox. He would listen to her. He would do something about it. He'd probably come through himself and make an announcement. She felt herself on the side of responsibility, of virtue.

Had there been a free seat, she would have moved. It was forty minutes before the receptionist called her through. The surgery was on the ground floor of a big old house half-way up Fishergate Hill. When she and Bert moved to Penwortham, he'd said they should register with a local surgery, but she wanted to stay with the doctors who knew her, who knew her family, who had known her mother. Dr Fox was too young to have treated her but his colleague, now close to retirement. had attended her at home many times. The consulting room had once been someone's living-room. Someone much better off than she'd ever been. It retained its original oak panelling and the imposing, serious, dark, high, polished, uncluttered mantelpiece beneath which once must have burned the coal fire that kept the residents warm. Now there was an electric heater with a curled white flex, at the other side of the doctor's desk, by the window.

The desk too was dark and from a previous time; one of those writing-bureaux with little drawers and compartments Bert had always insisted on calling an *escritoire.* As she entered, Dr Fox was writing, bent over the folded down board supported by two limbs which pulled out from the body of the desk. She stood and waited to be told to sit down. He turned his head and looked at her from over his glasses and under his heavy brows which always made her think of Denis Healey.

"Sit down, Mrs Lang," he said in his deep, easy voice, "I shan't be a moment."

"Thank you, doctor."

She at once felt self-conscious and out-of-place. Her rehearsed speech turned to steam. What should she say? What was wrong with her? It wasn't like having a sore throat or housemaid's knee. She was tired. How could she say that? How could she say she was weary of her life? How could she tell him the days followed one another and she inhabited them like a Jew living in Berlin in 1935? The very flow of time mocked her. How could she tell him?

"Well, Mrs Lang, what brings you to see me?"

He swivelled his chair to face her. His half-moon glasses were golden and slipping down his nose. His eyes were fixed, confident, questioning. She had the sudden sensation that he would see through anything she said. He was an educated man. He understood all kinds of things about the human body and medicines she had no inkling about. She could easily make a fool of herself.

"I've had a fall," she said.

"Ah. How did that happen?"

"I was crossing the bridge, on my way home from church, and I just went. I felt as if I was being pushed. I just went. Down on my knees."

He nodded, turned away and wrote on a little pad.

"Has this happened before?"

"No."

"Any dizziness?"

"No."

"Any pain?"

"No."

"Any problem with your waterworks?"

Waterworks? What was he asking that for? And what kind of problem? The question stunned her.

"No. Nothing like that."

"Tiredness?"

"Yes."

"Thirst?"

"No."

"Your father was diabetic, wasn't he?"

"Yes."

"Do you eat well?"

"I think so."

"Plenty of exercise?"

A FALL

"Exercise? Well, I don't have much time. I work. I work in a training kitchen. It's hard. It's hot. I'm jiggered…."

She stopped herself.

"Mmm. No pain in the chest or the upper arm?"

"No."

"Any coughing?"

"Well, I do cough a bit. I do get sore throats and colds."

"Often?"

"More than I used to."

"Let me just listen to your chest," he said, putting the stethoscope in his ears.

She breathed in and out. He put two fingers of his left hand on her chest and tapped them with his right hand. She opened her mouth and said Ah as he held down her tongue with an over-large lollipop stick. He wrapped the tight, rubber cuff around her arm and pumped the brown, stiff little bladder till it tightened, then watched the hand of the dial, descend and pause. She stood on the weighing scale as he moved the metal weights to make it balance.

"Well, Mrs Lang, your chest is clear, your blood pressure is fine, nothing obvious. I'd like you to bring in a urine sample. Sterilize the bottle first. And I'm going to send you for a blood test. Give this to the receptionist. She'll tell you the days and times."

"Thank you, doctor."

She took the P5 home. The disappointment of her consultation was exacerbated by the crowded bus. There was no one she knew. They were people going home from work. Who were they? Where did they work? Why wasn't there a single face she recognised?

She'd hoped for a long conversation with Dr Fox. She would have liked to pour her troubles out to him. Wasn't that what doctors were for? She recalled the day the old physician had called her *a very disturbed woman*. Yes, that was what she wanted to hear. Bert had left. She was unable to function. Shouldn't a doctor see to that? All she'd got was tranquillizers and she'd had to wean herself off those when she realised they were turning her into a zombie. She should have been helped. She needed help. Where should help have come from?

My help cometh from the Lord..The words drifted through her mind. Why didn't the church help her? She had been utterly alone.

As she walked along Crookings Lane, she replayed the consultation. What could a doctor hear through a stethoscope? Why did he tap her chest with his fingers? How was blood pressure measured? Dr Fox understood. To him, she was just another body. If he could lift this horrible tiredness from her, so much the better; she would forgive him for treating her as something to be prodded and measured. Yet the strange feeling came over her that he understood her body more than she did. It was her body. Why didn't she understand it? How odd it was to put yourself in the doctor's hands, to have your very existence depend on his knowledge. She wished she knew. She wished she could treat herself in the way she could make up her own mind. As far as her values were concerned, she'd bow to no one. She had her Methodism. She was unflinching in her rejection of the ideas which disturbed her. She was surrounded by snobs in Penwortham; people who voted Tory because they had a semi, a garage, a garden and a car. She considered that cheap, vulgar and despicable. She was virtually the only Labour voter in Woodland Grove; but she experienced no irresoluteness or doubt. Let them think what they like. She made up her own mind.

When it came to her body she had to cede. There was something wrong with her. She knew that. She could tell Dr Fox thought so too. Yet what was going on in her own cells was as hidden from her as the depths of the ocean. Her body was alien. It was acting against her. It was hard to feel that whatever was making her tired was part of her. It seemed to come from elsewhere. She'd always been at one with her body. She'd never been ill. Pregnancy aside, she'd never been in hospital. Her body was reliable and kind. How it could it suddenly work against her? When she said "I'm tired", what did she mean? Her body was tired, but it didn't feel like her body anymore. She wished she could have her body back. The real body.

What could Dr Fox tell by testing her urine? And how did they find out anything from the little bit of blood they took? Jimmy's lad, her nephew, would know. He'd studied chemistry and pharmacy at university. Perhaps she should ask him. He might be able to explain it in simple terms. It was hopeless. She didn't have the education. She had to accept that Dr Fox and the hospital and strangers in a laboratory looking into microscopes would know her body better than she did. They would know before she would what was wrong. She experienced it as a kind of theft and a submission which was against her nature. She was a Craxton. Resistance was in her marrow. All the same, in this she must submit.

She made steak and chips for herself and Sylvia who disappeared upstairs as soon as she'd eaten, coming down half an hour later, her hair brushed, her face made-up, the collar of her maroon coat turned up:

"I'm just going round to Heather's."

"No, you're not. Not tonight."

"Why?"

"Because I say so. You can stay in for once. Take your coat off."

Elsie was disappointed by her own unreasonableness but she forgave herself. Why shouldn't the girl sit with her? The dreadful thought gathered in the rear if her mind, like black clouds amassing over the sea, that she might not have much longer to live. She wanted Sylvia to be opposite her so she could tell her all about her visit to the doctor's. She had to have tests. She would convey it gloomily; but her daughter stayed in her room. She wondered if she should flush her out. Her tenderness triumphed. She ought to have let her go out. The girl was young. She needed her friends. She needed them more than her mother.

The thought woke her up like ice water being poured over head. Was it true? Did all her children now need strangers more than they needed her? Mary was living a life she knew little of. Day by day she was going to work, talking to people, elaborating relationships Elsie knew nothing about. She always believed the closeness of the community she came from would never dissipate. When she was Mary's age she was still living in her father's house. She saw her parents every day. They knew everything she did and everyone she met. There were no strangers in the streets neighbouring Talbot Road. She knew everyone and was known to everyone. The possibility of her children moving away had never occurred to her. Mary was in Skelmersdale, a place she had never thought about before Ted sprang up like a jack-in-a-box. Andy was in Lancaster, a place she'd never been. She'd lived in Preston for fifty years. Lancaster was twenty miles north, yet it was as unexplored as Tierra del Fuego. Her children lived lives quite separate from her and always would. How could it be? She could never have detached herself utterly from her mother. The world had changed. She'd been left behind. Her feelings belonged to a different age and place. She wanted to go back there. She wanted to be little Elsie Craxton, at home in the terraced streets, safe amongst her family; but she was Elsie Lang, alienated from her community, overcome by a sense of loss.

Mary.

She must tell Mary. Why shouldn't she? The thought of her daughter's pregnancy retained her for a minute. She mustn't cause her anxiety. Nevertheless, she might be ill. It might be serious. Her daughter must know.

"Hello, luv, it's your mum."

She recounted her visit in every detail: the coughing woman, the crowded waiting-room, Dr Fox's glasses, his pen and pad, the stethoscope, the blood pressure check, the weighing scales, the urine sample and the blood test, the P5 home and the possibility of serious illness. Mary was reassuring: it was probably something and nothing; maybe her age; perhaps a passing anaemia; the doctor would get to the bottom of it; he'd prescribe something and she'd be okay; it might be nothing more than a course of iron she needed.

Elsie took up her position in the corner of the sofa, her leg swaying like an eternal pendulum. Yes, Mary was probably right. A woman of her age: it was common enough to be anaemic. It might come and go. There might be nothing to worry about. She paid attention to the news but the ebbing of her anxiety slowed down her functions and when Sylvia came down five minutes later, she was asleep, her head lolling back, snoring.

Mary put the phone down and went back to tidying the kitchen. She was quick and decisive. Her ability to search out a truant crumb beneath the toaster or spot a splash of grease on the tiles was undiminished. It was a matter of principle. Had she sat down next to Ted to watch the television, her long-postponed cup of tea in her hand, knowing there might be a pea which had fled from the packet as she took it from the freezer and taken refuge under the oven, she would have had to get up, pull the cooker away from the wall, pregnancy notwithstanding, pinch the recalcitrant vegetable between her thumb and finger and drop it to perdition in the bin.

A FALL

Her pleasure, which was the refusal of self-abandonment, the pride that had made Tom Craxton never waste so much as a tack and his wife keep her house as clean as a hermit's diary, was diminished by worry over her mother. Oh, she knew her. She made the most of trivialities. It would be less serious than she made it sound. She'd fallen; but she wasn't injured. She'd seen the doctor. They were going to do a blood test. They would get to the bottom of it. In any case, whatever needed to be done would be available. This was 1973. It wasn't like the days when her grandma had been bed-ridden and every doctor's visit was a strain on the family's petty income. The NHS would provide. She would be well looked after.

She couldn't quite convince herself. There was always the chance of something serious. Suppose it was cancer. Perhaps within her the process was silently destroying. It would have to be faced. Sylvia would have to be looked after. At least there would be no worry about money. Her mother owned her house. All the same, just now, just as new life was growing within her, to receive news which might point towards death, to have think of her mother's mortality troubled her to fretfulness.

She laid her hand on her belly. Oh, for god's sake, calm down. Whatever happened, she would cope with it. What mattered was this child, her child. This was the chance to make amends. When she looked back, there was the horrible matter of her parents' divorce, the fact of her alienation from her father and her mother's decline into congealed bitterness. Ahead was a good life for the boy or girl within her. She would make sure of that. This child would never suffer as she had.

It was some days later before Andy Lang found out. The letter was the only one in his pigeon-hole. His mother's writing made him smile but the brief note with its portentous:

I had a fall and had to go to the doctor. They're going to do a blood test. Let's hope for the best...

shocked him. The following Sunday he cycled home on the big, heavy, clunking bike he'd bought for a couple of quid, the three Sturmey Archer gears sticking as he pressed or pulled on the chrome-plated lever. It was an easy ride straight down the A6 but the traffic was incessant and some of the cars or vans left hardly any room so he found himself raising two fingers as he wobbled close to the kerb.

"All right, Syl?"

"Hia."

"How's mum then?" he said dropping into the armchair opposite his sister.

"She's all right. She cut her knees."

"Where did she fall?"

"Coming home from church. On the bridge. She said it felt like someone pushing her in the back."

"God, was she mugged? What did they get, her glasses and her hymn book?"

There was the inevitable chicken dinner, carefully prepared, hot, tasty and wholesome. They ate at the table in the bay of the back room, his mother coming and going for pepper, more gravy, an extra spoon.

"Sit down and eat, mum," he said.

When he questioned her she began her diatribe, in spite of the food in her mouth, and he knew it would go on as long as they were to listen, even though they didn't:

"For all't world," she said, "I'd've thought it were a hand on me back. Shovin', just like it, between me shoulder blades. Dear heaven, I went down wi such a bang. Me knees were in shreds. And what bothered me most were folk were passin', cars, one after another and no one stopped, not one. I coulda died on't spot and no one'd come t'elp me...."

A female blackbird was in the middle of the near lawn. He watched her, unable to attend any more to his mother's attempt to reel in his sympathy. The little rockery, from the square of crazy paving down to the lawn edge, was still in place. He remembered how they jumped it in their summer games, the garden full of the grove's children, the days waning slowly, the lovely odour of sunshine on his skin. Even the odd behaviour of Robert Jones couldn't diminish the joy of those days and evenings. It was always open garden. His mother allowed as many children as wanted to come and play. They invented their own endless games whose rules could be changed to fit their needs. Before Sylvia was born he and Mary and all their friends had experienced carefree, wild, the-garden-is-our-own-world-

and-we'll-do-what-we-like afternoons and ends of days, while his mum and dad stayed in the house, distant, silent, letting them disappear into their imaginations.

The image of Mary in pink slacks and a white blouse, her face freckled from the sun, smiling in that warm wide way which had been so reassuring to him as a boy came into his head and at once he saw himself too in a yellow, short-sleeved shirt with a collar and one button at the throat which he never fastened, his hair cut short-back-and-sides by Smokey Joe who occupied a wooden building behind a house beyond *The Daintee* where he bought bubble gum and gobstoppers, utterly happy, oblivious of the tension which existed between his parents, secure in the love of his elder sister and with no inkling of the horror to come.

"There'll be a nest somewhere," he said.

"Eh?" said his mother, startled at the interruption.

"The blackbird. They'll nest in the garden. There were always nests in the back hedge and the rhododendrons. We had wrens one year, do you remember?"

"Wrens?" said Elsie. "We've never 'ad wrens to my knowledge."

"Yes, John Rutherford found the nest. There were eggs."

"John Rutherford? I don't recall that."

"He's at the Natural History Museum now. Entomologist."

"What's that?" said Sylvia.

"Someone who loves beetles."

"Ugh."

"Don't talk about beetles while we're havin' our dinner." Elsie gathered the plates, went to the kitchen and took the browned rice pudding from the gas oven.

"Not only beetles," said Andy when she'd gone, "leather-backs, cockroaches, centipedes…"

"Stop it."

"Anyway, she seems okay," he said. "I think it'll be something and nothing. She'll live to be a hundred and seven."

He set off back at three o'clock. There was a chill breeze in his face all the way and as he hadn't bothered with gloves, his fingers began to turn numb. He uncurled them from the black-taped bars, one after the other and blew into his fist, rubbed each tip against his thumb and began to dream of a warm shower. When he emerged from the steam, a little, worn, yellow and white striped towel around his waist, Jane was standing by his door, smoking.

"Waiting for a bus?" he said.

"I saw you come back."

"You should have let yourself in. It's open."

"You look like a chicken," she said.

"Cluck, cluck, cluck," he went and waved his folded arms.

Inside she took off her jacket and laid on the bed.

"You do. You have a chicken's chest."

"All the same," he said, rubbing his hair, "I'm still cock of the walk."

"You're not very masculine, are you?"

"That's what my psychiatrist says. She suspects me of surreptitious hermaphroditism."

"What's that?"

"Being neither one thing nor the other. Facing neither east nor west. Neither believing in god nor in a godless universe. Eating neither meat nor vegetables. Representing, in short, in the flesh, Mr Heisenberg's uncertainty principle: if you know where I am you can't know what I'm up to, if you know what I'm up to, you can't know where I am. Which is most convenient for mischief."

"You're not hairy, like John Redford. He's masculine."

"Ah, you've inspected his body for hirsuteness then?"

"He's got hairy legs and arms and a thick beard. I bet you couldn't grow a beard."

"I bet I could grow one faster that you."

"And he's sporty."

"He is, but he needs to work on his ground shots."

"What?"

"Tennis is not his forte."

"Have you played him?"

"Indoors."

"Did he beat you?"

"Not quite."

"What was the score?"

"Love and love."

"I don't believe you," she sat up and ran her fingers through her mane.

"Ask him next time you're counting the hairs on his chest."

"How could you beat him, he's much stronger than you?"

"He is. You're right. In a scrum I wouldn't have a chance, but his hand-eye coordination isn't quite up to scratch and he snatches at shots. There it is, strength isn't everything."

He was about to pull on his underpants. She turned and propped herself on her elbow.

"Don't get dressed."

"I thought I'd better conceal my unmasculine, hairless, chicken's body before it made you sick on the floor."

She sat up once more, pulled her sky-blue polo neck over her head and in seconds was naked.

It infuriated her that she found him so attractive. She said to herself in the moment of her acute desire as she stood, thin, white and unclothed, like a boy, an adolescent, a mere seventeen-year-old, that he was beautiful. Now, in front of the mirror, blowing smoke at her own reflection she hated herself for it. That she was a fool for his body was bad enough, but that she craved his affection, that she sank into helplessness when he touched her, that his attentiveness melted all the defences her parents and her school had installed against men like him, disgusted her. She should have been able to dismiss him: he was a northerner with an odd accent, his family had no money, he was a socialist, he came from a town she'd never heard of before being sent to Lancaster. He was the kind of man she should despise.

That morning she'd received a package from her mother. It contained the usual, silly, rambling letter full of inconsequential gossip and coy, dubious references. Along with it she'd included a two-inch thick note pad of coloured pages, some containing salacious *double-*

entendres. She took it from her bag which she'd dropped on his armchair with her coat.

"My mother sent me this today," she said, handing it to him.

He flicked the pages, then opened it at a pink one bearing in big, black print:

COMING SOON: NICHOLAS GURLZ.

He paused, looked up at her, smiled and said:

"Your mother sent you that?"

"Yes."

She stood beside the bed, naked, exposed in every way. She felt she had handed him her life. All her shattered confidence escaped from her. She was telling him how dreadful her mother was, how disappointing her family, how little she had to rely on; she was asking for his help. She was asking for his love.

His eyes were lowered, looking at the vulgar item. On his face was that seriousness behind which there lingered a little smile which so captivated her. She waited an age for his response. He looked up, his face softened into a wide, deliberate smile. He got out of bed, dropped the pad in the bin under his sink, took her in his arms and said:

"Never mind."

She kissed him and at that moment wished she could never be apart from him for a second.

In her room, as the evening drew in and the darkness she dreaded gathered, The Cretin at her desk scribbling at some essay, she lit a spliff. Normally, she smoked dope only when her room-mate wasn't there, but today she didn't care. Let her report her. What did it matter? What would they do anyway. They had no more chance of stopping weed being smoked on campus than stopping the rugby club drinking Newcastle Brown. She'd written to her mother telling her she was in love with a red-hot socialist from Preston. The letter was in the envelope and addressed before she ripped it up. She wrote another telling her Lancaster was an awful place, full of northerners and Labour Party people and accusing her of cruelty for having sent her there.

She wrote to Jean-Claude in melodramatic terms: she was falling for another boy; she was sinking; if he didn't rescue her, he would lose her.

She pulled the curtain aside to see if the light was on in Andy's room. She wanted to go down and pummel him with her fists. She was disgusted by her weakness. She tried to summon all the troops of her upbringing to defeat her attraction. She was at a loss to understand why she was driven. From the first time she'd seen him she wanted to get to know him. Why? He'd shown no interest in her. He was polite and distant. Boys crawled after her like flies on a cream cake. Why did it have to be the one who fascinated her who didn't? Fascinated? She rebelled against the idea. She was in control. Who did he think he was? Oh, he had nice blue eyes and a charming smile but she couldn't be won by such trivialities. She'd let herself down, again. Waiting outside his room. What did she think she was doing? Well, that was the last time. He'd better not think he could have her when he liked. She'd show him. She'd shut him out so suddenly he wouldn't know if it was last Wednesday or next Saturday. She had Jean-Claude. Ah, Lang was a fool. As if she'd be giving herself only to him. She was cleverer than that. Men had to be played with. A woman had to use everything at her disposal. A phrase came into her head: *On ne badine pas avec l'amour*. Where had she read that? In one of the authors she was supposed to study, but which? She couldn't recall but she liked the idea. Love was a serious business. Not to be toyed with. Yes, she agreed. A man mustn't toy with her feelings, which was why she so resented Jean-Claude. She knew he was doing it with other girls. He'd never admit it. He'd declare his love for her. They were fated to be together. She believed it. She wanted him to be the great love of her life; but he was far away and she was lonely.

Was Andy Lang falling in love with her? Maybe. Was he telling her when he said "Never mind" that he would take care of her. She relished the idea. Let him fall for her. She'd encourage him. Yes. That was it. What did it cost her, after all? Sex. She could give him that without being involved. She could stand back from herself and if he was stupid enough to think she gave him her body because she was giving him her affection, that was his look out. If he thought she was going to take his feelings into account he was an idiot. She had her own feelings to think about.

His light went out. Where was he going? She had an irresistible impulse to rush down and find him. Was he going to meet Sue Border? He mocked her when she accused him. Sue was Rob's interest; but she didn't believe it. She was an attractive girl. She was bound to fancy him. If they were alone together....

Now she wished she'd stayed with him. She drew on her spliff. It was such a relief to feel at a remove from the reality which so confused and grazed her. Cannabis was her great friend. Alcohol could wipe out a sense of responsibility and send her worst inhibitions to Mars, but dope was the eiderdown. She'd tried cocaine too. It had made her hyper-active and madly confident. It was fine for a short-term burst of absolute confidence, but she preferred a drug that let her lapse, which withdrew her from contact with the saw-tooth of the dismal every day. She wondered if she should try heroin. It was supposed to make you utterly ecstatic. She'd become an addict. She'd do anything for money. She be thin as a starved cat; her eyes would bulge in their darkened sockets. Men would take advantage. She'd be free of sexual desire. Her sex would become a thing. She'd sell it for the next hit. The idea of being completely asexual attracted her like a rumour of gold brings fortune-hunters. To be liberated from dependence. Never to have to put your trust in another person. To be able to trust to a substance that would never let you down. How wonderful.

Yet in her exorbitant conception of herself as a tragic heroine, she was unaware of her pusillanimity. She didn't know she was no different from the domestic tyrant who controls her husband like she controls her oven. She was oblivious to her petulant and unjust need for dominance which sprang from her cowardice: her inability to trust. She accepted as given the superiority of her background. Her father was a minor diplomat. She'd been educated privately. She belonged to a privileged minority. She had no notion that her upbringing was as emotionally incompetent as it was prissily snobbish. Like all young people of her class, sent away from their families to be educated, she had to evolve a compensatory identity to nullify the hurt of separation. She'd been educated among girls who thought themselves superior. They were not like the town girls who went to State schools and were common and ignorant; girls who would work in *Woolworths* or as shorthand typists and marry bricklayers or lorry drivers or teachers. They had a right to higher things. A right that was as much theirs as their bones or their toe-nails. They would have money and big houses. They would marry Managing Directors or men who ran their own businesses or barristers or diplomats or politicians; people who had a right to govern and to tell others what to do. All of them had had to develop this sense of election, this cast-iron belief that they had a right to money, power and status, because without it they would have had to accept that their parents loved them so little they sent them away to a school where they were regimented, processed and abused.

She had her black moment like so many of the girls. It was almost impossible to avoid. She was nine. The geography teacher, whose face had pulled into an ugly sneer, asked her take down her knickers. It was what happened. It was what you had to accept if you wanted a special education. It was better than being a common town girl.

She'd never told anyone. There was no point. It was the way things were. Her parents stressed how important it was to have a private education, how it was the guarantee of not having to breathe the same air as *undesirables*. She was befuddled by the desirability of Andy Lang. She despised him for making her want him. How did he do it? She began to think of him as an evil force which could control her emotions. He needed to be wiped out. She would like to kill him. She would club him over the head or drive a blade into his heart. That was what he deserved. That would set her free.

She was divided between her desire to possess Andy and her wish to have done with him. Her need for him was as tormenting as her craving for dope. The latter was easy to satisfy. She told her mother things were more expensive than she'd expected. There were books she absolutely must have. Food in the little *Spar* on campus was cynically marked up. She needed more money. She knew her mother. Recklessness with money was part of the way she tugged on her father's nerves. He was the one who had to be responsible. His hair could turn white worrying over her lavish dresses, her eccentric hairdresser's bills, the sudden throwing away of furniture no more than a year-old and the arrival of impossibly costly mirrors, little tables, rugs, curtains, bedclothes. She knew her mother danced her sexuality in front of him like a flirting teenager but kept him emotionally distant by her secretive spending. She discussed nothing with him. There was no question of partnership. She flew off into unhinged expenditure and the first he knew was when the bills arrived. His pleading or anger were hopeless. She was like a recalcitrant pupil who delights in infuriating the teacher. Had he been indifferent she might have worried, but she would have responded by driving him to bankruptcy. She had to jab at his nerves. It was the way she related to people. It was what she was. She was a pest, a nuisance. That was her self-definition. It was how she related to everyone. She could never be ignored because she was itching powder, the fly buzzing round the kitchen, the tiny chip of grit in the sock, the garrulous drunk at the bar, the salesman with his foot in the door, and she loved it.

The cheque invariably arrived. Jane found her dealer and replenished her stock.

That was simple. She could come back from a lecture on Aragon, go straight to her supply and soften the nails of reality that were scratching her face or digging into her thigh. The impossible tension which rose in her every day, the scorching need to outdo others, the bottomless sense of emptiness if she felt she wasn't keeping up, if someone had an advantage over her, could be made misty and remote. The world seemed ranged against her and she must fight back.

Dope was a good and reliable prop. It was under her control. So long as she had money, she had dope. So long as she had dope she had escape. The problem with Andy was he wasn't so subject to her power. He could make his own decisions. He could do things she knew nothing about. She needed some of her mother's technique. Her father might be the diplomat, he might earn the money, but in the home, he was at her mercy because she was sly and cruel. Andy must be brought under her complete dominance. She felt she'd struck a fatal blow when she told him: "I can't say no." She expected him to crumple. Her mother drove her father to the edge of insanity by provoking every man who came her way. That was how to drive a man down, to make him fearful and dependent. It was disconcerting that Andy seemed barely troubled. "You could be in difficulty if you're propositioned by Leonid Brezhnev," he'd replied. "Except if you like going to bed with fat, old totalitarians."

He had a space in which he could escape her and she loathed him for it. She was determined to drag him down, to bring him to that level of supplication which would put him beyond any release. As she sank further into stupor, she was assailed by two images: Andy was walking away from her, looking over his shoulder, laughing, and out of nowhere appeared Sue Border who took his hand and looked back at her mockingly, her face radiant with delight; he was knocking on her door begging for access while she was submitting to Jean-Claude; she opened to him in her dressing gown, a cigarette between her lips, while her lover lay beneath the covers, his hands behind his head.

When the desire to eat became irresistible she went to the kitchen and made herself toast, scrambled eggs, tinned rice pudding, a cup of coffee. Two of the girls from her floor were there. She ignored them. Who were they? What did they have to do with her? Where was Andy Lang? She ran her plate under the tap, put on her coat and went to knock on his door. Rob Green appeared. He smiled at her in the way she found silly and indulgent, as if she was a child in need of humouring.

"Hello," he said. "looking for Andy?"

"Is he in?"

"No. Don't know where he's gone. Not be long I wouldn't think. Come and wait in the kitchen if you fancy."

"I'll come back," she said.

The Cretin was still in her room. Jane was furious that she could find no privacy and what did Andy think he was doing going off without telling her? She needed another spliff.

"Jane's been looking for you," said Rob when Andy came into the kitchen.

"I'm not hard to find," he said.

"She can find a lad if she wants," said Mike.

Andy looked at him quizzically. He blinked in his usual rapid way, his long lashes noticeable, and appeared discomfited.

"You mean the poseur we saw her with yesterday?" said Steve Bancroft.

"Yeah."

"Who was that?" said Andy.

"You know him, don't you, Rob?" said Mike Darley.

"Yeah, he does French and Russian."

"Oh, him," said Andy.

"Doesn't bother you?" said Steve

"She's free to do what she likes," said Andy. "I don't own her."

The film society was showing *Saturday Night and Sunday Morning* at seven thirty and they were all going. Bowland lecture theatre was packed. The black and white images flickered and failed. They waited ten minutes. Johnny Dankworth's slightly suggestive theme started up, Albert Finney's young face evoked the period and the milieu. His cocky demeanour, Andy thought, was a bit exaggerated, and his Nottinghamshire accent not quite convincing. Why didn't he rely on his Salford roots? Maybe because he was a grammar school boy and the street habits of the northern, lower class young had been swilled away in the disinfectant of middle-class ambition.

Andy was irritated at himself for not having read the novel. Sillitoe was one of those names he associated with the emergence of the common people into literature. His admiration for Lawrence rested significantly on his treatment of the people he'd grown amongst as worthy of a place in literature. In spite of the neurotic clinging of Paul Morel to his possessive mother, the portrait of Lawrence's father in *Sons and Lovers* was charming. He might have turned into a drunk and been ugly in the home as his marriage failed, but his warmth, his delight in simple things, his love of flowers, his affection for his children and his ability to go to his physical satisfactions without guilt or hypocrisy, made him a literary character it was hard to forget and not like.

There'd always been in Andy's mind a half-worked out association between Lawrence and Sillitoe. Without having read him, he'd assumed Sillitoe must have absorbed something of his fellow Nottinghamshire writer. It was impossible not to be influenced by a writer of genius who had walked the same streets.

Watching Arthur Seaton run for the bus and swing onto the open platform brought back the atmosphere of the fifties and sixties. He was only twenty-two and already he was nostalgic for his lost life. How odd it was that memory made reality so vivid. He thought at once of *Combray* and *la petite madeleine*. Proust twisted his feelings because his style was so wilfully aristocratic. The very pompous, corseted, stuck-up, hypocrisy Proust was spiking was validated in his prose. Reading him made Andy long for the simple sentences of Hemingway.

He found himself sinking into a soppy retrospection which clashed with his reservations about Seaton. Was Sillitoe proposing him as typical? Was he suggesting that working-class young men were all brash, drunken, adulterous, cheating egotists? There was much about Seaton that reminded him of Ted Franks. It was true, there was a culture of hard-drinking, gambling, sexual irresponsibility, cynicism, self-abandonment and living for the moment which was offered to the people at the bottom; it connected them to the wayward habits of the aristocracy. In a way, it was more attractive than the zipped-up, fancy-hatted, clean-the-car-on-Sunday, goldfish and budgerigars, regular, frugal, keep-your-nose-clean, ways of the middle-classes; yet Andy baulked at the notion that men like Seaton were capable of nothing better.

Was Sillitoe pandering to a middle-class readership? Was he saying, "Ah, well, you can't expect any better from the working-class." Or was he kicking the shins of an Establishment which offered most people nothing better than the pub, the bookies, furtive sex and impotent rebellion?

There was appeal in Seaton's behaviour, just as there'd been for Andy in Ted Franks'. Why was it seductive? What was it about the idea of indulgence, lack of restraint and cynicism which could summon identification? Wasn't it because on the surface it looked easy? It was a way out of responsibility and it offered a false absolute: all doubt and vulnerability could be hidden by the need for the next pint or the certainty of the next winner.

What was queer was that Andy knew he was nothing like Seaton and never could be. Nor, in spite of his liking for Ted Franks could he ever have been like him. He was more like his grandfather. It was much harder to create an appealing fictional character out of a man like his grandad: taciturn, principled, hard on himself, frugal, self-disciplined. The superficial sociability of a what's-your-tipple bar-propper stirred people's sympathy more readily; but it was a cheat. There was a fear of life at the heart of it. A running from responsibility which was incompatible with the facts of existence.

When the showing was over they went to back to Rob and Mike's room, poured wine and beer, lounged on the beds, chairs and floor. Rob and Mike played their guitars.

"I wish I'd read the novel," said Andy. "I'll have to get a copy."

"I thought it was accurate," said Steve Bancroft, "that's what life's like for a lot of working-class lads."

"Yeah, but he's a loud-mouth and a brute, isn't he?" said Mike Darley, between chords.

"That's normal in his environment," said Steve.

"Is it?" said Rob.

"Lots of scousers would identify with that, even today," said Steve.

"Plenty of Brummies too," said Mike.

"Yeah, but he glorifies him to some extent doesn't he," said Andy.

"Not really," said Steve. "He's just showing how people like that have to get by."

"He doesn't have to screw other people's wives," said Mike.

"No, he doesn't, but that's what happens, isn't it? I mean, it's dead common," said Steve.

"Maybe," said Rob.

"I don't know, I felt I was being manipulated a bit by the film," said Andy.

"How?" said Rob.

"Well," said Andy, putting down his bottle and leaning forward, his elbows on his knees trying to make his thoughts turn into words, "I found myself liking Seaton, You know, that kind of life. Easy-going. Couldn't care less. Have a drink, have a smoke, find a woman. As if life is just one pleasure after another…"

"Why shouldn't it be?" said Rob.

"Because it can't," said Andy.

"It is for Seaton," said Steve with a laugh.

"He got himself beaten up though," said Mike Richards

"He deserved it," said Mike Darley.

"I don't think so," said Rob. "But his story was funny: jumping off a gasometer for a bet."

They all laughed.

"Reality was closing in on him. Is that the choice? Hedonism or capitulation?" said Andy.

"What's hedonism?" said Mike Richards.

"The pursuit of pleasure," said Rob.

"Oh. Well, sounds all right to me," said Mike Richards.

"We all want to fight against the system but we have to live in it," said Steve.

"They've got us by the balls," said Mike Darley.

"He wasn't fighting the system, he was just enjoying himself," said Mike Richards.

"I'm out for a good time, everything else is propaganda," said Rob.

They all laughed. Phil Ripon appeared, a can of *Carling* in his hand.

"What yer doin' yer dog shaggers ?" he said, brushing his fulsome curls from his face.

"Talking about you," said Rob.

"No better subject, lar," said Phil. "Bin here all night?"

"Film Soc," said Rob.

"What d'you see?"

"*Saturday Night and Sunday Morning*," said Steve.

"Shaggin' and a hangover, eh?" said Phil.

They laughed again.

"It's about you," said Mike Darley, "a bloke who just wants to enjoy himself and ignores whatever gets in his way."

"That's me," said Phil."Anyway, what's Jane Bentnick doin' outside your door, Andy?"

"Is she?" said Andy.

"I offered to shag 'er but she wasn't interested."

"What a surprise," said Rob.

"Better go and see," said Andy.

He turned the corner into the five yards of corridor. She wasn't there but he heard her voice, high, exaggerated, drawing attention. She was in Tom Dyuzbinska's room. He was tempted to go back to his mates, but it was late and he had a lecture at nine. In his room, he heard her wild laughter, little screeches of pleasure, her talking far too loudly so he could make out every word. He put himself to bed and pulled a pillow over his head to deaden the sound. Fifteen minutes later there came a sharp rapping at his door. He let her in.

"Where did you go tonight?" she said taking a drag on her long cigarette.

"Film Soc."

"With Sue Border?"

"No," he said, scratching his scalp, "Albert Finney."

"What?"

"He's from Salford, Finney . Albert that is. Not Tom. He's from Preston. My dad knows him. He came to our house when I was a little kid to weigh up the plumbing. Imagine that. Bit like George Best popping in for a drink. Though if he did you'd have to carry him out on a stretcher. Funny that isn't it, two blokes called Finney from the north-west and both at the top of their trees. They wanted him to change his name, you know. Albert, not Tom. No reason a winger shouldn't be called Tom Finney and play for England; but acting, that's a different matter. They have their eyes on Hollywood, the agents and whatever. Albert Finney. Could be a lad from Manchester whose dad was an illegal bookie. I suppose they wanted him to call himself Johnny Strong or something. Do you know Billy Fury's real name? Ron Wycherley. He was a twitcher. Bird-watcher. Girls won't wet their knickers over that, will they? 'Ladies and gentlemen, put your hands together for Ron Wycherley performing his latest release *There's A Blue Tit Nesting In My Garden*.' Would you throw your knickers at him, Jane?"

"I've been going insane with jealousy," she said.

"What?"

"I saw you with Sue Border."

"When?"

"Yesterday."

"*Yesterday,*" Andy began to croon, "*I had all my bloody bills to pay...*"

"Who did you go with?"

"I need to get some sleep," he said, "Malcolm Lowry at nine in the morning. They should be reported to the *National Society for the Prevention of Cruelty to Students*. Have you read *Under The Volcano*? Don't say 'No, but I've written on top of a mountain.' It's too corny."

She ran her cigarette under the tap, dropped it in the bin, threw her coat on his chair and undressed quickly.

"Decided to stay," he said, pulling the covers round him.

"Don't you want me to?"

"I want you to."

He woke entangled with her, warm and sleeping. He strained his head to look at his alarm clock. Half past eight.

"Christ," he said.

She stirred and opened her eyes.

"What's the matter?"

"I've to be in the lecture in half an hour."

"Miss, it."

"I could."

There was a gentle knock.

"Who's that?" she whispered.

"Probably Rob wanting to see if I'm ready," he said, equally sotto voce. "Hello," he called.

"It's Rob. Going to the lecture?"

"Yeah. Give me five minutes."

He kissed her and climbed out.

"Better go," he said. "Stay there if you like. I've nothing on at ten. Well, I've nothing on now, but I can have nothing on again at ten or shortly after if you like."

He splashed himself, cleaned his teeth, ran the electric razor over his barely visible stubble, inspected his spots in the mirror. dealt with the ones he could and pulled on his cords, a poloneck, a jacket, his desert boots.

"Just going to grab a drink," he said.

"Okay."

He gathered his file and was about to leave.

"Andy."

"Yeah."

"What I said last night."

"Yeah."

"I was pissed and stoned."

He paused.

"Well, as they say, 'from the mouths of babes and pot-heads..'"

"I'm going now."

She emerged from the covers and stood by the bed a defiant, sullen look challenging his facetious, untroubled mood. She saw how her nakedness affected him. She could have persuaded him back into bed with a tilt of her hips.

"See you in a bit," he said.

"Bye."

As soon as he was gone she got back into bed. The smell of him was on the pillow and the sheets. It was an odour she was starting to rely on. She lay quietly for ten minutes thinking how it might be if this scent became her everyday security, if she woke every morning with her arm round him and her legs between his. When she got up and dressed, she tidied his room, wiped down his sink, straightened the orange rug. How might it be if she kept the house neat for him, if he came home to find she'd taken the trouble to make things comfortable and nice? She lit a cigarette and sat in the armchair. Perhaps she would wait. Perhaps she would be here when he got back. She could put her arms round his neck, he would kiss her, they could get back into bed. She could make some lunch for him in the kitchen. They hadn't eaten together. How odd. They'd slept together but hadn't even shared a table and a sandwich. Yes, she could make something nice for him and after…

His friends would be there. All of them. In the kitchen. They would all know. The thought infuriated her. She got up and stubbed out her cigarette in the bin. What she'd said to him came back to her. Her confidence seeped from her like pus from a wound. *Je t'aime. Je n'ose pas le dire sauf quand je suis ivre.* She was horrified. She turned to survey his room, kicked the rug so it was askew and its corner upturned. As she tripped down the stone steps which smelled of cold and loneliness, she resolved never to enter his room again.

SOMETHING SIMPLE AND ESSENTIAL

William Hardcastle was reading an item about the Watergate Trial. Bert Lang hadn't paid much attention to the details. The investigative journalism of Carl Bernstein and Bob Woodward had sparked his imagination. He could have imagined himself doing that: ferreting out the dirt on people in power. He would have enjoyed it and it would have been appropriate: back-street urchins like him had an instinctive dislike and suspicion of power; but he wouldn't have had any idea of how to find his way into such a job. He'd always liked writing. He was still proud of the high marks he got for *composition*. Maybe he could have made a good journalist. Yet his mind failed when he tried to imagine how these two blokes had found the right stones to look under and how they knew which dark-loving insects were the ones to go for.

He was alone in his kitchen at that thankful hour when he could focus on preparing something pleasant and wholesome. The radio connected him to the outside world, the mad events he wanted to keep at a distance, but the walls of his little bungalow provided asylum. Nixon he'd concluded was as guilty as a burglar caught with the swag, a shop assistant found with her fingers in the till, a straying husband whose wife found a pair of strange knickers in his suit pocket. It was outrageous, yet he wasn't outraged. He wasn't even surprised. That was how power worked. It was what you could expect from the powerful. He'd read *The Observer* week after week. Watergate was a great scandal: as if it was taken for granted that politicians were high-minded and honest. The only high-minded honest folk he'd ever met, were at the bottom, and they weren't clean because of their status; his grandparents were at the bottom too and they would have sold him to slave traders for the price of a bottle of gin.

All the same, he couldn't help tilting to the idea that the common folk were more to be trusted than the rich and powerful. Once people had money or status , they changed. The most straightforward people he'd known were the get-by-and-keep-going folk of Marsh Lane and Talbot Road, the blokes like himself in the RAF, the people he'd worked with when he was a flour-boy at the Co-op. Like him, they trusted to democracy. He still had faith in Harold Wilson and he liked Michael Foot; but the Labour Party had changed. When he listened to Nye Bevan on the radio, he would have been willing to fight for what he offered. Bevan made him want to march in the streets. There was something *behind* what he said which stirred him, the feeling that Bevan really didn't give a monkey's fart for power. He was interested only in what power could do.

Now when he listened to Jim Callaghan or Denis Healey, Shirley Williams or David Owen, Roy Hattersley or Reg Prentice something was missing. They had no fire. They didn't speak to where he'd come from. They weren't offering a different view of society. He had the feeling always they were telling him the present arrangements must be adjusted to; there was no means of radical change; he had to diminish his expectations; the so-called *real world* denied the possibility of equality; he must settle for something soggier, like a man who was hungry and wanted fresh meat or bread, crisp vegetables and fruit and was offered warmed over meat and potato pie and a chocolate biscuit.

The sense that things were kiltering down and the politicians were accepting the decline; that their self-imposed task was to defeat idealism, to quench the thirst for justice, to stamp on the hands that reached for the fulfilment of the best in our natures made him squirm. He heard nothing but talk of crisis, of how little the country could afford, of how everyone had to tighten their belts; yet the country was in a far better position than it had been in 1945. Had he heard then what he was hearing now; had he come back after six years in Egypt and Italy risking his life to defeat fascism to be told the country couldn't afford a National Health Service, he would have participated in revolution. He would have been willing to seize the assets of the rich with his bare hands. He'd had his hands on bombs, loaded them onto planes, he'd participated willingly in killing to defend democracy. He'd seen battle and death. If he'd had to pick up a gun and take over the Bank of England to see the plain folk looked after, he would have.

In those days, there was a mood of uplift. The war was over. The battle against tyranny won. Now the people were to enjoy what they had fought for. They rejected Churchill because he equated doctors and hospitals for the common folk with Bolshevism. Bert had listened to his speeches and scoffed. There was a new world to make where the common people, at last, would have what rightly belonged to them.

Now, any sense of aspiration to the common good and justice seemed wildly subversive. Heath couldn't govern without shutting down the factories for two days a week. The mood was wary, gloomy, frightened. He sat at his little bar with his bowl of lentil soup. How good it was to eat his own cooking. He thickly buttered a wedge of his home-made bread. His mouth relished its consistency and flavour. It soaked up the hot soup and warmed him. Hardcastle was talking again about Watergate.

Though Bert understood how power could drive people insane, push them to act against their professed values and their natures, he could never have contemplated what the accused had done. Democracy was a principle. The people had to decide. To cheat to try to settle the outcome of an election was as low as mugging an old lady, or having sex with a child. It offended the most elementary sense of responsibility.

He didn't think of himself as a man above the norm in his morality. He was seeking spiritual strength and enlightenment through the Satsangis, but that was no different from everyone who went to church on Sunday. Virtually everyone he knew would have rebelled against the idea of theft or fraud or vicious exploitation. They weren't moral geniuses. They were just ordinary folk. Yet here was the most powerful man in America, perhaps in the world, behaving like a petty crook, a spiv, a gangster, a shop-lifter or a scally ripping lead off the church roof at midnight.

Talks had been going on in Paris to bring an end to the Vietnam War. There was mention of that in the news too but it barely registered. He was concentrating on his food. He was happy, for the moment. All that was missing was company. How odd it was. Why had he ended up alone? He was the last man who would have chosen to. Perhaps that was why. All his relationships had finished in estrangement: family, friends, colleagues. It was the one constant of his life, the predictability he could rely on. Perhaps the exception was Andy. Yes, he still felt connected to him; and there were his new friendships among the Satsangis; but it was hard to establish at fifty the kind of key-in-the-lock, mortice-and-tenon, perfect-pitch liaisons which come so easily early in life.

He'd imagined he would always have friends. He'd believed he would have a family. He'd liked Elsie's brothers and their children. He was uncle Bert. He was dad. What was he now? A bloke past middle-age, unattached, as lonely as a runt, working for a man he despised at a job he had no true belief in to try to put enough in the bank to secure his old age.

In his warm lounge he sat in his armchair, stood his mug of tea on the tall, three-legged table by the window and took up the previous Sunday's *Observer*. A piece about the Paris peace talks caught his eye. What had he heard on the radio? He pushed his glasses up his nose. America was losing. That was sure. Their direct military involvement was coming to an end. Vietnam, it was clear, would become a united country. Would it be communist? What if it was. Leave them to it. Let them make their own mistakes and learn their own lessons. What threat could they be to America? Or Britain. They were a poor country.

He found himself befuddled by references to the French intervention in the nineteenth century. What did he know about the history of Vietnam? Virtually nothing. How could he know in detail the history of every country in the world? It was always the detail that mattered, yet he was ignorant. He set the paper on his lap and drank his tea. His curtains were open because once he closed them he was utterly alone for the evening. While he could see Queensway there was a chance someone would pass he could wave to, or kids would be playing out and he could stand and watch them or go out and take them a couple of biscuits. He wasn't entirely alone while he could see what was going on outside, see the lights in the neighbours' windows, watch the odd car pass. Someone walked by with a Labrador on a lead. He didn't recognize her. She didn't look to the window. Had she done, he would have waved. It was easy to make contact. If you smiled and said hello, almost anyone would chat and from there you could get anywhere. How was it than that he was alone?

He looked at the paper again, briefly. He could find out. He could go to the library and borrow books on Vietnam. He could cram his little skull with facts and command every casual conversation with his out-of-the-way knowledge; but that wasn't the point. If he knew all there was to know about the history of Vietnam, there'd be other places about which he knew nothing. He liked to think of himself as informed. Ignorance was to be ashamed of. It was a stigma, like the poverty of his early years. He listened to the news and discussion programmes, he watched documentaries and read intelligent journalism and he had a library of five hundred serious books. All the same, peace talks had been going on in Paris and he was unaware of what they were discussing in detail. He didn't know how the debacle in Vietnam had come about. First the French, then the Americans. Colonialism, communism, the domino theory and hundreds of thousands of deaths; napalm, agent orange and in the end, failure.

It was important to be informed. You had to know the facts. Yet there was something else. He couldn't get hold of the idea and shape it with language. It was about principle. Somehow all the myriad details which no single person could possibly master, just as no one could learn two hundred languages or be an expert in Physics, Sanskrit, Italian literature, Baroque music, anthropology; could be subsumed to principles. There was something everyone could know. Something simple and essential. He had no doubt the Vietnam War was wrong. What did he mean? Politically? Tactically? No, morally. That was where the simplicity lay. Moral genius had the capacity to extract simplicity from complexity. *Thou shalt not kill*. He believed it. He'd been an airman, loaded those bombs onto planes to help kill the enemy; but he believed killing was wrong. Absolutely. Why was it so hard for humanity to accept that as a principle? Most people had no desire to kill. Those who did were usually demented and were very few. Why was it so difficult to outlaw violence? If he had a dispute with a neighbour, after all, he had no right to shoot him or even punch him in the mouth.

If violence could be prohibited between neighbours, why not between countries? Why couldn't heads of State who prosecuted war be brought to trial? Why couldn't it be part of international law that disputes between nations had to be resolved peacefully?

He'd been involved in war and he knew its propaganda. It was glory. It was the triumph of right. It was heroism; but he knew what it was: fear and despair and boredom and an urgent longing for it to be over, to be done with weapons and death, to be free to live.

The principle was simple. Everyone could understand it. Everyone could embrace it. Yet somehow it escaped humanity.

Queensway was quiet. The lights glowed behind closed curtains. He drew his own. His neighbours were in their living-rooms, their kitchens, their bedrooms. They were watching television or dozing or reading or eating. They were a kind of company. It was reassuring to know they were there. Yet how odd that he couldn't knock on a door, be welcomed in and spend a few hours chatting before going to bed. If one of his neighbours had come to him, he would have welcomed them, put on the kettle. He would have been glad to have three or four of them in his living-room. Yet he was alone and at a loss to understand why.

He enjoyed a kind of belonging in Queensway. Everyone knew him. He was Bert Lang. He worked in estate agency. The children called him uncle Bert. Everyone gave him the time of day; but no one, not even Dereck and Betty knew about his past. What was known to them was a recent and superficial Bert Lang. He was assumed to be respectable because he'd bought his own bungalow. He went out to work every day. He kept his house and garden neat. He was a helpful neighbour if help were needed; otherwise he kept himself to himself.

What did he know about his neighbours? Only what was on show. The joys or tragedies behind the well-painted front doors and the expensive curtains, he was oblivious to. He lived among strangers. They were inordinately important to him. During the winter, he barely saw them. The spring and summer brought people into their gardens. There was a chance of conversation; and the children were on their bikes and playing ball in the road. It almost began to feel like a community. How odd that in the winter, merely because of the dark and cold, people should allow months to pass without speaking to one another.

The disturbing idea occurred to him that he was made to live alone. Where did he come from? He had no ancestry. He knew who his mother was, though he hadn't seen her for years. His father was a sergeant at Fulwood barracks. His grandparents were a pair of feckless dipsomaniacs. Apart from that, he knew nothing. Where did his grandparents come from? Who were their parents? He knew more about Elsie's family than his own. He'd wanted to. He'd wanted to become an adoptive Craxton. The Langs were dangerous people.

It wasn't given to people like him to have an ancestry. That was for aristocrats. He laughed to himself. Royalty could trace its line back centuries, but people like him, born at the bottom, intended to be factory ants and flesh to be shredded and scorched in war, dispensable people, people who, even in a democracy, had little power, didn't need to know who they were. It was better if they didn't. They weren't supposed to feel at home in the world. They were thrown into life and could be blasted out of it with little ceremony. They needed to know themselves only as defined by others. True identity belongs only to the rich and powerful.

He tried to convince himself things weren't too bad: he owned his own home. He was earning well. He was warm and comfortable. He could do what he liked with his life, apart from the need to work. He turned on the television: another connection to the outside world. Yet he couldn't quell the sense that things were badly wrong. Maybe it was thinking about Nixon and Vietnam which had brought on this mood. Why should he bother with the news? What control did he have? Things happened round the corner he had no control over. *They* were building a new road. *They* had decided to change the opening times at the library. *They* had agreed to flatten a nice, old building in the town centre to create more parking space. Who were the *they*? The council? The MP? Some authority or other. Oh, he had the vote. The leaflet dropped through his letterbox. There was the smiling face of the young woman who wanted to be his County Councillor. Yes, he would vote for her; but would she ask him before she voted in chamber? What power did he have? His overriding sense was that the world was controlled from *out there*. A crook like Nixon had the nuclear codes. Men who had no idea why were sent to Vietnam to find death in the jungle.

He could be wiped out in an instant by a decision made far away by people he had never met and he had no influence over.

The television was showing *Are You Being Served*? It was the kind of empty entertainment he hated and avoided, but he watched because he knew John Inman came from Preston. Bert found his character ridiculous, like all the others. Foolish stereotypes which confirmed prejudice and reassured people in their thoughtless convictions. Most of the homosexuals he'd known were nothing like the fey, mincing, effete Mr Humphries. There was Stan Hogg in the RAF, for one; a big, muscular, taciturn bloke, who smoked and drank heavily and betrayed no hint of effeminacy. Inman's ambiguous call of "I'm free" was one of those juvenile innuendos which irritated him. Yet what fascinated him was Inman's success. How had he managed it? There was a curious surprise at finding someone from your own banal town lifted into a different realm. In spite of his disdain for the cheap, manipulative programme, Bert was intrigued by his own response. How old was Inman? Maybe forty. He could have run into him. Maybe he did. How did a lad from Preston get to be an actor who appeared on the telly and who earned more in a month than he did in a year?

Inman was a model of success. Yet what kind of life was it? Who would want to spend their time acting in something so superficial and dim? The adolescent references to Mrs Slocombe's pussy, the refusal to dig beneath the epidermis were disappointing and depressing. What choice did Inman have? If the script came along, was he at liberty to turn it down? Bert's guess was that actors who did would find work drying up. How was it that such stuff got on the television? Who made the assumption that people were worth nothing better?

He knew well enough such programmes were popular, but so was smoking. It was easy to exploit people's ignorance, vulnerability, insecurity, their need for a shared culture, their healthy desire for laughter, their fascination with other people's lives, their simple nosiness and love of gossip; it was no struggle to give people fags and booze and the bookies, *Coronation Street*, Tommy Steele and *Opportunity Knocks*, instead of engaging in the tough effort to raise the level in all things. Smoking was illustrative: people liked it, it was sociable and reassuring; offering someone a fag was generous and friendly; but no one liked it when they were crippled with bronchitis, or dying in pain of lung cancer or hobbling under the curse of angina at the age of forty-five. It was a cheat organised to make money. That was the way culture worked and it was despicable.

He changed channels in search of something worth watching and finding nothing switched off. The only sound was the hum of the gas fire. He pondered ringing someone. There was Paul, the Satsangi organiser who looked up to him as older, wiser and cleverer. He was thirty-five, had a wife, two young children and worked in insurance. They'd had several little discussions about the emptiness of work, the desolate sense of serving some monster whose purpose was money. He could ring him. He could pretend he'd forgotten the date and time of the next meeting. The phone squatted on the table by the window, silent, inert but a means of connection. What was Paul's number? He would need to look it up. It was in his address book in a compartment of the drawer of his bureau which tucked into the corner behind the door. He bought it with his matching, glass-fronted bookcase when he moved to Woodland Grove. How long ago was that? Eighteen years. He thought of it as a single chunk of time, the minutes, hours, weeks, days, months congealed into a blob, a mass. It had been a series of moments, but most of them were forgotten. He could bring some of them back. He could reminisce and a vivid picture could be revived but it was static. The moment by moment experience was gone. Eighteen years and he could think of it as the passing of a few seconds.

His intention withered and was consumed like a dry leaf in a flame. Paul would be with his family. To ring was intrusive. No, someone should ring him. Maybe Andy. He could be relied on. He called now and again and was patient. Bert could talk long and not fear he would make some excuse to hang up. It was right his son should stay in touch. Yet at once an awful thought came to him: was he reliant on Andy because he had few friends? You couldn't relate to your children in the same way as to your adult mates. Parents had a moral duty to their children, but no guarantee they would like them. The resonance between parent and child could never be like that of a freely chosen rapport. The truth was he lacked friends. Or maybe a friend. One good friend was worth a thousand acquaintances. That was his problem. He no longer had one good friend.

He put a record of Beethoven piano sonatas on the turntable, went to his bookshelf and tried to choose. *Portnoy's Complaint*. Yes, he could read that again. It was hilarious and beautifully undermining of pomposity. *Anna Karenina*. Or *War and Peace*. He'd never got to the end of it. The array of characters was too defeating and by the time he got to page 500 hundred he'd forgotten what happened on page 10. *The Decameron*. He enjoyed dipping into it. It reminded him, in a way, of *The Canterbury Tales*. He liked irreverence and a bit of bawdiness. Short stories by Lawrence. That might be an idea because it would give him something to talk to Andy about. How long was he going to read for? He knew he would tire and risk nodding off in the chair. It was pleasant enough to be ambushed by sleep but he felt it better to choose something short. He pulled out his unread copy of *The Whitsun Weddings*. People made a fuss about Larkin. He could read a few poems and feel he'd made headway. He sat down and put on his glasses.

Swerving east, from rich industrial shadows…

He stopped over *stealing flat-faced trolleys*. Why stealing? Was he suggesting all the cut-price folk were thieves? He couldn't make it work. It made him feel ignorant. It was a simple enough word. Yet he couldn't get the image in his head. He put the book on the chair arm, face down. Was it his failure? Was he just uneducated? Maybe Andy would explain to him in a sneeze what it was supposed to mean. He read it again. No, he couldn't make it work. It was out of place like a thoughtless remark. He gathered his confidence and concluded it wasn't his ignorance but a clumsiness by Larkin. Then *consulates* made him pause again. In Hull? In the plural? In the 1960s? It didn't fit. Why had he chosen that? And why were the wives *grim*? All of them? What did he mean? That they bore grim expressions because of the cramped lives or that he found them grim? Probably the latter. Wasn't that just snobbery? *Loneliness clarifies*? The formulation shocked him. There was nothing clarifying about loneliness. The *Moonlight Sonata* was playing in the background. Its simple beauty softened his feeling. If only he had someone to share the music with. Was Larkin saying loneliness is our truth? What were these lives supposed to be removed from? The city? Urban life? *bluish neutral distance*. Neutral in what way? Because that's how Larkin perceives it?

Bert wasn't one of those people who believe that truth lies beyond the urban. He didn't like Larkin's notion of the town as a place where only salesmen and relations come; as if all voluntary relations have broken down. He was lonely. He was lonely as hell. He wished he was one of those blokes who go to the pub, pour four pints into their pot bellies and talk to whoever's at the bar about football, horses or the state of the country. The pub had no attraction for him. He disliked beer and he wasn't inclined to listen to pale-ale politicians. He didn't share the culture of the plain folk he came from but he didn't like Larkin's suggestion that the plain folk are forever cut-price, cheap, interested only in the next bargain, led by their desire for white goods and tat. Wasn't Larkin a private-school, Oxford product? How did he know what the lives of the people crowding through the plate-glass doors are like? Why shouldn't they shop for bargains? They don't earn much.

What he really baulked at though was the pulling away from the human at the end of the poem. It was an offer of a false liberty. There is no *unfenced existence*. Of course it is *untalkative*. You can't talk to the sea or a beach. He was irritated and wished he hadn't read the poem. The image that came into his head was of Larkin looking down his nose at the common people of Hull, or any other town, dismissing them for their vulgarity and staring off into distances as if he belonged to a higher species. Bert was alert to snobbery because he'd been its victim. He didn't blame the common people for their vulgarity, he blamed the manipulative culture which exploited them and offered them nothing better.

He shoved the book back into its tight slot.

At least there was Beethoven, and jazz. When the arm lifted and clicked back into neutral and the turntable stopped, he took Count Basie's *Encore! April In Paris* from its still pristine sleeve. He'd bought it in Brady's in the days when they still stocked jazz, before rock became so profitable they had nothing but a tiny box containing no more than thirty or so 33s. The cover showed Basie apparently receiving a bouquet from a female admirer, a no longer young woman in glasses, her hair in a bob at the back, the two of them smiling pleasantly and in the background an out-of-focus Parisian scene.

He loved the title melody. The Thad Jones and Benny Powell solos lifted his mood. It was hard to feel alone with such generous music filling his living-room. Basie himself was delicate, clever, funny on piano. Jazz connected him in a different way then classical music. Beethoven was marvellous but there was thunder behind his work, a keyboard-smashing, insurrectionary feel which was at once bracing and intimidating. Mozart was as natural as a sparrow on a rose bush, as if melody, harmony and dynamics were as instinctive as walking. Stravinsky had a sharp edge and a wonderfully modern feel; but jazz had something else. He was in no doubt it was a lesser music when compared to Haydn or Shostakovich, but at its best it rose enormously high and throughout it was suffused with a soft acceptance of life, an utter absence of snobbery or pomposity, a gay embracing of the multiplicity of individuality and a rejection of the will to control. He closed his eyes and lay back his head as Frank Foster played *Did'n You*? A memory came to him. He was in the back room at Woodland Grove. It was evening. The children were in the garden. He was listening to this very tune. Elsie came through with mugs of tea. "Listen to this solo," he said to her. She disdained his interest in jazz. She had no feel for music, but she loved hymns, because she was supposed to. Bert had nothing against a good hymn, but he wanted her to share his love of big bands, Freddie Greene, Clifford Brown as well as Borodin and Berlioz.

It wasn't the music she denigrated. She had no instinct for it. He puzzled over it. He loved to whistle a tune and they stuck to his brain like chewing gum to a shoe. Yet a lovely melody seemed to have no effect on her. He'd never heard her say: "Oh, what a charming song." Was it because she just couldn't hear the beauty or was it some instilled resistance? He couldn't know, but he knew she sought to belittle his delight. She had nothing against Count Basie. Her negativity was towards him: his liking for music, his playing tennis, his attempt to educate himself about literature.

His disappointment returned to him. He'd coped with it as he always did: by hiding it. He wanted to share something with her and she rebuffed him. He wouldn't complain or sulk. He let her get on with reading the paper and listened to the music alone.

The horrible thought came to him that he'd always been alone in his marriage. He fought it off: his children had loved him. He'd had a good relationship with his father-in-law and with Elsie's brothers and their children. Yet the heavy feeling embedded itself in his abdomen: he'd always been alone. Elsie had always kept him caged.

Tomorrow he would have to work. He wished he could talk to Wickham about jazz; but he was a philistine and proud of it. Whatever didn't make money had no appeal for him. He would have thought of jazzos who barely make a living as failures. He would have assumed Ringo Starr was a better drummer than Sonny Payne because he was a millionaire. It was hopeless to try to talk to such a man about culture. He thought a ten pound note a greater work of art than *The Night Watch*.

When the music ended he went to bed. Somehow, he had to find a way out of his crushing loneliness. As he stepped into his pyjamas the pain in his right thigh made him wince. Christ, he thought, I must go to the doctor.

The thought was maturing in Elsie Lang's mind that when Mary had her child, she would need her. A carrying and nursing woman always wanted her mother near. It was natural. Elsie was a great believer in nature, which was another way of saying God. She had sung *All Things Bright And Beautiful* so many times as a child, had brought to life in her imagination the utterly beneficent, gentle, caring, loving, selfless, eternal father who made the flowers and trees, the birds and butterflies, the mountains and rivers, the innocence of children and the blue skies of summer but had nothing to do with viruses, bacteria, disease, earthquakes, volcanoes or sex, that she had convinced herself it was a truth beyond question that everything natural was good.

With a baby in the house, there was much to do. She was glad her daughter had decided to give up work. A child needed someone to look after them; a person who would always be there. In the early years, it was vital. Elsie was wary of nurseries. No doubt they could be well-run by dedicated staff; but it wasn't the same as spending your days with someone who loves you. That's what a child needs. Mary was right to make the choice to stay at home. Yet, at the same time, almost secretly, without admitting it to herself, she wished she'd decided to carry on working then she could have taken over care of the child.

It was true she still had to work. She had ten years to the pension. Yet half-formed, hazy, ill-defined, like a figure emerging from a night fog, she permitted the wish to arise in her that she could go and live with Mary and Ted. Sylvia would have to come too. Andy was old enough to sort himself out.

"I expect I'll 'ave to be coming and going once baby's 'ere," she said as she ate with the women of the training kitchen at lunchtime.

"It's a bit of a way," said Miss Bamford.

"Well, it is. It's two buses. That's true enough. But if it 'as to be done it 'as to be done."

"Isn't his family nearer?"

"Eh?"

"His family. Doesn't he come from Skelmersdale?"

"Oh yes, but his mother works."

"So do you."

"But I don't have a husband to look after," said Elsie, bridling.

"Husbands can look after themselves, I'm sure."

Elsie felt Miss Bamford was spiting her. What did she know? She'd never been married, had no children. Elsie was tempted to spill her bitterness. She would have liked to say: "And what do you know about it? You've never 'ad a husband and will never 'ave children. You've no idea what it feels like." She had to padlock her tongue out of fear for her job. Miss Bamford had power. If she found fault with a woman's work she could have her dismissed. Elsie had watched how she'd picked on Gloria Heywood. She disliked her from the day she started, one of those irrational dislikes which is rooted in a difference of character and for which people find justifications whose hysteria is in proportion to their flimsiness. Gloria was an unmarried mother. Pregnant at seventeen by a lad in the merchant navy, she'd had the child, prevailed on her parents for a while and now lived in a council house on the Kingsfold estate: one of those post-war, sprawling, woefully optimistic developments, bare of amenities, created by councillors and town planners who would have lived in a caravan rather than move there. It was remarkably salubrious, benefitting from the ingrained ability of the people at the bottom to make a meal from scraps, a home from a slum and a life from demeaning circumstances.

She evinced no sign of apology. Miss Bamford, who believed motherhood outside marriage one of the worst shames a woman could suffer, disliked her easy-going confidence, her cheerfulness and her unwillingness to act as if she belonged in the shadows, thought she was an insult to respectability. She knew it was becoming common among young people to have sex before marriage, but it was one of those modern phenomena, like the legalisation of homosexual acts or abortion which she deplored. She associated these with Harold Wilson, Jack Jones, Joe Gormley, strikes, CND, demonstrations: the entire gamut of loose, liberal, I'm-as-good-as-you-are, insurgent, irreverent, long-haired, tight-jeaned decadence which was ruining the country.

Worst of all was the well-fancy-that manner in which Gloria responded to being upbraided.

"No, no, no," said Miss Bamford, nudging her aside and grabbing the sieve and the bag of flour. "Like this. It has to aerate. Tap the sieve gently, let the flour fall slowly into the bowl. Look at that. Look. She how beautifully fine that flour is. Full of air. Now that will make a gorgeous mixture."

/

"Mmm," said Gloria, surveying the peaked heap of white powder, "you're a genius. You should be on the telly. You could be the next Fanny Craddock."

Miss Bamford needed her little, daily victories over the women she trained to sweeten the bitter pith of her evenings alone. That Gloria refused to treat her as a superior, that she spoke to her as if they were friends meeting for a drink, that the threat implied in criticism didn't make her deferential, drove the supervisor to intense inspection. Like a rat sniffing out food at a hundred yards, she was alert to every less-than-perfect action.

"You should join't union," Elsie said to the young woman.

"I don't know much about that kind of thing," she said, her big, brown eyes smiling.

"Well, they'll protect you, if you need it. You never know."

"Yeah, thanks. I'll think about it."

Gloria was given notice. Elsie was outraged. She should have joined the union. Miss Bamford wouldn't have got away with it then.

That night she dreamed she moved house. A great horse-drawn cart arrived and her brother Eddie piled in her furniture. There was no room in Mary's little house for her double bed, wardrobe, dressing table, the good dining-chairs she'd inherited from her father. Ted made a bonfire in the garden. She was nursing the baby but her breasts were dry. Ted was hammering on the front door. She had it locked and barred. The baby was crying. Mary was making pancakes. She fed them to the baby which grew in an instant. Elsie was outside. Mary, Ted and their child were at the window laughing and shooing her away.

She regretted every day that Mary didn't live nearby. It wasn't natural for a daughter to be far from her mother. Why hadn't Mary insisted they live in Penwortham? She'd complied with Ted's wishes. She'd converted to Catholicism and gone to live where he was at home. There stirred in the depths of Elsie's consciousness the hint of the beginning of a doubt: was Mary too generous? Was she too willing to bend to the will of others? Had Ted spotted her stem-in-the-wind nature and known he could make her bend to his insistencies? She dismissed the suggestion before it could become a realised thought. All the same, she could never have left her mother for a man. Bert had understood that. He was being welcomed into her family. How had it happened that her daughter now seemed to be more part of Ted's?

Andy Lang was sitting in Lonsdale Lecture theatre with Rob Green, Mike Darley and Mike Richards. They'd seen the posters and decided they should come along. The speaker was a Chilean based in London. Andy guessed he was probably twenty-five or so. Dark-skinned with thick, black hair and a moustache you could have swept the floor with, he spoke fluent English with a heavy, charming accent. Andy knew little about Chile. He'd read the odd piece in *The Guardian* about Allende and felt positively about his socialism. The South American explained the involvement of the CIA in Chilean politics. It went back a long way. Allende had come to power in spite of their machinations but now the evidence was mounting they were conspiring to bring him down. International support was needed. Allende was democratically elected. The support of democratic regimes in Europe was vital. The Chilean military were ready to act. Any time they could mount a coup, democracy would be shut down, opponents arrested, silenced, disappeared. The British government could make a difference by standing with Allende as the legitimate President. The Trade Union movement could offer solidarity. The British people needed to know what was happening. The Chilean military was supplied with British-made weapons. That trade must be stopped.

Andy was convinced. Whether Allende was a good or bad President wasn't the point. He was elected. If he was to be removed there should be an election. Heath was a twerp of a Prime Minister, but he was in power until he was voted out. Andy was stirred enough to take action. He would join marches, hand out flyers, write to his MP and the papers. Small stuff but if millions of people do it, big stuff.

Yet what preoccupied his thoughts wasn't the broad political landscape, but the man in front of him. He was a bloke a few years older than himself. Just a bloke. He was a socialist who did the same kind of things Andy had done and took for granted; but he was facing the possibility of imprisonment or death. If the coup came and he returned to Chile, he might be arrested, tortured, possibly murdered by one of the hired goons of the potential dictatorship. He might be wiped out for doing the things Andy thought of as routine. Here he was, a living human being, an intelligent, vital, energetic man; a man with decades of life in him who should have children and be a good father, take up his role as teacher or doctor or engineer or whatever he was going to be, enjoy his life and grace the world by his charming, generous presence. How could it be that such a man, an obviously principled, high-minded democrat might be battered, broken, bruised, electrocuted, starved, kicked, whipped and killed, simply for engaging in the banality of political campaigning?

When the time for questions came, Andy asked:

"If there is a coup, will you go back to Chile?"

"Yes, the man replied.

He elaborated that it was his duty to resist tyranny. If he stayed away and saved his skin, that would be mere cowardice. He would go home and do what he could.

In Bowland bar afterwards, Andy said to his mates:

"Would you go back?"

"I dunno," said Rob Green, "I like to think that I would."

"You'd have to," said Mike Darley, "you couldn't claim to be on the side of democracy and walk away."

Mike Richards was forming a delicate roll-up, his long, fair hair falling across his cheeks and hiding his face.

"What about you, Mike?" said Andy.

"What?" said he friend, tossing his head to see beyond his locks and raising his dark brows in that surprised way he did when he preferred not to be disturbed.

They laughed. Mike licked the thin paper and glued the skinny fag, tugging a few scraps of trailing, auburn tobacco from the end.

"What I think," he said, in that quiet voice which they had to lean in to hear and with that hesitant delivery which concealed the blade of his intelligence, "is I wouldn't be brave enough. It's the right thing, but if I could save my life, I think I would."

He pressed his lips together and brushed his hair aside with his free hand before taking his blue briquet from the cluttered pocket of his brown jacket and lighting up.

"I think you're right," said Andy. "If I were him and the coup happened while I was here, I'd seek asylum. I'd campaign from London, but I wouldn't go back to face torture or death."

"What about the people who can't get away?" said Mike Darley.

"I know," said Andy, "but my instinct would be to stay out of harm's way."

"Cowardice," said Rob.

"I am a physical coward," said Andy. "I'd run ten miles to avoid a fight."

Over the next months, they all did what they could: handed out leaflets, attended meetings, wrote letters that didn't get published. It was easy. There was nothing to giving up a couple of hours on a Saturday to hand out leaflets in Market Street; and when they'd done, they went to *The Blue Anchor* or *The Ring O' Bells*, for a sandwich or pie and chips and a few pints. Always, in Andy's head, was the image of the Chilean. He hoped he would stay in England. He hoped he would be safe.

"I can't see the point," said Jane, naked before his mirror brushing her thick hair.

"The point is democracy," said Andy pulling on his black cords.

"Well, my father says only the businessmen know what the economy needs. I think we should leave it to them."

"I think we should leave it to the goldfish," he said.

"You always say something facetious."

"That's a big word, Jane Bentnick. You're getting educated. You'll be quoting Noam Chomsky before long."

"What's linguistics got to do with it?"

"Mr Chomsky is a syntactic structures man from Monday to Friday, at the weekend he's an anarchist. He and your father would get along like chickenpox."

"Anarchist? Don't they throw bombs and shoot politicians?"

"They do. Some of them. The lunatic wing. Every political movement must have its lunatic wing. The Tories have Enoch Powell and Gerald Nabarro, for example. So as you say, anarchists have been guilty of outrages. However, there is what you might call the buttercups and apple blossom wing of the movement, represented by Kropotkin who would have agonised over killing a fly. Chomsky is definitely an apple blossom anarchist."

"Anyway, I think my father knows more about these things than you," she said, fastening her bra.

"He should write a book or stand for parliament, then we could all have a laugh."

It was the penultimate day of the year. They'd received their results. Jane had M2s in all three subjects, Andy an M1 in French and M2s in English and Russian. She was simultaneously stunned and unsurprised that he'd done better. There were no more than half a dozen M1s in French. She knew he was clever, but at the same time, he came from the north and the working-class. It didn't fit. People from his background weren't supposed to be among the most intelligent. She wished it weren't true. There was a terrible conflict between her assumptions and her experience and she willed her assumptions to win.

"Where are you going to live next year?" she said.

"Morecambe."

"It's horrible."

"It's not Biarritz but it isn't horrible. The sunsets are fabulous and you can swim in Half Moon Bay at Heysham, so long as you don't mind a dose of radiation."

"Radiation?"

"There's a facility nearby. It's what provides your lights"

"Who are you sharing with?"

"Rob, Mike and Mike, Steve, we're getting holiday flats. It'll be like the summer holidays all winter. We'll breakfast on candy floss and have a donkey ride before bedtime."

"Well, I'm staying on campus."

"Have you fixed it?"

"Yes. I claimed special circumstances."

"What are they?"

"I don't have anyone to share with. Campus is safer. Anyway, Mrs Calland has given me a single room."

"That's handy. I'll have somewhere to stay."

She turned away, looked in the mirror and ran her fingers over her eyebrows.

"I'm going now. I might see you later."

"You might."

The long summer vacation meant separation. She was anxious for what it could bring. She was going to Bilbao. Jean-Claude would visit. She'd go with him to his parents' house in Nancy. His father was posted to the consulate in Athens but his mother would spend several weeks in their northern home. She would supervise them and try to stop them sleeping together but they could easily outwit her. They would travel; maybe to St Tropez or Monaco. In any case, it would be three months away from Andy. She would be able to put him decisively behind her.

She was brisk in packing. She wished she was leaving Lancaster for ever. The year had been a terrible trial. She was tortured. She was tormented. She'd closed herself against the university, its students, the town. Yet her fiercest rejection couldn't prevent liking, charm, pleasure even, at times, delight seeping through like sunlight finding its way through a nick in tight blinds. One thing she'd relished was the staff. She noticed, one morning, edging round the table to her seat, Tim Madden, the linguistics lecturer, glancing furtively at her breasts. She was wearing the tight, light blue polo neck which accentuated her curves. She was quite used, of course, like all young women to the greedy eyes of men; yet more than most because of being extraordinarily good-looking and well-made. Yet Madden wasn't a bloke on the street or some sleazy, middle-aged chap with a bald head, a double chin and thick glasses on the train pretending to read *The Times*, while taking crafty looks at her chest: he was her teacher. He was married.

He was a tall, gangling man with big limbs, straight shoulders, a large head topped with a wild mop of curly hair and a face which while not remotely good-looking had strength and character. There was a hint of her father's build in him. He too was tall and had arms and legs which might have reached to Africa. She was immediately shocked by his licentious glimpse but quickly adjusted her feeling. For the next seminar she wore her navy-blue and white hooped top with the deep V-neck. He couldn't fail to notice. Such exposure always made her slightly embarrassed. She had a strong desire to keep her flesh concealed, an almost puritan impulse never to let a man see her utterly revealed. Andy had read her Donne's line about being as liberal as to the midwife but she couldn't respond to it with a sense of it being natural and innocent. She preferred undressing in the dark, conjoining without the means being seen. All the same, the thought of seducing her tutor was too darkly attractive to stop her.

She'd read *Jane Eyre* and one of her friends in the sixth-form had introduced her to Ann Radcliffe. Jean-Claude had read aloud passages from *Justine*. She knew passion was at its zenith when it was illicit or associated with madness or extreme emotion. There must be cruelty, heartbreak, tears, violence, suicide or the threat of it for sex to have real zest. What was it otherwise but mere physical sensation? Adultery, she knew, because it had been taught in her religious education classes, was the ultimate sin. What could be more exciting than the ultimate?

She would have been astonished to learn there are young women who have easy, simple, affectionate relations with young men and have no need of a sense of transgression. For Jane, sex that wasn't a sin was flat as a punctured tyre, dull as a wet Sunday and no more to be pursued than a rabid dog. If she could have sex with Madden! His wife might find out. There might be a court case. She would be cited. It might be in the papers. Everyone would know. She would be famous on campus as a *femme fatale*, a *fallen woman*. That would-be status worth having. She mentioned the notion to Andy. He laughed out loud and said:

"Carry on like that, you'll be mad, bad and dangerous to know."

She watched for signs that Madden had noticed her provocative attire. She hung around at the end of a seminar to ask if she could come to see him to discuss the essay she had to write, but he had to be elsewhere and disappeared. All the same, the lurid images of assignations, of sex in the back of his car, in bushes, in public places in the dark, in the very bed he shared with his wife, haunted her. Oh, if only she could torture Jean-Claude with stories of her adulterous affair, if only she could become thoroughly experienced in vice, a corrupt, cynical, risky woman all timid people feared and secretly admired.

The end of the year had arrived and she had seduced only Andy. Now that she was about to re-join Jean-Claude, she despised utterly her northern lover. It had been an act of desperation and it was the desperation which gave it meaning. It was true she'd told him she loved him. It was true she was besotted and jealous to the point of murder if she saw him with Sue Border. She'd been driven to extremes by loneliness and frustration. She liked herself in the role of seductress. Andy had fallen. She'd worried before she got him in bed that he might have the will to resist. He'd showed no interest. Had he refused her she would have had to resort to exorbitant measures. She might have threatened to throw herself off Bowland Tower. She would have been the thoroughly desperate woman. If she killed herself, it would be his fault.

The next day she was taking the train to London. She had a taxi booked. She would leave without saying goodbye. That ought to torment him over the summer. When she came back, a prospect which distressed her, she would shun him. He would be hurt and confused. He was in love with her, of course. She'd played the devoted woman. She was aware of the power of her beauty. He would pursue her. She would be bored and exasperated. He would plead, she would be as unresponsive as granite. She would smoke, tobacco and dope, wallow in her misfortune, exhibit a haughty *ennui*. She was convinced he was held in orbit and could no more escape her than the earth might depart from the sun's command.

When Andy was at home, he gave half his income to his mother. He signed on, but he wasn't going to spend the vacation without working. In the *Daily Telegraph*, whose jobs pages he looked through in the Harris Library, he found an ad for hop-pickers, sent off a letter and was accepted. That was the last four weeks settled. In the meantime, he looked in the *Lancashire Evening Post* and spotted a job at a paper mill. He began within days. It was dirty, routine, chaotic work. The place was filthy, disorganised, badly managed. There was a core of skilled men who serviced the machines and understood the processes; the remainder of the staff were unskilled and casual. His first task was to clean the polluted stream the factory had dumped waste in for years. The water was black and at points where the stinking silt stopped its flow, crawled up the banks and flooded the footpath to one side and the field to the other. Andy guessed the business had been ordered to do the clean-up. It wasn't the kind of place to be responsible without a kick in the rear.

He was provided with a scoop on the end of a six-foot pole. He had to stand in the water which threatened to sneak over his wellingtons, dig the metal half-sphere into the thick, dark, viscous, nasty, poisonous, pungent mud, lift the weight through the water and dump it on the banks. He'd been working half an hour when a rat swam towards him, its snout poking into the air. He paused and stared at it. It halted and stared back. He swung his heavy pole in an ungainly effort to whack it. It ducked beneath and disappeared.

On the banks was a profuse growth of thick-stemmed, big-leafed plants. His second tool was a kind of small scythe. He had to slice through the sappy integuments close to the earth and heap up the cut specimens.

The following morning, his forearms, exposed by his rolled sleeves, were full of small blisters. He went into work but resolved not to cut the weeds. The other lads who'd been on the same job had the same affliction. One, who'd worked shirtless, had been to the hospital, his torso covered in enormous sores. The culprit was giant hogweed. They were ordered to keep their skin covered, were given gloves, face masks and goggles. Later, an official appeared to inspect the work.

His second job was helping a welder. There were pipes here and there which were leaking. The welder tied a rope, told Andy to stand with his legs either side and tug to bring the two ends into line while he lit the oxy-acetylene. As he turned to apply it to the metal, Andy let go of the rope and jumped back.

"What the fuck you doin' ?" said the welder.

"Don't point that thing at me," said Andy, "you're gonna set my bloody pants on fire."

"Ah, you fuckin' cissy, get 'old o' that rope."

"Find someone else to do it," said Andy walking away, "I'm not having my bollocks fried."

The same man had a job to do high up, where thin pipes ran close to the roof of the main building, beneath the machines which were fed with the liquid pulp and miraculously turned out broad sheets of coarse brown paper. He climbed a ladder, scrambled across the roof of a little office, shinned up a pipe, edged along a ledge and looking down at Andy who stood with his hands in his pockets shouted:

"Come on, follow me."

Andy shook his head.

"What the fuck's the matter wi' you?"

"I've got a brain and I like being alive," said Andy.

The huge vats in which the waste paper was pulped needed their filter plates replacing. They were thick steel, almost wedge-shaped but curved at either end to fit the outer rim and the inner circle. Inch diameter holes had been drilled to let the liquid drain and keep what wouldn't pulp behind. They were lowered into the tubs by block and tackle, a single nut and bolt through one of the holes. Andy and three other lads were standing in a vat as the first plate swung overhead. The managing director, a thin, grey man in a pin-stripe who strutted as if he knew what was going on and was on a rare visit to his profit-mill, was giving orders. As Andy watched the great metal pad sway, out of control of the men who were trying to direct it to where it should lie, he noticed the bolt was bending. He backed against the side, moved to the ladder and began to climb out.

"What are you doing?" called the suited boss. "Stay down there. Stay down."

"That bolt is going to snap," said Andy.

"Get down there," said the boss.

Andy continued to climb. He was almost at the rim when the plate was lowered and the three lads were told to direct it into place. They struggled with its weight, pushed and tugged. The bottom end was brought into the centre. The outer edge was moved further down, bit by bit. When it had another two feet to descend, Roger Brewer who was now reading Sociology at Keele, and who liked to push himself forward, as if he knew how to command any task, wrapped the fingers of his right hand round the edge and tried to pull it to where it should be. The bolt snapped, there was a shout, he tried to pull his hand free but his middle finger was trapped. He let out a scream, men scurried into the hollow and managed to lift the corner enough for his mangled hand to be pulled out.

Still on the ladder, Andy looked up into the face of the managing director who stared down at him, grim and stern.

"You should have stayed down there," he said and hurried away.
Two days later Andy picked up his last wage packet.

BABY BLUES

The baby was born in August. Since the due date had been known, Elsie had seen it as an omen: her own birthday was in the same month. It was common in her family. She ran through all the relatives born in high summer. It must mean something. It didn't occur to her that though she and one of her brothers were August babies, the other two weren't. Nor did she reflect that people might deliberately aim for a summer baby; nor either that the relaxations of Christmas might have an influence. Her mind had been formed in revelation; the forces that made things happen were incomprehensible. It was an omen.

The signal she wanted it to be was that she should become indispensable to Mary's family. The boy had arrived relatively easily. The hospital stay was short. All the same, Elsie went to the local shops, stocked up the fridge and the cupboards and cooked for Ted while Mary wasn't there.

"He can look after himself for two days," said Mary.

"It's no good buying a pie from the bakers and heating some beans. He has to go to work. He needs to eat properly."

"Well, he wouldn't starve."

Reluctantly, Mary had provided her mother with a front-door key. She'd tried to persuade her it wouldn't be necessary, but Elsie had argued that, being August, she wouldn't be working full-time, and in any case she could arrange to take her two weeks. It would be a help. She knew how much there was to do when a baby arrived. She knew how tired a new mother could be. Someone to look after the little things was invaluable. That was why it was a good idea for daughters to live near their mothers. When she was a girl there wasn't all this moving away. All the lasses she grew up with stayed local and they were glad of it when their families came along. It's good for the children. It stands to sense. Her grandma had been round the corner, and her aunties. It gives a child security. What's more important than that?

Ted was relaxed about his mother-in-law being on hand. He had no feel for domestic niceties. If she made a steaming cottage pie or steak and chips and a hearty apple crumble, he could put up with her odd, never-ending, knotted, round-in-circles wittering about the training kitchen. It troubled him, marginally. It was queer how she would spurt like a broken main and be unaware of how little interest what she said held for him; but he was a new father, nothing could undermine his joy.

Elsie was installed in the little, second bedroom which had been decorated as the nursery. She stayed for two weeks. At first, Mary thought her strange mood was because her mother was in the house. She assumed once she'd left, her typical resilience would return. She was surprised to find that day by day her mental state worsened. One afternoon, alone with her son who was sleeping in his cot, she broke down and wept for an hour without knowing why. She wondered if she should tell Ted. What would he say? He'd probably make a joke of it. It would be a *woman's thing*, that category into which he placed whatever puzzled or disappointed him about the opposite sex. The worst was, she couldn't tell him why she'd cried. She had no idea. There was no straightforward cause. She was sad. Unaccountably sad. Was that how a new mother was supposed to feel?

The local Methodist church ran a new mothers' club once a week. She went along and was delighted to meet the other women and their babies. Holding someone else's child in her arms permitted her a distance she couldn't achieve from her own. She could see this little life as charming, dependent, in need of love and care and temporarily the overwhelming sense of inadequacy which swamped her when she was isolated with Patrick receded. The Wednesday morning two hours became the fulcrum of her week. If she could have been with new mothers every day, if they could have brought their babies up together, she felt she might have avoided the bizarre thoughts that came to her: the thought she might harm her child; the fear he would be taken from her; the sense that whatever she did for him, it could never be enough.

"Baby blues," one of the mothers said to her.

She was a dark-haired, dark-skinned lass, very pretty and with an athletic way of moving; one of those people you would never imagine could suffer mental conflict. Yet she told Mary for the first two weeks she'd been *all over the place*.

"You should've seen me. Well, you shouldn't. I was a mess. I couldn't be bothered with anything. I didn't wash my hair for a fortnight. I didn't take my dressing gown off. Poor Barry, he thought I was going to be like that for the rest of my life," and she laughed. "But it went as quickly as it came. Three weeks and I was back to my old self."

A month passed, two, and Mary felt no different. What had once lifted her now left her heavy as an iron saucepan. She thought she'd bake a fruit cake. Following a recipe attentively and producing a perfect outcome had always cheered her up and made her feel proud. She took the flour, dried fruit and spices from the cupboard, the butter from the fridge and the mixing bowl from under the sink. She stood and looked at it all for a minute before being overcome with an absolute sense of pointlessness. What was the point of a cake? She sat on the sofa and cried for forty minutes.

When, finally, she was sobbing as Ted came through the door at six, they had to talk.

"Maybe t'doctor could give you summat."

"But there's nothing wrong with me."

"Aye, but there must be like, if you start crying for nowt."

At *snap time*, he confessed to his workmates. It was necessary to secure male support. They were sympathetic. It was hard for a bloke to work all day and go home to a crying wife. For Ted, it was an incontrovertibly woman's problem, one of those mysteries which men need to defend themselves against. He couldn't keep it to himself. He was vindicated by the lads' agreement that a man shouldn't have to put up with that sort of thing. He hadn't sought or expected anything more, but an older man, an electrician with a stammer who said little and had an odd habit of reading a book as he ate his sandwiches, put his hand on his shoulder as he was heading back to nails and skirting-boards: his wife had suffered post-natal depression. He should get Mary to a doctor. It had to be taken seriously. It wouldn't go away by itself.

Ted asked him what treatment his wife had received. She was given tablets and *a talking cure*. Was she all right? The electrician shook his head and looked hard into Ted's eyes. No, she killed herself.

Nothing as serious had ever invaded Ted's mind. He'd grown up playing football and cricket, getting by at school, indulging in the usual mischief and had imagined his life would roll like a wood on a perfectly-tended green. Why should this trouble come into his life? It was a woman's thing. Why should it bother him? Yet the melodramatic possibility had installed itself in his consciousness. Going home to a sobbing wife was bad enough, but the idea of going home to a body on the kitchen floor was beyond anything he'd ever had to respond to. He didn't have the appropriate feelings.

He experienced an impulse to ask the electrician about the details. Perhaps he could get away with it by insinuating his worry; but he backed off. The bloke wouldn't want to relive it. Ted couldn't clear from his head how other-worldly strange it was that a man he worked with, who sat quietly, his back against the wall, unwrapping his sandwiches from their greaseproof package, could have lived through an experience whose horror it was impossible to imagine. It was the kind of thing that happened in films or on the telly. It was never real. It was always presented in a way which didn't leave you troubled. It was entertainment. You might see a dead body in a tv drama, a woman who had shot herself or taken too many pills, but it was just a bit of fun; something you could relax in front of. It was meant to scare you but only in a way which made you feel good. Hearing about the electrician's wife terrified him in a way which drove him to absolute loneliness. If such a thing happened to you, you were entirely alone. Might it happen to him? He felt resentment that he should have to think about it. Why should this woman's problem have come into his life? Most women had babies and got on with it. The high joy of fatherhood which made him feel as if the universe were made for him, was dragged low by this peculiar ailment.

"Anyway," he said as Mary brought his mug of tea to the table and cleared his plate, "there's a bloke on site whose wife had t'same. Doctor gave her pills and suchlike. Make an appointment."

"And did it do her any good?" said Mary.

Ted paused, blew on his tea and raised his eyes to hers.

"Aye, she's right as rain."

Mary was strict about not pestering the doctor. She'd been brought up to respect the NHS and to use it responsibly. Her mother had told her stories of people rushing to surgeries in the early days expecting to be given prescriptions for disinfectant or toothpaste. She never went to the GP without a slight sense of guilt: it was costing money; was she really in need of treatment? She'd worked with women who at the first hint of a sniffle demanded a prescription. She thought it cissy and selfish. A cold or a cough were just things to put up with. The Health Service was for serious matters.

In the waiting-room, she was suddenly struck by embarrassment. What was she going to say? That she began crying for no reason? That she'd lost interest in things? How would the doctor respond to that? No doubt the people around her had real illnesses. The man opposite, thin and silver-bearded, had to open his mouth to suck in each breath, his chest rising with the sudden inspiration. He might be close to death. What was she doing here? She was fit and healthy. She was twenty-five. Oh, it was ridiculous. She should just grit her teeth and get on with life. She was about to leave when her name was called.

Doctor Delafield was thirty, tall and slim with one of those faces which look as if they have just come in from the fresh air and sunshine of a beach or the hills. Mary put the brake on the pram. The baby stirred and gave a little cry.

"How is he?" said the doctor, standing to shake her hand.

"Fine," said Mary.

"Good. Pleased to see you Mrs McIlwaine. Now, how can I help?"

Mary crossed her legs and pulled her skirt over her knees. The doctor was smiling at her pleasantly.

"Well, I don't know where to start really. My husband pestered me to get an appointment."

"I see."

"I don't really think there's anything wrong me. Not in the normal way."

"No. That's fine. Just tell me what it is."

The thought went through Mary's head that the doctor wasn't much older than her. Perhaps she could have been a professional. The sudden, odd feeling that she'd let something slip from her troubled her.

"I suppose the main thing, I know it sounds stupid, is that I get weepy for no reason."

"No, that doesn't sound stupid at all. You've done the right thing in coming to see me."

"People say it's just the baby blues, but it doesn't seem to be getting any better."

The doctor shook her head.

"Baby blues is just a passing mood caused by your hormones being in confusion after the birth. I think your complaint is something else. Tell me about it. Take your time."

The fear of being dismissed cleared. Mary tried to put her odd moods into words. It was difficult because it was as if she was talking about someone else. There was Mary before Patrick's birth and Mary afterwards. She'd always been one of those people who find life interesting, even in its banality: she found washing-up interesting, ironing, shopping, cleaning the bathroom. There was an inner positivity which transformed the most redundant task into a pleasant activity, especially if it was shared. Ted would wipe the dishes, if she jabbed him a bit, and she liked that; the two of them in the kitchen, chatting, joking as the necessary tasks got done. Or she would go out into the garden, which he thought essentially his preserve, and help him clear weeds from the beds or push the mower a bit while he laughed at her and mocked her slowness, squeezing her biceps and telling her she needed to saw some timber. They were delicious, deliquescent, hilarious moments when they descended into their intimacy where they could poke fun at one another affectionately.

Life had never seemed to her anything but essentially delightful. Even her parents' divorce, which had pushed her under water for a short time, hadn't robbed her of her *joie-de-vivre*. Suddenly, this other creature had crept into her skin who woke up and wondered what was the point of getting out of bed, who ironed blouses, shirts, sheets and trousers, and looking at the pile, fresh and smelling of heat and cleanliness, felt nothing but weariness and lack of motivation. Even wiping down the kitchen surface took an effort of will.

This wasn't her. She was the Mary who'd loved to go to school in her neatly pressed blouse and skirt, who took infinite pride in the neatness of her exercise books, who tidied her room to perfection without thinking about it, who cooked a three-course meal, served it, cleared, washed up and had the kitchen looking pristine and felt she'd done nothing.

She told the doctor she couldn't be bothered with things. She felt useless. She had odd ideas that she might harm her baby and the dam of lovely equanimity which she always lived behind broke and through it gushed the wish to sit and weep and do nothing else. She felt right when she was crying; it was all she was fit for.

"You will have heard of post-natal depression?"

"Yes."

"It's common. It won't clear up on its own. We'll have to do something. There's medication. It takes a bit of time to kick in, but it will raise your mood. That's a good idea for dealing with the acute symptoms; but you can't take pills for the rest of your life. I think you'd benefit from what's often called a talking cure. Have you heard of that?"

"Yes."

"I could refer you to someone, a clinical psychologist, or if you like, I could make some time available. I'm qualified in counselling as well as medicine."

Mary had the feeling the doctor wanted to offer. She was leaning forward and her crooked little smile reminded her of her brother. The idea sprang into her head that they could be friends: they were close in age, they lived in the same locality. Yet she'd always felt people like doctors existed on a higher plane. In the terrace streets where she'd spent the first eight years of her life, there were no doctors, lawyers, accountants, headmistresses, bank managers; her neighbours were factory workers, bus drivers, joiners, dustmen, roofers, painters, shop-workers, cleaners, women-who-did. The hangover of that apartheid still lingered.

"If you don't mind, I think I'd prefer you. I already know you and that feels better than going to someone I've never met."

So the sessions began. Mary was astonished at how simply talking could make her feel much better. Doctor Delafield was informal. It felt almost like meeting a friend; but she said remarkable things:

"What did you expect being a mother would be?"

"I don't know?"

" Did you imagine killing routine, tiredness, not being able to think about your own needs much?"

"No, I don't think so. I think I was imagining the baby"

"Yes, you weren't thinking about you were you?"

"I suppose not."

"And you thought the baby would be wonderful."

"He is."

"Of course, but he's also hard work."

"Yes, I suppose so."

"And you worked hard anyway."

"Not really."

"Not really? Who did the housework?"

"I did."

"Who did the shopping?"

"Me."

"Who looked after the household finances?"

"Me, I suppose."

"Who made sure the milkman knew what to leave and the coalman was paid?"

"That's not very difficult."

"No, Mary, but can you see what you do? Whenever it's a matter of your effort, you think it's nothing. Looking after a new baby is incredibly hard work. Much harder than what your husband does every day. And you've taken it on as if it's nothing, as if you should just be able to cope and keep on. You need to recognize how hard you're working and you need to think about your own needs a bit."

"Well, I do."

"Yes? How?"

"I go to the mother and baby group on a Wednesday."

"Of course, but with the baby."

"I can't go without him."

The doctor laughed.

"No, and he can't go without you, can he? That's what you need to think about: time away from the baby, time for yourself."

"But I like being with him."

"Yes, you're a good mother, but what I think is this. There's a gap between what you thought being a mother would be and the reality, and that's where the depression invades. In thinking about having a baby I bet you never said to yourself: 'This is going to be really hard and I'm going to be exhausted.' You feel guilty about being tired. You feel guilty that you need to hand the baby over to someone else for a bit. That's what you should do. Be a bit selfish, if you like. I think you've wanted things to be too perfect. That's your nature. You do everything as well as you can. But having a baby is different from ordinary things, it absorbs the whole of your attention and energy."

"I don't like the idea of being selfish."

The doctor laughed again.

"No, badly expressed. What I mean is, just say I need some time to myself. I need to be free for a few hours, and it doesn't matter if the ironing doesn't get done for once."

Mary had never experienced someone being able to crawl inside her head and see what was going on, but she knew the doctor was right. She'd been so intent that everything should be perfect for her son, she'd never imagined patches of blank weariness or boredom. As the weeks went by she found her desire to cry was a distant, tiny voice.

"You look after Patrick tomorrow," she said to Ted, "I'm going to Liverpool to do some shopping."

"All day?"

"No, I'll go in the morning and be back by lunchtime."

"We could both go."

"Do you want to go shopping?"

"No, but I could walk him in't pram for a bit."

"If you like."

Her reasonableness deterred him. He stayed at home. She took the train at nine.

She'd never liked Liverpool much, in spite of the glamour of *The Beatles*, but it was a city, it looked out to sea, it had a history of trade and emigration and the people were of her kind: folk from modest circumstances sometimes suspicious of wealth and power. She walked from Lime Street to the docks, because she wanted to see the water and it attracted her as the source of the city's energy. Shocked by how clinging-to-the-edge it looked she didn't stay long. Walking towards the shops, she recalled what the news reports she'd heard and the bits she'd read in the paper about how recession was hitting the city. The image of Bessie Braddock addressing a crowd came into her head. She was one of those Labour people her mother spoke well of. What had gone wrong? How could it be that despite Harold Wilson, Liverpool could give off the atmosphere of the sick room, appear as lacking in energy and future as the old man she saw shuffling along, a fag in his mouth, struggling for breath? What was *recession* anyway? It was one of those words which made her feel immediately ignorant and quickly annoyed. Politicians, journalists, television presenters, used such words as if everyone knew what they meant, as if everyone was agreed; but in truth, she had no idea. A recession was people not having jobs, factories and shops closing, money being withdrawn from hospitals and schools, but why, when there was so much money around?

She went into *Marks and Spencer* to look at the blouses. She was glad to find it was busy. The shoppers were mainly women. She enjoyed being amongst them. It was a great feminine activity, looking for just the right colour and style at the right price. Ted had no feel for it. His idea of shopping for clothes was to go to John Collier and buy the first pair of trousers that fit him. The less time he spent in the shop the better. Most men, she assumed were like that, though her dad had a sense of style and liked to choose carefully. As for Andrew, he'd joined the dressing-down brigade and was as eager to put on a suit as climb into his coffin.

She didn't buy anything. As usual, she thought carefully about spending. She would never buy anything as an extravagance. To leave with a new blouse if she couldn't convince herself she needed one would have left her disgusted with herself. She had to convince herself the purchase was necessary, reasonable, well within what she could afford before she would even think of opening her purse.

More than anything, she wanted to look around. She could have said that to Ted. He would have been more likely to come along if he'd thought she wasn't going to be trying on skirts or twin-sets. She needed to be alone. Doctor Delafield was right, she couldn't always be doing things for other people. One of her comments sounded in her head:

"It seems to me you've grown up having to be excessively sensitive to someone else's needs. It's made you very caring and generous. But people sometimes exploit that."

Did the doctor know she was evoking her mother? Was she just too polite to be direct? Being caring and generous were qualities, if she possessed them, Mary was proud of; but the doctor was right: she had, even as a little girl, always been attentive to her mother's thin skin. Had it made her a *soft touch*? Was that what Titch had taken her for? Was there something of that in her relationship to Ted?

"You know," Doctor Delafield had said, "not everyone responds to kindness with kindness. There are some who see it as an expression of weakness."

At any rate, what was without doubt was that her sessions with the doctor, her growing sense of having someone to confide in who understood her and the sanction from someone she respected of her right to space and time of her own had lifted her mood and put the despair of her weepy period behind her.

She passed the *Everyman Theatre* and it occurred to her it might be nice to go and see something. She might persuade Ted, if it was the right kind of thing. He enjoyed a show if it was funny or musical or a crime drama or thriller. She would prefer Shakespeare. She stood a moment and examined the posters and was reminded of her lessons with Mr Duck on *Julius Caesar* and *Richard III*. It had been a great pleasure and source of pride to get her essays back with a good mark and positive comment. The complete Dickens she'd won as the English prize sat on a shelf Ted had put up in the alcove in the living-room. Maybe she could have made more of all that. It was too late. Her bed was made.

After an hour and half she found a little café which looked clean and competent but the coffee was instant, thin and undrinkable, the sandwich hard at the edges and her scone apparently held together by Portland cement. There was a framed picture of *The Beatles* in their 1962 manifestation, looking fresh, innocent, cheeky and affectionate. What had happened to the atmosphere of those days? Now there was panic over the price of oil and the sunny prospect of a life as cheerful and uncomplicated as *She Loves You* had turned into a grim forecast of job losses, cuts, rising prices; a long, chill night of fog and ice.

The Beatles had made her laugh, though she'd never bought any of their records like Andy. He had much more interest in music than she did, like her dad, and was now listening to Mozart and Gershwin and things she felt she didn't understand; but *The Beatles* weren't really about music: the songs were catchy and bright, but the response to them was more about uplift. They were products of the forties, like her; a few years older but nevertheless part of the same atmosphere of retreat from violence, a culture of collective effort and, for the small-means folk of the north-west, a life centred in affection. Among the people she grew up alongside in her early years in Talbot Road there might have been ambition: her brainy cousin won a place at Preston Grammar though uncle Jimmy was a plumber and they lived in a tiny terrace in Plungington; there might have been the neurotic expectation of a windfall or some sudden transforming *deus ex machina*, but day by day people had one another. Neighbours were people to get along with not get ahead of. That's what *The Beatles* were about: neighbourliness and everyone getting along and helping one another, and of course, adolescent love which is the springboard to those enduring affections which create the bonds which guarantee the stability needed to bring up children. That's why they were popular. They sang in major keys of positive emotions and for kids who remembered rationing and were stuck in the unimaginative routines of school with nothing to look forward to but forty years in a factory, a shop or an office, they were a sunny bank holiday, a day on the sands, a walk over the hills, a night out with friends who would never lose touch. Their message was that the folk with empty pockets could enjoy life and deserved to. They were popular for the same reason as chocolate and candy floss: because they appealed to easily satisfied, undemanding and unsophisticated impulses which ignited memories of the nursery. Like indulgence in toffee apples at the fairground, they valorised self-abandonment. Their music required neither emotional not intellectual effort.

How strange it should all have evaporated so quickly. They were no longer cheeky upstarts who knew what it was to have egg and chips for tea and ride home on the bus; they were multi-millionaires, far out of reach of the fans who had made them rich; and while they took off into the thin atmosphere of the masters of mankind who own private jets and luxury yachts, the kids who handed over their paper-round money for *Penny Lane* or *I Feel Fine*, were experiencing the world turn against them; inflation was rising, there was talk of jobs losses, a sense of more or less permanent crisis. Just as chocolate, candy floss and toffee apples bring toothache, so cultural indulgence leads inevitably to pain.

Why was it so difficult to make life pleasant? She tried to attend responsibly to political debate. She listened to Edward Heath, Keith Joseph, Robert Carr and gave what they said serious thought; but it always defeated her. It always seemed immediately emotionally wrong. Everything resolved into economics, which she felt was a cheat. She always felt she was being told people couldn't make choices. The economy decided for them. The market determined one thing or another. It never convinced her. What was *the economy*, for god's sake? What was *the market*? She couldn't escape the feeling she was being manipulated. The point was, people could choose. They could choose to be generous rather than greedy, kind rather than nasty and if people made those good choices all the time, life would be pleasant. She couldn't rid herself of the sense that Heath and his people used economics as a way of hiding greed and selfishness.

The café was disappointing and out in the streets again Liverpool saddened her. Shabbiness was round every corner. There was a sense the place was being dragged down. It made her think of the house in Talbot Road where the old man lived (what was his name?), whose window-frames were rotting and whose lace curtains were black and shredded. She'd always felt the impulse to renovate. It was so easy. It took so little effort and so few resources. A bit of paint. A needle and thread. Things could quickly be made clean and nice.

She had the same feeling about the city. Would it really be so hard to spruce things up? Why was the place going downhill? Oh, she was back to the economic explanations. If economics couldn't work out how to make people's lives pleasant, what good was it? What she knew, in her feelings, was that Edward Heath wouldn't accept living in a place like this. Economic laws or no economic laws, if he and his kind lived in such places, something would be done.

She bought some towels, because they were good quality, reasonably priced, and they needed some; and a toy for Patrick, a rattle with a face which smiled when the thing was shaken. She was glad of her morning out but she wished she'd been with a friend. She'd barely noticed how, in her time with Ted, she'd let her contacts with the girls she'd known for years wither and become nothing more than the dutiful Christmas card. She resolved she'd get back in touch. She had a need for something other than Ted. Friendship was lightened of the burdens of fidelity, child-rearing, all those fatal impositions which defined the character of marriage. She'd enjoyed such lovely friendships. Why had she let them go?

"What d'you buy?" said Ted.

"Some towels, and this for the baby. Where is he?"

"Upstairs. Is that it, Mary? What you bin doin'? You coulda bought them in't village, lass. Eh, you've not got a fancy man in Bootle 'ave yer?"

"Stop it. What d'you want for your dinner?"

"Steak and ale pie, roast potatoes, carrots, peas, apple pie and custard and mug o' tea."

"I'll make some cheese on toast."

"Well, y'asked what I want and I told yer. Is that not on't menu today?"

"Stop bein' daft."

"I am daft. Come on lass, there's football on't telly soon."

The baby began crying.

"There we are," said Ted with a mock melodramatic gesture, "that's me afternoon gone."

"I'll see to him. You'll not miss your football."

"Aye, but what about me steak and ale pie, lass?"

Elsie never knew about her daughter's depression. Mary didn't tell her because she didn't want to worry her nor have her feel she must step in. More and more Elsie' thoughts turned to the baby. She had an odd feeling there was an authenticity about Mary's marriage which had never characterised her own. They were a real family. Without knowing it, she found a compensation for having failed in what she thought of as life's essential relation, through her identification with the new family. Before Patrick's birth they were a couple. Now, they were a family. She had her position. The pity was the distance. Over and again she regretted they weren't living nearby. She wanted to be an everyday presence in their household. If she could do one or two indispensable things, if she could become relied upon, little by little she could spread her influence.

She was aware of Mary's competence. She needed no one to help her run her home. She was quick and orderly without thinking about it. Nor was she unable to handle her relationship with Ted. Elsie knew she had produced a mature, self-possessed, equable daughter. In a way, she was sorry.

Herself, she'd never been able to think of marriage as a real relationship; not like her liaison with her mother or father. Who was Bert Lang? A stranger. That was the fact. He was unfamiliarity made flesh. The horrible fact was, that to have children, you had to be intimate with a stranger. What had to be done couldn't be done within the family. Yet emotionally she couldn't attribute to a husband what she granted to her mother, father and brothers. They were blood. A husband was water. It was only the terrible fact of sex which made a husband necessary. Sin. Yes, it was better to marry than to burn, but there was no escaping the fact that a husband was associated with the sinful act. Of course, the innocence of children swept away the dark facts of how they were conceived. Why had God made it necessary to do the work of the Devil in order to perpetuate his Creation?

The advantage of her new family was she had nothing to do with its sinfulness. She was the sexless matriarch. She should preside. She went to Skelmersdale when she could. Sometimes, she was invited. At others, she turned up unannounced. Ted opened the door at midday on a Saturday and there she was, with a packed shopping bag in her hand.

"Hello, luv. Come in. Is Mary expectin' you?"

"No. I just thought I'd get on't bus, as it's a fair day. I've brought some things for the baby and I can help Mary clean up a bit."

"You'll be lucky. There's not a speck. Mary," he called up the steep, narrow stairs, "your mum's 'ere. Sit down, luv. D'you want a cup o' tea?"

Already, still in her coat, Elsie was unpacking the disinfectant, oven cleaner, cloths and wipes from her bag and starting to attack the surfaces of the pristine kitchen.

"You should have asked me," said Mary, appearing with her son in her arms, "I'd've come and picked you up."

"Nah, it's no trouble on't bus. Not if you time it right. You've got to time it right. If you get off at Burscough and you miss that connection, and you can miss it if you don't watch out. It comes round that corner, whoosh, you've to 'ave your wits about you, if you don't you can be left standin'.."

Ted and Mary, having listened a hundred times to Elsie's tale of her fabulous peregrination from Preston to Skelmersdale, exchanged glances.

After tea, Mary would give her mother a lift home in spite of her protestations that the bus was no trouble, her checking the clock, her assertion that if she left now she would make the seventeen minutes past five, get the twenty to six in Burscough and be home before seven.

In the armchair, her left leg swaying with the regularity of a cradle as usual, Elsie reviewed the events of the day. She had held her grandchild close to her breast and she was sure he'd responded. Yes, he knew her and cleaved to her. She had a new connection. This babe of no more than a few months who might live another eighty years granted her a future. He would love his grandma with that pure, immeasurable love which is possible only among the innocent. She let herself believe she was as important in his life as his mother and father. She would be more. His father had to work. His mother had the house to attend to. His grandma could make him her one and only focus. She would be love incarnate. The child would depend on her. She, more than anyone, would be security and warmth in his life. If only she could live with Mary and Ted. They should invite her. Perhaps they would when they got a bigger house. It was the duty of children. She had accommodated her father. It was natural. Yes, surely they would. For the time being, there was Sylvia. She would soon be grown. Then she, Elsie, could assume her place. There would be more grandchildren. They would adore her. She would be fulfilled.

Andy discovered he was an uncle when his mother poked her head round his bedroom door on a bright, August morning. He lay with his hands behind his head wondering when he would get to see the boy. It was few weeks before he and Sylvia met him. New life. There was nothing like it. It made him question what he was doing. He was twenty-two and nowhere near fatherhood, yet as a teenager he'd imagined he'd be married by twenty or twenty-one, in his own house and with children on the way. It was what lads did: an apprenticeship at Leyland Motors, a motorbike and girl riding pillion, a second-hand car, early marriage and settle down. Now he was reading *Les Liaisons Dangereuses* and was no more likely to be married and father in the next few years than to be Foreign Secretary. It felt like a postponement too far, as if life itself was being postponed. What was there about being a student, developing intellectual skills, which could match the wonder of that new little baby he held on his knee at Mary's?

He spent September hop-picking in Goudhurst. Most of the workers were cockneys who were housed in miserable, low, damp, corrugated iron shelters without electricity or running water, while the students were accommodated in a purpose-built chalet with bunk beds, heating, a kitchen and a bathroom. The glamorous job in the fields was tractor driving, tugging the long trailer with the crow's nest at history's pace through the bines, then smoking off to dump the load at the hop-stripping machine. Students alone were permitted to apply to be drivers. The cockneys were allocated the low-level work. Andy hadn't driven for years after passing his test while at F.E.D. so wouldn't have felt confident about climbing on a tractor, but even if he'd been driving every day, he wouldn't have applied. He would work alongside the cockneys.

They were in the fields by seven. Whillock, the farmer, owned sixty acres. The family home was big, ancient, charming, ivy-clad, surrounded by lawns and flower beds. In the corner, some three hundred yards from the house was a grass tennis court. Andy worked at three tasks: polling, gathering and the crow's nest. The first meant following the trailer with a long, heavy, wooden pole topped by a metal hook. As the bines were cut by the crow's nest man, as close as possible to the chessboard of wires which ran between the uprights separating the bines into lanes, inevitably small clumps were left behind, hooked over the cable, or trapped beneath it. The lads with the poles had to scavenge these left-overs and ensure they fell onto the load. Gathering meant walking alongside, catching those bines which missed and tossing them over the wooden sides. In the crow's nest, a tubular platform fixed to the rear, you swung a sickle left and right to sever the clinging fingers.

They worked in the rain, the sun, the wind. At half past nine there was a thirty-minute break. Andy would hop on a trailer which took him part of the way to the chalet, make himself cheese on toast or a fried egg sandwich and cup of tea, make use of the bathroom and hurry back. The cockneys ate their sandwiches and drank from their flasks in the fields, as they did at lunchtime when the students trooped to the house to sit around a huge, rough, wooden table pushed under the eaves if the weather was unkind, dragged out onto the lawn if the sky smiled. Lizzie, the eldest daughter, was an expert chef. Educated at Benenden along with what she referred to as *your actual PA*, she was training in London with the intention of setting up a top-class restaurant. Every day the students were treated to a three-course meal: tomato and basil soup or courgette and coriander , minestrone, lentil and bacon, leek and potato, red pepper and tomato, cream of asparagus or cauliflower or mushroom, beef consommé, garden vegetable, pea and mint; great, glaze-crusted steak pies, ten pound dressed salmon, sides of beef carved into thick, succulent slices, fillets of pan-fried sea bass, piled dishes of roast potatoes, green beans, sprouts, carrots, parsnips, broccoli, green cabbage; over-full, silver gravy boats; apple pies, gooseberry, blackcurrant, rhubarb, with geological crusts drowned in custard or topped with thick cream.

One hot day, arriving in the field replete, one of the cockneys Andy had got to know a bit said:

"Stuffed, eh mate?"

He was a dark little man, wiry and very strong, always smiling as if he feared punishment should he assume a serious expression, with very white teeth, who always wore a laughable, black, felt hat perched on his balding head.

"Yeah," said Andy. "You should come along one day."

"Not for the likes of us," said the little man with a laugh, "all that posh stuff."

"What d'you mean, the likes of you? You're as good a man as the next."

"Ain't a fancy student though is I? No brains you see," he pointed to his head and laughed again. "Your privilege ain't it?"

"Tell you what," said Andy, "I'll swap with you one day. You go up to the house and eat and I'll stay in the field."

"Ain't gonna get away with that, mate. You enjoy it."

Andy contemplated staying with the cockneys at lunchtime but the truth was he was so eat-his-own-leg hungry after the morning he couldn't resist the thought of a girding meal. He took to filching slices of steak or apple pie, wrapping them in a serviette, shoving them up his jumper and taking them to his workmates.

"Here, get your gnashers round that."

"You're a wide-boy, you is mate. You'll get your cards if you're caught."

"Don't worry. I'll bring you the cutlery tomorrow. Real silver. You can flog it in the Portobello Road."

They laughed.

"You're a wide-boy all right, you is mate."

Of the twenty-one students, seven were from Oxbridge. One was a medic with a taste for literature. One evening Andy spotted him reading *Felix Krull*.

"Interested in German literature?" he asked, leaning against his bunk.

"Not particularly," said the tall, thin lad whose hair was a mop of thick, black curls."

"I haven't read that one."

"No."

"Do you know *Death In Venice*?"

"Yes."

He didn't want to engage. The Oxbridge boys formed a group from which the rest were excluded. In the evening, if most of the lads walked the two miles to the nearest pub, they sat in the corner away from the rest.

Andy got to know a lad from Glasgow who was studying engineering in Sheffield, a Brummie who was doing fine art in London and another lad from Preston who was a chemist at Durham. The only foreigner was a German, Kurt, almost stereotypical by his short blond hair, eyes as blue as a jackdaw's and his fresh, alpine complexion. At the end of the day's work, when everybody wanted to get into the bathroom, he would stand before its door, a towel round his waist and announce:

"I am going into ze bazroom. I will be in there two hours. Do not disturb me. I will not open ze door. If you urgently need to use the toilet do so now, please."

The others stood and laughed and shook their heads.

"Ten minutes, Kurt, then we'll kick the bloody door in."

"Two hours," he said with absolute seriousness. "I will not accept being disturbed."

"You are disturbed. Get in there and get out fast or we'll break in and duck you under cold water."

The younger daughter was Rosalind. She was seventeen, pretty, excited to have so many young men on the farm and quickly warmed to Andy. He was surprised because, like her sister, she was familiar with *PA* and some minor royals, very much part of the public-school, Tory, Kentish elite. He imagined she would have an instinctive aversion for a northerner of obvious low origins, but she hung by him when she joined them on their excursions to the pub. She was quiet and almost shy, but like a dog or a rabbit who knows when it will be fed and petted, nestled by him, let her upper arm touch him, smiled and asked him questions. Andy was surprised to find her congenial. He liked Lizzie too. They were purblind Tories, the kind of people who had no idea what Salford smelt like or what it meant to clock on in a factory at seven thirty every morning, but beneath their acquired prejudices, they were gentle and sweet. Every time he heard Lizzie say, *your actual PA,* he felt like responding: "Come to Preston, I'll introduce you to your actual JJ."

Trade union leaders weren't the kind of people they valued. Mrs Whillock, a short, blonde, stocky, energetic woman with thick calves who hurried around at an Olympic pace, had a group photo taken because: "You never know, one of these students may be Prime Minister one day." "If I'm Prime Minister," Andy whispered to the Glaswegian, "she'd better watch out."

Walking back from the village, in the utter darkness, pulling into the hedges when they heard a car coming, Rosalind beside him, very charming and without any edge of snobbery or disdain, it occurred to him that had she grown up in his circumstances she might well be a socialist. Was he like Lizzie and her? Had he simple absorbed a view of the world and failed to work things out for himself? Had he been born the son of a wealthy Kentish hop farmer, would he have been a Tory? He hoped it wasn't true. Without doubt there was plenty of tribalism in the north. There were people who voted Labour like they went to the pub or the bookies or the football. Was there something of that in him? Yes, but merely a residue. He'd worked out his position. He could have rejected socialism like he rejected the religion he was raised in if he found it wanting. The essential fault of Toryism was its naturalisation of what was cultural. No economic system was natural. Slave-owning economies, feudal economies, capitalist economies, they were cultural formations. No one argued Britain should be a slave economy? Why not? Because slavery had been recognised as morally abhorrent. Why? Because it denied the humanity of the slave.

Yet much of Britain's wealth had been made from slavery and in the seventeenth and eighteenth centuries, it was naturalised. That was the Tory mistake: once they'd believed a slave was a slave by nature. Now they believed a capitalist was a capitalist by nature. The relation of an employee to an employer was no more natural than that of a slave-owner to a slave. He was sure he could never have fallen for Tory prestidigitation.

The essential question was: how had society become divided between slaves and slave owners or lords and vassals or capitalists and workers; a difficult question because the antecedents were lost in pre-history, but a simple one in another sense. Violence. Without coercion humanity could never have lost its original unity.

A sports car arrived at screeching speed round a severe bend. He put his arm across Rosalind's shoulders and pulled her to the verge. She turned to him so he felt her breasts press against him. She lifted her face which he could barely make out in the impenetrable dark. He stared into her eyes and saw her soft lips slightly parted.

"You're very nice," she whispered.

"So are you."

She wrapped her arms around him and drew him. He kissed her. Her lips were very soft, warm and innocent and her kiss very still and gentle.

"Come on," he said, "we've got left behind. We'll get lost."

"Don't worry," she said, "I know these lanes. I could walk back with my eyes closed."

They held hands. Her skin was very soft and delicate. He took her to the farmhouse, under the eaves where they ate lunch.

"Goodnight. See you tomorrow."

"Yes," she said, lifting her face to him again.

When he was back at his bunk, the Brummie turned to him and said:

"About time you two got together and stopped pussy-footing."

Andy smiled and picked up his towel. In the bathroom, he wondered about the comment. Pussy-footing? What was he talking about? Was he jealous? Did he fancy Rosalind? He supposed it wouldn't be unlikely. She and Lizzie and the friends who came to visit them were the only girls around. Deprivation can make a man see beauty in the ugliest face, but Rosalind was pretty in any company.

What puzzled him as he settled down was what Rosalind meant. Was it just a young girl's swooning at his blue eyes and his nice face, in spite of its dartboard acne? Or did she mean she found him nice as a person? If so, why? What would she think if he told her he was a raging leftie who believed all enterprises should be collectives, the State be reduced to a minimum and the kind of differences in wealth which allowed her dad to be a millionaire abolished? Would she think him a nice person then?

He thought her a pleasant person. She was kind and modest. There was no vulgarity or nastiness in her. Her assumed political opinions he thought laughable; but she was a sort of insouciant Tory, not like those people he'd known who enjoyed putting others down, who retreated into a vicious snobbery, like Robert Jones's mother.

It was odd. It made him think of Jane. He hadn't heard from her since the end of term. He'd written to her. Weeks went by. Before he left for Kent he sent her a note letting her know where he'd be for September. He assumed things were dead.

The next day, when he was sitting down wearily at the long, burdened table for lunch, the sun burning his back through his thin shirt, Mrs Whillock came hurrying:

"Andy, a letter for you. Gerald, one for you. Charles..."

He looked at the thick, white envelope and saw Jane's writing. The postmark was Spain. He turned it over. Her address was on the back. He set it by his plate.

"Who's it from?" said the Glaswegian, swinging his foot over the bench.

"Girl from university."

"Your girlfriend?"

Andy turned to him. He was smiling. He was a big, friendly, easy-going Hellensburgh teddy bear with a woodbine hanging from his lips.

"Kind of."

"You're doing well."

Once he'd eaten he left the table, walked out onto the road and crossing to the chalet read the letter. It was one of those spill-it-all-out missives, as voluble and urgent as a child who must tell her mother the events of the day; five pages of gushing, how-close-you-and-I-are inconsequentiality. He was at once charmed, flattered and shocked. It was what a man might receive from a woman he was about to marry. Oozing through every line was an importunate emotional tone of need, an almost desperate plea for affection, reassurance and commitment; and with it, of course, an implied offer. She finished with love and three kisses.

He folded it, dropped it in his rucksack. Part of him rose on the between-the-lines submission; part of him was revolted. It was hard to hold back pride at the thought of a beautiful, intelligent young woman effectively declaring her love, treating him as if he were hers and she his. Yet there was a disturbing sense of invasion. He wished she could be more reserved and ironic. There was something untethered about her tone, as if some retaining cable had been severed, as if all reservation had been set aside, as if there were no need to hold different forces in balance, as if the rocket had been launched and was on its way out of the stratosphere with the possibility of stupendous success or gut-melting failure.

He wrote back but no further letter arrived. Throughout September he was troubled. He'd assumed he would go back to Bailrigg and they would have become strangers. Now he would have to make a choice: reject her or behave as if they had a future. The thought of the distress a repulsion might cause her was the lesser of his motivations in deciding on the latter. In spite of the queer feelings her letter engendered, he let himself believe she might be capable of steady commitment.

One evening there was a violent storm. He, Rosalind, Lizzie and a few of the students were chatting in the garden when the sky turned blue-grey, the thunder drummed and the rain came down in drops big enough to hurt. They sheltered under the eaves and watched the display; great, white electrical streaks across the black sky, a wind that summoned all its muscle to break the trees and biblical amounts of water. They'd been there ten minutes or so when Mr Whillock appeared with a flashlight. He shone it into their faces as he stood beneath the torrent. He was a big, barrel-chested, balding, awkward man with something undeveloped about him; a forty-five-year-old child who always looked as if he was about to be called to the Headmaster's study for a beating. He had great, wide, brown staring eyes, as if everything he saw were shocking.

"What are you doing here?" he called.

He was dressed in his usual trousers and tweed jacket which were absorbing the rain as resolutely as the grass. No one spoke. Rosalind nestled close to Andy.

"We were just watching the storm, Mr Whillock," he said.

"Well, come inside," the man called, "it's dangerous out here. You could get struck by lightning."

Lizzie led the way. When they reached the door Andy said:

"Maybe I'd better go back to the chalet."

"No, it's okay," said Rosalind. "Come in."

They congregated in the kitchen, a huge room, with an Aga, copper pans hanging from racks, more cupboards than Andy thought it possible to fill, a stainless-steel fridge and freezer. Lizzie quickly began making tea and coffee, slicing cake, arranging biscuits on plates. Andy was astonished by the wealth of the place. Everything his eyes settled on seemed the most expensive of its kind. He thought of his mother's little kitchen with its one cupboard, its lino, the gas cooker and the sink. He'd never thought of it as poor, and Woodland Grove was hardly the bottom-end; but compared to this, it was miserable. These people were wealthy in a way he'd never experienced. Not even Matt Ross's family, who he'd thought of as fabulously well off, was quite at this level.

They drank and ate and were glad to be warm and together. Lizzie was very attentive to her guests. She offered toast or crumpets or scrambled eggs and refills. She was very generous and Andy thought how odd it was that he was in this money-clad kitchen with a girl who'd been to school with Princess Anne being offered hot buttered crumpets and tea. He and Lizzie were from different sides of the class divide, but she was lovely. How crazy it was that people were set apart by money. They were young, happy people glad of one another's company. At this moment, money meant nothing to them.

He wondered what Lizzie and Rosalind would think if they saw his mother's kitchen. He realised he would leave them behind. It could never happen that they would be long-term friends. The horrible fact of class, the vicious separation of money would stop them.

When the students began to drift off, Andy said he'd better go.

"No," said Rosalind, grasping his forearm, "stay. It's not late. We can go into the living-room. My parents are always in bed by nine because dad has to be up so early."

She led him through. It was a long, wide room with old beams across the ceiling, furniture of a quality he'd never sat on, thick carpet and a log fire roaring in the hearth.

"This is a lovely room," he said.

"I'm glad you like it," she said.

She lay on the sofa and he sat beside her. Lizzie appeared to say she was going to bed and not to forget to lock up. Rosalind looked up at him longingly so he bent to kiss her warm, dry lips. To his surprise, she sat up pulled off her jumper, unfastened her blouse and lay down with her bra exposed. He smiled and ran his hand over her tight belly.

"Oh, that's nice," she said.

"What do you want me to do?" he said.

"I don't know," she said.

"Do you want to have sex?"

"I don't know. I don't know if I want to have sex. I want you to touch me."

"Touch you?"

"Yes."

He did what she asked.

"Just a minute," she said.

She sat up once more, unzipped her jeans and pulled them off. Her bra and knickers were silk.

"Are you okay?"

"Yes," she said, "touch me. Touch me, Andy."

He went back to the chalet at eleven. Most of the students were asleep.

"You took your time," said the Brummie as Andy passed his bunk.

"Yeah, I'm fond of crumpets."

Rosalind was a sweet and charming girl. He would have been glad to establish a liaison with her; but he knew it was impossible. Did she? Her father would have chased him off the farm with his shotgun if he knew what he'd just done. He had to go back north. She had to finish the sixth-form. Shame. He would write to her. Maybe they could meet up in London, or *town* as she called it. Yet there was Jane to think about. Was he being unfair to her? Maybe, but he'd come clean. If she flipped she flipped.

Early in October he moved into the pink-eiderdown holiday flat he Rob, Mike Darley, Mike Richards, Steve Bancroft and Norman Evans had found in Morecambe. He was in the basement, in a room with a bed which folded into the wall, but the sunsets were sometimes remarkable. Jane had a room on campus. He went to see her in a mood of wary expectation. It was early afternoon. She'd invited people from her floor and the floors above and below. There was much coming and going, some booze, some snacks, some card games, a chess board. She appeared looking as taut as a mother superior with PMT, walked past and ignored him. He hung around for ten humiliating minutes then went to Furness bar to look for Rob.

THE EMMA BOVARY OF BAILRIGG

Bert made a visit to Bailrigg during the first weeks of term. He was free to use his time as he liked so long as he brought houses onto the books for Wickham. He turned up at lunchtime, parked on the periphery, facing the M6, had a stroll round Alexandra Square before heading for Furness College. The atmosphere of the square was charming and thrilling; the long-haired young, mostly dressed down, with books and files under their arms; the sense of being at one remove from the banal preoccupations imposed on the majority; the heady feeling of being able to devote yourself, day after day, for years, to minute study of a particular subject. Lancaster was one of the universities founded by Harold Wilson. Bert saw it as part of that post-war revolution which had transformed social relations. In the twenties and thirties, the class divide was as difficult to breach as the blood-brain barrier. The idea of him going to university was as likely as him being the first man on the moon. No one he grew up with got a degree. Of course, Elsie's brothers Jimmy and Eddie each had a lad who made it, but they were born late enough to benefit from 1945. People like him, in the pre-war world, were required to know their place. There was a strict hierarchy and they were at the bottom. If they needed a doctor, they had to pay. Society was a tight conspiracy to do them down; but it truly had been transformed. His son was at university studying English, French and Russian. If someone had asked him when he was young if such a thing were possible, he would have laughed with derision.

He thought the campus a lovely place. It had the feel of a village. He stopped before the bookshop and looked at the volumes written by Lancaster's own academics. Maybe, one day, Andy would publish a book. His spirits were buoyed by association with the place; its high-mindedness; its unembarrassed promotion of learning. It was true he was a mere visitor. A few hours and he would be back in the grim and grubby world of estate agency, the shifty, doctor-the-milometer arena of buying and selling whose principles could have been written by W.C.Fields; the here-comes-a-mug, gull-who-you-can culture which ultimately tainted and depressed everyone who had anything to do with it.

He met Andy in the Furness college foyer. His son stood up from his chair. He was dressed in grey flares and a skinny-rib, wine-coloured polo-neck. His hair had grown onto his shoulders. His face was still producing acne like geysers produce plumes. They shook hands. Bert smiled widely. Andy was one of the few people he could genuinely smile at, someone he trusted and felt he belonged to. It was strange to think the little boy who'd kicked a ball around the scruffy back-alley in Talbot Road, whose hand he'd held as they walked to the shops from Woodland Grove, who'd sat beside him on the beach in Blackpool and who he'd held as he jigged on a smelly donkey, was this gangly, budding intellectual in whose hands were a fat, blue, French-English dictionary and a book whose title Bert could neither pronounce nor understand: *Notre Jeunesse*.

"Find it okay ?"

"Yes, no trouble. I had a look at the square. I could do with a brew."

"Yeah, we'll go to the library café if you like and I'll show you round."

Rob appeared, his head a mass of blonde, unbrushed curls his heavy-framed black glasses, one of whose arms was lost, slipping down his long nose.

"Oh, hello," he said in his usual apologetic way.

"Hia, Rob. This is my dad."

"Pleased to meet you," said Bert and Rob shook his hand.

"Rob comes from Rochdale," said Andy, "which is a good place to come from. His dad owns a string of supermarkets."

"Bugger," said Rob, turning to Bert. "He runs a corner Spar."

"Yeah," said Andy, "he makes millions from selling past-its-sell-by-date milk to undiscerning customers."

"He does. Sell sour milk, that is. Not make millions. I'm trying to educate him but he thinks making money is making money. There's no right and wrong about it."

"I'm taking my dad for a brew and a wander. Want to come?"

"No, I've got a German lecture. I just wanted to see if you're going to the Chile meeting."

"Ah, viel Spass. Yeah, I'm going."

"Danke. See you later. Nice to meet you, Mr Lang."

On their way to the café, Bert spotted posters taped to brick pillars advertising the meeting.

"What's it all about the Chile meeting?"

"Allende. You know, the CIA-inspired coup. The USA, the great defender of democracy spending millions over decades to keep the right in power in Chile. Allende was elected but they brought him down and now the goons are in charge. If they can do it in Chile, they can do it here."

Bert thought it an idea from the other side of the moon that the CIA could bring down an elected government in Britain; but he was inspired at the thought of Andy being active for justice. Like most people, he hadn't followed the events in Chile closely. He'd read of the coup and thought little of it; one of those things that happens as a matter of course in far-away, undeveloped countries. At once, it came into focus. The students were right. Elected Presidents shouldn't be deposed by secret services. He wished he was going to the meeting too.

Andy showed him the library, the indoor recreation centre, the lovely old house that was now the medical centre, the Great Hall where you could hear concerts of the classical music Bert loved. On their way back they passed a man on *The Spine* who nodded and said hello. He was hurrying along with books in his hand. Bert assumed he was a teacher.

"That's Peter Greig," said Andy. "Do you remember the Greig Affair last year?"

"No."

"It was in the papers. They tried to sack him on the grounds he was indoctrinating students. The entire campus went on strike. I'm doing his course, *Modern Life In Literature, Film and Sound*."

The so-called *Greig Affair* had been reported when Andy was at the Harris College. John Swallow had mentioned it, saying Greig was an intelligent man but didn't know when to keep his mouth shut. Andy had baulked at that.

"I thought democracy was about not having to keep your mouth shut," he said to John White and Nick Drake at break.

"Yeah, but he's a communist isn't he ?" said John.

"So what ? Doesn't democracy give the right to communists to express their point of view ?"

"Communists don't believe in democracy though. They want us to be like the Russians."

"Maybe some do, but we should hear what they have to say. If we don't like it, we can argue."

Andy had been attracted by the story of the campus-wide action. Lecturers, students, ancillary staff, pulled their work and shut the university down. Greig was reinstated as Senior Lecturer without Departmental Responsibility. The five other staff kept their jobs too. To Andy it was a great example: most people were employees. That's how the economy works. People can't be slaves or feudal vassals. Capitalism needs them to sell their labour in the market; but doing so gives them power. It seemed simple common sense to Andy to use that power for the common good. Sacking people on specious grounds was about control rather than justice. Andy wasn't a communist. His instinct was to support Labour. It was a mass party that had won elections and made a difference. He liked Bevan's observation that people who want to do everything at once do nothing at all. He wasn't for revolution. Violence was always a mistake. The images from the Latin Quarter in 1968 had stayed with him. Kicking policemen in the face just gets you hit over the head with a baton or tear-gassed. He agreed with Martin Luther King: non-violence is not only morally right but tactically sensible.

Nor was he a Marxist. He'd read, with great relish, Volume 1 of *Capital* and loved its discussion of the nature of money, surplus value and its witty, funny, excoriating language in response to the appalling conditions people suffered at work in the nineteenth century; but he didn't accept the idea of historical inevitability. That was a hangover from Hegel and a mistake. That everything is inevitable before it happens seemed to him contradicted by life in its most banal manifestations. He was going into his room one day with his overcoat unbuttoned. The window was open and the breeze lifted one of the wings and as he moved forward the door handle slipped into a button hole and yanked him to a standstill. He laughed to see it but it made him reflect that he could have tried a thousand times to make it happen and not succeeded. It wasn't inevitable. It was one of those events which can happen but aren't bound to. That's what life was like. The strict laws of determinism gave rise to the most extraordinary contingency so that nothing was inevitable until it happened.

That fact was the ground of freedom and the basis of the nervousness of possibility which was the psychological condition he loved. If everything was settled before it happened, people were no more than iron filings moved by a magnet. That wasn't his experience. Every second brought choice and every choice made a mockery of the notion of an inescapable teleology.

Andy had signed up for Greig's course as his *free ninth unit*, a choice of course outside their principal area of study, which allowed students, if they wished, to add a bit of spice to the plain intellectual fare. What attracted him more than anything was that creative writing was acceptable as coursework rather than the usual, too often clever-dick, essays. Rob and Sue signed up too.

"Fancy trying to sack a man like that," said Andy after his first seminar, sitting in Bowland bar with the two of them.

"What do you mean?" said Sue, pushing her black curls away from her pale cheeks with her slender fingers.

"He's obviously not a threat. He's open and generous and mild-mannered. He wouldn't indoctrinate a parrot."

"Yeah, I like him," said Rob.

"But," said Sue, with a little nervous laugh, "he's a Marxist isn't he? I mean, he could, you know, impose his view."

"He didn't impose anything in the seminar I've just been in. He let us talk. Compare that to the experience I had last year with the born-again, homosexual Jesus-chaser. He shoved Manley Hopkins down our throats as if there was no other English poet in the twentieth century. And he wanted to get his hands on my arse."

Sue rocked back on her stool and brought her hands to her mouth.

"You should have reported him," said Rob.

"To Jimmy Perry? He'd've had me sent down. The fact is they went after Greig and the others because they don't like intellectual freedom. They want universities to operate like businesses. There should be a free exchange of ideas in universities, that's what they're for."

"Yeah," said Sue, brushing her hair again, "but, you know, would we let fascists speak? Like The Monday Club. We protested about that didn't we?"

"I'm for freedom of expression," said Andy. "Let them speak, but to protest against their racism is right. There's no rational defence of racism. It isn't an idea it's a denial of ideas. The test has to be that ideas will stand objective scrutiny. Racism simply has no basis in fact."

Greig was one of the first lecturers appointed when the university opened in 1964. Initially he was one of three staff in English along with Professor Jimmy Perry who was Head of Department and the young and brilliant Frances Bracken. The department grew rapidly and by 1968 there were nearly twenty staff. Like Greig, a number of them were young, idealistic and excited by the prevailing atmosphere of questioning. Across the Channel they'd seen an uprising begun by students leading to de Gaulle fleeing the country and ten million workers on strike for a month. The occupation of factories and the establishment of worker-organised supply chains led to the slogan *imagination in power*.

Greig was a convinced Marxist and member of the Communist Party. He liked Marx's materialism and he was inspired by the idea that people who produced wealth should benefit from it and decide what should be done with it. Quite willing to vote Labour, sympathetic to Labour figures like Michael Foot, he nevertheless felt the party was too inclined to manage capitalism, rather than reform it out of existence. He was impatient with Labour's patience and suspected that behind *the inevitability of gradualism* was a sly trick to engage the votes of millions in order to secure the careers of a few.

The spectacle of the drunken George Brown disgusted him and Barbara Castle's *In Place of Strife* seemed exactly the wrong intervention. It blamed the unions. It vilified workers. It granted the divine right of management. It seemed obvious that the correct thing was for the workers to take what belonged to them. Their labour was theirs. When they employed it to produce value, the value should be theirs.

There was nothing grim about Greig's vision. He despised the Soviet Union with its insane displays of weaponry, its grey, dullard apparatchiks, its ludicrous control of literature, its cruel gulags and its absence of democracy. His was the prospect of a joyous, smiling, sunny uprising; an uprising not of guns and violence, but of laughter and easy-going relations.

Professor Perry was wary of the younger, liberal staff. The ambience of the sixties troubled him. He claimed descent from Scottish aristocrats, liked to wear a kilt, spoke in the accent of the upper classes and couched his erudition in a flamboyant style which made much of what he said incomprehensible to the youngsters, especially those from lowly backgrounds who'd been hoisted into grammar schools by the 11-plus. He liked to run the department as his fiefdom. What was the point, after all, of being Head of Department, if he couldn't make the decisions? He was one of those people who think all challenge to established authority a kind of treason. He had his status legitimately, lawfully; any subversion was illegitimate.

When half a dozen staff produced suggestions for changes in assessment, the way the department was organised, representation of students in decision-making and experimental methods in teaching, Perry experienced it as a threat to his position. He dubbed them a *pressure group*, which was the sharpest insult he could think of, pressure groups being composed of feckless, irresponsible malcontents unable to secure their aims through legitimate channels. Greig having done most of the work to develop the course in modern literature, where it was suggested the experimental methods could be tested, and being particularly articulate and energetic, Perry identified him as the ring leader and when he complained to the Vice-Chancellor, claimed Greig was lowering academic standards through an ideological approach.

The Vice-Chancellor, fully aware of Greig's political affiliations and sniffing the chance to be rid of a wasp in his beer, responded complaisantly. In due course, Greig was humiliatingly demoted, removed from the convenorship of the Modern Literature course and forbidden to teach it, being required instead to focus on the Victorians. The moderns course included Ibsen, who Perry considered a dangerous adherent of women's liberation and a promoter of decadence; Beckett who he believed had destroyed the tradition of English theatre through his depressing, meaningless works which were no more serious than executive toys; Albee who was a known homosexual whose major play reduced the governance of America to the level of an endless, domestic row between queers; Lawrence, who as everyone knew was a heretic, an ill-educated, bumptious oik who should never have been allowed to force his way into English literature; and Orwell who Perry thought of as a traitor to his class, a man granted the advantage of an education at Eton who used it to write about the chaotic lower orders.

Greig appealed. It got him nowhere. He called in the union. They fought his case diligently but expected him to sign up to the loyalty oath the university presented to him:

Do you now and for the future term of your service at this University in the Department of English, agree and undertake, to accept, abide by and faithfully act upon....

To Greig and his colleagues this was no better than McCarthyism.

"The only thing that surprises me," said one of the lecturers also required to sign the statement, "is that they don't shine bright lights in our eyes and begin: *"Are you now or have you ever been..."*

This same lecturer was accused of having missed seminars and lectures. He defended himself by pointing out he had missed only one seminar and that because the university required him to attend a meeting.

Perry sought to inveigle the external examiners to his cause and sent them an unusually large sample of students' work, much of it given very high marks by Greig and his colleagues. The external examiner, the respected Professor Williams, upheld all the marks.

When the press got hold of the dispute in the spring of 1972, they labelled it *The Greig Affair*. In their reports, they ignored almost entirely that six members of staff were threatened with dismissal. Finally, Greig received the letter spelling out the grounds of dismissal:

In that you on divers days in the month of March 1972 within the premises of the University of Lancaster

> (a) *Exhorted and incited students members of the University to absent themselves from and/ or boycott lectures and seminars, coursework and/or project work.....*

The campaign for reinstatement began with staff in the English Department, quickly drew in the students and widened to History, Politics, Sociology, French, Classics, Financial Control, Physics, Chemistry, Economics, Philosophy, Educational Research, Religious Studies, Russian and Soviet Studies, Czech and South-East European Studies and German. Some two thousand students boycotted lectures and seminars.

"Good that he won," said Bert.

"Yeah," said Andy. "Good that people supported them. If it hadn't been for that, they'd've lost their jobs."

"I might lose mine before long."

"Really?"

Andy looked at his dad who was sitting looking out at the paved area between the foyer and the bar. He had that hint of nervousness beneath his cockiness which, since he was a little boy, Andy had puzzled over. His face betrayed his anxiety and alienation. Andy had always known his dad didn't belong. His mother had a family. He'd lived with his grandad for seventeen years. He was fond of his uncles and aunties. His cousins were interesting; but all this was on his mother's side. From his father's forbears there was nothing but loneliness, neglect, drunkenness, abandonment, chaos. Yet his dad had come through. That glib notion that people who grow in bad circumstances turn out bad, become criminals or wasters, was denied by him. He'd made something of his life. He wouldn't have pinched a stale loaf if he was starving. There was a possibility of facing down circumstances and his dad had made a good choice in the Craxtons. Yet it was true there was an emptiness at the heart of him, an essential hurt he'd been unable to heal. The illegitimate child abandoned by his mother at the age of five and given nothing more than a roof by his wild and feckless grandparents; of course he lacked what love and security engender in a child.

His dad shook his head.

"Ken Wickham, he's a fool. A wheeler dealer. All show and no work. He'll destroy the business sooner or later."

"Why don't you get out before he does?"

"I'm thinking of it. I might set myself up. I fancy a vegetarian restaurant. I know a bloke who runs one in the Lakes. I'm going to have a chat with him. I might go into partnership or I might set up on my own. I've got enough behind me."

Andy liked the idea. He was proud when his dad ran his coffee bar in Preston. It was uplifting to have a sense of ownership. The idea of *being your own boss* was pleasant; but it was a confused idea: if you worked on your own account, if your effort produced the value, there was no boss. The notion of alienating a part of yourself to supervise yourself or even exploit your own work was daft; but being in control, not having to comply with arbitrary authority, to do what is characteristic of human beings: to act according to your own decisions, was far preferable to what Andy had experienced at F.E.D.. Being part of a system, a corporate body, a machine which ran according to its own logic when in fact it was driven by human wishes, expectations, theories, fears, doubts, mistakes, was at once nightmarish and laughable. People submitted to a monster of their own creation, as if it had a life of its own; as if businesses and corporations had existed since the start of time. It seemed to Andy that was how the economy was organised. It was a beast into which people fed themselves, as if it was made for them. Why should people expect to find their slot in the economy? Why should he? Why should there be the least correspondence between what he wanted to do with his life and jobs the economy offered? The economy wasn't organised to make people happy. It was run to make money.

That was why Peter Greig and his colleagues had got into trouble. John Swallow's pusillanimity in dismissing Greig as a loudmouth was typical of the vulgar response. The truth was, Greig's passion was literature. He wanted to devote his life to it, but in his own way. He was searching for the hints which might reveal how particular historical conditions give rise to literary forms. Why was that threatening? Applied to modern literature, it came too close to exposing the festering wound of injustice and irrationality. Hidden from view by the bandages of ideology, the glib notions of *a free country*, *the spirit of fair play*, *getting on*, all those platitudes which were supposed to sum up what it meant to be British but which had no explanatory power, the gaping sore was not to be mentioned. As for literature, in the hands of people like Jimmy Perry it was a proof of the necessity of hierarchy, order, rule by an elite. It was the product of a few great minds. The secret of literary form lay in their genius, not in the conditions of life of the masses, who were mostly too ignorant to appreciate poems, plays or novels. It was a fact of life that the few had talent and the many didn't. It was there, in the biographies of the great writers that the explanation of changing literary forms must be sought, just as history was the story of decisions made by great men. The Elizabethan five-act drama was the product of men steeped in Seneca who understood that only through its architecture could the space be created to deal with the great events set in train by great men. In the same way, the modern poem, whose greatest example was *The Waste Land*, required a degree of opacity to protect it from intrusion by the semi-literate: regrettable creation of mass education; as well as a heavy dose of pessimism to hold at bay the ignorant cheerfulness of the lower orders.

Greig was dangerous because he wanted to relate Conrad's obsession with espionage to the power struggle between the Great Powers and his evocation of horror in *Heart of Darkness* to the racism which was intrinsic to the creation of Empire; because he wanted to trace the link between Lawrence's style and his working-class, non-conformist upbringing; because he recognised in Eliot the defeatism of those who feared democracy and harboured the fantasy of a return to a society of fixed hierarchies.

What was wrong with letting Greig get on with it? Students could make up their own minds about his teaching, and his influence was balanced by that of his colleagues. Was he indoctrinating his students any more than Jimmy Perry? To offer a view of literature consistent with Christianity, which nodded towards the view that the existing economic arrangements were eternal, which insinuated that to challenge them was tantamount to subverting the natural order, raised no objections. The university authorities yawned sleepily over the idea that teachers in the English Department might define the nation's literature as intrinsically Christian but were thrown into near hysteria by the suggestion that there might be a relationship between literary form and relations between the rich and the poor, the powerful and the rest.

Andy hoped his dad would start his own enterprise. He recalled with inward amusement that in his last year at school he'd talked animatedly and enthusiastically to Wheels about setting up a café. The example of *The Minotaur* in his imagination, he thought it would be entertaining to set something up with a good mate. They could earn a living, have a laugh and stay good friends; but they were sixteen: where could they get the capital ? The manager of the Midland Bank wasn't going to hand over a few thousand to a couple of scallies with five O levels between them; and business wore a serious face, while what they wanted was to put fun and friendship before money. The system separated them and sent them down that dismal alleyway which is called a career; that long, lonely corridor where delight in human contact is diminished and the rewards of money and status are supposed to compensate for a diminished humanity.

At F.E.D. he'd been offered advancement. He could have become like Dickins, a ridiculous corporate man, a jumped-up, look-at-me-mum-I'm-the-manager apparatchik who served the interests of Unilever as if they were his own. He'd scoffed at the idea. He wanted to be a rebel voice, an outsider. He wanted Lawrence's willingness to face down his entire culture. That was the only way to be able to say what you believed. What it got you was what had happened to Peter Greig. Insiders made the decisions; insiders had power and they would use it; insiders were legion. Outsiders were few and powerless.

Allende was an outsider because he refused to suck on the teat of American capitalism. The insiders were murderous. Yet fear didn't overcome him. He was determined to live his life. What would be the point of lying on your deathbed saying: *Well, I stayed out of trouble, I made money, I got on*, if the price was the renunciation of your autonomy. Greig was right, not in the sense that there was no possible intellectual challenge to his position, but that he followed his own path; he was bold in pushing the ideas he thought right; but he was in favour of freedom of thought; he was a democrat. The system was stupid to try to silence and be rid of him.

His dad was working for a cavern-skulled conformist, a self-regarding mirror-gazer who believed money was the measure of individual superiority; he drove the BMW he hadn't paid for as a way of asserting his pre-eminence; he owned a yacht because that was what the super-rich did and they were obviously the caviar of humanity. It was clear to Andy the strain of running the enterprise responsibly while his boss behaved like Billy Bunter in the cake shop was wearing him down. Was he going to lose his job? He knew he would take it badly if the set-up folded. He believed in hard work and restraint. He subscribed to the notion, now becoming old-fashioned, that you had to produce more than you consumed to ensure well-being.

"You should get your own thing going," Andy said. "Get away from Wickham. He's a fool."

"Yes, Andy, I think you're right. You know, here I am, the other side of fifty, and I still don't know what I'm supposed to do with my life."

"Enjoy it."

His dad laughed.

"That's what I've wanted to do but there's always been some bastard trying to stop me."

The bastards had stopped Allende. The Chile meeting attracted a hundred or so. The same faces. They were addressed by an Allende supporter in exile. Pinochet was rounding people up. They would be tortured or disappear. What did Heath have to say? The Tories were complicit in the subversion of a democratic regime because it believed there was an alternative to capitalism. Walking back with Rob he reflected that maybe in a century's time, maybe longer, the reforms Allende wanted would be taken for granted. Posterity would look back on his suicide and shake its head. Humanity was constantly looking over its shoulder and regretting its brutality and ignorance, while finding new ways to be ignorant and brutal. The essence was violence. That was humanity's great mistake. There were laws against punching someone in the nose, but not against dropping an atomic bomb on Japan. You could be sent to prison for kicking a policeman in the shins, but dropping napalm on peasants in Vietnam might get you a medal. If it was sensible to have laws against fights in the pub, why not against war ? Wouldn't that be the greatest advance for the common people of the world? If war were forbidden in international law and heads of state who prosecuted it brought to The Hague, wouldn't that free people from fear; wouldn't it ensure all disputes had to be resolved democratically and by words?

He tried to articulate his thought but Rob was sceptical.

"The Americans! The Russians! They'd never wear it."

Andy sat in the library reading *Les Fleurs du Mal*. What an odd mentality Baudelaire had? His technique was extraordinary, but Andy quickly wearied of his sulky wallowing in misery and the perverse celebration of the unhealthy. He couldn't identify with it at all. The unhappiness of the poet's childhood, his resentment of his mother's re-marriage, his disappointment in her, these were real bitternesses;

but to stick out your bottom lip till a cat could sit on it as a grown man was feeble. How odd that Baudelaire could be so gifted and expert and at the same time so regressed. It immediately reminded him of people he'd known; Robert Jones for example who developed his intellect because his parents and teachers said he should, but who was poor in his relations to other lads, lost in a dead-end of self-regarding go-getting, incapable of the simplest conversation on the street without boasting and too much of a snob to have friends who left school at sixteen and worked as plumbers or joiners. There were girls from Penwortham Grammar who were the same, sticking their noses in the air and treating him as a lower form of life because he went to the secondary. How odd it was that the intelligence to play with calculus and learn Latin principal parts could co-exist with such stupidity. It was stupid. To be unable to chat to a bus driver or a school cleaner, to find some little patch of common ground to occupy for ten minutes, to be so walled into your sense of superiority that eighty percent of humanity was beneath you, was about as stupid as you could get. Andy would have thrown over all learning in an instant if it implied snootiness.

Someone spoke.

"Hello," he said.

Jane sat beside him, a sense of furtiveness in her movements; but once she'd set her bag on the floor, kissed his cheek as if she had squatter's rights.

"I saw you with Sue Border," she said.

"Guilty."

"Are you having sex with her?"

"I've told you, six times a day."

"What are you reading?"

"Baudelaire, the biggest sulk of the nineteenth century."

"I haven't read it yet."

"You'll love it. He'll cheer you up no end."

"Have you read *Madame Bovary*?"

"Twice."

"I'm like her," she said.

"What? You're going to marry a failed doctor, have affairs with cynical aristocrats and callow young romantics and poison yourself because of your debts?"

"No, I'm a bored woman."

He wanted to laugh out loud. A university campus, thousands of people of her own age and lots of free time and she was bored. Boredom was working in *Woolworths*. As for being a woman, she had all the physical attributes, but was a little girl in respects that mattered.

"Fuuny you should say that because I'm a bored man. I need to stretch my legs. Fancy a walk?"

"A walk wasn't what I was thinking of," she said, standing up.

He'd jumped up and was facing her. She really was extraordinarily beautiful. She was wearing her light blue, angora, polo neck which hugged her breasts and her flat belly; the grey jeans which were a second skin on her turgid thighs; her green eyes fixed him; her lovely face with its charming pointed chin, pale, inviting lips, her little, slightly abrupt nose, her high cheekbones and arched brows was almost impossible to reconcile with her inner landscape of jealousy, tidal moods, despair, panic and importunity.

"There's plenty of time," he said changing to a more tender tone. "We've never walked together. Come on. Let's go."

On the way down to the lake, he stopped at the huge horse chestnut and ducked under the low branches full of reddening leaves.

"Wow," he said. "What a tree"

He was looking up into the black, twisting arms. She was annoyed almost to fury. Part of her wanted to kick him but she was overcome by what she thought of as weakness. She unbuttoned his coat, thrust her arms round him and pulled him to her. He had to kiss her. He may have avoided getting into bed but he couldn't not kiss her. It was what she wanted but she hated herself for it. Why did she want him? It was all wrong. He was the wrong kind of person. Yet he was just right. Kissing him was exactly right. She wanted to fall back into her weakness, depend on him, let her emotions be regulated by the way he treated her because he was kind and funny and affectionate and passionate; but she was afraid of tumbling, of being dependent, she wanted to force herself onto the world and to control her own emotions. She was a Tory. She despised socialism. She hated the north because it was a backward place where people were unsophisticated and dim. It was place of factories and docks and poor housing and people who spoke with stupid accents. She loathed it. She excoriated Lancaster as a petty, ignorant, poor town where people lived only because they couldn't afford to move to the south. That was the truth of the north: only failures lived there. Anyone who could, got out, went to live in London or Kent or Surrey or Berkshire, changed their accent and concealed their origins.

He was exactly the wrong person yet he was so right. She wanted to go straight back to his room. She knew how susceptible he was to her intimacy and she knew he was too honourable to betray her. The fool. Yes, he was a fool. She was two-timing him and would carry on. He was a weakness she must learn to overcome. She would marry Jean-Claude; but Andy was nicer. There was no doubt she was happier kissing him. She was happier in bed with him. It was all wrong. It shouldn't be that she could fall for a northern socialist with a gormless accent. He talked like a backward northerner but he was clever. Cleverer than her. Cleverer than Jean-Claude. It was too confusing. She cursed the system for sending her here. She should have gone to Oxford and met someone with money, class, perfect RP who would take a job in the City, make millions, buy a mansion in St John's Wood and allow her to live at the centre of her sense of election; one of the elite who had money and power by virtue of their natural gifts.

Nothing in her upbringing or education had prepared her for this. She'd never imagined she would have to live further north than London. That she might be madly attracted to a socialist and jealous of every girl who came within a hundred yards of him had seemed as likely as diving with Jacques Cousteau.. Her parents and teachers had formed her mind for a reality which didn't exist. In her Tory eschatology, socialists couldn't be charming, intelligent, gorgeous, loving, irresistible. They were the enemy.

She was trapped between her undeniable out-of-the-universe desire for Andy Lang which was as delicious as strawberries, and the cramped, severe, snobbish voice of her education which, no matter how she tried, she couldn't silence.

They walked back to her room hand in hand and during those minutes she was more at home in the world than she'd ever been; but standing in front of her mirror, brushing her shining auburn hair, dressed again, her need satisfied, the inevitable contempt began to arise.

"What's that?" she said.

"A flyer about the Arab-Israeli war."

"My father says the Arabs are terrorists and communists."

"A balanced view he has of the world, your dad."

"I'm sure he knows more than you," she said, pushing the wooden handled brush into her bag and taking out her cigarettes.

"No doubt."

He wasn't paying attention to her. He was on her chair, his left leg hooked over his right in his characteristic way, scanning the page. She despised this interest he took in political events. She had no idea what the Arab-Israeli war was. She'd been educated to accept the perspective of the Home Counties. She wanted it to be true that what you read in *The Daily Telegraph* was all you needed to know; but Andy would insist on thinking. Everything made him think. She had a set of ideas in her head other people had put there and which she didn't have the means to challenge. He said to her: "People always think what is is because it has to be, but they are very bad at distinguishing necessity from contingency." She had no idea what he meant. She loved him for it. His seriousness and his ability to think about everything was a strength; but at the same time she wished he were like the girls she knew at Ashford School who took Toryism as much for granted as the sunrise. It made life so much easier.

She sat in her chair, pulled on her cigarette, tossed her hair and tried to look sophisticated. She felt weak and excluded by his attention to big, serious questions. She wanted it to be undeniable that there was a simple set of assumptions which could be applied to every case: power and wealth were always justified; people who challenged them were jealous; people had money and power because they deserved them.

"What's the war about anyway?" she said hoping he would look at her so she could make big eyes at him and shift his mind in her direction.

"Whether you should put milk in tea or tea in milk," he said, looking at her, smiling and sliding the flyer across the desk.

"Whose side are you on?"

"Me, I'm on the side of black tea. It's better for your health."

"Tell me," she said trying to appear as if the question interested her.

"Well," he said standing up and going to the window, "the Jews have been badly treated. For centuries. It's a terrible, terrible thing. But I don't think the State of Israel is the answer. I think its creation was a mistake. I think the idea that Jews must all live in one place or have a place that they can forever say is theirs is wrong. As it would be for Christians. I think a democratic State can't be founded on religious or ethnic identity because it has to treat everyone as equal before the law. I think that's the mistake. And I think the way Israel, not the Jews, but the State of Israel treats the Palestinians is appalling."

In spite of herself, she liked to listen to him. He had what seemed to her an odd capacity to leave himself behind which she'd never met. People said what was in their interests. As her mother put it: "Everyone looks after themselves first. That's human nature." Yet he seemed to be able to escape. He could see beyond his own interest. Her mind jumped back to the previous hour. He was attentive and put her first. At once the disturbing image of her mother and father in bed sprang into her head.

"Why should it bother me?" she said, hoping he would come and kiss her.

"It shouldn't, Jane," he said, relaxing, "be carefree and gay. Sigh no more. Turn all your sounds of woe to hey nonny nonny."

She stood, doused her cigarette under the tap, threw it in the bin and turned to him.

"You should go now."

"Okay."

She approached him to be kissed. She had an overwhelming wish as his lips met hers to make a declaration. To tell him she loved him infinitely, to pledge herself to him for life.

"See you later," he said.

"Maybe."

As soon as the door was closed she began a letter to Jean-Claude: she was desperate. If he didn't come for her he might lose her forever. The boy here wouldn't leave her alone. She was only human. They should be together. They were made to be together. He must rescue her. He might have to beat the boy up to put him off. She sealed the envelope, addressed it and took it to the post. She made a detour to buy some dope. In her room, she rolled a spliff and lay on her bed.

A demand was being made of her she couldn't respond to. Why had she approached Andy Lang? Why had she hissed at him in the newsagents? She knew he wouldn't have approached her. He had shown no sign. She had offered herself. She'd thought she could be in control. He would be her lover. Her beloved was far away. She needed someone in her bed. That was the way sophisticated women behaved. She'd seen it in films. She identified with those unhappy heroines who were torn between two men; women whose inner lives were forever in chaos, who smoked compulsively and drank heavily. She wanted to be one of those glamorous women who recklessly give themselves to one man after another in pursuit of a love that can never be fulfilled. A tragic heroine was something to be. She would rather be Emma Bovary than a contented woman with a fulfilled emotional and sexual life. To be wild, hysterical, fraught, suicidal, to be unpredictable, a woman no one could pin down; to live on the edge, to risk your health, to toy with pregnancy or venereal disease, to be even a whore was better than to be an ordinary woman, a commonplace person, someone books or films couldn't be based on.

She hadn't imagined she could love Andy. He demanded to be loved. She loathed him for it. She would have liked to murder him. That would be a fitting end, if she stabbed him through the heart with a pair of scissors and was on the front page of the newspapers. Oh, how wonderful to be guilty of a *crime passionnel*. Or if Jean Claude arrived, they met, they fought and one of them was killed. To be the woman a man was prepared to die for, that was a life worth living.

She sank into her cannabis stupor her head full of fantasies of anguished lovers, conflicts, knives, impossible vows, tears at midnight, heartbreak and tragic death. She was happy.

"Let's get on with it."

A roar went up from the forty-odd students who had slunk into the Furness television room to watch Edward Heath's election address.

"Looks like he'll win, though," said Rob as they headed for the bar.

"Yeah," said Steve Bancroft, "making it a who governs - me or the unions - election will clinch it."

"Three-day week and the Tories claim they know how to run the economy," said Andy.

"People vote with their pockets," said Steve. "There'll be a Labour landslide in Kirby."

"Is that what we're like," said Andy, "mean-minded creatures who use democracy to hang onto to petty advantages? My garage is three square feet bigger than yours so I'm voting Tory. It's a dismal picture."

Steve laughed.

"Most people aren't idealists, Andy."

"Anyway," said Mike Richards, "when they are look what happens. Allende."

Andy was depressed at the prospect of Heath's win. When Enoch Powell intervened calling on people to vote for whoever would renegotiate the terms of membership of the Common Market (which obviously meant Labour) he was disgusted at the thought that the infantile egg-head's emotionally cramped orientation and backward notion of sovereignty might win votes for Wilson.

Andy wasn't in favour of the Common Market. It was a club for capitalists. Its aim was to entrench capitalism and to make an alternative impossible; but Powell's view of self-rule was outdated. Internationalism was the correct outlook. Its purpose wasn't profit, but peace, cooperation and equality. The huge inequalities between nations weren't the product of glib *uneven development*, but of deliberate, wilful, vicious conquest and exploitation. There was a madness at the heart of Powell's call for sovereignty: he would have been the last person to argue that the British Empire violated the sovereignty of people across the globe. Pulling back into our own borders was risible after we'd made ourselves rich and powerful by piracy, colonialism, imperialism, slavery, slaughter and exploitation. If we wanted to live within our borders, we should never have left them; but then we would be a nation of sheep farmers and fishermen living in stone cottages and drawing water from the well every morning.

The nations of the world had to come together. Humanity had to define itself as one. Everyone's first definition must become human, not British or French or German or American. That was the great task of internationalism and it meant the rich countries, which had all become rich through violence, had to cede some sovereignty in order to make amends, to leave the world of conquest and exploitation behind and create a future of co-operation in equality.

Heath had taken Britain into the Common Market to enhance its competitiveness. His concern was for business. Europe provided a plentiful harvest for capitalists. Managing directors would get richer. Shareholders would do well. The majority would take the crumbs, as usual. In Powell's voice Andy heard something more sinister: a retrograde nationalism which could light the blue touchpaper of racism and xenophobia. Powell was a stupid man. One of those highly educated, public school Oxbridge specimens who can read Latin and Greek but whose emotions are stunted; who can translate Herodotus but can't hold a conversation with the milkman .It was what Lawrence was always scratching at: the emotional incompetence of the middle-classes and above. There was more intelligence in Walter Morel, the barely literate miner, walking home from the pit across the dew-moistened fields with cherries dangling from his ears to delight his children, then in the schoolroom and supervision, exam-passing, instruction of the official system whose purpose was to turn out plum-mouthed brain-boxes with the emotional responsiveness of a gatepost.

The report was released showing that miners had fallen behind other industrial workers in pay. Andy felt it was a blow for Heath; but he was still going to win. When the result came and Wilson had a four-seat advantage he was astonished and relieved.

He sent a note to his mother: it was a good result. There would have to be another election soon. Wilson might get a majority, and that for a manifesto calling for *a fundamental shift of wealth and power to working people and their families.* Her reply was glad of the victory but she told him his cousin's wife, his uncle Jimmy's lad, had died of a brain haemorrhage at age of thirty-two, leaving him with three young children. He was stunned to realise he'd never met Katherine. He knew of her. She was in the background, one of those family members who was part of his landscape without him ever talking to her. He regretted it. He should have knocked on their door. He should have known her. Only ten years older than himself, and his cousin left with the kids to bring up and they with no mother.

There was a horrible cruelty in life. Yet to call it cruelty was a mistake. There was no malice in nature. There was imperfection. Nature didn't want to kill Kathleen. It didn't want anything. It was process without motivation. Only people were cruel. Powell was cruel in stirring people up to racial hatred. Heath was cruel in favouring the rich over the rest. Nature was simply blind, if tragic.

When Wilson won the election on 10th October, Andy was in Paris. He, Rob and Mike Richards had put a preference for the south on their application to the Bureau for Educational Visits and Exchanges, Montpellier in particular. They hoped they would be sent to the same region. Andy got Saint-Denis, Rob Bagneux and Mike, Carmaux, a small mining town near Toulouse. It didn't pass their notice that almost all the girls were sent where they asked for.

"Yeah," said Rob to Andy, "we come from the industrial north so they think we're hard-cases. We'll cope in the poor banlieues."

"Bastards," said Andy, "does class fail to govern anything in this country ?"

He wrote to the Head of the school he'd been allocated introducing himself and asking if there might be any help offered in finding accommodation. A reply arrived from the existing assistant saying he was staying in a *foyer des jeunes*, that Saint-Denis was a slightly difficult place, that settling in was a bit of a strain but it was worth it. Andy wasn't attracted by a foyer. He wanted independence. He sent another letter asking the Head if it would be okay if he sent some of his belongings in advance. No reply came so he sent his trunk anyway.

He arrived during lunchtime, his rucksack on his back and a holdall in his hand. He'd set off at midnight, taken the coach to Victoria, the train to Dover, the ferry and train again to the Gare du Nord. When he emerged from the station in Saint-Denis he hailed a taxi because the school was at the other end of the town, he was tired, hungry and didn't know the way. As he paid the driver, a horde of jeering kids came to the fence to watch. He went through the gate and they formed a line behind him and followed him, jeering all the way, to the main entrance.

"Bonjour. Je suis M.Lang, votre nouveau assistant anglais," he said to the receptionist.

She told him to sit on the single chair against the opposite wall. He was there an hour before the *Directeur* appeared; a small, rotund, sweating, flustered, impatient man dressed in crumpled brown trousers held up by a narrow leather belt around his bulging belly, a white shirt with brown stripes, and a wide, blue tie.

"Ah, c'est vous l'assistant anglais?"

"Oui."

In spite of his unappealing manner, Andy hoped the man was going to shake his hand, welcome him and his introduction to the school would begin.

"Attendez là," he said and disappeared through a door beside the receptionist's window.

Five minutes later he returned, accompanied by the caretaker wheeling an upright trolley on which sat Andy's dark blue trunk with the brass corners.

"Cette malle est à vous ?"

"Oui."

"Ôtez la de mon collège."

"Mais je n'ai pas de logement."

"C'est un peu votre faute."

Andy stood up and, not wanting to protest, insisted that with two bags to carry and nowhere to go, taking the trunk away was impossible. The little man told him to leave the bags, pointed in the direction opposite to the one Andy had come from saying the *Foyer des Jeunes* was there: he should go and get himself a room. The caretaker pushed the trolley so it rested in front of Andy, turned and left. The *directeur* told him to come back for his bags once he'd got a room, disappeared into his office and shut the door.

The yard was still full of pupils. Andy wondered if he should wait till the lunch break was over, but the receptionist came out of her office and held the door open.

"Vous suivez la route principale, monsieur," she said. "Filez tout droit, le foyer est à gauche."

He leant on the rubber-covered handles, the trolley tipped. He banged down the step and began to push towards the gate. The pupils came running, hundreds of them. They jeered and clapped, lined up behind him and followed him; then they began to chant: *taxi, taxi, taxi*. No member of staff appeared.

The trunk was heavy. He was tired and thirsty. His arms hurt. He walked a few hundred yards but there was no sign of the foyer. Half a mile, still no sign and he began to wonder if he was going the wrong way. The cars flew past in both directions. Drivers and passengers gave him odd looks. He stopped to rest. What was he doing here? What was this to do with him? He was living out experience which wasn't his own The sun was warm in spite of it being the start of October. He was sweating. What if he didn't find the foyer? Could he take the trunk back to the school? His strongest instinct was to abandon the trolley and his trunk, retrieve his bags, get a taxi to the station and head back home. A car went by containing four young men, it slowed, the windows lowered; they hurled abuse, spat and sped away.

He thought of Rob. They'd arranged to meet at the *Odéon* metro station. Maybe he would begin to feel he was in the right place. Yet the desire not to be there, the feeling this had nothing to do with Andy Lang was so intense he began to experience his body as not belonging to him. He pushed on. He was ridiculous. He knew the passing motorists were looking at him and asking themselves why that idiot was pushing a trunk on a trolley along the main road. He was thoroughly alone and humiliated. He told himself it would pass but he didn't believe it. It was wrong to carry on. He should go back to the school and give the *directeur* a mouthful.

He pressed on and after a mile the foyer came into view. It had the look of a barracks. He followed the long, curving concrete path to the entrance. There was a flight of thirty steps. He stopped. A man of forty or so in a *bleu de travail* came trotting down. He looked at the trunk and said:

"Il est coupé en deux ou en quatre ?"

They both laughed. The man asked him if he wanted a hand and together they carried the trunk to the top. Andy thanked his helper who pointed out the trolley was still at the bottom. Andy shrugged and said it could stay there.

Inside he approached the reception which lay to the left in a big, empty, modern, concrete and brick entrance hall. A thin-faced woman with black hair and a cigarette in her fingers was on duty. He explained. She shook her head, raised her palms and told him there were no rooms. He looked her in the eyes and paused, pointed to his trunk which he'd dragged inside and told her it was staying there. He was going into Saint-Denis to find himself somewhere to stay. He'd come back in a taxi for the trunk when he'd found somewhere.

The woman stood up and he noticed how slim and shapely she was. She began to remonstrate, wave her arms and shake her head. Coming out of her office she confronted him; it wasn't possible; no; he must take the trunk away, now; she had no rooms; he must leave.

He shook his head and reiterated what he'd told her. She went quiet, stared at him as if she was going to slap him across the face, told him to wait and ran up the stone stairs which faced the main entrance.

Half an hour later he had signed up for a year, handed over almost all his money and hauled his trunk into his tiny room. She told him the rules: leave the key at reception; the main doors are locked at eleven, no visitors in the room overnight; no females allowed in the rooms. He lay on the bed feeling as if he'd been imprisoned.

When he took the trolley back, the *directeur* told him to take his bags and disappear. Andy pointed out he was supposed to be starting teaching. The little man made a Gallic gesture of indifference, said he hadn't even begun to think about his timetable, suggested he should go and do a course at the Sorbonne for a fortnight. As Andy was about to leave, he called after him telling him to open a bank account the next day and give the details to the receptionist.

Almost broke, alone, unoccupied, he loitered around the foyer, walked the streets of Saint-Denis and wondered how things would be when he started at the school. He would have to write to his mother for money. If he didn't start his job for two weeks, those were two weeks without pay. He had barely enough in his pocket to buy a coffee each day.

On the Wednesday afternoon of the second week he was in the television room, wasting time, when an announcement came over the *Tannoy* that there was visitor for him at reception. He assumed it must be Rob. It was his dad. He'd had the offer of a stay in a monastery in Brittany and had decided to drive to Paris to see Andy on his way home. At once Andy thought of escape.

"I can't stay here," he said.

"Well, it's up to you, Andy," said Bert.

Andy knew if he told the *directrice* he simply didn't want to stay, his deposit would be lost.

"Mon père est là. Je dois rentrer en Angleterre. J'ai des chagrins," he told her.

She softened at once, became fulsomely sympathetic and took the francs out of her drawer. He had no compunction about lying to her nor about leaving the school without an assistant. He'd come in good faith. He wanted to make a success of the year. He wanted to meet the staff, get to know the school, start working, settle in and feel he belonged, for the year. He'd been treated as an encumbrance, an intrusion, a wasp, a fly, a pest. Well, he would pester them no more.

He got a room in the little hotel in the Latin Quarter where his dad was staying. For three days they visited the city. Andy did the talking and interpreting, showed his dad the Marais and the Buttes-Chaumont. His dad paid for his ferry ticket. When they arrived at Woodland Grove they carried the trunk into the hallway. Elsie appeared and was shocked.

"Well, I'll leave you to it, Andy," said his dad and they shook hands.

His mother retreated to her kitchen. He went through to speak to her.

"I couldn't stay," he said " it was appalling."

"All right," she said, without looking at him.

He went up to his little room, the place he'd been so happy when they first moved in. He leaned on the window sill to watch the tall trees of the tennis club swaying in the October breeze. He would have to tell the university. He would have to find some work. His high expectations of a year in Paris had come to nothing. He lay on his creaky bed. Was he to blame? No, as usual it was the system. What Rob had said was true: they'd been sent to Parisian banlieues because they were from the industrial north. He'd been sent to Saint-Denis because some dumb southern bureaucrat assumed all people from Preston were the same: rough, insensitive hard-knocks who would be at home in a poverty-stricken dump full of ill-treated immigrants, crime and drugs.

Some months later he watched a documentary about the school. The teachers had barricaded themselves into the staff-room in protest at the chaos and violence. It was deemed the worst school in France. He'd been right to come home.

A REUNION, A START, A DECLINE

Elsie wasn't glad to have her son home, nor would she have been glad had he made a success of his year in France. The former she experienced as something of a burden, the latter as beyond her experience and interests. All the same, he quickly found work and, as when he began as a clerk at sixteen, handed over half his pay. The money made things considerably easier but she still felt that at twenty-three he should be established. She was married at twenty-four, but the war had slowed things. What bothered her was how long this need to come home would last. He had a year to fill, then another at university and what after that? It was odd to experience her son as a burden. She tried to tell herself it would soon pass, but the life he was living was remote from what she knew. The business of studying seemed to drive away the urgency of finding an income and setting up a family.

On the one hand, she was relieved by Harold Wilson's victory, small though it might be. She was puzzled why people didn't vote Labour in the way they had in 1945. What had changed? On the other, she was troubled by Andy's return. He was a stranger to her in some ways. She'd never imagined she'd have a child who would be lost in books. She hadn't wanted it. Her expectation was that, if she had a son, he would be like her brothers: a joiner or mechanic or plumber. That she could understand.

Things settled down. Andy got up every morning and went off to his little job at the Ministry of Agriculture and Fisheries offices in Cop Lane; established a table for himself in the back room where he read and wrote and went out to the pub or to see a play or a film once or twice a week. He didn't get under her feet. He'd always been a quiet boy who could be in the house while she would hardly notice.

As her anxiety about him calmed, her thoughts came back to the election. There was talk of the government not lasting because of the small majority. She feared it would collapse and Heath would get back in. Perhaps Wilson could get through the five years with support from the Liberals; but she loathed Jeremy Thorpe. She'd thought Jo Grimond a decent man, but Thorpe she considered sly and untrustworthy. The Liberals, in any case, were essentially Tories in disguise. The core of her politics was what she'd absorbed from her father: when people work, what they produce should be theirs. That was what the NHS was about: returning to people the wealth they'd created.

She was perplexed, though, as to why people didn't vote Labour. George was outraged by the result. She had her customary disputes with him which she knew made no difference: he couldn't change her mind she couldn't change his. She ruminated compulsively over why a man who drove a van for the school meals service, was always down to his last quid by pay day, had no savings nor property, could imagine the Tories were on his side. It occurred to her it was a kind of gratitude. He was grateful even for the little he had, as if his betters had permitted him to be a van driver and he must reward them with deference. She could understand how folk with money could think that way. Most of the people in Woodland Grove, for example. Mr Lingard and his family were obvious Tories. He was a solicitor with his own practice. No doubt his house was paid for. He ran a nice car. He probably had plenty in the bank. He was one of the few people in the Grove who never spoke to her. One of those snobs so precious about their status they have to respond to people of lower status as if they are trees or lamp-posts.

Yes, she could see how someone like that, with a comfortable, three-bedroom house in a nice part of Penwortham, his own business, a good income and status could be grateful for his opportunities and his well-being and vote for the hand which he assumed fed him. She couldn't agree with it. Had she been twice as rich as Lingard she would have voted Labour because there was a moral duty to think about people less fortunate. A sense of gratitude for your own good luck might be positive, but it was negative if it meant you voted for policies which would harm those lower down. She couldn't agree with it, but she could understand it.

It was much harder to comprehend how someone like George, and there must be millions of them for the Tories to win, could vote out of gratitude. He seemed to think it was thanks to businessmen, bosses, shareholders, speculators, investors, wheeler-dealers, bankers, merchants, City traders, stockbrokers, middle-men, he had a job. All these people, she'd learned at her father's knee, lived from the work of others. It was work that made wealth. The sense of gratitude she believed in was horizontal. It was the gratitude of one worker to another. George's was vertical. It was gratitude to what he called "the high-ups". He believed if it wasn't for stockbrokers there would be no coal miners whereas she knew it was the other way round.

It was all a trick of money. She'd read *The Ragged-Trousered Philanthropists*, one of the collection of a few hundred volumes her dad had in his little oak bookcase. She'd kept in her head the notion that the money-manipulators were parasites. Money was a shape-shifter and the people who devoted their lives to it were no better than stage magicians. George and millions like him were tricked. They applauded as the white rabbits appeared from the top hat, a string of handkerchiefs was tugged from the performer's cheek and the lady sawn in half stood in her glittering costume.

The thought that people voted Tory out of gratitude softened her feeling. If they were genuinely grateful for their good lives and if they wanted everyone to be able to share the same, that was benign and morally reasonable. If, however, part of their motivation was to deny to others what they had, that was wicked. George, of course, wasn't in a position to look down on and fear the advance of those below him (except for his racism). He was fawning. He was a bootlicker. He prostrated himself before those he thought his betters. He had no sense that he and people like him were quite capable of making a decent life. They had no need to lay their coats in the mud for the passing feet of managing directors.

There must be millions of them, she reflected; millions of Georges, people whose lives were immeasurably improved by a free, universal education system, the NHS, old age pensions. Her son could go to a publicly-funded university thanks to a grant. In her view, the NHS alone was enough for her never to vote other than Labour. The Tories had opposed it. Had it not been for Nye Bevan, there would be some insurance system or nothing more than an emergency service for the poor. What she loved about Bevan's system was that it put George on the same level as Mr Lingard. If either of them had a heart attack, the NHS would take care of them. There was no question that was morally superior to a system which relied on the ability to pay.

She talked to Andy about the election.

"People are fed Toryism by the press every day," he said. "If we had five Labour supporting daily newspapers, we'd never lose."

His temporary job was routine. He filed documents. Took messages from one manager to another. Ensured the huge maps in the big drawers were always in order. This was the sole point of interest. The staff who visited farms needed very detailed charts. They were about three feet square. Now and again he got the chance to lean on the sloping desk with one of the blokes who was about to make a visit and search for a farm hidden in the hills of The Trough of Bowland or tucked away on the moors beyond Todmorden. He'd never seen anything so topographically detailed and was amazed to find names given to tiny copses, ponds, hillocks, minute parcels of land.

The only other interest, and also cause of some alarm, were the women. All the serious jobs, the core functions, visiting farms, making decisions, were done by men; but most of the employees were women. They carried out functions slightly more complex and responsible than those Andy had to deal with. Almost all of them were married and most beyond thirty. One morning he was sitting in his swivel chair at his desk when Mrs Brewer from the neighbouring office brought him a file. She stood close to him.

"Here, Andy," she said, "can you put this in order."

He took it from her and opened it. At the same moment she pushed up closer so that her belly was pressed against his shoulder. He thought he should pull away but didn't want to be impolite; perhaps it was inadvertent; maybe she was unaware she was virtually rubbing her crutch against him. He said he would sort out the file. She laid her left hand on his other shoulder. One of the higher officers came through the door, smoking his pipe, and she subtly withdrew.

"I'll pick it up this afternoon, shall I ?"

"Yes, that's fine," he said, looking up at her.

She was a short, rather dumpy women of about thirty-five with one of those bosoms which look like a pillow. She wore glasses whose frames had curious, little wings. Neither ugly nor attractive she had one of those undistinctive faces like thousands of other you might see in passing. She was smiling complaisantly, almost in the way an adult humours a child.

When she came back later, he made sure he was standing but she brushed her ponderous breasts against his arm. The incident made him acutely conscious of how the women related to him. Previously he'd noticed the odd glance, or that self-conscious demeanour when one of them passed him on the corridor which suggested she might have noticed him; but this was on a different level. Mrs Brewer was a conventional, married woman with a couple of primary age kids. Was she trying to entice him? Did she really want to inveigle him into a liaison? He wouldn't have entertained it in his most distant fantasy.

Little by little he came to realise, that being the only young man in the place, most of the permanent male staff having celebrated thirty some time ago, he was an object of special attention for the women. Not the most unprepossessing man on earth, in spite of his acne, he'd sparked up a bit of feminine competition. He became aware of the odd, neurotic atmosphere. These were women who worked all day, five days a week in a preponderantly female milieu. If Sean Connery came amongst them, of course it would cause a stir; certainly it would arose the demon of female sexual competitiveness. He was no Sean Connery, but he was young and good-looking enough.

There was a woman whose name he never learned, dark, slim and pretty who worked in the office at the far end of the corridor. Occasionally they passed one another and he noticed how her walk became more slinky, how her face took on a coy, serious expression, how she looked hard into his eyes and in spite of his wide smile and his cheery greeting, maintained her serious poise. She was a very nice-looking woman, but he wanted to laugh out loud. It was all too ridiculous. What was wrong with these women? They all had husbands. Why did they have to respond to him as if he was the only male on the planet?

The experience made him excessively aware of his celibacy. There was Jane in the background. She'd written to him in August, a long, rambling, emotional spilling out, suggesting they could meet in Paris at the rendezvous for assistants he'd never intended to attend. He didn't reply and resolved to leave her behind: trying to track her mind was like trying to read a bee's wiggle dance. He was troubled at being unattached but it stayed in the background; he read, reflected, went to the pub and found someone to chat to and was working hard at trying to write something which didn't make him nauseous when he re-read it.

The more he thought of Mrs Brewer and the tense atmosphere amongst the women, the more it aggravated his loneliness. Matt Ross had married Linda Lowther. Matt had asked him to be best man but his family had intervened. He was invited. There was a nuptial mass at St Mary's and St Michael's Garstang where Matt's dad had bought a huge, old house, followed by a splendid reception at Barton Grange. Andy came away weighed with a sense of loss and sadness. He had enormous affection for Matt but he wasn't convinced Linda loved him. He felt she'd been drawn by money. He had a horrible fear the marriage wouldn't last.

Stu Archer got married too. His bride was the pretty, bouncy, clever Angie Windsor, daughter of a Durham miner; a linguist who he'd met at university and been inseparable from since the first term. Andy was best man at the reception held in the miners' welfare hall, where the fare was plain and alcohol not permitted. Stu had dropped lucky and chosen well. Angie was delightful, affectionate, reliable, charming and unaffected.

Andy was puzzled by his own ill-luck in love. He thought back to Maggie Swift and wondered if he'd made a terrible mistake. He was too immature. She, at twelve, was already nearly a woman. Too late, anyway. She would be married now. His infatuation with Janice Eaves now seemed laughable. The on-off business with Carol Berry had fizzled out like a roman candle in the rain and then there was Jane. He was at a loss to understand why things had gone so badly.

The winter was slow to pass but when the spring arrived and his job had come to an end, he busied himself painting the outside of his mother's house. It was a relief to be able to pass a few hours sandpapering window-sills, priming doors, climbing the heavy wooden ladder he could hardly manage, removing bits of rotten timber and making the best repair he could manage. It was a healthy diversion from his intellectual work and it made him aware of how a physical task has clear limits and an intellectual-moral task doesn't. All the questions he worried away at were without simple answers, or even answers at all. Yet they demanded attention.

The tennis season started. He was glad to help setting the courts to rights; laying new shale, dragging, rolling, hammering the nails in the tape; and he was free to play whenever he liked. The standard was below the university team, but he was as at home on a tennis court as Albert Camus on a football field.

When September arrived and the days began to cool and the nights draw in he was eager to get back to campus. His pals who were on three-year degrees would no longer be there, but he would meet up with Rob and Mike again; he could pick up the lost thread of serious study and maybe find a girl.

One Friday night, at a loose end, having read and tried to write a poem all day before playing tennis from six till eight, he told his mother he was going out and walked into town. He went to the *Fox and Grapes*, a busy, little pub in Fox Street run by the handsomely moustachioed Arthur, a diminutive bloke of fifty who rode a Triumph 500 supported the National Front and tried his best not to serve blacks. Andy was fully aware of his insane political views but he liked him. He was a friendly little man whose mad affiliation came from a profound lack of confidence. Andy had struck up a warm if superficial relationship with him and on a couple of occasions invited Asian or West Indian lads he knew for a drink.

"This is my mate, Ravi," he would say. "Ravi, this is Arthur, the best landlord in Preston," and in spite of himself the stocky barman would smile, shake hands and pull the pints.

Crowded from front to back, noisy, full of that fuck-it-it's-Friday mentality of the masses who earned their livings at boring jobs which required suppression from early on Monday till five o'clock on Friday, the hint in the atmosphere of self-abandonment combined with the good-natured desire for enjoyment gave him a sense of possibility together with a feeling of belonging. He nodded to a couple of people he knew: a lad who'd been in the year above him at Penwortham Sec but whose name he never knew; one of the old *habitués* of *The Jolly Farmer*, a pub rat who could always be found in town at the weekend and who exhibited that disconnectedness typical of his breed.

He intended two pints and a brisk walk home but as he was ordering his second, Carol came through the door with Elaine and Gina, two of her old friends from the days at *Great Universal Stores*. All three had married at twenty. Carol had two little children. All the same in the way she looked at him approached him and spoke to him, he could detect her wish to be alone with him. They chatted inconsequentially as people do while in the background gurgles the stream of enormity.

"I was going to go home after this," he said. "Fancy a walk?"

She was so quick to accept, to make her excuses to her friends who smiled conspiratorially and cast intrigued glances across the pub as they left, he knew she was a woman whose marriage has gone wrong. They walked through Avenham park, stopped on the tram bridge, came back into the bowl of the huge lawn which dipped from Ribblesdale Place to the river. She took his arm and when they stopped, lifted her face and he kissed her as he had eight years earlier when he was innocent and loving sixteen and she eager for experience fifteen.

They met a few times before the start of term and when he went back to Bailrigg she began to catch the train to come to see him twice a week. Usually, he met her, they jumped on the bus to campus, spent a few hours in his room and then walked down to the A6 where she could get the late bus which would have her back in Preston just before midnight. It was normal for her to get home at twelve or beyond when she'd been out with Elaine and Gina.

One Wednesday, early in November, they decided to have a drink before going for the bus. They sat in Bowland bar which was sparse and chilly. She kept her coat on and her fur collar turned up. They restricted themselves to a half and were about to leave when Andy looked up to see Jane coming in with three people he didn't know but assumed must be from her floor. She was dressed in a full-length, green, cloak-like coat, elegant and expensive looking. She looked in their direction as she arrived at her seat, lowered her eyes quickly, flushed and hesitated.

"Come on," he said. "Can't miss that bus."

Walking back alone, climbing the sweet path up from the road, in the dark, on the campus he loved, where he felt more at home than since he was a little boy newly arrived in Woodland Grove, he thought about Carol on the bus. It was terrible she should have to travel alone. He wondered where things were going to lead. She was unhappy in her marriage but that she was prepared to leave it she hadn't said. He was glad to be back with her but there was an odd sense of trying to live what he'd missed. He wasn't sixteen. They couldn't recapture what might have been. He thought of Proust and laughed to himself.

His thoughts switched to Jane. Seeing him with Carol had caught her off guard. He was astonished. She'd spent a year in France with her lover. Was she so out of touch with her own feelings she was still in love with him and had denied it? At all events, that was nothing to do with him. She'd run her bath and would have to wash in it; but what fascinated and appalled him was the glimpse of her chaotic inner life. How could a person become so remote from their own emotions? How could a mind be so divided against itself?

He found an item he'd read in the paper coming back to him: Pasolini had been murdered by a teenager who claimed he'd made advances to him, who'd clubbed him over the head and run over him with his car. It brought back the incident in Jane's room shortly before the end of the second year when she'd told him about Jean-Claude and derided him for thinking she was committed to him. They'd rowed and when he turned his back, she picked up the nearest object and hit him over the head. She was left holding the handle of her mug and he rubbing his crown.

Sylvia was always glad when her brother came home for the weekend. It relieved the atmosphere. Her mother descended more and more into the deep pit of her resentment, the churning well of miasma where she'd chosen to live. She would begin to talk about her ex-husband and the long charge list of his abysmal crimes would be run through over and over: he was a miserable devil, mean, selfish, vain, incapable of thinking of anyone but himself. He'd had a good job with ICI but what did he do? He threw it away. That was him all over. Big ideas. Always big ideas. She should have had more sense than to marry him.

It was a terrible strain for the teenager to have to listen. She wanted to say: "Well, what's it to do with me? That's your life. I've got my own life to live." It was impossible. When her mother had lapsed into one of these states of extreme self-pity and accusation, her eyes glazed, her left leg pale and slightly obscene in its nakedness rocking, rocking, as if to stop would arrest the earth's turning, she couldn't be reached. She wasn't a distinct person you could talk to but a morass of conflicting, regressed, infantile, unsublimated impulses which must spill out like the innards of a gutted cod.

Andy made her laugh. He managed to push seriousness into the background and say something warm and amusing; and he could talk to her mother so didn't have to be the eternal interlocutor.

"I don't like her one bit," said Elsie as she and Andy were watching the news on Saturday evening.

"She's driving them to the right, that's for sure," said Andy.

"I didn't like Heath but she's worse. She's artificial as plastic daffodils."

"So was he."

"I know. She's a right snob, pretending to be better than she is. She's a shopkeeper's daughter from Grantham and she tries to sound like the queen herself."

Andy laughed.

"That's right. People like it. They fall for it. Everyone has a superficial mind and a deep mind. Appealing to the superficial works. People identify with posh accents, an arrogant attitude and smart clothes. They think it ensures authority. But they don't look through the mist to the policies"

"You don't need to tell me, I have to listen to George. By heaven, "George," I say to him. "Y'aven't sense you were born wi'. You don't like Jack Jones because he talks rough and wears a flat cap, but he'll do more for you than Edward Heath ever will"."

"People always identify with the elite of wealth of power. The problem is they don't ask where it came from. The truth is, it was built by violence. Democracy is capitalism's afterthought. It'll take a long war of attrition to wear away the ingrained deference."

Elsie wasn't sure what he meant. What she knew was Harold Wilson had increased the old age pension by twenty-five per cent and was building plenty of council houses. She read too that he'd introduced benefits for the disabled. She was glad she'd never lived in a council house and proud that her parents had scrimped to pay off the mortgage on their little terrace as early as possible. She was wholly in favour of everyone owning their own home; but she'd seen the pre-war slums of Preston and she knew the council houses built by Bevan and Macmillan had given millions a decent home. She felt no snobbery towards council tenants, though she was glad she owned her own fine, three-bedroom semi in a comfortable suburb. Her ideal was that everyone should be able to live in a good house in a nice area, but till that came about, people must be protected from jerry builders and Rachmanite landlords. She'd been lucky and she had exceptional parents, people capable of unusual self-discipline and frugality, but circumstances could have forced them into difficulties. It was right that homes at reasonable rent provided and looked after by the council should protect people from squalor and exploitation. As for disability, it was right people should be looked after. Her dad had been diabetic. He might easily have suffered something worse. A good society was compassionate. It looked after its most vulnerable.

"Well," she said, "I hope Harold Wilson can stay in power. He needs a proper majority to get things done."

"Yes," said Andy, "and he's up against the international monetary system. They'll wring him dry. They'll force him to make cuts in public spending. We vote Labour but the IMF has the power."

Elsie didn't know what the IMF was. She had a naïve and trusting view of democracy. She believed everyone was as principled as she was and accepted that if a government was elected, it must be allowed to do what it promised. She would have been astonished to discover there were people willing to see the economy crash into recession or be scorched by inflation if that's what it took to bring down a social democratic government.

Sylvia was going out.

"Be back by ten, think on," said Elsie.

Andy went to see her off.

"Where you going?"

"The Fleece."

"God, under age drinking. Don't tell her. Who you going with?"

"Some friends from Lune Street."

"Want me to come and meet you at ten?"

"No, someone'll walk me home."

To meet her at ten he would have had to alter his arrangements. He was aware his mother didn't like being left alone. Sylvia was her last link to life. She hadn't made friends after her decision to kick Bert out, she hadn't found her way into organisations or clubs which could give her contact. Apart from church she was isolated and as

Lune Street was a bus ride away and she was nervous about coming home in the dark alone, she missed many evening events. What was happening to both his mother and Sylvia was terrible: the mother was clinging to the daughter as to a lifebelt and she was trying to swim away, against the impossible eddy of her mother's manipulation. It was impossible. There was nothing he could do except encourage his sister to break free. That had to be the principle; young life must prevail.

He knew what was ahead for his mother would be awful. She was fifty-three. She could yet, if she was minded, find herself a husband; but the idea was as practical as growing tea in the Highlands. She hadn't simply let the path which led to that possibility become overgrown, brambled, nettled, impassable without serious work; she'd built a twelve feet high, two skin brick wall at its entrance. She didn't know she was destroying her mind. Her Christian eschatology told her her self-righteousness would bring the ultimate reward. She had no intuition that driven to the extreme she was pursuing, it would lead to madness.

Andy washed his face in water as hot as he could stand it, squeezed the whiteheads in the crevices of his nose, dried himself, pulled on a polo neck and brushed his hair. He knew his mother was heading for a terrible end. He would have liked to tell her:

"Listen, mum. You mustn't do this. Let Sylvia go. Let her build her own life and you attend to yours. You need to find a life that can sustain your mind. You could find a man, but if you don't want to do that, you must at least have friends, people who come to the house. Who ever comes here? My mates. Syl's friends. But not yours. If you carry on as you are it'll drive you insane."

It was hopeless. All he could do was be a good son. He knew that what she needed was way beyond what that could offer. It was a crushing, demoralising thought that his mother was destroying her mind. He blamed religion, poverty, poor education and the domination of property. As the vicar at Penwortham Congregational used to say: you can't be so heavenly-minded you're of no earthly use. That was his mother: too heavenly-minded to be of use to herself.

Her fate was a terrible weight on his life, but he had to make something of himself. He had to find some route to happiness out of this morass of neurosis and delusion.

He met Carol on Avenham Park. They had a walk and found a quiet spot then went for a drink in the *Lamb and Packet*. Little by little they were moving towards an understanding of a possible future. She let him into the secrets of her unhappiness. He wondered if she had married because she was pregnant but it would have been mercenary to ask. He wished it was simple, that they were both free, that they could set up their tender bower in some who-cares-if-it's-down-at-heel flat and in joyful enjoyment of each other gather themselves to some level of comfort; but there was a marriage and children and they agreed that above all their well-being must be looked after.

She noticed someone eyeing her from the crowd at the bar.

"Oh," she said, "I know him."

"Yeah."

"He's one of my husband's friends."

"Shall we go ?"

"Too late now."

Part of her wanted collapse, for the whole sorry edifice of her marriage to dissolve and for her to be able to begin again. There had always been within her this sense of fate taking it course. She wanted to give in to it. It was delightful to feel yourself dragged along by the inevitable movement of events and not to have to choose, be responsible, bear the burden of your mistakes. Yet that was just what had led her into difficulty. She thought back to meeting Andy. How sweet she'd thought him. A charming, almost pretty boy of sixteen all the girls agreed was worth looking at. Yet the very sense that she would be envied put her off. He was too nice and his seriousness made her wince. She was fifteen. She didn't want *to be tied down*. She recalled saying that to him and her feeling sank. If she could go back eight years, she would accept him. She would enjoy the boy-and-girl affection which at the time she disdained as old-fashioned. She would stay close to him and be good to him and marry at twenty or twenty-one; but when he was sixteen, she didn't believe he could become what he now was.

He was an unassuming, shy, polite boy and though the general opinion was that these were essentially positive, or at least not negative, she found herself sneering. What kind of man would he make? She couldn't see him as anything but passive, undemonstrative, the kind of person who gets left behind. It was 1967. The world was alive with psychedelia. *The Beatles*, madly successful very young, rich as only lunatics wish to be, so famous they couldn't open the door without being mobbed, were an example of how life might be. She never thought she'd be worth millions, but something of the glamour and stardom might rub off even on the daughter of a lorry driver from Much Hoole. She might smoke dope on a beach wearing a kaftan, throw over the restraints of routine and responsibility. Yet at the first try, she ended up pregnant and married, under duress.

She drew on her cigarette. Had someone told her then, on one of those Wednesday or Sunday nights at St Mary's Youth Club, that Andy Lang would go to university to study French she would have been shocked. She thought he had nothing like it in him; but he had moved beyond her. That was how she felt. She was left behind in a marriage as stale as last week's loaf while he was enjoying himself on campus and learning things she'd never heard about. He had potential. He told her he might try university lecturing and she found herself wondering why she had been so convinced he was going nowhere.

Part of her wanted collapse, but Andy said they needed discipline. It wasn't going to be easy and they would have to take things slowly and carefully. She knew it was good advice, but she found it hard to adjust her feelings. She wanted to set up home with him tomorrow, for the tension of secrecy and deception to be over.

"Come on," she said, stubbing out her cigarette, "let's go."

They sauntered down Friargate, took narrow Cannon Street down to Winckley Square and separated in Mount Street which was a short walk from the pub where she lived. Neither of them knew that his doctrine of discipline and patience and her will to have it all over and done with would clash and overturn the boat of their temporary bliss. They both went to bed expecting they would spend the rest of their lives together. They both woke in the morning satisfied and happy.

Sylvia had decided to train as a nursery nurse. Andy was aware the choice was influenced by his mother and her sentimental attitude to children. On the one hand, she was genuinely caring and sympathetic; but at the same time, she'd carried over a Victorian sensibility she'd learned from her parents. Andy sat on his mother's sofa with a mug of black tea and a copy of *Le Malade Imaginaire* reflecting how strange it was that a way of feeling instilled in his grandparents when they were children in the 1890s should influence his sister's decision in 1967. It was a pre-Freudian view of childhood: children were little innocents, but at the same time they should be controlled, *seen and not heard.* It was the sickly attitude he found in Dickens; Oliver Twist and Tiny Tim were supposed to evoke sympathy, but really they flattered the well-meaning middle-classes in their view of themselves as moral guardians. There was something roundabout and dishonest in it, that neurotic inability to be straight about anything. Middle-class Victorian ladies dabbing their eyes with expensive handkerchiefs as they read *A Christmas Carol* made him nauseous. There was something of that in his mother's attitude, an inability ever to leave herself behind, to see things other than through the distorting prism of her own factitious emotions.

"What's the training then ?" he said to Sylvia.

"NNEB."

"Sounds posh. How long does it take?"

"Two years."

"Crikey, you'll be a genius by the time you've finished."

"Ha, ha."

"How's it going ?"

"Fine. I like it."

"What's the pay like for nursery nurses?" he said, knowing full well but not wanting to offend.

"Oh, it's not great, but that doesn't bother me. I just want to work with children. Little ones. I'll manage."

" 'Course you will. You've made a good choice. You'll be great at it."

He was tempted to ask whether she'd set aside her idea of living in America. His feeling was she'd become more oriented to reality, to what was available to a lass leaving school at sixteen with a few O Levels, in Preston, in 1975. Yet at the same time he wondered if the fantasy might not be rumbling in the background like an ill-serviced boiler. The discipline of getting to college every morning, focusing on the work, being up to scratch, was a good means of damping down the elaborate, compensatory delusions popular culture was designed to evoke. Everyone was subject to them. Sober-suited bank managers whose regular habits would have strained Kant, harboured secret visions of themselves as Arctic explorers, Hollywood sex-symbols, heavyweight champions, super star centre-forwards of the First Division; diligent primary school teachers with colour-coded key-fobs, mark-books with prim rows of red numbers and sensible shoes, entertained mad illusions of torrid affairs with monosyllabic, impossibly handsome foreigners; young blokes who stood at lathes eight hours a day delivering five hundred identical parts without much sense of where they would be used in the engines they were destined for, thrashed at amplified *Stratocasters* in their garages at the weekend, imagining they might be the next Keith Richard, until their mothers called them in for fish fingers and chips; middle-aged bus drivers with pot bellies, high blood pressure, yellow fingers and a smoker's cough, let themselves believe that one day Sofia Lauren might be waiting at the next stop ready to be charmed by their dirty jokes and bad breath.

Andy knew how the grim dullness of his teenage routine, the paucity of his home life and the cultural nullity of his milieu had permitted pop culture to generate the same kind of destructive, exorbitant expectations in his own closed-bud mind. Without being fully aware of it an idea of rapid, glamorous success had insinuated itself, a sense of crossing into the higher world of the rich, famous, adulated and emulated. It struck him, in retrospect, it was akin to the belief in the afterlife. In both cases, what might have been realised here and now had to suppressed, postponed, projected onto a realm you were excluded from. The insane banalities of F.E.D. had woken him from a living partial reverie. In his late teens, he'd experienced revulsion from popular culture, its spatchcock products, its exploitation of the young and vulnerable, its persistent refusal to engage with life as it is, its constant offer of what could never be provided. He came to loathe pop music, soap-opera, dim-witted films; all those sub-artistic genres whose intent was not to challenge, educate, provoke to thought or genuine feeling, but to drag thought down to idiocy and feeling to neuroticism, and all, he felt, for the purpose of preventing people taking control of their lives and making them fulfilled, today.

Literature had fatally dislodged all those inedible fruits ripened in immaturity. Working hard to get his A Levels and now at university was a spade-in-the-earth way of dismissing foolish expectations and concentrating on effort. He hoped the same would happen to Sylvia, that striving to accomplish skills and taking a get-the-nappies-changed job would relieve her of the need to live half her life in a false paradise of trans-Atlantic glitz.

When he left for the train, Sylvia was slightly sad; but her world was opening out and she wasn't thinking too much anymore of how it was when her elder brother and sister were at home and her grandad alive. She'd entered the arena beyond the house where her mother's ego was as pervasive as the smell of rotten eggs. She had a life of her own that she had chosen. At school, she was processed. What you had to learn was laid down and you were carried by the conveyor belt of instruction to the quality control department of exam passes. She'd enjoyed some of it, but the inability to choose was as heavy as a satchel full of dictionaries. Now, even if she found a class boring or wondered what the point of a piece of work was, she was buoyed by having chosen. It felt responsible and she had longed for that for years. Soon she would be sent on her first placement and would have other people's children to look after. That was a real task, an adult task. It meant putting aside childish indulgence and adolescent pretention. She was ready.

Then there were boys. She started seeing John Durran, from the youth club who lived on Leyland Road in Lower Penwortham. His dad worked as a fitter at Leyland Motors and was one of those men who can fix anything and master any manual task. He'd trained as a bookbinder, emigrated to Canada in his twenties in search of the expansive life of a big, varied country where a man was free to make of himself what he could, but had come back when his wife became homesick during pregnancy. Arthur Durran had married Betty because she was, as he indulgently put it, "a good soul", which was his way of avoiding criticizing her for her sixty-a-day habit, her excessive drinking, her incorrigible spendthrift ways and her negligent housekeeping. She married him because he called her "a good soul" and didn't care about her fags, booze, empty purse and unwashed dishes.

The first time Sylvia visited their friendly, untidy home, she was charmed. Told that Arthur had sought a big life on the borders of Alaska, she felt an affinity and Betty's loose-corseted habits were at the other end of the see-saw from her mother's Craxton abstemiousness and almost-beyond-human self-discipline. Arthur's practicality was also a contrast to her brother's which-end-of-this-screwdriver-do-I-hold feebleness in fettling. She liked John. He was easygoing, kind, affectionate but he had his mother's taste for drink so she never got beyond holding hands before she transferred her interest to his elder brother Barry who was better looking, training as an electrician with Tom Finney, played guitar and sang in working men's clubs on Friday and Saturday nights under the stage name of Johnnie Strong and had a car they got around in.

The atmosphere in their home was a relief from the tension of being alone with her mother in what more and more seemed like a mausoleum. Apart from Mary and Ted, visitors were as rare as polar bears in Africa. Uncle Eddie and Aunty April turned up one Saturday teatime. Sylvia was glad to see them and sat on the sofa beside her mother in expectation of relaxing chat; but her mother headed off on one of her rants, an endless diatribe which flipped from subject to subject and made more detours than a getaway car. Her brother and his wife sat politely, their cups and saucers in their hands, listened, nodded and smiled but were unable to contain their dismay and once they felt they'd stayed long enough for departure not to be impolite, got up and insisted they must go in spite of her mother's pleading offer to make something to eat.

The Durran's house was a thoroughfare. Neighbours, friends, relatives, work-mates, old school pals, Arthur's bowls and darts chums, Betty's bingo pals, the regulars from *The Bridge Inn*, the milkman, the window cleaner, wandered in, sat down, had a brew discussed the customary regrettable state of the world, used the facility, shared a bottle of beer and a joke or settled in the corner of the sagging sofa and stayed to watch the television all evening. To Sylvia, accustomed to the force field of isolation which surrounded her mother's house, it was as good as the circus. She loved and laughed at the way people tapped once on the ever-open front door, walked in and were immediately at home. They greeted her, patted her on the back, engaged her in talk as if they'd know her since Adam.

Her mother was much more fastidious and though she knew there was a discipline and a high-mindedness in that which Barry's family lacked, her inability to combine superior discrimination with enough inconsequentiality to attract people into her living-room, seemed more a failing that Arthur and Betty's lack of reinforced steel in their moral make-up.

She had a world beyond that of her mother and she was growing into it. Elsie, of course, disapproved of Barry. She would have disapproved of Cary Grant, Gregory Peck, Charles Dickens, Shakespeare, Charles Wesley, Clem Attlee, Saint Paul or Christ himself. It was true that Barry's I'll-be-friendly-with-anyone demeanour, oily hands and unceremonious way of dealing with everything and everyone, was a long stride from the taciturn principle of Tom Craxton; but what lay behind her disapproval was that Sylvia was her last bond.

Her daughter knew it as children always do, but like a horse broken too soon, they find a way of rearing up, unseating the rider and galloping off to where they want to be. The art of parenting which lies in binding your infants to you to give them security and gently pushing your adolescents away to ensure their independence, Elsie almost put into reverse. The importunate demands of her infants had often made her cross; so did the bid for independence of her adolescents, particularly her last.

On the train, Andy reflected on Sylvia, his mother and Carol. He loved all three of them but his mother was destroying herself and there was nothing he could do to stop her. All her life she had exerted her extraordinary will to resist what was harmful: she'd never smoked nor drank. She ate sensibly, always had plenty of fruit in the house, kept indulgent treats to a minimum; but her will was useless against what she didn't perceive as destructive. She was like a man who fits intractable locks to his door and windows, an alarm system, security lights, but forgets the greatest threat to his property is from fire.

As for Sylvia, he was glad she was finding Houdini ways to untie the knots his mother had pulled so tight. Yet at the same time, he felt she was capable of more. There was nothing wrong with being a nursery nurse, in fact there was everything right with it; but Sylvia could easily have established and run her own nursery if her confidence were boosted. If he was approached, his dad would stump up the funds; but of course, to Elsie, that would have been as bad as taking money from a pimp or the devil himself. He feared his sister would be put upon, poorly paid because her mother had denied the I'm-as-good-as-the-next-girl chutzpah that could have saved her. Mary had done much less than she was capable of. She was a terrific wife, housemaker and mother; but she could have done those things and run a primary school without moving out of third gear. He'd failed at school for want of a peck of encouragement. His mother's shadow hung over all of them.

Carol, he thought was his future. He'd known at sixteen they were suited. He couldn't have pinned down exactly why, any more than a man can explain why the taste of beetroot disgusts him. Those unconscious forces which are as accurate as a compass, tell us where to go and all too often we ignore them in favour of conscious whims, flimsy desires, arrogant ambitions, self-regarding schemes and when our unhappiness faces us like our silhouette at noon, we blame fate, or others or circumstance for what is the outcome of our hubris.

He didn't blame Carol. She was fifteen when they met. Who knows their own mind at fifteen? Yet he felt it was true that if she'd managed to follow the promptings that lay below her girlish fancies, they could have come through. He was glad they'd rediscovered one another, but in the background was the fret of scandal. He knew only fools believe they can keep an affair eternally secret; but all they needed was enough to time for him to complete his degree, maybe qualify as a teacher, get a job and be able to provide. The threat was that the crumbs of the midnight feasts would be seen by the wrong eyes and the repasts have to end.

He was in his room for five minutes when there was a knock and Mike Richards appeared in his usual hope-I'm-not-butting-in way. He had his *vade mecum*: his tobacco tin. Andy stretched himself on the bed while Mike settled into the armchair and began the ritual preparation. Of the nine lads who had shared the ground floor and much else in the first year, only Andy, Mike and Rob, the linguists, were left. Rob spent almost all his time with Sue, his lover, his companion and his pupil. Finals were on the way. Her can-you-help-me-with-this-essay and can-I-have-a-look-at-your-translation way of scraping by which had brought her bare 2:2s in most of her work, wasn't going to prevail when she had nine three-hour exams to sit, hadn't read Laclos, wasn't sure which century Heine belonged to and could no more recognise *style indirect libre* than a reed warbler. Rob effectively did her work for her but patiently tutored her so she would know what to say about *Buddenbrooks* or Kafka, had the essential dates in her head and knew how to define *Sturm und Drang* and *La Belle Époque*. She, nervous of failure, of having to face her father who had financed her four years of dizzy fun and idleness, clung to him for his kindness and his knowledge. They were inseparable.

In this way, Mike and Andy, who had rooms next to one another became close friends. Every day they spent hours in one another's spaces providing that essential antidote to mind-shredding loneliness: someone to talk to. It wasn't that they didn't like one another or had little in common: they shared a sense of humour and bubbled with off-the-leash laughter for long minutes; they were lefties and could always find a defensive position to share from which they could snipe at Thatcher, Keith Joseph, Willie Whitelaw and the glib band of purveyors of the commonplace benighted self-interest of the fortunate; they liked music and Mike had introduced Andy to *Fairport Convention*, Martin Carthy and his beloved Richard Thompson. Andy hadn't attended to them previously; the folk revival struck him as slightly pretentious and he had little affinity for small gatherings in upper rooms in dingy pubs where people with their finger in their ear sang about taking the horse to water or kissing girls at Truro agricultural show; but he was impressed by Carthy's guitar playing and some of Richard Thompson's songs were witty, socially penetrating and emotionally accurate.

Most of all though, it was a matter of being a mate. Had Mike been a fan of Val Doonican he would have found it hard to share his enthusiasm, but the folkies he liked were accomplished musicians and for the sake of friendship it was easy for Andy to put aside his petty, too-pernickety reservations.

"How are things at home ?" said Mike, as he lay the brown strands on the flimsy paper.

"Insane," said Andy.

Mike let out a brief guffaw which almost blew his tobacco onto the floor.

"Worth the trip then ?"

"It is our moral duty to bring comfort to the demented."

"Well, I bet they're not as mad as my family."

"What's the cause ?"

"Beats me, but my god did my parents row."

"Money."

Mike snorted again.

"Why d'you say that, Andy ?"

"It'll be either money or sex. The latter is easy to sort out but money, boy, if that goes wrong the marriage is in the dustbin."

"Well," said Mike," I-I-I guess they shouldn't have married. They can't get on with one another."

"My mother can't get on with herself."

"Anyway, I bet she was glad to see you."

"I was glad to see her, Mike, and my sister."

"Oh Christ, I wouldn't be glad to see mine."

"What's the matter with her ?"

"She-she-she goes on at me. She always did. She thinks I should get my hair cut and be like her. I can't stand her. She-she-she's a snob and her husband is even worse."

"Well, you should invite them up here. We could educate them."

"You can't educate a brick. Anyway, did you see Carol ?"

"I did."

"That's good."

"Yeah. We were in a pub and she was spotted by some bloke who's friendly with her husband."

Mike let out a yelp of surprise.

"You're in trouble now."

"I hope not. I hope the bugger keeps his mouth shut."

"You-you-you want to be careful. An angry husband."

"I don't think he'll come after me with his revolver."

"No, but all the same. Now the cat's out of the bag things won't be so easy."

Andy suspected Mike was right. When he told him, at the start of the year, his new girlfriend was a housewife, Mike had splurted his coffee over the rug. During his year in Carmaux, he'd taken up with Patricia, the daughter of a miner, an Italian immigrant who married a young woman from the south, fluent in the patois of the region. Patricia was their second child, a pretty, slightly shy, unassuming, kindly girl who Mike met shortly before Christmas having spent most of the first term as lonely as a socialist in Texas. His only other contact was an American who was the assistant in a rural school and claimed to have been a classmate of Bob Dylan. He was a Democrat and they rubbed along relatively well, but he had that typically American optimistic, can-do default setting which clashed with Mike's sceptical sensibility: raised in an unhappy, working-class family in Bletchley, sent to Bedford Grammar where he was poor at the sport which seemed to dominate the culture; tight-skinned, thick-thighed rugby players, broad-shouldered swimmers, and never breathless athletes being the ones who were always up on stage in assembly to receive awards and applause; he was inclined to the sad, ironic perspectives of Richard Thompson and felt his pulse race at the nothing-can-get-in-my-way mentality of his companion.

His final year weighed and moved slowly. He was going back to Carmaux once it was over. He'd get what work he could, in the mine if necessary.

"Bloody hell, Mike," said Andy, "coal mining. That's hard work. You need muscles and you can't stop every half hour for a roll up."

Mike nodded in his slow way as he drew on his fag.

"I know. I-I-I'll just have to do it. There'll be some work I can manage."

"You could get the CAPES."

"That's not easy."

"It's bloody easier than wielding a fucking great pick axe at a seam three miles underground for eight hours a day."

Mike laughed.

"Patricia's dad will be able to get me work in the mine. Straightaway. I'll need money. Doing the CAPES takes time."

"Patricia not fancy coming to live over here ?"

"She doesn't speak English. She wouldn't want to leave her family. In any case, I want to live in France."

"Yeah."

Andy regretted his anticipated year abroad had come to nothing. He Rob and Mike had been badly served. Carmaux was a small, working-class, somewhat insular place without much culture where, especially during the winter, people relied on their families and close friends and spent most of their time outside work in their homes. It had been appallingly hard to break into the community. They were generous, tolerant, easy-going people. Jean Jaurès was a hero amongst them. They didn't exclude him deliberately, but few of them spoke English, he was, in their eyes, a teacher and therefore on that slightly higher plane than most of them which can become an impossible gulf. They didn't know he was lonely to despair and spent his evenings in his *chambre meublée*, smoking, drinking, listening to Richard Thompson and wondering if he should pack his bags and get the train to Paris in the morning.

Yet once he'd met Patricia, been invited into her home, eaten with her parents he had more friends and acquaintances than a man who's come into money. Her cousins, her aunts and uncles, the neighbours, the people she'd been to school with, her dad's fellow workers in the mine, her mother's friends from church, the blokes her dad went to the café with to *prendre un pot*, his fishing companions, the old blokes who played *pétanque* in the square and knew Patricia's dad through work and the union, the women who ran the market stalls where her mother bought meat, vegetables and cheese; all of them were suddenly his friends. He could hardly walk a hundred yards without someone shaking his hand and offering him a *verre rouge*. He was invited to eat in someone's house every weekend. He had never felt more welcome and cared for.

Andy was glad for him. He was in love with Patricia and her family made much of him. He would visit him in Carmaux. Yet at the same time he regretted that at the end of the year they would part. He was starting to feel there was something wrong with the way people were left behind. He had no contact with his old pals from school. He hardly ever saw Matt Ross. Stu Archer was embarked on his married life and they no longer wrote to one another. It was strange to make friends, for people to be an important part of your inner landscape, and then for them to disappear. Tom, Steve, Mike Darley, Phil, he'd liked them enormously in spite of whatever disputes had come along; but now they were gone.

Maybe it was right; perhaps that was the way people built a life; but he had an opposite sense: the drive to get on, to progress, to move up, to achieve was the essential reason. A curious foreboding came over him: what was to guarantee it would work out? If it didn't, and life went wrong for many people, maybe he'd find himself wishing he'd kept his good friends close. Maybe he'd wish he was here in his room with Mike, happy, at home and more or less carefree.

Mike's prediction was accurate. Carol's family knew. Her mother spoke to her. She was under terrible strain. She continued to come to see him twice a week, but now there was a black cloud of disapproval and conformity in the sky of their erstwhile bliss. For him, it was easy; but for her was the daily pain of sharing her home with a husband who was aware of being betrayed. What had been theirs alone, was now shared by many and most of them thought it should come to an end. Time had been taken from them. Yet what could he do? He had to sit his finals at least. What had been a matter of discretion and patience was now a question of urgency and decisiveness. He wondered if Carol had wanted revelation, if she wanted to push things to a resolution. If so, what would it be?

SACKED

The first Bert knew was that Wickham was trying to sell his yacht. He realised at once.

"Well, Ken," he said to him, "what's going on?"

"Nothing's going on, Bert. You know me. Haven't I always been straight with you? The business is in good health."

"You're selling your yacht."

"That doesn't mean a thing. That's personal, Bert."

"And you owe me four thousand quid."

"Am I the kind of man who doesn't pay his debts. I'm not Shylock, Bert."

"Nor am I. I don't want your flesh I just want my money."

"And you'll get it."

"I haven't had a payment for months. You signed a contract. I can enforce it, Ken, if I go to my solicitor."

"No need for that kind of unpleasantness," said the big man, laying his hand on Bert's shoulder. "We do things man to man me and you, Bert. We're friends. A handshake is enough between people like us."

"You owe me commission as well. If things are going wrong I need to know. This is my job. If it's under threat, you have to tell me."

"What are you talking about, Bert? Honestly, you're a worrier. I tell you, never worry. Let things sort themselves out. They always will one way or another."

"Yes, and that means people like me get it in the neck. One way or another won't do. I've put money and graft into this business and if you've let it go to the dogs by spending like a pools winner on amphetamines, I need to know."

"Now, Bert, let's not get to the level of insult."

"It's not insult, Ken. There's Sandra too. Have you said anything to her?"

"She's just a receptionist, Bert. I don't have to tell her about the business."

"Yes, you do. She works here. She relies on her wage to pay her bills. You have a duty to tell her."

"Bert, this is my business. I run it the way I like."

"And that's the way I don't like."

"I'm sorry to hear that, Bert. I thought we were good friends and colleagues.."

"Be a good friend and give me my money, Ken."

"It's business, Bert. You know that. Just hard-headed business. There's nothing personal about it. Cash flow. It'll right itself. These things always do. It's the business cycle. You know what, Bert, you should take a course in economics…"

"You should take a course in philosophy, Ken. What I want to know is, am I going to be in job in six months, because if I'm not, I'm going elsewhere."

"How could the business do without you, Bert? You're a genius at what you do. Truly. No one can bring houses onto the books like you."

"I don't want flattery, I want my job to be secure."

"It is, Bert. It is. I guarantee it. There is no question of bankruptcy. No question."

"Good. Can I have the commission I'm owed."

"'Course you can. I'll see you get a cheque tomorrow."

The cheque didn't appear. Over the next few days, the pain in Bert's thigh became much worse. He hoisted his foot onto the chunky pouffe and resolved to see the doctor.

Since registering with his practice, Bert had got to know Cliff Tucker well. They'd met through charity work for *The Lions*. Bert had got involved by a neighbour's invitation and because it seemed a way to do a bit of good and get to know people. The first event was a children's Christmas party. Dr Tucker had donned the red suit and white beard and when his daughter's little girl had come to collect her present she'd said: "My grandad has shoes like those" Bert and he got on well. He was a widower living alone, one of those rare working-class lads born before the war who managed by brains and hard work to get into a profession dominated by the middle-classes. An inveterate Labour man, he and Bert found it easy to chat, and being unattached and lonely, struck up an instant sympathy.

"Hello, Bert. Good to see you. What's the problem?"

He was one of those highly accomplished people who, because they know the objectivity and sheer graft needed to do what they do, wear their achievement as naturally as their socks. Like a lot of people from his background, he aimed lower than his capacity. For a boy from the backstreets of Blackburn, familiar with bread and dripping and worn out clogs, the idea of being a doctor was as out-of-the-stratosphere as opening the batting for England. He was conscientious and kept his frustration hidden, but he regretted not having pushed himself to become a consultant. Paediatrics was his passion. He read the recent papers. He was abreast of the research. Nothing pleased him more than to see a sick child back on his or her feet thanks to his intervention.

Bert stretched out his leg and grimaced.

"I don't know what I've done, Cliff, but I've got this terrible pain in my right thigh."

"You haven't done anything, Bert. Illness isn't retribution."

Bert laughed.

"I didn't mean that. I thought I might have pulled a muscle or something."

"Let's have a look. Ever had an injury to the leg?"

"Yes, I broke it playing football."

"Oh, the follies of youth. Where was the break?"

"Here," said Bert indicating his shin.

The doctor made him bend it, push with his foot against his hand, palpated the thigh muscle, asked him to indicate exactly where it hurt.

"Nothing obvious, but I'll tell you, Bert, this isn't my specialism."

"No, but you're a doctor Cliff, you know what's going on in the body."

The physician laughed.

"As much as the average G.P. There's more going on we don't understand than we do, otherwise the undertakers would go out of business. When did it start?"

"Oh, I don't know. Two years ago."

"And it's taken you that long to get to the surgery."

"I thought it might pass off."

"You'd be surprised, Bert, how many people I see who have had heart attacks or strokes or surgery for cancer who say exactly the same. If your roof leaks, you call a builder. If you're leg hurts, see a doctor."

"What do you think it is ?"

"No idea. Done anything unusual lately?"

"Unusual ? I made a short trip to India."

"Really?"

"I've become involved with the Satsangis. My friend Tessa is from India and was going to visit relatives. She invited me along."

"Anything happen ? Accidents, illness ?"

"No. Nothing."

After a thorough examination, Tucker concluded he couldn't find anything that looked like the culprit and on the grounds that where there's pain there's inflammation, prescribed anti-inflammatories and told Bert to come back in a week.

The tablets brought some relief. He sat with his leg elevated, his out-of-time mug of tea on the table beside his chair and *The Power and The Glory* in his hands. Andy had mentioned it to him when he studied it for A Level. Bert had never read Greene and thought he'd give it a try. The whiskey priest was an appealing character because of his weakness. It was odd how that made people attractive. A man who was the victim of his desires was much more likely to be popular than someone of Tom Craxton's will power. It seemed to Bert, people wanted to look up to men like Tom, but not to be like them nor friends with them. It was easier to be friends with the bloke who supped seven pints every night, lost half his wages in the bookies and lusted over every woman who didn't look like Ena Sharples. It was queer and confusing. People seemed to have a need to distance from them the qualities they admired, as if to have them near was a reminder of their shortcomings.

The novel was easy to read but he couldn't help feeling he was being slightly manipulated: behind the whiskey priest's terrible dependence, Greene was insinuating a Catholic message. He set the book on the chair arm, thinking of his childhood. The thought of the Catholic church still riled and humiliated him. The whack of the ruler across his knuckles might have happened yesterday and the priests were addicted to something much darker than whiskey. Above all, though, he despised confession, that ritual in which you had to deny your capacity to decide for yourself, and are forced to demean yourself to receive absolution, when humiliation was the *sine qua non* of forgiveness.

He rubbed his thigh. The pain was much more in the background now. He wondered about the trip to India. It was true the pain had become much worse on his return. Or was it the same pain? He'd had the twinge for a long time, but it had come and gone and seemed to be related to movement. He'd assumed it was muscular, but this was something else. Was it the trip? How? Next time he saw Cliff he would tell him.

Bert had high hopes of Wilson's 1974 government. The promise of a shift of wealth and power to working people and their families he took seriously. For himself, it was too late; but for his children and their children a world of equality was possible. When Wilson resigned on 16th March 1976, Bert was shocked. He'd come to think of him as almost indestructible. Prime Minister meant Harold Wilson. A flat-vowelled, Yorkshire man of the common folk who looked as comfortable on a football terrace as at the despatch box. Who would take over? There was talk of Callaghan. Bert didn't dislike him, but he lacked that bite and flair, that willingness to seem ready to expel the money lenders from the nursery which Bert thought a socialist should have. Jenkins impressed him because of his erudition, his literary ability and his capacity for argument, but he didn't trust him fully either. He was too much the type who see politics as a career, an opportunity and not a moral crusade. Bert's favoured candidate was Michael Foot. An obviously highly intelligent but modest man, he had principle as well as fire and he'd been close to Bevan, Bert's model of what a democratic socialist should be.

Callaghan's victory disappointed but didn't dishearten him. What did were the cuts that quickly followed; Denis Healey's argument that it was a matter of arithmetic; the sense that agencies beyond democratic control, the IMF or the World Bank or whatever other huge, distant, incomprehensible institutions could seize the wrists of Prime Ministers or Presidents and twist them up their backs, were forcing a settlement he hadn't voted for. The so-recent promise of a transfer of wealth and power evaporated. It was hard for Bert to retain his feeling for Labour. He listened to Callaghan or Healey justify public sector stinginess and felt he didn't want to be associated with it. It made him anxious. If Labour was doing what he expected the Tories to do, where was the alternative? If it was true the public sector had to be given a short-back-and-sides, where was the promise of a society whose wealth was in the hands of the ordinary folk?

He arrived at the office at eight one Tuesday morning to find Ken Wickham already there.

"Bed catch fire, Ken?"

"Come into my office a minute, Bert."

The big man sat gravely behind his desk, as if he were a physician about to deliver bad news or a Prime Minister on the verge of appearing before the cameras to tell the country it was at war. Bert wanted to laugh out loud. How odd it was that when people with a pinch of petty, passing authority used it to diminish and injure others, they always assumed the demeanour of a headmaster expelling a boy for flooding the toilets. This was the seriousness of those who were determined to inflict pain on others and avoid it themselves. That's why they hid in smart suits and behind big, uncluttered desks; it was why they were full of regret for having to humiliate, degrade and destroy others, but never regretful enough not to do it.

Wickham's attempt to look like the anxiety-burdened executive, the self-consciously powerful and superior man-who-makes-things-happen, increased Bert's disdain. He knew what he was: a spoilt baby, a regressed, the-world-is-my-nipple-and-no-one-else-can-suck-on-it, lazy fantasist who imagined great wealth could fall into his be-ringed hands without effort; a believer in the capitalist myth that prosperity is created by those who move money from one place to another or sit in boardrooms making decisions intended to pack their pockets with twenty pound notes. Bert experienced a sudden loss of faith and realization of error. He'd always been a socialist, at least since he began to think seriously, which was no later than 1945; but he'd always assumed too that equality and the common good could be bundled up in business. He'd run *The Minotaur* out of that conviction. Looking at Wickham he knew it wasn't true. He thought he knew too what Wickham was going to say. How wrong he'd been to work for such a man. What a fool to think his own commitment to hard work and responsibility wasn't mocked by the kind of enterprise men like Wickham ran. What an idiot to lend such a man money.

"This is a very sad day for me, Bert," said the boss, looking up from the desk.

"Is it, Ken?"

"I consider you one of my closest friends."

Bert pressed his lips together and nodded.

"You know me, Bert. I'm the kind of man who values his employees."

"Not enough to pay them their commission," said Bert.

"Now you know that's not true, Bert," said Wickham stretching his arms wide in one of his expansive gestures that were intended to convince the world he was as harmless as a new born child. "I may get a bit behindhand, but I always pay in the end."

"Let's stop beating round the bush shall we? You've got something serious to tell me."

"You know how business works. You're a man of the world. There are ups and downs. The business cycle. We all know that. It's the what makes the world go round."

"I think you may have things in the wrong order there. It's because the world goes round there can be business."

"You know what I mean. There's nothing personal, that's what I'm saying. It's just hard-headed business and you and me both know there's nothing personal about that."

"So you're going out of business."

"No, it's not as bad as that. It's bad. The bank is calling in the debts. I've sold the yacht. The car will have to go. I may have to move house, but I'll keep going."

"What am I here for then?"

"I can't afford you any more, Bert."

"You can't afford not to have me."

"I'm going to have to be a one-man operation for a while."

Bert scoffed.

"You haven't brought a single house onto the books. Do you know how hard you've got to work to do what I do?"

"I'm not afraid of hard work."

"How do you know, you've never done any?"

"I've been the executive, the man who makes the contacts, oils the wheels, but I can get my hands dirty."

"You've been the long lunch, short days and golf course man, Ken. I've made this business work. The essence is to bring houses onto the books and sell them fast. It's because I do the first so well we've been able to do the second. I've made thousands for this firm."

"I don't deny it, Bert. Haven't I always said you're brilliant at your job? You're a genius at it, but the money's run out. I can't keep you, Bert."

"And you think you'll stay in business?"

"I know I will."

"I know you won't."

"We'll see."

"It's a month's notice then ? What else do I get?"

"What d'you mean, Bert?"

"You're making me redundant. You've got to offer me a package, and you owe me commission and four thousand quid. If I'm not working for you anymore I want my money back."

"We've signed an agreement."

"Which you've broken."

"I'll see you get your money. You know me, I'm a man of my word."

"When do I get the commission I'm owed and what's the redundancy deal?"

"I'm a small business, Bert. This isn't ICI. I can't afford redundancy deals."

"You could afford a yacht. You have responsibilities as an employer. You can't just sack me given the length of time I've been here and the money I've made."

"I wish I could afford it, Bert. You know me, I'm a generous man. The truth is, you'll have to leave today."

"Today."

"I'm sorry, Bert, but that's how it is."

"Today."

"It's nothing personal, you know that."

"Give me my commission."

"I can't do that right now."

"But I'm sacked right now."

"It's just hard-headed business, Bert. We know how that works. We're men of the world."

"And my four thousand quid."

"Now, let's be reasonable."

"You're not even giving me a month's notice. What do you think I'm going to live on?"

"Man like you, Bert, you'll walk into a job."

"You know I could take you to law over this."

Wickham looked suddenly crestfallen. A blank look of depression crossed his face.

"You can't sue a man of straw, Bert."

Bert got up, left the office, gathered what belonged to him, said goodbye to the tearful receptionist and drove home.

It was good to be in his own kitchen. The kettle boiled, the water spurted into his cup. He was glad to be free of Ken Wickham. He had no need of him. He had no need of an employer. He resolved he would never be employed again. Employers were cheats, manipulators, exploiters, liars, dissemblers, deceivers, self-obsessed, self-pitying money-grubbers who would say or do anything to get their own way. He would work on his account. He needed to work.

He took his tea and inevitable, thick slice of his homemade, wholemeal bread into the living room to sit in his chair by the window which allowed him to watch whatever happened outside. As he sat down the sharp pain in his thigh make him wince and groan.

"Christ," he said aloud, "what the hell is that?"

His foot on the pouffe, the pain ebbed away over the next few minutes and became a somewhere-in-the-distance pain which made him wary of moving. Was this going to remain for the rest of his life? He had a sudden horrible sense that his death might be much closer then he'd imagined. Like most people, he'd assumed he would grow old. He'd have his three-score-years-and-ten. After that, every morning was a bonus. He was in his mid-fifties and the idea seized his mind that whatever was causing this pain might kill him. In a year? Two? He thought of the will neatly stored in his desk along with his other papers and which left his estate to Mary, Andy and Sylvia. Should he tell Andy where it was?

He fought against the gloomy thoughts. Cliff Tucker would find the answer. In a few months, he might be striding down to the newsagents for his paper as vigorously as when he was twenty-five. He switched his thoughts to money. He had about fifty thousand in savings. He was in no immediate danger. He lived almost frugally. He could get by for ten years without any income and by then he'd be picking up the State pension; but he didn't want to live on that. He wanted an old age in which he could afford to pay for comforts and conveniences. He would have to start a little enterprise. Maybe a vegetarian café or perhaps, if he could find a partner, something more ambitious: a restaurant with a hundred covers, somewhere that attracted lots of visitors. Maybe the Lakes. He'd start looking for opportunities straight away.

He was confident about his position. He had the funds and he'd run a café before. He knew he could do it and make it pay, if he chose the right place and offered what people wanted. Yet beneath his self-assurance he was wounded in a way he hadn't known since he was a child. Not only had he suffered the humiliation of being sacked, he was dismissed by a man he considered a fool, a braggart, a spendthrift, a mirror-gazer, a pompous, arrogant over-estimator of his capacities, a snob, a preening, witless bird who had no idea of the damage his attitude and behaviour did to others. Even worse, his basic rights had been trodden in filth: no period of notice, no redundancy pay and not even payment of his commission or the debt he was owed. Though he tried not to think about it, the effort of his conscious brain couldn't overcome the response of his nervous system. He found himself aware of his racing heart, he broke into a sweat. He was once again that neglected child who had lived in fear of his grandparents' drunkenness, whose life was daily humiliation, yet now he had no future before him, no long years in which to rectify the hurt done him.

He couldn't believe it. How could he be brought low by a man like Wickham? Yet it had happened. He'd walked into the trap. His heart gave a strange leap he'd never experienced, seemed to halt a second, and re-started with a heavy thump. The curious idea came into his head that his heart was beating against life. It was no longer pulsing with happiness and pleasant expectation but with a tense, deathly rhythm. Death was coming for him. He stood up to try to calm himself but the pain in his leg bolted upwards into his groin. He steadied himself against the window sill. He was alone. The terrifying thought came to him that serious illness was going to claim him and he would have to face it without a hand to hold. The fifty odd years of his life condensed into a tableau of major events: childhood, the war, marriage, divorce, and now this. No. It couldn't be true. He would fight it and get back his health.

Every winter he suffered a chest infection. Sometimes he'd been able to carry on. At others, he'd had to take to his bed for two weeks. He knew it was the result of having spent his early years in a damp, poorly heated house. What would happen next time? Was he reaching an age when he wouldn't be able to defeat the infection? Would he die here, alone, in his bed, coughing, sweating, unable even to get to the tap for a glass of water?

He hobbled to the kitchen. The pain receded a little. He would write to Andy. He wondered if it was fair, but he was his son. He needed him and he knew Andy wouldn't want him to be ill and to say nothing. He would write to him. Just in case. A man could live alone but no man could face death alone. He would write to him.

As finals approached, Andy Lang worried more about Carol. She was under pressure now the secret was out and he felt it robbed them of time and relaxation. Something needed to be done fast. She came to see him one Wednesday and as they left his room to go down to wait for her bus, she responded to a stray comment by taking his arm, pulling him to her and saying: "Come here, you fool." There was something in the gesture and comment which provoked a little shock. He was surprised at himself and tried to set his reaction aside. On the way back up to his room having kissed Carol and seen her safely on the bus, he examined his response. Its disproportion suggested it had touched off some lingering anxiety. A comment Rob had made returned to him: "Don't you have doubts about her mind?"

He'd been surprised by that too. He thought Rob and Sue over-estimated him. They commented on his depth and Sue would say: "There's always something going on in that mind of yours." He thought it odd. Wasn't there always something going on in everyone's mind? Yet Rob's comment alerted him to a possible truth and a consequent problem: Carol wasn't an intellectual. She was intelligent, but she wasn't like him, forever turning ideas over and searching through literature for insights. Would that doom their relationship? Was Rob telling him he was setting too much store by their physical relation?

The idea began to trouble him. It was true, their relationship was nothing more than meeting, going to bed and parting. They had no opportunity to spend long hours together, to eat together, to watch a play or film together, to simply enjoy being in one another's company. Perhaps Rob was right and if they lived together the discrepancy between them would be magnified and his feeling would change. The thought began to haunt him that he might be about to take her away from her husband only to be unable to offer her a long-term alternative. Yet how could he close things down after she'd come to see him loyally for nine months, got into his bed and in those few hours made him so happy?

The need to do something urgently produced those wayward ideas which everyone's mind generates when external pressures make moderate thinking impossible: he could forget doing his finals, get the first job he was offered, find a flat; he could do his finals, reject the idea of a PGCE or any other post-grad course, jump into whatever employment he could find; he could persuade her to come to France with him, he could make a living teaching English; but when he dragged himself back to the facts, these were chimeras. Her kids needed their family. They needed to stay close to their grandparents, aunties, uncles and cousins geographically. He couldn't ask her even to move to Lancaster and the thought of going back to Preston depressed him.

He was in the kitchen one evening with Mike. It had been one of those blue-sky, hot, May days which make you hope the summer will be long and rainless. They were making a meal together as they sometimes did. Their friendship had coalesced around these simple shared activities. Mike was preparing a Spanish omelette in the way Patricia's mother had taught him and Andy was gathering a bit of desultory salad as he imitated a television chef, a cross between Fanny Craddock and Philip Harben, the two of them breaking into mad laughter as Mike beat the eggs and Andy doused the lettuce leaves with French dressing, as if he were trying to put out a fire.

They heard the door at the top of the stairs squeak shut and a voice call. They looked at one another.

"Jane Bentnick," said Mike.

The two of them moved to the entrance and at the end of the little corridor they saw Jane, thin and anxious, in a short skirt and low-cut top, an unlit cigarette in her hand. Andy noticed how her thighs, once well-formed and turgid, had lost their bulk. On her face was a curious, pleading, what-am-I-to-do expression and she appeared cramped and tense as if she was about to explode. They stood still, beside one another.

"I wondered if you'd got a light," she said, holding up the cigarette like a choirboy carrying a candle through a nave.

Mike and Andy looked at one another.

"I'll get my lighter," said Mike and headed down the corridor towards his room as Andy went back to his drenched, limp leaves.

Mike was back in two minutes.

"Sort her out ?"

"Yeah."

They said no more but the incident troubled Andy. She didn't need to come across the quad to get a light; he knew her: she always had a *briquet* in her bag. The thought she was trying to re-establish contact shocked him, as did her loss of weight and demeanour. He couldn't keep from his mind the thought she regretted her behaviour; but he had no inclination to go back to her, even as a friend.

She seemed desperate and tormented. How odd, given she'd had the opportunity to establish a relationship with him and had disdained it. Thinking his way into her mind was disturbing. Anyone could make a mistake, but that wasn't it. There was some terrible disjuncture between one part of her mind and another. That odd feeling he'd had with Janice Eaves, Geraldine Bone, and Carol too that he knew their minds better than they did made his heart beat anxiously. Was it true of him? Did other people read his mind and see what was hidden from him?

What would he do if Jane knocked on his door? It wasn't his instinct to turn people away, but he couldn't let her in. She'd probably drop her clothes on the floor and lie on his bed. He stayed out of her way. One morning he was heading for a revision seminar on Rabelais when pushing though one of the doors in Lonsdale College which seemed made to test weightlifters she appeared in the corridor at the other side. He held the door to let her pass. She lifted her chin, stiffened and went on her way.

Thoughts of Jane and her disturbed mind mingled with the nagging, bothersome urgency to resolve things with Carol. She rang him one Thursday, at lunchtime, to ask if he she should come in the evening. Without thinking about it, he said she'd better not.

"Don't you want me to come any more?" she said.

That hadn't been his intention at all. He was merely postponing a visit because he had a dozen books waiting to be read and in the back of his mind was the notion that if the intensity of their liaison eased a little, he might better see a way through; but her sudden conclusion that this first refusal meant absolute rejection sparked the thought that she wanted a resolution and had entertained the belief that things were now hopeless.

"Maybe not," he said.

"Okay, then. 'Bye, Andy."

"See you."

He didn't hear from her again. He worried that he'd been cruel and thought of ways to contact her. It would be easy enough. He could find a means to bump into her; but at the same time he wondered if she hadn't reached the point where the tension between her affair with him and her love of her children had become unbearable. Perhaps she'd leapt on his turning down her offer as the way out she needed. Or was it she just wasn't sure of him or that his reservations had found their way into her mind and she'd precipitated the break she was afraid of?

The hard work for finals pushed all this from his mind and when they were over and he and his mates relaxed, spent their days in the bar, playing tennis, kicking a ball around, chatting about what they were going to do with their futures, a fresh, clean, happy, generous, spirit of hope arose in him. There was nothing he could do about the past. He enjoyed a few weeks of utterly light-hearted joy, and the weather proved better than hoped for. One day he was lying on his back on the grass by the big sycamore above the lake, Sue Border by his side in her charming, long, Indian cotton skirt and skinny white top which showed off her lovely breasts, when she plucked a long stalk and tickled his belly, exposed by his shirt having pulled out of his jeans.

"Sue," he said, "stop it."

"Don't you like it?" she said, leaning over him so that when he opened his eyes and raised his head her face was two inches from him, pretty, young and expectant.

"I like it a lot," he said. "So stop it."

He took the grass from her hand. She gave a little indulgent laugh which showed her lovely, white teeth and kissed his forehead.

He sat up.

"Where's that bugger Green got to, anyway?"

"Here he is," she said.

Andy turned his head to see his mate coming over the brow, his long, curly, fair hair lifting in the breeze, his blue shirt outside his faded denims with the holes in the knees.

"What you been up to?" he said as Rob sat next to Sue.

"Just been looking at Bergson's *Le Rire* to see where I went wrong in the exam."

"That must've been a laugh."

"I'm knackered," Rob said, lying down. "Did you read it?"

"Yeah, *du mécanique plaque sur du vivant*. It's good as far as it goes but it doesn't get to the physiology. What goes on in the brain that triggers laughter?"

"Every joke is the death of an emotion," said Rob.

"That's sounds very clever," said Sue.

"Herr Freud," said Andy "the hysterics' nemesis."

"Don't we think Wilhelm Reich is better than Freud?"

"Have you built your orgone box yet?" said Rob.

"I'm still trying to break through my character armour."

They'd had a flirtation with Reich, *The Mass Psychology of Fascism* being the book that impressed them most. It tallied with ideas which had found their feet in the sixties and it seemed in keeping with their instinctive sense that people who were loving and easy-going in their relationships were less likely to be attracted by the hatred and violence of fascism; but their enthusiasm had soon waned and Reich's theories began to seem simplistic and mechanistic. Rob had punctured the affiliation by saying that orgasms don't give rise to ideas; thinking does.

"You need more climaxes, mate," said Rob.

"Yes, I think I'll go and look for one. Do they sell them in *Spar*?"

He got up, shoved his thin, blue and white striped shirt into his jeans and waved goodbye. He was glad to leave Rob and Sue together, but slightly disturbed. Sue was very attractive. He was sure he could resist her, if she was being anything other than affectionate to a friend. In any case, the end of term was near, he'd decided to take up the offer of a PGCE at St Martin's, Lancaster's teacher-training college. Rob was doing the same but Sue was provisional. She'd been offered a place but wasn't sure she was going to accept, so in the autumn, she might no longer be around.

On the last day of term, when his trunk had been dispatched to his mother's and his rucksack and holdall were packed, he was struck by how quickly the time had gone. He'd been at home at university. The atmosphere was congenial. In spite of his difficulties with Andrew Steiner and having ended up with a degree in French rather than English, to be in a place where asking fundamental questions was taken for granted was uplifting. He didn't realize that by choosing to become a schoolteacher he was leaving it behind; that schools are more petty-minded, more obsessed with discipline, more conformist and determined to drive adolescents through the exam system rather than open their minds to the excitement of thinking.

He entertained the delusion that the intellectual values he cherished would be welcome in school. He didn't know that most people disdain intellectuals and that they need places of protection; he was unaware that what he should do is fight with every cell to spend his life where the free pursuit of truth was given a high value, where no one thought it odd to spend hours every day reading and where your hard work was done at a typewriter.

An odd impulse came to him. He wandered over to Block 3 and climbed the stairs to the top floor. Jane's was the last room on the left. He thought he'd knock and if she was there, shake her hand, smile and wish her well; but the door was wide and the room bare. All that was left was a magazine on the desk facing him. He went to look. It was a glossy, empty-headed Sunday supplement folded on itself, the spine pressed straight and firm. He stared at it for a few seconds. In that compressed seam he could see the unbearable tension of her leaving. How odd, when she had so disdained the place. He turned and left.

What was it she found so hard to leave behind? He didn't want to think about it.

He, Rob, Sue and Mike went to the railway station to see Mike off for France. There were promises to visit him, but Andy knew the keen, sustaining friendship he'd relished for the past nine months was over. He had no desire to lose it. How strange it was that life must take people away from what they cherish. Mike was going to Patricia, of course, and she was much more important than he was; but circumstance and ambition could be great disrupters of inner peace.

Rob and Sue were making a final visit to the *Etna* for lunch. He shook Rob's hand and kissed Sue's cheek. Alone on the bus back to campus to collect his belongings and walk down to the stop to wait for the number forty for Preston, he was caught between nostalgia and anticipation. He could hardly believe that what was to come would be as good as the delight of Bailrigg; he had a horrible sense that in his mid-twenties, perhaps the best of life was already behind him; but like all young people, he had to believe the future would be full of possibility. For the time being though, was the anti-climax of going back to Preston, to his mother's and of finding some job to bring in a few quid.

Elsie was glad to see him, but depressed at the thought that at twenty-five he still wasn't established in his own home. It didn't occur to her that she'd lived in her father's house till she was thirty-three. She made allowances for herself: her bed-ridden mother had needed her; the war had made houses hard to find. Mary was married at twenty-one. She expected the same of Sylvia; but Andy, would he still be relying on her for a roof when he was forty? The culture of study, of reading much and earning little was alien to her. She came from the working-class. In her day, there was none of this university business. You got a job and started earning as soon as you could. *Our lads*, as she always called her brothers, were out of school and on a wage at fourteen. What was the point of all this study if it didn't get you a job?

Sylvia was now enmeshed with Barry. Andy liked him: he was a straightforward, working-class lad, obviously intelligent, one of those millions the education system had cut down, like a lawn mower spurting the tough, tall grass into its box to be dumped on the compost heap. His intelligence wasn't like his own; he had no feeling for language or literature, but at practical or mechanical tasks he outshone Andy by miles. The thermostat on the immersion heater had been faulty for some time. Elsie, anxious about expense as usual, had stalled. She flicked the switch when no hot water was needed and to the gurgling of the tank responded with insouciance: it would be all right.

Barry diagnosed the problem as soon as he was told.

"Let's have a look," he said and after five minutes in the bathroom came down the stairs two at a time. "Yep, thermostat. I can get one tomorrow. I'll pop round after work and fit it."

And he did. At no cost. Elsie tried to force a pound note on him but he dismissed the idea with a laugh.

The calm operation of the repaired water tank made Elsie realise she should have done something about it long ago. Sylvia and Barry were out together and Andy was in the back room hammering away at the typewriter. She sat alone on the sofa letting the television drivel spew over her, like a woman trapped in a sewer. Her attitude to Barry was transformed. She'd disdained and despised him from his first visit. He was vulgar and presumptuous and what she learned of his family disheartened her: drinkers, smokers, spendthrifts. She brought her daughter up a Methodist. How could she have strayed? She had no inkling that nothing appeals to people more than the opposite of what they are forced to endure: a bread and water diet brings a craving for cream cakes and champagne.

Now she began to say to herself he was a *grand lad*, the designation she'd always applied to those boys and men from her early days who worked hard at essential jobs for modest pay, were sober, modest, responsible and reliable. The very opposite of Bert with his big ideas, his fancy clothes, his pretentions about music and books. Barry was as handy as a pen-knife. Through her mind began to pass all the jobs that needed doing: the garage door hung drunkenly from its top hinge; the pebbledash by the front door was crumbling; the cold tap in the bathroom dripped as regularly as the tick of doom; the woodwork in the front upper bay that Andy had repaired needed replacing; there were two slates awry; the storm door caught on the tiles; the pipes in the loft needed lagging. She would have liked to have given him a list.

Little by little she insinuated into Sylvia's mind the idea that he could busy himself:

"There's that garage door needs repairing," she'd say for the ninth time, "it's been hanging like that for I don't know how long. I can't open it, way it drags. It'll be falling off one of these days and then what shall I do?"

Barry arrived with timber, brought his tools from his boot and after three hours with the saw, the plane, the screwdriver and the hammer had the cracked and damaged tongue and groove repaired and the door swinging as easily as a hammock. While he worked, Elsie prepared food. He left his overalls outside and came to the table for steak and chips.

"Oh, I'm ready for this," he said, "hungry work."

"You've done a good job, Barry," said Andy. "Is there anything you can't do?"

"We have a go," he said, reaching for a slice of white bread and margarine," but nowt's easy."

It wasn't long before Elsie's incantation became:

"I shall 'ave to find someone to go on that roof. If them slates slip down they could have your 'ead off."

Barry lifted his dad's wooden ladder from his car, climbed up, exposed a bare square and replaced the slates so they were firm and symmetrical once more.

"You could do with some waterproof underfelting," he said. "I'll get some and do the whole roof for you."

"Ee, there's no need for that, Barry," she said. "No rain's getting in. I were just bothered about them slates hitting someone ont th'ead. That's all. It's right now, Barry, you don't need to go to all that trouble."

He fitted new taps in the bathroom, brought his float, mixed cement and fixed the hole in the pebbledash, cut out the rotten timber from the front bay and replaced it as neatly as if he was time-served joiner; took the storm door from its hinges, planed the bottom and sweating and struggling with the weight, single-handedly re-hung it, and disappeared through the loft access with a bundle of sacking in his hands. He wouldn't take a penny. Elsie began to think that her long-held fear that she wouldn't be able to stay in Woodland Grove because the cost of maintaining the house would defeat her, could be set aside. In her imagination, Barry became almost her estate manager. She painted the new panels in the garage door herself (though Andy had offered), she even threatened to get up the step-ladder and paint the landing ceiling, but Barry covered the carpet in old sheets and had it done in an afternoon.

She became fond of him and was glad to cook for him if he stayed long enough or to regale him with a mug of tea, a plate of cakes and a-thousand-and-one-night stories of the training kitchen if he was in a hurry.

Andy was glad for Sylvia and his mother. Barry was a good presence. Sylvia had a chance of breaking free. His only regret was that she was unlikely to move away. Mary was distant enough for his mother not to intrude and he lived a life that baffled her; but if Sylvia ended up living close by he feared his mother's regression would make her an interloper.

One evening, Sylvia idled into the back room while Andy was clacking the typewriter keys. Beside him were two piles of A4, one of carbon copies.

"What you writing?" she said, standing by him.

"It's a novel," he said.

"Why two copies?"

"One for me, one for the publisher."

"Is it going to be published?"

"No."

She looked at him and they both laughed.

"What's the point, then?"

"Well, that's literature. Not Agatha Christie or Mickey Spillane, they're just high-quality typists. Real writers spend years producing books that get turned down by every publisher on the planet. After being rejected nine thousand times your book gets published, sells fifteen copies and disappears. Then five thousand years after you're dead it gets discovered and everyone weeps over its appalling neglect and shakes their heads in dismay at the stupidity of publishers."

"What's it about ?"

"Life in the cage that is contemporary society."

"Why is it a cage ?"

"Because it suits the rich and powerful. They live in the cage of their own delusions, so they think everyone else must do the same."

She picked up a page and began to read. He watched as she stood silently, following the fuzzy black letters. She was a young woman now and he could no longer easily put his arm round her, cuddle her and kiss her cheek. She was still his worry as she'd been when his dad was kicked out. Through all the years he'd tried to be a barrier between his mother's straight-for-your-nerves way of relating and the tender stem of her developing self-hood. He'd liked to believe he'd succeeded: without him she'd have lacked humour, irony, fun. The house would have been filled by his mother's self-pitying, demanding, stiff, factitiously serious inwardness.

Yet looking at her, he knew the damage had been done. She'd learned to layer over her terrible inner confusion, isolation and despair with a somewhat strident, too-cocky, voluble, loud self-assertion. He understood that what lay beneath could never be rectified. There was only one chance to grow up. A tree that is bent by the wind will never be straight. He came back to language as his model. He'd read Chomsky's *Language and Mind* and flitted about among books and papers on acquisition. What had penetrated was the recognition that the capacity for language is innate, but requires a social trigger. He wondered how much of our minds followed the same rule. A new-born child kept away from human community wouldn't speak or comprehend, even though everything required was delivered by natural selection. If it was true that something as fundamental as language needed a social trigger, might it not be true of most of our capacities?

What might Sylvia have been had she grown up where there was relaxation, love and confidence? He knew part of her mind had failed to flourish, just as a child deprived of protein or sunlight or exercise would suffer some physical deficit. She might have been a splendid young woman full of confidence and *joie de vivre*; but the last thing his mother had wanted was confident children. He'd said to her, about his nephew, after a visit to Mary's:

"He's a confident little boy."

She'd turned away sullenly without a word.

Yet he didn't blame his mother. Had someone sat her down and explained to her, someone wise and educated; had she been shown that her behaviour was damaging her children. Had she been told that to deprive them of a relationship with their father was to rob them of something they had a right to; that her relationship with him was one thing, theirs another; had she been made aware of the way her resentment had twisted her mind and was driving her mad and could only injure her offspring, she would have changed. She was uneducated, alone, lost, and she interpreted everything through the only powerful, over-arching set of ideas she'd ever been offered: Methodism.

She was a victim of poverty, inequality, absence of real democracy and of her gender. He blamed the society which had formed her because he knew that none of us could be anything except through society. Without it, we couldn't even speak. Beethoven born ten thousand years ago couldn't have played the piano, Shakespeare born before the emergence of theatre couldn't have been a dramatist. Music and theatre were social accomplishments. Even genius was impotent without the right social context.

His mother was born a working-class female in a society which exploited and sneered at its workers and abused and denigrated its women. What chance did she have? He couldn't save her. He had tried hard. He'd been the best son he could but his mother's problems exceeded a son's love. So did Sylvia's a brother's. He hoped Barry would be her salvation. He hoped in his love she would find something of what was denied her and become a fulfilled woman. He hoped she would treat her own children with kindliness and a smile, *slow to chide and swift to bless*, as his mother would often quote.

She had been often indulgent; but indulgence is lazy and sentimental. It's love that's hard. Some fear held her back. Somehow, she was irrevocably trapped within herself.

"I don't understand it," she said.

"'Course you do. All the words are simple."

"I know, but it still doesn't make sense to me."

"It doesn't make sense to me either and I wrote it."

She laughed.

"How can it not make sense to you?"

"Well," he said, "think of a dream. You know, you're flying over the houses, then you're on the bus. An elephant comes to take your fare. You find yourself running so fast you overtake all the cars. Then the dentist is pulling out all your teeth. You look into his face and it's Reginald Maudling. It doesn't make sense, but it came from your brain. Writing is a bit like that. It taps into things going on beneath your normal, in-control consciousness."

"How do you do that?"

"I've no idea. You just have to work at it. Get going and work at it. If you're lucky, it'll come."

"Do you think you've been lucky with this?"

"Not yet. When I read through it I want to be sick on the floor. I'll have to re-write it six or seven times."

"Six or seven. That'll take ages."

"I know. If I get to ninety-three and haven't moved from this desk call an ambulance."

"All that work and it might not even get published."

"Ars longa vita brevis."

"What's that mean?"

"It means art lasts much longer than we do as individuals. Art is social. That's why we still read Sophocles and Shakespeare."

"You do, I don't."

"Well, you should little sister, you should. They're good for you."

He wasn't at his mother's long. He responded to an ad in *The Guardian*, was called for an interview in Didsbury, sat for an hour with Paddy Devlin in a chaotic office in the converted front room of a Victorian semi and was appointed as a teacher of English for eight weeks with *Albion North International* at their centre in Morecambe.

ANI had been set up three years earlier by Devlin and his partner Steve Dowling, teachers from an adult education college in Southport who had a side-line in private lessons for Italian waiters and other foreign workers in need of emergency skills. It had occurred to them one morning break over tepid coffee that there might be market for lessons and activities for foreign kids during the summer. They took out adverts in the French press, got a stunning response and realised they could be on their way to millions. They employed whoever they could (Andy was the sole linguist taken on for the Morecambe centre), kept the costs low and raked in plenty. Dowling, easy-going and liberal, argued with the older man over his skinflint approach.

"For fuck's sake, Paddy, the kids have to be entertained in the afternoons. If it's raining and we have to pay for them to go to the cinema, we'll just have to bear the cost."

"A hundred and twenty kids," said Devlin, scribbling on a scrap of paper, "do you realize what that comes to? There's a gym isn't there?"

"Have you seen it? A table tennis table and two bats. Come on, Paddy, this is asking for trouble."

"No. They can't go. Tell them they have to stay in the gym. Send them back to the families early."

Dowling shook his head.

"This is no way to run a fucking business, Paddy."

Andy was pleased to be able to return to Lancaster. It had a different feel from Preston. Industrial to some degree, its past wasn't as marred by mills, terraced streets and brutal architecture. It advertised itself as an historic town. Visitors came to see the Castle and the university imbued it with a sense of learning, cosmopolitanism and values less utilitarian than those of commerce. He thought he'd try for a room on campus, but when he went there for a day, spotted a flyer advertising a room in a shared house in Bare, on the outskirts of Morecambe. He made the call, found the rent was cheap, jumped on the train, met Tony Eccleston who looked after things with the landlord and moved in the next day. It was a standard three-bedroom, inter-war semi, roomy and well-cared for with a small front garden and a big rear lawn, flower beds and a blossoming cherry. He had the back room downstairs where there was easily space for the bed, a desk in the bay window, a wardrobe and a chest of drawers. The other residents were Gordon Daniels, a management trainee with National Bus; Diane Bannister, a devout Catholic primary school teacher who seemed to think it was her mission to save the rest of them from perdition, and Wendy Brown, a promiscuous bank clerk whose room was above Andy's and whose bed shook nightly from her vigorous activity with whoever she decided to bring home.

"I suppose," she said to him airily soon after he moved in, "love is having sex with someone you like. I'm afraid it's never happened to me."

The summer was hot and dry. Day after day not a hint of rain. Andy bought a second-hand bike, a big, heavy, straight-handle-bar thing and rode back and forth to the centre where in the morning he taught English to his class of fifteen French and Spanish teenagers and in the afternoon, took them to *Happy Mount Park* to play tennis or bowls, swimming if Paddy Devlin could be persuaded to release the money, or sat with them in the hellish gym where they became bored and badly behaved as the sun beat down and they were forbidden to leave.

SACKED

The other students who'd been taken on as teachers included an engineer, a PE man, an artist, a mathematician and a physicist. Every day, at least one of them came to him to ask for help and resources. No books were provided. Andy produced his own teaching material each evening.

"Some of them know hardly any English at all," said John Whittle, the tall, broad, pleasant athlete, "where do I begin?"

"Here," said Andy, "try this. It's a simple gap exercise. They just have to find the right verb from the list at the bottom to complete each sentence. Once they've got through it, you can show them how the verbs are formed.."

"How are they formed?"

"Well, look. For example, this one. *We built* is irregular. You know, the regular form is we played, we danced, we watched; but to build doesn't use that *ed* suffix."

"Christ, I don't understand that. I think I'll just play some games with them."

And he did. While the others made an effort with tenses, adjectives, adverbs, gerunds, he moved the desks aside, carried the kids on his back, had them doing press ups and sit-ups.

Andy enjoyed being with the youngsters, liked his colleagues and got on well too with Tony Eccleston whose life at the time was dominated by a failed love affair. They went to the pub together and Tony told him the story. They were to be married, but she ran off with one of his friends. Tony was a trainee architect unsure about his choice of career.

"Well, there's plenty of time, Tony, both to change your mind and to find another woman."

"Yeah," said Tony and he laughed in the charming way which screwed up his sympathetic face. "Rats."

And the two of them roared and drank their beer.

GERONIMO

In January 1977 Andy began his term's teaching practice at Witton Park High School, Blackburn. When he was allocated the school, he called at his dad's, the first time he'd been there, to tell him.

"Well, you can live here," said Bert with alacrity.

Andy hadn't intended to suggest moving in, but he was glad his dad was eager. He hadn't lived with him since he was eleven. He was aware of the absence in himself. There was the embarrassment, of course. He was the only person at school whose parents were divorced, the only one among his mates at university. When he'd first got to know Blackie and they'd been at his house, kicking a ball in the garden or messing in the garage or lying on the lawn in the sun after a game of tennis, his mate had noticed the lacuna and had said:

"Why is your dad never here?"

It was mortifying to say the word *divorced*. It was shameful and indicative of failure, irresponsibility, loss, outsidership, even degeneracy. Yet none of his mates were ever cruel or mocking. Once they knew, they said nothing. Except Marek, who was aware his dad had left and said to him one day when they were following a path through the school woods:

"I saw in the paper about your parents' divorce. My mum spotted it. Sorry to hear that."

He still suffered from the stigma. If possible he avoided talking about his parents. Yet that wasn't the cause of the inner blank. He knew that having lived in a house dominated by his mother had shut down some activity in his brain. Had his dad been there, an everyday presence, a masculine presence, he would have responded to him and across all those years it would have made a difference. He knew he was marked by a passivity which was derived from his mother's character: she'd been formed by the male-dominated culture of working-class Preston in the twenties and thirties. Her domestic dominance was the compensation for the narrowness of her possibilities. Then there was Methodism with its replication of the work disciplines of the economic system and schooling which had implanted fear of authority at the core of her.

In some barely acknowledged corner of his mind, Andy hoped that by spending time with his dad, what had never developed could be recovered. Yet in the full light of consciousness and beneath the glare of intellectual inspection, he knew it was hopeless. The damage he had suffered had to be lived with.

Elsie, of course, was livid to hear he was staying with Bert. She didn't want to blame her son. She didn't want to revile him, yet she found it hard to forgive him. It was a betrayal. She was the victim. She was innocent. All sympathy should be hers. She calmed her anger by telling herself it was an arrangement of convenience: Andy needed somewhere to stay in Blackburn; he could avoid rent. That's all it was.

Andy walked to and from school, carrying his packed, brown leather briefcase. The children were largely from Mill Hill, a working-class area replete with the problems thrown up by poverty and lack of hope. On his introductory visit, a Deputy Head, a tall, ungainly man with thick, dark brown hair combed into a half-accomplished quiff, had regaled him with melodramatic statistics: fifty per cent of the pupils came from homes where there was no one working, or alcoholism, or drug abuse, or domestic violence, or a parent in prison, or child molesting, or mental illness. Andy almost wanted to rehearse the mantra of his ex R.E. teacher: "Are you bragging or complaining?" The man had a curious, self-indulgent smile as he recounted the misfortunes. He was one of those professionals who feel they must always be justifying themselves, letting everyone know how hard they work and how difficult their life is. His wife taught Geography in the school. On his first day, she said to Andy in the staffroom:

"You'll be lucky to survive."

Andy liked the pupils. They were children who knew what the world was doing to them. They were destined for factories, building sites, shops, offices, driving buses, sweeping hair, wiping tables. They knew they lived in a rigged society and they took it philosophically. Their attitude to school was grudging tolerance. It was something that had to be done, like cleaning your teeth, but they had no enthusiasm for it. They didn't see it as the route to fulfilment or self-justification. They knew where they were. Universities were for the kids who went Queen Elizabeth's Grammar, or Westholme or Stoneyhurst. There were limited places and those kids would get them because they were prepared for them. The Witton Park kids didn't have a chance. If a teacher was sympathetic, got on with it and was relatively interesting, they'd give her the benefit of the doubt; but they scoffed at the idea that school was their escape from routine, low-paid work.

Some of them had dads who worked for themselves: plumbers, joiners, electricians, plasterers. They did okay, so the sons assumed they'd take on their mantle. Some of the mothers were nurses or midwifes or ran their own hairdressing salon and the daughters believed that would be their life too; but no one believed that if they did their homework, listened in every lesson and revised like donkeys for exams, they would be reading Greats at Balliol. They'd never heard of either.

No one had ever spelled out to them what their position in society and the education system was. They didn't need to. No one needs to be told it will be cold in February. They breathed the air and drank the water of inequality and they knew they were near the bottom. What astonished Andy was how biddable they were, how little trouble they caused, how, essentially, they wanted to be good children, to belong, to be loved, to be well thought of.

In his second year English class was a boy with an emotional age of three and an intellectual age of five. Jason Carter lived with his mum and three older sisters. His dad had left when he was a baby and he'd never seen him. His mother got by on tranquilizers, booze, fags and benefits. He found it hard to stay in his seat. If something went through his head, it had to come out of his mouth. When Andy took in their books for the first time, he realised the boy was functionally illiterate. He sat next to Neil Bancroft, a tall, blonde, slow, patient, bespectacled lad who tried his best to help his classmate:

"Sit down, Jason, come on. Let sir get on with it."

When his mate dashed to the back of the room to look out of the window because he'd heard voices in the playground, Neil would push his glasses up his nose, look at Andy and say:

"Shall I get him, sir?"

"If you would, Neil."

The class would wait and watch. Neil, a foot and a half taller than Jason, would put his arm round his shoulders and coax:

"Let's sit down. It's nowt. It were someone crossing't playground, that's all."

Jason would set off, run three times round the room, bang onto his chair out of puff, while the rest of the pupils applauded and cheered.

Last thing on Friday he took them for their reader. It was a *Day of the Triffids* type book for teenagers called *The Arrival*. After the first restless lesson he decided he would get them to act it out. They shifted the tables, he allocated parts and let them improvise their lines. Jason ran around wildly, called out while the scenes were underway.

"Shut up, Jason," they told him.

"Yeah, shut up, we can't hear."

It was difficult to organize and keep within bounds and by four Andy was exhausted; but the kids liked it and it was a good way to end the week. Walking home one Friday, he heard running footsteps behind him. A breathless girl, her hair swept by the wind, appeared at his side.

"That were great, sir," she said.

"You liked it, did you Ruth ?"

"Yeah, it were fantastic, sir. I like actin'"

"Well, maybe I'll see you on stage someday, eh?"

"I don't think so, sir. I'm too thick."

"You're not thick at all. You're a clever girl. You were brilliant."

She gave an embarrassed laugh, blushed and ran ahead.

"See you on Monday, sir."

His supervisor came to see him teach them. She frowned through the lesson and in the feedback said:

"That was chaos."

"They enjoyed it though."

"It was appalling. Pupils were running around. Some were chatting. Most of them didn't take part."

"They all get a chance. We change roles each week."

"That's not the point is it? It's supposed to be a reader. They weren't reading they were playing."

"Last thing on Friday," he said. "They need to let off a bit of steam. But they're more interested in the characters now than they would be if we just read it aloud and answered questions. They get bored by that."

"You weren't teaching," she said. "They were making far too many decisions for themselves."

"What's wrong with that?"

"I have to assess your teaching and there wasn't any in that lesson."

Andy wondered if he should abandon the idea. She'd failed his lesson and if she came to see him teach the same class again and did the same, he might be kicked off the course. Sitting in his dad's kitchen, eating the stuffed peppers he'd made, listening to the news on Radio 4 about IRA bombings in the West End, he was repelled by his pusillanimity: what did it matter if they threw him out? If he was going to be a teacher, it wasn't to do what three-bags-full, teacher training college, my-job-before-all-things, time-servers wanted. He was going to challenge the very nature of the education system. His conviction, through reading Piaget and John Holt, John Dewey and A.S. Neill was that education must be voluntary: a place must be available for every child, but no one must be forced to learn. Let children choose. They'll find their way to what interests and inspires them, and then they'll learn quickly and deeply and most importantly, learning won't be experienced as a penance.

His dad got up from the stool beside him.

"Oh, Christ."

He was bent, rubbing at his thigh, grimacing and unable to move.

"All right, dad?"

"God knows what this bloody thing is."

"You'd better sit down in the lounge."

Bert hobbled through and took up his beginning-of-time position by the window with his leg elevated.

"That's a bit better."

"Want some painkillers?"

"No, I've taken a couple."

Throughout the term, his dad winced, groaned, moaned, shook his head, limped but didn't go back to the doctor.

"You should pester him," said Andy.

"He doesn't know what it is."

"Get a referral. Pay if you have to."

"There speaks a good socialist."

"Okay, I'm a hypocrite. In principle I'm opposed to it, but we are where we are. I'd like private practice shoved out of the NHS. For the time being, if you're in as much pain as you are and you've a few quid in the bank, get to see someone who can help."

"Who does he refer me to as he doesn't know what's wrong?"

"Well, you know, G.P.s are well-trained, but they're what the title says: generalists. And they aren't geniuses. You need someone who can take time, find out about you, your health record, your habits, your diet. The devil's always in the detail."

"You might be right. I'll make an appointment with Cliff and chat it over."

Andy had no idea what the problem might be. When his dad had first mentioned it, he thought it was probably muscular, but now that was ruled out. Something was wrong deep in his thigh. What could it be? Could cancer start in the thigh? Maybe. Bone cancer. Or maybe something to do with nerves or circulation. Whatever it was it didn't seem trivial or passing. Nevertheless, apart from his leg, his dad seemed vigorous and thriving. Surely, he'd get over it. He just needed to nag the physicians till someone got to the bottom of it. Andy wondered if he should tell his mother; and Mary and Sylvia. If it was going to turn into something serious, he should. Maybe his sisters would soften and visit. He even wondered if Elsie might discover enough sympathy to come and see him if he was hospitalised; but he dismissed the ideas as melodramatic. His dad would be okay if he got the right intervention quickly enough.

The weeks went by quickly. He was up at seven, out of the house by quarter past eight, back at four thirty, his head down over lesson plans by six. He had a thick file but his supervisor, on her two visits hadn't asked to see it. He lifted his head from his writing: was it worth the effort? Should he give it up on the gamble she wouldn't ask for it? If she did and he had only half a term's plans and reviews, he'd definitely fail. Tush. How lousy it was to have to do what you knew to be unnecessary because some apparatchik with the imagination of a slug insisted on it.

At half-term he met Rob in *The Sawyer's Arms*, Manchester. He'd had his hair cut so it no longer touched his shoulders.

"So, how are things at Hutton?" said Andy.

"Pretty antediluvian."

Andy had laughed when he heard his mate had been allocated the school some of his old mates had attended.

"Watch out for Fatkegs," he'd said.

"Who?"

"Head of German and notorious for his inclination to little boys' genitals."

Having been sent to Bury Grammar at eleven, Rob was familiar with the atmosphere of boys' grammars with pretentions to private status. He knew the unnaturalness of the segregation of the sexes, the unspoken odour of homosexuality which hung in the corridors, the masters boys knew to be wary of.

"In what ways?"

"Oh, every official document addresses staff as Masters. *When completing the register Masters must ensure*..But there are four or five female members of staff."

"You should organise them. Have a little coup and force the place to slither into the nineteenth century."

"The women don't complain. Everyone goes along with it."

"How'd you get on with the staff of stiffs?"

"They're okay. I don't not get on with them. Some of the younger staff are lefties. There's an English teacher, Mick Nixon, he's okay. The place frustrates him and he kicks against the pricks. Only been there two years. I get on with him."

"Got to know Fatkegs."

"Yeah, my timetable is mostly German."

"Has he propositioned you yet?"

"I'm too old."

"Still at it, is he?"

"Not the only one, I guess."

"Kids all right?"

"Yeah. Cocky because they're middle-class. Some real arrogant little gits, think they're entitled to pre-eminence; but they get on with the work and don't cause trouble, so the job's easy. Bet you can't say that about Witton."

"They're not middle-class and brimming with entitlement. I like 'em. Kids are kids. They all need the same things. They're full of life and they're funny. Take the piss out of everything. I heard a kid on the corridor singing to the tune of that bloody awful "*I am a linesman for the County* thing: *I am a dustman for the Council*. That's clever and irreverent. They're clever but they don't know it, because they don't use their intelligence in the way the system demands. How's Sue doing?"

"Doddle. Gets me to do her lesson plans, but Lancaster Girls', not exactly testing."

"Well, good for her."

Sue, scion of a middle-class family from Croydon, educated in a girls' grammar had been allocated a school which tallied with her background. It was obvious the college hadn't picked schools at random. Rob had got Hutton Grammar because he'd been to Bury Grammar, and he, Andy, Witton Park because he'd been consigned to Penwortham Secondary. He mulled it over on the train: wouldn't it have been better to do the opposite? They were training to teach in a national system; shouldn't they get a taste of its variety? It was like the allocation of schools for the year abroad: ingrained assumptions drove people's behaviour. Wittingly or otherwise, the college was reinforcing class divisions and attributing its students to categories. He was working-class, Secondary Modern, up-by-his-bootlaces and so best kept away from grammar school pupils. Sue was middle-class grammar, so too precious to have to handle the scuffed-shoe and no-breakfast kids from Mill Hill.

The first half-term had convinced him he didn't want to be a teacher. He enjoyed the work. He liked the youngsters; but the sense of being part of a system fuelled by the wrong values dragged him down. The staff at Witton were for the most part honest, hard-working folk who put the children first. The Head of English, Yvonne Edmondson, was a Labour councillor; one of those committed idealists busy from five in the morning till midnight trying to improve the lives of the left-behind. She seemed to have no time for herself. Andy liked her because of her lack of self-absorption, her modesty, her inexhaustible energy and her way with words. To one of her colleagues who was going camping over the half-term, she said as she drew on her cigarette:

"You'll be bivouacking in the hills then, Bernard."

She could often find some slightly unusual way of expressing herself and her vocabulary surpassed most. She was in her mid-forties and had three children. Andy would watch her as she diligently marked a set of books, a three-cigarette task, or listen in on her conversations while pretending to read the paper. She was the kind of woman (apart from her tobacco habit) he would like for a wife. The kind of woman he could both love and admire.

Yet she was also the kind of woman who wouldn't be a Headteacher or Deputy. She was too independent, too willing to speak her mind, too intent on spiking injustice, too unwilling to nod to bureaucrats or to tear out her own heart for the sake of a pension.

The place was run by a male trio: John Kellet, the dapper, greying, dark-suited Head who joined the staff for coffee every morning break in an effort to seem accessible and one-of-the-workers, but who spent most of his time behind his office door and cultivated the demeanour of superiority managers employ to conceal the fact they are often less competent than those they manage; Colin Southworth who had responsibility for discipline, worked like an ant, got on well with the staff and was as unpretentious as a rose; and Gerry Watkinson, who had given Andy the how-bad-it-is-here talk and who little by little he had come to despise.

Watkinson was the more senior of the Deputies and acted as Kellet's guard-dog. He sent his own children to private school and was one of those comprehensives-have-wrecked-the-grammar-schools throwbacks whose view of education was predominantly nostalgic. Neither he nor his wife tried to conceal their silk-purse-and-sows'-ears view of education for kids like those from Mill Hill. To Andy, Yvonne Edmondson was everything that was right about schools and Watkinson and Kellet everything that was wrong; but it was the latter who had the power.

During the second half of term, he thought more and more about what he would be entering if he became a teacher: if you stayed in the classroom, like Yvonne, arse-licking, no-pole-is-too-greasy-for-me place seekers would overtake you and rule over your work; if you wiped your nose every five minutes and climbed into senior management, you had to be as dutiful to your masters as a whore to her clients. It twisted his democratic sentiments till he was tormented. What was wrong with democratic schools?

The idea of thirty years graft in a system prone to the whims of governments populated by men and women who couldn't think their way to the bathroom, made him recoil from his previous decision. He'd thought it would be easy. He liked his subject. He liked kids. He was committed to the public sector. He thought he could find a job in a congenial school with congenial people, make good friends and be happy; but that now seemed naïve and hopeless. There was deadness at the heart of the system. It was founded on a military model: discipline was its essence. They were taught about *the hidden curriculum*, which made him laugh: what was hidden about it? It was as obvious as light. He'd been thrashed at school with plimsolls, canes, cricket bats, a child's plastic spade, cuffed round the head, humiliated, bawled at, insulted: what was hidden?

He was glad that at Witton Park physical punishment virtually didn't exist. Kellet granted the right to administer it solely to Southworth, who did everything he could to avoid it; but a small minority of the staff, Watkinson's wife chief amongst them, sent boys to him regularly and insisted they should be beaten. Andy had joined the *Society of Teachers Opposed to Physical Punishment*. A long-haired maths teacher who described himself ironically as *a part-time Trot*, was also a member. They chatted about it now and again:

"The idea a boy's backside is the route to moral improvement seems pretty daft to me," said the mathematician.

"Thrashing children is an old English tradition," said Andy, "and they do it in the public schools so we're all supposed to join in."

The previous October, Jim Callaghan had initiated the *Great Education Debate*. Andy had read the transcript of the speech in horror: parents were worried if their children would learn to read and write, be bullied and fail to absorb social standards. There must be concentration on the basics. Standards must be raised, and oozing from every sentence, like pus from a wound, the implication that teachers were to blame. The flame of dishonesty and responsibility-shifting was picked up by Shirley Williams who talked of too many teachers being in the wrong job.

It was clear to Andy this was the start of a witch-hunt.

He disagreed viscerally with Callaghan and Williams. Callaghan's thinking about education was as faulty as that about homosexuality, which his religious upbringing had taught him was a sin. As for Williams, what was she but a typical opportunist careerist? The problem didn't lie with teachers, but with inequality. Nothing held a child back more than deprivation. He knew from his experience how hard it was to focus on schoolwork when your home-life was filled with worry, and what kids could avoid that if they knew they were at the bottom. Everything was a relationship. That's what Callaghan was failing to grasp. Enforcing rote learning of the basics, measuring children every thirty seconds, browbeating teachers if their results were a millionth of a decimal point short of a target, that was all demented Americanism. The essence was the nature of social relationships and most children knew their lives were limited by the economy: there was a need for millions of minions, low-level operatives deprived of responsibility and creativity, earning barely enough for egg and chips six nights a week. How was that supposed to inspire them to learn? What child from Mill Hill was going to work hard at French when they knew their future was working on a production line or driving a bus or serving in a supermarket?

The truth was, the education system was a failure because it served a society of rank injustice and irrational distribution of wealth and responsibility. Callaghan was more concerned to bundle the blame onto teachers so the electorate didn't accuse him than to help youngsters. His message was: "Look at me, I'm doing something about those lazy, feckless, left-wing teachers with their liberal views on education. I'll take us back to the good old days when children sat in fear at their slates and recited their tables for hours." It was pathetic and typical of a politician. What Andy saw, was that in a society of justice and rationality, where wealth and responsibility were evenly distributed, education could be relaxed. Instead of pursuing bits of paper, children could be encouraged to follow up their interests. He'd retained a gnomic sentence from Piaget: "In the moral sphere as in the intellectual, we only genuinely own what we have conquered for ourselves." What did Callaghan and Williams understand of that? Any idiot can wave a certificate for having jumped through hoops, but only people who have found their own way through learning are truly educated.

Yet Callaghan's speech was taken seriously. Andy would have given it three out of ten and told him to do some proper reading and thinking. The education system was going to move in exactly the opposite direction from the one he believed in. Measurement, supervision, State intrusiveness, obsession with results, the kind of lunatic culture which had made a mangled wreck of American education. Callaghan stressed the need for education to serve industry, which Andy despised. What it meant was schools must serve capitalism, they must turn out dutiful, obedient workers. How did that fit with being educated? What thinking person could fail to put in question society's turning most of its citizens into dumb robots?

He had to get out, but where to go?

What he truly wanted to do was write. He could accept teaching in order to pay the rent, but he could have accepted driving trains or cleaning windows. The only thing he couldn't give up was writing. Yet he'd published nothing more than three poems in the university literary magazine, and though people had complimented him, the constant rejection of his work by back-bedroom publications which featured pieces he thought inferior was dispiriting. His model remained Lawrence. Flaubert and Joyce were better stylists and *Madame Bovary* was supreme in its architecture, but no one touched on what Lawrence was insistent about; not the mechanics of sex, which Andy had come to think of as the risible part of the work, but the emotional crippling of middle-class life. Somehow it was true: we had created a culture which had shut down part of our minds, made us purblind and manic, destroyed tender feeling and replaced it by a crackpot imposition of our own bright-light view of ourselves, as if we could know ourselves better than others, as if we didn't need others to fulfil our natures.

He was unaware that his retrospectiveness was holding him back. The world in which Lawrence had made himself a writer was long gone. Andy didn't know that without contacts, you were doomed; that the young writers who were getting noticed were slick operators; that Carol Duffy didn't get into bed as a teenager with the thirty-nine year-old Adrian Henri out of adolescent love; that Ian McEwan's early Gothic stories were deliberately aimed at a market. He was still naïve enough to believe good writing would find its place. He had no idea how murderous literary culture can be.

In the final term, he went along one Friday evening to the inevitable college disco. The noise and jigging were unattractive, but Rob would be there and people he knew in passing but could chat to for two minutes at the bar. It was a way to beguile a few idle hours and not be alone. He was becoming more aware of how his central preoccupations were solitary. Reading and writing were done alone. There was nothing quite like the self-encounter of hours at the typewriter, but it brought the danger of self-obsession and diminution of easy-going rubbing along.

By the time he arrived, Rob was tipsy. He spied him following Sue into the girls' toilets, which on these occasions often became unisex. He climbed the stairs to the airless, pounding, sweaty room where lights flashed and spun and the dancers threw themselves around as if they lacked motor control. Some of the girls followed little routines of their own invention and looked more like they were trying to shake bees out of their hair than dancing. He stood at the bar with his pint. A few lads nodded or said hello. He was on his way to a table at the far side when arms circled his waist. He turned to find Sue, afloat on three or four vodkas looking into his face. She put her arms round his neck and kissed his lips.

"What you doing?" he said.

"It's all right."

She kissed him again.

"Where's Rob?"

"He knows."

"Knows what?"

"I've been wanting to do this for some time."

"Where is he?"

"Don't worry."

She took his beer, put in on the nearest table and came back to him, her arms round his neck, her body pressed against him. Over her shoulder her saw Rob wander in, obviously looking for her.

"Look, Rob's here."

He pushed her gently away and walked towards his friend. She came alongside him and took his hand. Rob approached, nodded and said:

"I get the picture."

Sue gave a little, girlish laugh and pulled Andy towards her. He extricated his hand, took her by the waist and guided her towards Rob, turned away and went to collect his beer. Looking back from his seat by the wall, he saw them leave and was relieved; but five minutes later she came back, sat on his knee, put her arm round his neck and said:

"It's okay. I've explained."

It was very odd and confusing, but the weight of her on him, the warmth, the tenderness of her dry kiss which reminded him of the first time he kissed Carol, her charming prettiness, the soft pressure of her breasts against him were hard to resist in his overwrought state. He wondered if it might be no more than a tipsy flirtation and tomorrow she'd be apologising to Rob and things would be restored between the three of them. They danced. She laid her head on his chest. When the DJ began to pack away, they went down the stairs together.

"How are you getting home?" he said.

"Walking."

"Okay, I'll come with you."

She smiled, hooked her arm in his as they followed the incline out of the college grounds and stopped half way to kiss him, after which she gave another little, schoolgirl laugh and looked fondly into his eyes.

At the door to her house he said:

"Got your key?"

"Yes," she said, delving into the pit of her cotton shoulder bag.

As she slipped it into the lock he said:

"I'd better get going. I've got to leg it to Heysham."

"But you can stay here," she said, and the little smile which had been on her lips all night, like that of a child who has just received exactly what she wanted for her birthday, expanded.

"Here?"

"Why not? Come in."

He wondered if she meant on the sofa or in a spare room, but she went straight up the stairs and into her room. He stood looking round him at the clothes she had drying on an improvised line, the few books in the alcove, the little table with two chairs by the window. She drew the curtains and turned on the bedside lamp, then as naturally as if they'd been lovers for years pulled her black sweater over her head, unhooked her bra and dropped it to the floor, stepped out of her skirt and discarded her knickers. She was white and sleek in the lamplight.

"Come on," she said, and climbed into bed.

Andy spent eight weeks during the summer working for *Albion North International*. He picked up sixty pounds a week, which was more then he'd ever earned, but the facilities were as poor as ever, he had to work every evening to produce materials, and Devlin's pursuit of profit meant the afternoons were often fraught. Every Saturday there was a trip. A corporation double decker took the students to Southport or Blackpool where they disgorged, disappeared to spend the day shoplifting or annoying shoppers on Lord Street or parents holding the hands of candy-floss kids on the prom. The staff hung around in cafes, stretched their legs and hoped the police wouldn't come to find them. One week, Andy turned up at eight, the bus appeared, the kids invaded, but the two other members of staff supposed to be there didn't show. The bus driver, bemused by the Babel his bus had become, drew on his fag as he turned to Andy:

"Where they from, like?"

"France and Spain."

"Aye," said the driver, "and do you understand all this jargon they come out with?"

There was no alternative but to set off. They were bound for Keswick. The journey was raucous. The bus rocked. The driver shook his head and lit another fag.

Andy was determined when they arrived he would give them strict instructions. He would divide them into groups, appoint a leader for each one, tell them where they mustn't go, have a rendezvous at one o'clock and assembly at the bus at four; but as soon as the doors were opened, they charged off like redskins attacking the cavalry, spread in all directions and didn't listen to him calling after them that they must be back at the allotted time.

His comfort was that Keswick was small. He could patrol and spot them, talk to them in trios, pairs and singly, make sure no one was pinching souvenirs. They proved far more elusive than he could have imagined and if he saw two of them on the street and headed for them, they turned and ran. He got fed up of sprinting after them only to find they'd disappeared up an alley.

He was back at the bus by three forty-five. They began to turn up in had-enough-of-this-place little groups. Some were showing off their swag.

"T'as piqué ça?"

"Oh," said the teenager, waving his hand beneath his chin in a typically Gallic gesture, "termes techniques."

They gathered like cattle for feed and he tried to count heads, but it was impossible. He had to get them to file onto the bus and try to count them as they entered, but they refused the discipline, nipped in in pairs, crouched, squeezed, shoved. He was three short. He struggled to get them to sit and stay, but after four counts, was one short.

"Alors," he shouted, "écoutez. Qui manque?"

"Geronimo," came the chorus.

A clever lad of Chinese origin whose English was much better than average, Andy had no idea how he'd earned his nickname. He talked to the lads he knew were his friends. They told him Geronimo and three others had taken a rowing boat out to the island in Derwent water. The three had rowed back but he'd decided to swim.

"Sans blague?"

"Oui, sans blague."

Andy got off the bus and stared across the water. Were they telling the truth? If so, what should he do? There was nothing for it but to alert the police. If the boy had drowned, what would his responsibility be? Would *Albion North International* be liable? Would he be, for having decided to supervise alone? Would it be manslaughter? A prison sentence? If so, it had to be. The important thing was to notify the authorities and find the boy.

He spoke to the driver.

"Listen, there's a kid missing. They say he swam back from the island. I'm going to have to get the police. Can you keep them on the bus?"

"That fuckin' lot."

"Shut the doors. I'll be back as soon as I can."

He set off at a trot, but at once heard a commotion from the top deck. Turning, he saw a mass of boys pressed against the front window, hammering, bawling and pointing to his left. He veered towards a cluster of shrubs by the lake shore. As he got within touching distance, Geronimo sprang up, smilingly widely, the bus began to rock and a rhythmic thumping of feet carried across the air.

"Petit farceur," said Andy. "J'ai cru que tu t'était noyé."

"Je t'ai eu," said the lad, holding out his hand.

Andy shook it.

"Dans le bus, petit fou."

The journey home was wild. They rushed away to their host families as soon as the bus was parked, their bags full of stolen tat; but Andy didn't care. He went for a pint in the *Bradford Arms* and never had beer tasted so sweetly of freedom.

Elsie expected her son to be at home for a few weeks. She knew he'd had interviews for teaching jobs in Whitehaven, Cambridge, Newquay, Blackpool, Colne, Wigan, Fleetwood, but had either not been appointed or felt they weren't for him. She was proud of the thought he would soon be a teacher. Such an elevated position would have seemed, when she was young, as impossible as joining the royal family. She could tan her ego in the reflected rays. She relished telling the neighbours, who were always duly impressed. Yet it was September and he hadn't found anything. Surely that couldn't be right.

He'd been at home a fortnight when he said to her:

"I really don't want to be a teacher."

She set the *Lancashire Evening Post* aside and took off her glasses.

"I don't know what I'm going to do," he said. "I want to try to find a job that involves writing. I'll maybe see if I can get a start as a journalist."

"Well," she said, resuming her reading, "it's up to you."

She went to bed disappointed, angry and confused. Her son was twenty-six. By that age she'd expected him to be married and looking after his own children. In her petulance at the sense of being imposed on, she forgot her old fear that her children would move away. It was characteristic of her mind that the present moment's obsession expelled all previous attitudes. She would have been astonished if some objective observer had been able to tap her on the shoulder and play for her on a magic screen, the scenes she had imagined when her preoccupation had been how to prevent her children disappearing. All her mental effort now was centred on her bemused and injured response.

If he could be living under her roof at twenty-six, why not thirty-six or forty? She knew of men and women who had failed to marry and had stayed with their parents till they died. There was John Crawley from Hartington Road who worked as a postman and lived with his mother till she expired at ninety-three. When he was the other side of fifty she was still washing and ironing his clothes and making his meals. Was that to be her fate? Would she be an old woman and still have to put his shirts in the washer and peel potatoes for him every day? He was just like his father. Big ideas. Writing. Who could earn money from that? She didn't know anyone who did. Why couldn't he get an ordinary job and be content? What was wrong with teaching? And she'd told all the neighbours. What would she have to say now. Oh, he showed her up good and proper.

It was part of her conception of things that submission in employment was unavoidable. She derived no direct pleasure from her work. It was what she had to do to live. The pleasure was secondary: the egotistic satisfaction of obedience, diligence, efficiency; looking at herself in the mirror of her own categorical agreement with what was demanded of her. The simple pleasure of a task undertaken voluntarily because it was necessary was confined to home. She was usually acting in obedience to an external injunction. Andy's wish for work to be other than walking bare-legged through nettles was incomprehensible. The Methodism that had formed her mind was substantially derived from work discipline. She could no more have imagined work as a pleasurable, collective endeavour than she could have believed the tides wouldn't turn. Like millions more, she celebrated what oppressed her because it permitted a tiny, compensatory, self-regarding pride. She had no idea her son was striving to avoid exactly that.

He didn't find a job but signed on, which troubled her: how he could he accept the shame of the dole when he had a degree and a teaching qualification? She would have cleaned drains with a toothbrush before she would have accepted a State handout. The dreadful shame attached to the being unemployed in the thirties didn't flood her son's mind. His attitude was that he was looking for work; he'd trained as a teacher but decided against it; he wasn't robbing the State while being idle; he was trying to find work that would mean something to him. In the meantime, signing on was a means of getting a bit of money for her. He handed over virtually all his benefit. His needs were minimal and in any case, he'd saved a bit while he worked. It was out of fairness to her he claimed the money, so that while he was in her house, she would be better off.

He spent his days writing, broken only by the need to exercise and eat. She looked through the sheets of A4 accumulating beside his typewriter. The sentences didn't make much sense. It was some kind of novel but it wasn't written in a style she could get hold of. To Elsie, literature was Charles Dickens. She'd read *The Mayor of Casterbridge* and *A Pair of Blue Eyes*, and if there was a Shakespeare on the television she'd watch it and try to stay awake; but Dickens was what had been read to her at school and had become the measure by which all literature was judged.

She would have been shocked by Kafka's judgement (she hadn't heard of him) that there was *heartlessness* behind Dickens's *sentimentally overflowing style*; that his *opulence and great careless prodigality* brought passages *of awful insipidity*. Her own moral and emotional orientation, derived as it was from parents, teachers, vicars, figures of authority of all kinds, born in the Victorian era, was a cistern of sentimentality whose overflow never stopped running; carelessly prodigal; insipid in its repetitions and essentially a concealment of heartlessness. Not that she was knowingly cruel. She would have given her life for her children and wouldn't have hurt a rat which invaded her kitchen if she could chase it away with a broom; but the culture which had formed her mind had to hide its viciousness and she had imbibed, without knowing it, its phoney moralism, an entirely factitious set of translucent attitudes whose sole purpose was to consign to the dark cellar of capitalism the fact that it generated inequality, poverty, division and misery like the sun generates heat.

She read the letter he was sending to newspapers along with his C.V. (she wondered what *curriculum vitae* meant). He was willing to start at the bottom. Any opening in journalism he would gladly accept. She read too a couple of the replies telling him it was impossible any longer to train journalists on the job and if he got himself a postgraduate qualification, they would offer him an interview. She wanted to talk to him about it, but didn't want him to know she'd read his correspondence.

The weeks and months went by. The pile of papers grew thicker. He was working at the typewriter for hours every day; but what was the good? It was Elsie's view that talent revealed itself without work. As it was God-given, He would ensure it was recognised. Though she knew well enough society was unfairly organised; the rich knew how to keep the best for themselves; the public school system, the old boy network, the Masons, all manner of clever schemes ensured the few were admitted and the many excluded, she clung nevertheless to her conviction that God would set things to rights. It was because the Devil was abroad that things were unjust. Yet it didn't occur to her that this injustice might mean that talent could go unnoticed; that a second-rate writer from Eton would find it easier to get published than a first-rate one from the back streets of Preston.

She assumed if her son had it in him to be a writer, they would have spotted it at school. Publishers would have come knocking. They would clamour for every paragraph he turned out. She had no idea that James Joyce had despaired over publication of his masterpiece.

To her it was pretension. It reminded her, inevitably, of Bert. He too had tried to write, filling notebooks with attempts at stories she disdained to read. In her mind, writers came from far away. They existed on a different plane. They weren't people you shared your house with or met in the fishmongers. Like most people, she believed she admired genius, but if Beethoven or Einstein had lived next door, she would have dismissed them as odd, ridiculous and idle. She'd hoped her son would take a down-to-earth, honest job. She would have been delighted if he'd been a plumber or joiner; but filling paper with words no one would read seemed to her no better than madness.

One day, when he'd gone out for a walk after tea and she was looking through the things on his table, she found a folded copy of *The Guardian* in which he'd circled an advert in red. The University of Hull was offering studentships. More study? What was the point? It vexed her till she would have liked to throw the paper in his face and say:

"For God's sake get yourself a job. What's all this study for? Haven't you done enough? You've been at it for six years. Do you think you can spend your life studying?"

A fortnight later he told her he'd been accepted. He was to start at Hull in October to work for an MPhil (she didn't know what that was). Her feeling softened. What did it matter? He would be off her hands. Oddly, she was surprised to find herself thinking she would miss him. Sylvia was out more and more often with Barry. She was nineteen and no longer on a short lead. Andy was a reassuring presence, and as he'd always been, undemanding. She would come home from work to find he'd tidied up and vacuumed everywhere. He weeded the garden and mowed the lawn and when the iron stopped working and she shook her head over the expense, the next day she found a new one, still in its box waiting for her in the breakfast room.

"What is it you'll be studyin', any road?" she said as he sat down to eat one evening.

"Flaubert," he said. "Nineteenth century French novelist. Wrote at the same time as Dickens."

"I bet he's not as good," she said.

"Well," he said, picking up a slice of white bread, "not as prolific, but his best is exceptional."

Elsie turned back to the television wondering what could come of studying French novelists. What kind of job could that get you? What call was there in Preston for folk who knew about that kind of thing?

During the summer, Andy took work again with *Albion North International*. He found a room in a house in Abraham Heights, Lancaster and became friendly with a pleasant couple who lived there. Ed Holmes was an historian and Rebecca Sandler a philosopher. They both intended to become social workers. He was surprised at how open and welcoming they were to him and puzzled over it. The thought crossed his mind that they were slightly sorry for him; he was a loner; he had no girlfriend; they were taking him under their wing. It was true, there was a great lacuna in his life. He was at a loss to understand himself. Ten years earlier, he'd've been astonished if anyone had told him he would be still unattached. Perhaps it was the very assumption that love must arrive, commitment follow and a stable, happy relationship establish itself as effortlessly as apples grow in summer that had defeated him. Maybe he should have been more wilful and calculating. Yet when he imagined that, it altered his feeling: love and wilful calculation cancelled one another out. He was glad of Ed and Rebecca, they were good people, even if he did feel slightly like a teetotaller at a booze up in their presence.

The other residents included Julian Booker, a small, dark, stocky cockney, who had been active in the International Socialists at university and who struck Andy as distinctly psychopathic.

"You might have noticed," Julian said, as Andy sat at the table a steaming plate of piled spaghetti bolognaise in front of him, " that I'm hard. I don't mean physically. I mean emotionally. You might have noticed that."

"No," said Andy.

"Well, I am. It's my upbringing. I was in an orphanage. Part of the time. My mother was an alcoholic. That's the cause of it. You might have noticed it about me."

"I wouldn't say so."

When he thought no one was around Julian used to sit in front of the television and imitate presenters, not mockingly but admiringly. Andy came in quietly one evening and found him watching *Three Two One*, flicking his fingers in an effort to be speedier than Ted Rogers. Andy watched him a minute and withdrew silently.

There was a young, attractive, blonde woman who didn't have a room but who appeared to be there more or less every day. She slept on the sofa. Andy walked into the living-room with his toast one morning to find her asleep, naked from the waist up. He turned to leave. She roused.

"Hello, do you want to sit down?"

"No, no, it's okay. I'll go to the kitchen."

"No, sit here," she said indicating the cushion she'd shifted her feet from. "Nice morning, isn't it?" and she stretched her plumpish arms above her head as she yawned.

Andy hovered. He didn't want to offend her by leaving, but to sit next to her seemed intrusive. She got up.

"I'll just go and make myself a coffee. Want one?"

"No thanks. I'll have a cup of tea in a minute."

She pulled on a t-shirt which reassured him, but it was her habit to appear topless. She would come out of the bathroom drying her hair and wander into the kitchen with a small towel round her trim waist, and every morning she was half naked on the sofa. Andy didn't get to know her name.

John Woodcock was a bearded, intense politics graduate who delighted in showing his knowledge in all areas, loved games and quizzes, rode a Triumph 500 and mocked anyone who didn't know the population of Ukraine or the average summer temperature in Peru. He and Julian were drinking partners who would come loud and hungry back from the *John O' Gaunt* or *The Blue Anchor* to raid the fridge and devour Rebecca's expensive paté or the apple pie Ed had baked at tea-time. He and Julian entertained the theory that revolution was imminent: the more Callaghan and Healey pressed on with cuts and money supply control, the more certain it was the working-class would rise up and destroy capitalism.

"Working people are more concerned about how to pay the rent and put shoes on their kids' feet," said Andy.

"You've fallen for Marcuse's illusion of the embourgeoisement of the workers," said John with contempt.

"No I haven't," said Andy. "I haven't read Marcuse. I come from the working class. They'll always make the best of their situation. They don't believe it's their historic role to replace capitalism. They elect governments to sort out the economy."

One evening, Andy was in the little room he occupied on the ground floor working on Spanish grammar, when there was a single knock, the door opened and the half-naked girl, her hair wet, her hips encircled by a towel which threatened to come loose and fall, stood in the door-frame.

"There's a phone call for you," she said. "Sounds official."

"Thanks," he said, getting up.

"That's all right," she said, rubbing her hair and loitering a moment.

It was his dad. His voice was grave and somewhat self-pitying. He was going into hospital for a biopsy. Maybe Andy might get to visit him.

A biopsy? Did they think he had cancer? Wasn't that usually what a biopsy was for? When Andy arrived at Blackburn General, his dad was coming round groggily from the anaesthetic. He couldn't speak more than a few words. Andy asked if there was anything he needed, anything he should do. Bert shook his head. On the second visit, Bert was propped up reading the paper, his glasses on his nose, his thinning, grey hair combed forward in a Bobby Charlton effort to conceal his pate.

"They haven't said anything."

"Probably good news," said Andy.

"Maybe," said Bert but Andy could see the worry on his face.

"Anyway, it seems I may be able to go home in a day or two, so I'll be glad of that."

"Yeah, get home, get on your feet, back into your routine and you'll be fine."

When Andy asked if there was anything he wanted him to do, Bert said:

"You could go to the bungalow and collect my post. There should be a cheque from Ken Wickham. That needs paying in but I suppose it'll have to wait."

"No, I can do it."

Putting the key in the lock and opening the door was curious. This wasn't his home. It had never been his home. He'd been a visitor here for a few months, no more. There was a pile behind the door, most of it redundant. As his dad had said, if the cheque had arrived, it would be in a white envelope with the firm's address stamped on the reverse. He used his finger as a letter-opener and took out the cheque. Two hundred and four pounds and seventy-six pence. How often did he get cheques like this? How much more did Wickham owe him?

He passed through the little, L-shaped lounge whose odour was his dad's and into the kitchen. From there he went into the spare bedroom where he'd slept and then, hesitantly into his dad's bedroom, where he'd never been. It was neat. By the double bed was a pine cabinet bearing a lamp with a blue shade and beside it a copy of *Mr Sammler's Planet*. He picked it up and read a few lines of the bookmarked page. It was a novel he didn't know, Bellow being one of those writers he'd dipped into but didn't feel the impulse to stay with. It was a hardback in mint condition. He wondered why his dad hadn't bought the paperback, or dug out a second-hand copy as he would. He knew his dad was attracted to the way things were presented; he liked what was best and often said *you get what you pay for*, which Andy thought a laughable cliché. Nevertheless, it was true: those with money did have higher quality things, like the shirt he'd bought in the sale at *Lingard's*, the posh Preston men's outfitters. It was reduced from some ridiculous price, thirty-five pounds or so, and as it was his size and dark blue, which suited him, he handed over a fiver. There was no doubt, wearing a high quality, well-tailored shirt was a superior experience to the cheap, ill-fitting things he had in his drawer.

His dad's instinct for quality was rational: everyone would drive a Rolls-Royce if they could. Yet as they couldn't, buses and trains were better. Produce a high-quality, technologically advanced train, and everyone could enjoy it. As for books, libraries should have the hardbacks for the same reason.

He opened the wardrobe, though he felt intrusive. His dad was failing. The biopsy might reveal he had little time. Andy might have to take responsibility for him. Who else was there? His carefully pressed shirts were on hangers, his beloved chunky jumpers folded uniformly in the drawers, his shoes lined up obediently at the bottom. He was remined of the big wardrobe in his parents' bedroom in Woodland Grove. His dad's clothes were always tidily stowed but his mum's were often over the back of a chair, across the bed, hanging over the wardrobe door, limp on the floor.

The key to the side door hung on a hook in the kitchen. He followed the little path to the small garden and stood for a few minutes looking at the hills behind. A voice from next door disturbed him and he reverted to a business-like attitude. Gathered what he had to and left.

On his next visit to the hospital, he managed to speak to one of the doctors: the biopsy was inconclusive. They were at a loss. He'd be able to go home but they'd have to do more tests. Andy brought him home in a taxi and stayed a few hours. The pain in his leg was much worse and he hobbled from the kitchen to his chair.

"They'll get to the bottom of it," said Andy.

"I had a dream," said Bert, "about my leg."

"About your leg?"

"Yes, they had to amputate."

"I doubt it'll come to that."

Andy felt he had to tell his mother, Mary and Sylvia. Elsie responded with a moment of shock. Her face became mask-like, but she quickly found her way to disdain:

"He always did eat wrong. Way he put butter on his bread. Eh, I'd say to 'im after t' war, that's rationed yet, you know. He'll've been eatin' too many pies and convenience meals. That's what'll've done it."

He didn't have the heart to tell her he was a vegetarian who baked his own wholemeal bread and ate more fruit and vegetables in a month than the average man in a year. She wanted to believe if she had cooked for him, he would be healthy. Her mind was depending more and more on delusion. It was getting more and more impossible to engage her with what was real. Andy experienced once again the terrible hopelessness of watching her destroy herself.

"Well," he said, "I guess we'll never know the cause."

Mary had given birth to her second son in June. Andy cycled over to the house Ted had built on the outskirts of Parbold. It was a pleasant ride through Eccleston and out along the lanes and it was good to feel his legs and to make the old, heavy clanking machine whizz along. The four-bedroom place stood on its own plot, surrounded by garden, an integral garage to the left of the front door, a big, picture-frame window at the front and a porch with a little, pitched slate roof to keep the weather out. Ted and his brother had worked night after night and weekend after weekend when the weather allowed till they were both exhausted. One evening, after he'd been finishing the roof timbers alone, Ted stopped on the way home to buy a packet of cigars at the newsagents. Heading back to his car, a stray Alsatian bared its teeth, barked and growled. He tried to ignore and circumvent it but it came at him from behind. He turned to swing his leg at the animal and found he was so tired he'd couldn't execute a kick.

All the same he worked on and they'd been in the new home for two years.

Mary was alone with the baby. She saw Andy arrive and opened to him.

"Hello. I thought you were working in Lancaster."

"Finished," he said running his fingers through his hair and wiping the sweat from his forehead. "I'm off to Hull next week."

"Yes, mum told me. Very good. You've done well. I'll make a cup of tea."

He was very glad of the few positive words. Mary was such a kind person. She put herself aside and said or did what was good for others. There was a kind of genius in it, but one society disdained. He followed her into the kitchen and the thought occurred to him that without her his life might have gone badly awry. In a way, he owed her his life.

The child clung to her. Andy made baby talk, widened his eyes, opened his mouth and chucked the lad under the chin. There was a shyness about him that was different from his older brother.

"Hello little James," he said. "Yes, there's a good boy. Where's that mummy, eh? Where's that mummy of yours?"

The boy looked at him with uncertain, blue eyes and clung harder.

When they were settled in the lounge, Andy said:

"Dad's been in hospital."

"Oh, dear."

"Biopsy. They didn't find anything. He's home now, but he has this terrible pain in his leg. They're going to have to do tests."

"That's a shame," said Mary. "Have you told mum?"

"Yes."

"Is she okay."

"She's fine. She thinks it's the absence of her good cooking has made him ill."

"Mmm. Well, who knows?"

Andy was glad Mary wasn't upset. She was focused on her baby. Her estranged father was ill and possibly seriously but she had another life. He was happy for her, yet at the same time troubled for his dad. Mary was his daughter. He knew she had been a greater source of pride to him than he had. She was diligent, responsible, ever-reliable Mary, while he was the kid who rebelled against school, did badly in his exams and had to pick up the pieces. He wanted to suggest she should visit, but he knew it was impossible. What had been between them had failed. It was terrible but it was true. His dad might die without ever seeing Mary again. She might see only his coffin. The only comfort he found in facing the pain of this estrangement was her attentive delight in her child.

But he wouldn't let his father die alone.

LA VIE EST AILLEURS

Mary was glad of her brother's visit. He'd often arrived unexpectedly to spend time with Patrick and they had a close and happy relationship. He would turn up on his bike and devote the day to the boy, always following whatever interest led him and in the evening the child would climb on his knee to be read to and fall asleep with his bent index finger in his mouth and his *cuttie*, an old, tattered blanket he couldn't be parted from, in his arms. She asked Andy to be James's godfather. He accepted out of love, in spite of his devout atheism and mockery of the Catholic church. She'd looked after him when he was a little boy, now she was glad he could help bring up her children. She recalled fondly how devoted she'd been and how she'd loved him without limit when he was a sweet, charming, biddable little boy but also how that had changed to distance and frustration when he became a teenager who confounded her. She'd been almost a mother to him. She knew it was partly because his actual mother was lacking. The horrible, dark thought of her mother's disturbance crossed her mind. She shut it down, lay the sleeping baby in his pram and went to busy herself in the kitchen.

Her mind was divided over Andy's future. She was pleased he was going to do a higher degree. She would be very proud if he became a doctor and lectured in a university. Her little brother. Yet, she knew it was unlikely. In his place, she would work hard and do just what was demanded of her; but Andy would rebel against the bus timetable. He had to question everything and nothing was beyond his irreverence. She had no doubt he could do the work, but his attitude would trip him up. She remained an unshakeable Labour supporter and adjusted her thinking to Callaghan and Healey's cuts, while Andy excoriated them:

"If we're going to have Tories running the country, let's have real ones," he said, "at least then we can have a socialist opposition."

In a way, she admired him, but his willingness to climb where hardly anyone was willing to go was perilous. What would he make of his life?

It worried her too that he wasn't settled with a lass. She'd watched from a distance when Maggie Swift had been besotted with him. She hardly knew Maggie, but she liked her. She would have been good for him. The fact that he never appeared with a girlfriend, never spoke of one, made her anxious for his well-being.

"D'you think 'e's queer?" said Ted

"Don't be ridiculous."

"At his age, and no woman. It's fishy."

"And what if he is? What's wrong with that?"

She had to force her thoughts away from him. He was her little brother, but he was a man now. He had to make his own way. She had two sons to bring up. Her happiness couldn't have been greater than when she thought of them. She escaped herself in minute attention to their needs. Washing and ironing Patrick's clothes, putting them in his drawers and knowing their exact location was an expression of intense love. Its quality was utterly different from work. There, she'd been conscientious. It was a matter of taking the tasks seriously and ensuring they were carried out properly; but there was no love in it. The parts of her mind which were engaged to make her a valued employee were quite distinct from those which made her a good mother. As a mother, love came first. As an employee, she was merely duteous. Love came from within. The injunction to duty from without. She'd enjoyed working. She'd been pleased to be good at her job and to be praised by her bosses; but as a mother, she needed no praise. She was her own judge. She knew what needed to be done and she did it thoroughly, not because she was being watched, because her pay rise depended on it, because a promotion might come from it, but out of love for her children.

She was determined not to go back to work till her children were grown up. Ted talked about her getting a job as soon as they were both in school.

"I might have another one," she said.

"Aye, but if you don't."

"Even if I don't, I'm not going back to work till they're sixteen."

"Sixteen? They'll not need their nappies changed when they're teenagers."

"No, they'll have other needs."

"Not as'll stop you workin'"

"You may not think so but I do."

Her near neighbour, Sandra Spencer, had a son the same age as Patrick. She'd gone back to her job as a teacher when he was two.

"I don't know how you stand it, at home all day, Mary. It'd drive me mad," she said.

Mary was tempted to reply:

"I don't know how you stand being in school all day. At least I can go out when I like or stop for a cup of tea if I want to."

She knew the pressure on women to take jobs. Ted saw the pound notes. She heard the argument from her neighbours that women shouldn't be confined to the home; that opportunities were opening up; she'd held the same view herself; but working had made her see its transparency: most people disliked their jobs. Ted did the pools and hoped for the win which would mean he wouldn't have to fit window frames or climb on roofs. Most of the women she'd worked with had been of the same view: they hoped the Premium Bonds might be their salvation. She had no desire to escape the life she was leading. She was content. She worked hard to make a good home for her children and bring them up well. Nobody told her what to do. She made her own decisions. At midday or one she might take James for a walk, bump into someone she knew, have a chat for five minutes, nip into the corner shop for a few necessities and, if it was fine, sit in the park for half an hour. She wasn't a prisoner in her home, she loved it. Nor did she feel any lack of contact or significance. What could be more significant than looking after your children well? It had far more meaning than a lot of the routine work she'd had to complete.

"And what did she say?" asked Elsie when Andy told her he'd spoken to Mary about Bert.

"Not much," he said. "She's got a baby to think about."

"Aye, quite right too. 'Im, he doesn't deserve thinkin' about.."

Andy was glad to be away and on the train. He hadn't seen much of Sylvia. She was obviously soon going to marry Barry. He hoped they would live far enough from his mother for the circle of their life to widen enough to keep her from daily intrusion, but he had a depressing intuition his mother might prevent it.

There was already snow on the Pennines. He'd never been to Hull. It was one of those places he didn't think of visiting. Its only pinpricks of interest were that Larkin worked in the university library and Alan Plater, Tom Courtney and Andrew Marvel were scions. The Larkin connection was likely to keep him away. Andy recognised his technical skill, but the sensibility was dismal. It was all that was worst about Britain: snobbish, narrow-minded, insular, fearful of democracy, dismissing the majority of people as cheap, vulgar or no more than a mob. It was the public school, Oxbridge view of Britain Andy despised. He was much more attracted by Marvel, and Alan Plater's best work had some power to endure, though he disdained the money-in-the-back-pocket writing for *Z Cars*. There was nothing wrong with a series of its kind in a way; you could flop in front of it after a hard day's work and its blade cut flesh wounds into the body of social injustice; but that kind of script writing could be done by low-level writers. Some of it was done by committee. Writers of any stature should stay away.

Tom Courtney he liked and admired as an actor. He and Albert Finney represented the northern, working-class vertical invasion which could subvert the established expectations.

He changed trains at York, caught a bus from the station in Hull to Cottingham and turned up where he'd been told. There followed several hours of bureaucracy: a form to register with the university; another to register with the library; another for the student house he was going to live in. He was sent to the house supervisor, a tall, serious, somewhat gloomy German lecturer, no more than a few years older who exuded a sense of impending tragedy. Colin Harding had taken on the role of looking after the house because he was provided with a rent-free flat and it was responsible and beneficial; but it had badly soured his feeling. For reasons he couldn't fathom, the students took against him, viewed his presence as an intrusion and were hostile and aggressive.

As he explained to Andy he'd be sharing with another student, an Algerian called Aisat and spelled out the essential rules, Andy didn't know that he wanted to tell him not to move in, to find his own place, that some of the people he was going to live with were malicious and their behaviour dangerous.

Andy was disappointed to discover he had to share, but at least the room was big. It was on the ground floor of an extensive house which must once have been the home of some upper-middle-class family. There were three floors and above them, Harding's flat. Twelve students shared the kitchen and bathroom. He shook hands with Aisat, whose English halted and spluttered like a misfiring engine. In French, their conversation flowed more easily. Andy wasn't much interested in making friends with the other residents. Most of them were second years and the age and experience chasm made them of little appeal. He had a thesis to write. His ideas were mapped out. This was an opportunity. He wanted to get his head down, get the work done and find a job in a university.

The day after his arrival, he met his tutor. One wall of his room was bookshelves, mostly French titles but Andy noticed too James Joyce, Henry James and plenty of English critics, including Leavis and George Steiner. At only thirty-six, Frank Jones's hair was already substantially grey. It clashed with his boyish demeanour and habits. They spent two hours discussing how Andy's thesis would take shape and after half an hour, Frank took off his shoes and folded his right leg under his backside, like Andy had done at school. He was a fairly small man with a slightly adenoidal voice, big, black-framed glasses, laughter which came easily and a charming habit of raising his chin, screwing his eyes slightly and peering into the distance through the window when Andy said anything which roused his curiosity.

Andy liked him immediately. He was an intellectual in every movement. One of those academics who hasn't given in to cynicism but retains a principled commitment to study, objectivity and a belief in the duty to seek the truth. What disturbed Andy though were his frequent references to structuralism and deconstructionism. By the end of the session, Andy was loaded with a burden of reading he hadn't expected: Saussure, Barthes, Foucault, Gothot-Mersch, Lacan, Levi-Strauss, Althusser, Greimas. He hadn't anticipated having to veer away from Flaubert into a labyrinth of dubious theory. He knew what he wanted to say. His ideas were already formed. The task was to diligently apply them to the books, in particular *Madame Bovary* and *Les Trois Contes*, to show how *figurative evocation* as he'd dubbed it, pushed aside narrative in Flaubert.

For the first few weeks he met Frank every Friday at ten. His supervision paper had to be submitted by Wednesday. His first took issue with Saussure: it was true there had to be a degree of arbitrariness about words, otherwise the thing with leaves couldn't be tree, arbre, Baum, arbol; but that didn't imply absolute arbitrariness. Why couldn't there be enough absence of necessity to permit a potentially infinite number of languages, and at the same time a measure of necessity? If there was a degree of necessity, then the idea that what gave words their form was the agreement of the linguistic community was flawed. In any case, how did such agreement come about? Sausuure had no answer. He was pointing to an emptiness which didn't really exist. Language is part of our biological inheritance and is likely therefore to contain strong elements of necessity.

Frank peered out of the window. Tucked his leg under his behind. Pushed his glasses up his nose.

"Yes, yes. That's very good. I see what you're getting at but doesn't it lead us to an impressionistic view of culture?"

"What's wrong with that?"

"Well, it lacks an organising principle."

"Who has identified one?"

"There must be one. I mean, isn't natural selection an organising principle? Doesn't it permit us to explain the extraordinary variety of species through a single and simple principle?"

"Only superficially. Genetics is much more complicated. But in any case, we aren't scientists. We're literary critics. Why should we try to pretend we can do what physicists do? We can't. We're engaged in a fundamentally different exercise."

"We can't do what physicists do, exactly; but we can approximate. The structuralist view is that behind all the variety there are simple organising principles. Literature is built out of the same stories, for example. A handful of plots, if you like, appear in literature from the Greeks to the present day."

Andy gave a short laugh.

"If you go looking for that you'll find it. But doesn't Flaubert subvert it? The story barely exists in *Madame Bovary*. You could summarise it in half a page. And you can't say the imagery in *Madame Bovary* has appeared again and again across the centuries."

"Yes, there's something in that, that's good, yes," and Frank tucked his leg a little more comfortably and peered a little more quizzically.

The session over, they adjourned to the Senior Common Room refectory where, as a post-grad, Andy was permitted to take advantage of the highly subsidised and superior fare. He could eat a lunch which would keep him going till the epilogue for sixty or seventy pence. They sat at a table with a group of lecturers and professors who were soon talking about their arcane areas of research.

"And what are you researching?" a female professor from the German department asked.

"Flaubert," he said between spoonfuls of tomato and basil soup. "Imagery. I'm interested in the way the web of images displaces narrative as a way of creating meaning."

"Kafka," she said, and bit into her bacon and avocado sandwich.

"Sorry?"

"Kafka thinks in images."

"Don't we all?"

"Oh, I don't think so. Oh, no. George," she said, turning to the bald on top but long-haired at the back and sides man beside her who had slopped some of his humous onto his wide, old, thickly-knotted tie, "what do you say? Do we all think in images?"

"What?" said the near-deaf emeritus.

"Images. This young man believes we think in images."

"Now, I was reading only this morning something in Spinoza..." he began.

Andy found it odd there was no small-talk. It was kind of daft. He didn't expect anyone but Flaubert specialists to have much interest in his area. Why should they? Yet, by and large the conversation didn't stray far from specialisms. He'd just spent two hours talking about structuralism with Frank and would have been glad to chat to someone about whether George Best was the best dribbler English football had ever seen. The atmosphere inhibited him. He wanted some of that inconsequential gabble which permits people to convey their character without being aware of it.

He could have eaten in the SCR every day, but he confined it to his visits with Frank. Though the food was less appetising in the student troughs, he felt more at home, even if most of the time he ate alone.

He walked from his student house to campus every day, ordered the books and papers Frank had told him to read from the library, trudged through them though they seemed as relevant as weather forecasts for the Galapagos Islands, and began to feel more and more at a distance from what he was doing. He'd hoped, when he wrote the five-hundred-word abstract which got him the scholarship, he'd be left alone to follow his own path, but he'd quickly come to understand that Frank had a stake. He had soaked up the structuralism which was infecting university departments like syphilis Napoleon's armies. He wanted Andy's thesis to bear the mark of his influence; but Andy was as attracted to structuralism as to Catholicism. It seemed to him to carry all the worst sins of French intellectualism. Much of it was empty jargon trying to pass as sophisticated theory. His strongest desire was to throw in all in the bin and write what he wanted to say about Flaubert; but Frank insisted that he must be *au courant* with the criticism and much of it was structuralist.

Andy liked Frank, but he felt he was mistaken in absorbing much of the nonsense peddled by people who were trying to pretend they were Einsteins of literary theory. Science was science and literature was literature. It wasn't possible to examine novels and plays and poems like you could the rotation of the planets or what goes on in an atom. The latter were given facts of nature, The former products of the human mind.

By the time he came home for the Christmas vacation, he was thoroughly sick of writing papers to dismiss the vacuous drivel which passed for thinking in the structuralist mafia. He found himself suspended in a limbo not of his making between deconstructionism and *The Morecambe and Wise Christmas Show*. He belonged nowhere. He wondered if he should simply throw up the scholarship and get himself a teaching job. The memory of the Witton Park kids cheered him, but the system depressed him. The children were processed to make politicians look good. He would have to see it through in Hull and hope he could land a university post.

One morning when he'd gone into Preston to distract himself for a few hours, he passed a girl he recognised from the university library. She met his eyes and he smiled and said hello, she nodded and smiled in return. She was a dark-haired young woman with a pale skin and big, blue eyes which reminded him of ice. Her broad shoulders made him think she might be a swimmer. She was very neat in her tight-fitting jeans , green polo-neck and dark coat and her confined, restrained demeanour made him think of Jane Bentnick.

For the rest of the holiday she came back into his mind every day. He had a reason to approach her. He would be able to speak to her. Perhaps his long, painful lack of easy, happy intimacy would end. The truth was, he could easily have found girls to go to bed with. The old strictures about sex and marriage had dissolved in the minds of most students. Had he been cynical enough, he could have satisfied his sexual needs as simply as his need for physical exercise or someone to go to the pub with for an hour; but he was committed to the high ideal of sexual love. In spite of things coming to an abrupt end with Carol, Jane's moth-around-a-candle mind, the odd, brief liaison with Sue which had made his last weeks in Rob's presence so confused and dispiriting; he was still as engaged with the notion that *l'amour c'est d'abord partir de soi-même*, which he'd found in Aragon, as when he was naively besotted with the perfidious and manipulative Janice Eaves.

Boxing Day was spent at Mary's. She was as organised as career bureaucrat but as welcoming as a puppy. It was a delight to be in her home. Elsie fussed around, offering to cook the sprouts or wash the plates, but Mary calmly sent her to the sofa with a smile. At tea-time Barry arrived to pick up Sylvia. It was the first time Mary had met him.

"Hello, Barry" she said as Ted brought him in from the chill, "lovely to meet you. Sit down and I'll get you a cup of tea."

The fire, part coal, part Ted's off-cuts roared in the fireplace below the stone chimney breast whose right side was straight line and whose left an angled descent to the polished wooden top which ran along a six-foot expanse of the same stone to the television corner; everyone was gathered in the living-room like the characters in the last act of a Restoration comedy. For Andy, this felt like a family and he was sure his mother and Sylvia had the same response; and what suffused it with its special feeling was Mary's extraordinary character.

Barry stayed for an hour before he Sylvia, Elsie and Andy shuffled through the cold into his car whose engine turned over with a spurt and whose heater pumped slowly. He'd bought it for seventy-five quid from a lad at work, fitted a new gearbox, replaced the head gasket, renewed the suspension and in place of the indicator lever, defunct because of the frazzled electrics, had mounted a switch on the dashboard: up for right, down for left. He was cheerfully proud of his work. To buy a well-past-its-obsolescence chugger, raise it on ramps, slide underneath, spend hours with the odour of old oil in his nostrils, rip out all the wiring, refit the brakes, hunt the scrap yards for matching parts and drive it for two years in defiance of the new-car-every-three-years culture of the manufacturers made him feel he was beating the system as well as saving money and enjoying himself.

He and Sylvia were going to the pub for the final hour. In the house, cold from having been empty all day, just the two of them, Elsie quickly up to bed with her timeless milky drink, Andy turned on the gas fire and sat on the sofa with *La Vie Est Ailleurs.* He'd come across Kundera when he'd visited Mike in Carmaux and he was reading the story of the young, idealistic Jaromil.

"Ah, is he influenced by Rimbaud?"

"No," said Mike. "He's opposed to that idea. His motto is more life is here and now."

Andy bought himself a copy, read it on the way home, found *The Joke* in a second hand shop, bought the other titles and was now re-reading them. Kundera's disillusioned ex-communism meshed with his own disillusion over capitalism. They met in the recognition that ideologies of perfection conceal a death-wish. Whenever Andy heard capitalist apologists spill their loose-tongued, dead-brained version of nirvana – only let so-called *entrepreneurs* make as much money for themselves as possible and everything will be as lovely as a rose-garden in summer because people are greedy by nature and giving free rein to greed is therefore the primrose path to social harmony – he knew he was listening to someone who had given up on life, someone for whom the corpse of money was more important than living human relations.

Tories were the true utopians. They genuinely believed what everyday experience showed to be false: that people's needs could be looked after by organising society around the unenlightened pursuit of lucre. It was as obvious as the sun that an ideological *parti pris* in favour of money and those who possess it must lead to the needs of millions being neglected. It was as undeniable as death that work was the source of all economic value and that for people to work themselves half to death to make other rich was madness.

Yet the communists had responded with their own insanity: only let the State own and run everything and, hey presto, as capitalism was no more, the result must be justice, equality and freedom. In fact it was entrenched injustice, indoctrination and misery.

The same was true of the State-capitalism passing as communism Kundera spiked, as of the capitalism of America and Europe. It was the doctrine of men in dark suits with black-and-white minds, men who had no joy in life but merely a graveyard love of power and hypocritical wealth.

What was wrong in Kundera's Czechoslovakia was what was wrong in Britain: people lacked the freedom to make choices over their own lives. Their dissatisfaction was displaced to a pursuit of money and things. People fought for wage increases as a substitute for happy control over their own actions; and the workplace was the forge where the handcuffs were made.

He set the book aside with a yawn after half an hour. He was half way through the chapter called *Le Poète Se Masturbe*. It was funny but disturbing. He thought of the dark-haired girl. How could he approach her? Recently, Matt Ross had been in touch. His marriage was failing. He wanted to meet up. Stu Archer was happily married but with no children yet. Blackie was married and had a son. He'd heard too that Wheels had married a girl he'd met in the bank and was happy as a fish in water. He was worried for Matt and puzzled about himself, yet beyond that was the sense, long fermenting, that something was breaking down which made the idea of a simple, happy liaison almost impossible. He was unaware of the subtle influences which had helped form his mind and didn't know that like the Jaromil of Kundera's satire his idealism in the arena of romantic love, like that of his politics, was wrapped in a naivety which undermined its effectiveness.

He turned off the fire and as the heat receded and he went into the cold hallway and up the stairs, the chill seemed a metaphor for the absence of love. His mother was not far from sixty. For nearly twenty years she'd lived without the comfort of someone to share her bed, to sit opposite her in the evening and talk about nothing, to go to the pictures with and watch something of no significance just for the sake of being together. In the bathroom he inspected his still virulent acne, swilled his face with hot water and dabbed it with a clean towel. How much longer?

Before going back to Hull he met Matt in *The Fox and Grapes*.

"It's falling apart," he said, "it's all falling apart around me, Andy."

He was distressed to see his old friend so troubled. What could he say?

"You'll come through it, Matt. Believe me, you will. It's bad now because you're in the middle of it, but you'll be okay. You're still young. You're a nice bloke. You'll find someone else."

"I can't understand it," he said. "She never said anything was wrong."

"No it's often like that, isn't it, Matt?"

He couldn't tell him, of course, that he'd thought from the outset Linda was more interested in his money than him. There was an artificial sense about her, as if she were always acting, as if she had to put on a show. Matt was a young man from one of the richest families in the town. His money had never bothered Andy. They got on well, never argued and the atmosphere between them was always buoyant and carefree; but he knew Linda was impressed by the *Triumph Vitesse*, the big house, the connections to money and its inevitable overtones of power. Perhaps he should have told him. He was his best friend and had been since they were seventeen. Maybe in those months before the marriage when Andy found her behaviour inauthentic and ulterior he should have said something. Could he have saved Matt this agony?

Someone put *Mull of Kintyre* on the jukebox.

"Oh, I love this," said Matt.

Andy understood how his fraught emotional condition would make the song attractive. He thought it feeble, dirge-like, cheap and sentimental. His teenage enthusiasm for *The Beatles* had soured into a disdain for their musical predictability, lyrical insincerity and pursuit of money. Pop stars, he now felt, were little more than capitalists with guitars.

"Thanks for meeting me, Andy," said Matt as they shook hands outside. "It means a lot."

"That's all right, Matt. Anytime. Anytime."

Week by week Andy's intellectual battle with Frank became more intense. The supervisor was determined to stamp his hallmark on the student's thesis, the student to follow his own path, free of the weighty and hampering luggage of structuralism. Andy felt bad in a way about taking Frank on. He would have liked to be able to agree with him, for the relations between them to be as sweet as an April morning. Yet, once again, where he'd hoped for ease and harmony, there was conflict, discord and struggle. It made him think of Andrew Steiner and the thorn of his disappointment in having to switch from English to French in order to protect himself. Now, here he was again, having embarked on what he thought would be a fulfilling and happy project, under water and fighting for breath.

Personally, he and Frank strolled along fine, but the skirmishes were getting him down. After each Friday supervision, he went away, his head buzzing, read a bit more of the nauseating, bet-you-can't-find-your-way-through-this-jargon theory and bashed out the following week's supervision paper on his rattling portable. By Monday morning it was done. He spent the week reading what he felt like, not thinking about Flaubert or deconstructionism. He worked steadily through the library's collected Freud; read John Berger's oeuvre; got to know Hermann Hesse and Heinrich Böll, whose sensibility appealed to him; feasted on Gunter Grass's novels and began to feel as out of place in Hull as a cow on a beach.

The dark girl smiled but was self-contained and never stopped to chat. Did she have a boyfriend? There was no evidence. He saw her almost every day. She would sit at a table in the open area before the library's shelves so that coming through the door after trotting up the stairs, he would see her with the big dictionary in front of her, digging at a translation or essay. He decided, as the chair was free, to sit opposite. She looked up and a smile as small and fleeting as a passing gnat appeared and faded. She kept her eyes lowered for the next hour as he read more tosh about the death of the author, as if books wrote themselves, as if the brain were nothing more than a vacuous conduit, as if mental volition an impossibility.

When she put away her pen, closed the dictionary and made her papers neat, he anticipated an opportunity; but she pulled on her green coat and went to the lift without a glance. Should he follow her? Would it be too outrageous to ask if he could buy her a coffee?

He sat for a minute then scribbled on his pad: *Shouldn't we Prestonians stick together? I'm at 22 Hallgate, 01482 235765. Andy Lang* tore it out, folded it and left it on top of her file. The result was she didn't smile or acknowledge him anymore. Had he made himself appear a freak, a pervert, the kind of dirty-mac bloke who follows young girls off the bus? Would she have responded positively if he'd simply leaned across the desk and said: "Excuse me, fancy a coffee?"

He signed up with the hiking club and went out for good walks across the moors on a few Sundays. Among the group was Judith Asquith, a tall, stately, handsome girl of twenty who he caught staring at him with that hard gaze of fascinated interest. She was also often in the library. He was slouching in an armchair with *Dog Years* when he looked up and saw her with her pen in her mouth, fixing him. He smiled, closed the book, got up and went to the table:

"I'm just going for a coffee. Fancy one?"

"No, thanks."

In May, the cold wind still whipping in from the East, came the dreadful general election. The day after, he went for a long, solitary walk from Cottingham into the city and along its streets. Thatcher spelled the death of hope. It was clear unemployment would rise, the public sector and the unions become the enemy. He expected she would engineer a showdown with workers, probably in the public sector and use the full force of the State against them. Her adulation of Churchill made him fear conflict. His grandad had always dismissed the putative great leader as a war-monger. It seemed obvious Thatcher was bidding for the same kind of saviour-of-the-nation status. Nothing could be more dangerous, especially in tandem with the rise of Ronald Reagan in America. He might win in 1981 and such a boost to the Right would be a disaster for equality and the idea of the democratic workplace. The one shaft of light, he felt, was that her policies were so out-of-touch she would become quickly unpopular. Promising people tax cuts and decent public services was candy-floss politics. She could be a one term Prime Minister and if the left could get someone less conservative than Callaghan in the leadership, a short period of bad Tory government might bury them for a long time.

He blamed Callaghan for the disaster. The Tories had the *Labour isn't working* posters showing the long dole queues on billboards from Durham to Dagenham in the autumn. Callaghan was an old man clinging to power. Half-dead back benchers were being stretchered into the Commons to give the kiss of life to his administration. It was demeaning. He should have had the courage to call an election. He should have said he couldn't govern without a majority and he should have offered a radical manifesto. Instead he had capitulated to the bankers, the *investors*, the *markets*: to the greedy masters of a corrupt system. His appearance on the television had appalled Andy. It was nothing less than a declaration that he liked being in power, enjoyed being important and that the country should serve him. Andy was convinced if he'd called an election in late 1978, Thatcher would have been denied a majority. It was rank cowardice and Sunny Jim would now retire to his Sussex farm with a million or two in the bank while people who had voted for him would be spit-roasted by the throwback policies of the neurotic daughter of a repressed greengrocer from Grantham.

That her father had been a Liberal who swung right because he felt the creed too collectivist: that his daughter bore a grudge against Labour for having defeated him as she did against the miners for their humiliation of Heath, pointed to a personalised politics of bitterness and revenge. Andy had seen her on television declaring in her poshed-up, artificial articulation "Don't cut down the tall poppies." He knew what that meant: trample on the daisies, let the cynical flourish and punish the altruistic. Thatcher was one of those people whose inner conflict was revealed in every move, every facial expression, every comment and intonation: she was fighting, second by second, those tender, generous impulses her ideology told her were a form of weakness. Their suppression returned them in the form of sentimentalism and preening narcissism. Thatcher's was a neurotic politics, one in which an outward pretence of control, superiority and objectivity concealed a regressive, vindictive, vicious and destructive unacknowledged motivation.

By the end of the third term, his nerves were shredded. When he came back in October, would he still have to battle against Frank? Surely he'd done enough in nearly thirty supervision papers to demonstrate he was too at odds with structuralism to make it the basis of his thesis. An idea came to him when he was in Lancaster working for *ANI* again. He wrote to Frank saying he needed to spend some time in Rouen to see the manuscript of *Madame Bovary*. Frank rang him: was there really any need to consult the original? Andy put his case that the deletions might have much to tell him. Frank agreed to think it over and eleven days later the letter of introduction to the director of the *Bibliothèque Municipale* arrived together with a note about what Andy had to provide for the university authorities.

When Bert found out his son was going to France for a term, it sent a shock of loneliness and fear through him. What if his condition was to worsen? Andy was the only relative he had. His neighbours were good, especially Dereck and Betty who kept an eye on him as if he were one of their own. Yet he knew, if he became housebound, if he needed someone who would attend closely to him, there was no one but Andy. Also, there was the chance he might die while he was in France. Over the past weeks, the idea had infiltrated more and more: this condition wasn't going to improve. The doctors were baffled. The pain was worse than ever. He was losing weight. His cheeks were sinking and he had to make another hole in his belt. Death couldn't be far away. His life now presented itself to his consciousness as a little package of misery. The best was his children, but his marriage to Elsie, he saw clearly now, had been stillborn. What would he do if he declined fast and Andy wasn't near?

Elsie was puzzled. Why did he need to go all the way to France just to look at a manuscript.

"Well," he explained as he ate the scone she'd brought with his tea, "it's the original. I'll be able to see just what Flaubert crossed out, just what he altered. I'll be able to discuss those changes in my thesis."

"Is it that important?"

"In a way. If you think literature is important."

What really sparked Elsie's anxiety was the thought that this was another postponement. She couldn't shift from her mind the notion that her son had followed one of life's by-ways. The true path was a job, marriage and children. Her Methodism encouraged a belief in the one true way. Not that she fell into prejudice. She was offended when she heard people insult *queers*; but tolerance towards strangers was easier than acceptance of what she found odd in her own family. Her son was twenty-eight and still came to inhabit his little bedroom during holidays. There was no girlfriend. Would he ever be independent?

Andy turned up in Rouen with a holdall and four hundred quid. He expected to spend a few nights in a hotel until he found *une chambre meublée* but when he called in a little café on the *rue de la République* for *un grand crème* and asked the *patronne* if there was an estate agents nearby, she speculated he was looking for a room, told him her mother-in-law had one for rent, picked up the phone and half an hour later he was inspecting the big bedroom in the nonagenarian's house in the *rue de la Glacière*.

"Je n'ai pas peur," the old lady kept saying. "J'ai le jeune ouvrier qui occupe la chambre à côté. Sa petite est souvent là. Mais je n'ai pas peur."

"Bien sûr que non," said Andy handing over two hundred francs for the rent, "il n'y a rien à craindre."

The ground floor, which Mme Dupin occupied, stank badly of urine. Andy quickly discovered he was sharing his room with a family of mice who appeared in the middle of the night to eat the crumbs from his *baguettes* and the bits of *gruyere* left on his plate. He tried jamming the holes in the skirting boards with thick twists of newspaper, but it did no good. Then one morning he spotted a cat prowling the enclosed courtyard, bought some cream, tempted it to climb the sloping roof and leap onto his window ledge, stroked it, grabbed it, shut the window and kept it till the mice came no more.

The young engineer who was the tenant of the neighbouring room had his girlfriend living there. She looked fourteen or fifteen and seemed to spend most of the day listening to music. Andy shared a bathroom with them and once or twice he crossed her on the gloomy, dank landing wearing nothing but a t-shirt which barely concealed her essentials and she would become coy and enticing. Sometimes the lad came home at lunchtime and the ecstatic cries of the girl in the midst of her climax sent Andy out to walk the old town. Their love-making was at least daily. Andy wondered if Mme Dupin was hard of hearing. If not her evenings in the kitchen in front of her little television must have been seriously interrupted.

He made his first visit to the Bibliothèque the day after his arrival. The director was a thin, pale man with a fixed, slightly smirking smile, dressed in a black suit, white shirt and dark tie, as if he'd just come from a funeral. He questioned Andy about his research before taking him to a large, unoccupied desk on the first floor, bringing the heavy *brouillons* in gloved hands, setting them down as if their weight might send the table crashing through the floor, and standing at Andy's shoulder as he began to look though them.

Andy turned the pages with preternatural delicacy, made notes on his pad and at one point when, with his pen in his hand, he ran his middle finger under a line of Flaubert's scruffy script, the director pounced, grabbed his arm, pulled it away and ordered in horror that on no account must he write on the pages. Andy looked into his face which was tensed into frowning anger. He explained he had no intention of making any mark: his pen was well away from the page; he was merely running his finger along the better to read.

On his second visit, the man stood at his shoulder for two hours. On his third, for three. Andy began to feel he was under suspicion and the close supervision was an intended insult. He decided to stay away for a while, sat at his portable in the mornings and hammered out what he wanted to write about the master of French prose; and then began a happy routine: breakfast in a nearby café, writing in the morning, strolling the old town in the afternoon like a latter-day water-drinking, *flaneur* who occupied the tiny, chilly mansard in some crumbling six storey town house; eating in the *Café de la Poste* or some other not-too-expensive place in the early evening, sitting with a single cup to watch the world go by for a couple of hours, maybe another little *promenade digestive* before walking back and inevitably encountering the prostitutes who hung around in doorways and on corners and threw a casual *ça t'intéresse* ? as he passed, and a bit of reading to bring the day to a close.

He made the odd trip to the cinema, bought a copy of *L'Humanité* or *Libération* every day, was going to get a ticket for the theatre but found it too expensive. His four hundred quid was diminishing like soap. He was frugal. He ate bread and cheese at lunchtime, bought no alcohol, chose the cheapest items on the menus; but he wasn't going to make it to Christmas.

His isolation was broken only by contact with the family of a lad he'd met while teaching for *ANI*. His parents owned a four-bedroom flat on the *rue Jean Lacanuet*, one of those huge, expensively appointed places in the heart of the city which afford luxury within five minutes of the advantages of the commercial centre. His father worked in finance, his brother had just begun his military service and Patrice was studying law in Paris but came home every weekend. His mother invited Andy for Sunday lunch: six or seven courses in their dining-room, a chandelier dangling over the expansive polished table. One weekend, they took him to their house in the country near Lillebonne: a five-bedroom *pavillon* in an acre of garden and orchard and because he was working on their home town's great novelist, they insisted on driving him to Ry and introducing him to the curé who, according to Patrice's father was *plus câlé en Flaubert qu'en religion.*

He was very grateful for their kindness, which was extraordinary. Patrice's mother, concerned to hear he was living in a room in an old lady's house where there had been mice and where he had no access to a kitchen and not even a bidet, offered to take him in: they had a spare bedroom, he would be more comfortable, closer to the city centre and she would feed him a proper lunch and dinner. Andy was stunned by her generosity but he couldn't have imposed on them without handing over any money and knew they wouldn't take any. Not that they couldn't have afforded to accommodate him. They were obviously wealthy; but that wasn't the point. Freeloading was demeaning. He thanked Mme de Rôme graciously but assured her he was quite comfortable and that the sound of his typewriter would disturb the peace of her apartment.

His weeks were lonely but it didn't trouble him. He'd found a congenial rhythm to his days and could have gone on in the same way for years. It was true, he missed a good friend like Mike or Rob, but the thought of the latter filled him with regret. He wished he'd turned down Sue's offer. What had it got him? Oh, she was beautiful and to see her white, sleek body set off by her full dark curls and the thick, black triangle at the bottom of her belly almost made him gasp; she was warm and accepting and making love to her was a delight; but they hadn't found that ground of shared feeling which raises the physical act to a level of emotional commitment. They'd conjoined a few dozen times and now there was no contact between them, and for that he had ruined a good friendship. He was to blame. He was older than Sue and in any case, if as she claimed her relationship with Rob was coming to a close, there was no need for him to deliver the *coup de grâce*. Had he gently turned her down, he would have risen but by behaving opportunistically he'd stooped.

He toyed with the idea of joining something. There were clubs advertised on posters and postcards. He could sign up for drama or table tennis and get to know a few people; but the ulterior nature of it put him off and it was bound to happen, if he became part of something hoping to meet fellow spirits, there wouldn't be any.

On his walks, he constantly compared Rouen to Preston. The populations were probably comparable but what had Preston to compare to the cathedral, the old town, the market, the cafes and restaurants, the *Maison des Jeunes,* the *Musée des Beaux Arts* and the historical and artistic inheritance of Jeanne d'Arc, Corneille, Flaubert, Géricault and Duchamp? He strolled the rue de Maupassant one bright afternoon in November. Preston had the cast of Francis Thompson in the Harris Library, but why wasn't there a Francis Thompson street or square? Why no A.J.P. Taylor avenue or house ? Why had Preston produced so few artistic figures of significance? There was a cultural assumption in Britain that northern, industrial places like the one he came from were artistic and intellectual nullities. Was it true, as it seemed to him, that the French took their writers, artists, composers more seriously? Was there anyone in Rouen who didn't know who Corneille and Flaubert were? How many of his fellow Prestonians had even heard of Francis Thompson?

The morning of his departure he had to be up at six. Mme Dupin insisted on making him breakfast: a big bowl of weak coffee in which floated soggy *biscottes*. He ate and drank as she stood by the table so as not to offend. As he bent to her and she kissed him on the cheeks, the penetrating smell of urine filled his nose. He realised she was sorry to see him go.

"Je n'ai pas peur," she said, "j'ai quatre-vingt-trois ans, mais je n'ai pas peur."

Had his presence been a comfort to her? He'd done no more than exchange a few words each day but it dawned on him as he picked up his holdall that at her age, having a young, male tenant who made little noise, was polite and friendly, paid his rent each week and followed a predictable routine might be comforting. The sudden realization of her loneliness made him feel almost guilty about leaving.

"Alors," he said, "je vous enverrai un petit mot quand je serai sain et sauf chez moi."

"Ah bon," she said, "et si un de ces quatre jours vous revenez à Rouen. La chambre sera disponible."

She stood at the door and waved as he walked away to the railway station. He would never see her again, this old, lonely, smelly, near-to-death woman but he was stunned to think that in the short time he'd been there he could have come to mean anything at all to her.

He handed over to Frank the wad of what he'd worked on. In the first supervision, the academic tucked his right leg under his bum, picked up the bundle and said it was clear there was no point going on with the structuralist approach; what he'd written was interesting and thoughtful.

"What's impressive though is the way you took on the big thinkers of structuralism. That's very good for a post-grad."

Andy wanted to laugh. The big thinkers? It seemed to him that some of them couldn't think at all and were obviously playing an academic game to win professorships and invitations to conferences at the other side of the world, with expenses paid by their institutions for standing at a lectern for an hour talking drivel; but he was glad Frank had relented and he could press on and finish his thesis. He had two terms. What he'd written in Rouen probably amounted to fifty thousand words, but it wasn't organised. Could he start from scratch and have the required sixty thousand words done by the summer? What then?

A lectureship became available at Hull and Frank was on the appointment committee. They were looking for a specialist in linguistics. Frank explained the sifting procedure: all those who didn't have a First, a Phd, publications and experience of teaching at degree level went in the bin. There were a hundred applicants. They interviewed four. Andy began to feel gloomy about his prospects of finding a post.

"Well," said Frank, "we could get you a Chair."

"What?"

"Colin Pomeroy knows everyone. He can pull a few strings and get you in."

Pomeroy was the Cambridge big-name who was Andy's external supervisor, an expert in nineteenth century fiction who had written the seminal study of realism and naturalism.

"But you don't have a Chair," said Andy.

"No, but I will. I can ring Colin and see what he can do, but I'm sure he'll be able to swing it. You may have to go to Cambridge for a chat."

Both Frank and Pomeroy were products of public school and Oxbridge. Frank had been educated at Manchester Grammar before his parents moved to Cornwall for the blue skies and he to Oxford. The hole-and-corner business of buttering up influential folk from the same background to secure easy passage to position was as natural to them as sabbaticals and marking finals. To Andy it seemed no better than house-breaking.

"Shouldn't these things be advertised ?" he said.

"Oh, don't worry about that," said Frank. "It's common practice. I'll tell Colin you're a bright, young prospect who's doing great work on Flaubert and you'll be home and dry."

Andy ran it through his head again and again: he was being offered a professorship for having done no more than bash out some supervision papers spiking the structuralists and cobbling together a a hundred pages about imagery in *Madame Bovary*. It was an extraordinary opportunity but it terrified him: if he took it, he would be forever looking over his shoulder; he would never feel he had won the post honestly and whatever he did in the future, that knowledge would gnaw at him and consume his self-respect.

"No," he said to Frank, "I can't accept a Chair in the way you suggest. I think there should be a proper application and interviews and everyone should get a fair shot at the bulls-eye."

Frank pushed his bottom lip up in a clown's expression which said "maybe you're right, but it's a pity".

"In that case," he said, "what about coming back to do a Phd next year. We could give you some undergraduate teaching. Or if you like, you could go to Perpignan for a year as our *lecteur*."

"Really."

The latter possibility appealed. He knew that if he went, he would never come back. After a year by the Mediterranean it would be impossible to live in Preston again. He'd see little of his family. Mary's kids would hardly know him; but it was a great chance and he decided to tell Frank he'd take it. That evening he was called to the phone in the hallway of the airy student house. It was his dad. He was to go into hospital again the next day. They were going to try abdominal surgery. He had a bit of good news though: one of his Satsangi mates was friendly with a woman who taught maths at Hutton Grammar. They'd appointed a French teacher who'd given backword. If he wanted a job for September, it was a ripe apple.

He took the train home the next day, went to see his dad before his surgery. He was grey, weak and fretful.

"Don't worry, it'll be okay. You'll be on your feet in few days."

The doctor he collared shook his head. They didn't know what they were looking for, but the outcome didn't bode well. Andy rang Frank and told him he was staying until things had resolved themselves. He rang the Headmaster at Hutton Grammar too. John Wellington had been there during Stu Archer's time and was retiring at the end of term.

"Can you get here tomorrow?" he asked in his croaky, clipped, high-handed voice.

"Yes, I can do that."

It was odd to think he was going to be interviewed by the Headmaster his teenage mates had mocked. Wellington's wife was called Phyllis and the common joke was to imitate Wellington's gruff, pretentious delivery in saying: "Anyone here see Phyllis?"

He turned up at ten, was asked to fill in an application form by the plump, bustling bursar and as he sat at the table in what she called the committee room, lifted his eyes to the painting of a dim-witted rural scene, a nit-wit's sentimental imitation of *The Hay Wain*. He put down his pen. Did he really want to take a job here, in the place where Fatkegs had preyed on first years, prefects used to have the right to beat younger boys, football was viewed a sport for ruffians and snobbery was as redolent as the smell of cabbage in the dining-hall? He didn't. He wanted to go to Perpignan but he couldn't leave his dad. He was sick, depleted and afraid. He was his son after all. It was his duty to stay. He completed the form.

Wellington came to collect him. He was a stocky man whose demeanour suggested impending violence. On his face was an expression made up of suspicion, disdain and disgust. Andy stood and faced him. He was begging no one for a job. He wasn't going to be intimidated by a time-serving Headmaster who was used to exacting absolute obedience from his pupils and staff. Facing him a memory sprang into his head: Alan Madison telling him that Wellington had interviewed him in the fifth year, just before O Levels, as he did all the boys to discuss their prospects, and had suggested he should join the Marines. Madison's dad, outraged, had made an appointment and expressed his dislike of his son being pointed in the direction of the armed forces. He was doing well and should try for university.

"What makes you want to work here, Mr Lang?" he said when they were seated in his study.

Andy was perfectly aware the man could see through the opportunism of his application, but he wasn't going to say: "I don't, but my father is on the verge of death and I just need a way to earn a bit of money for a while until things are finished and I can move on."

"It's a good school," he said brusquely. "Some of my best friends came here. It has a good reputation."

"Yes, and you didn't come here. You missed out on the 11-plus, eh?"

Andy wondered if he was about to say something demeaning and was ready to get up and leave.

"That's right."

"All the same, you've done well. Are you sure you wouldn't be better off teaching in a university?"

"I don't think so," Andy lied. "I've enjoyed doing the post-grad work but I've been in universities long enough."

"Well, Mr Lang," said the man whose face wore the same ugly expression he'd greeted Andy with, "I don't have anybody else in mind."

Andy almost laughed out loud. He wanted to say: "I'm not taking the job on sufferance. If you don't want me, say so. I can get work elsewhere perfectly easily."

He didn't reply.

He was appointed.

At home he lay on his bed wondering what he'd done. He was filled with dread and an overwhelming desire to flee. He comforted himself with the thought it would be for a short time. A year at the most. He would ask Frank if the job in Perpignan would still be available the following October. He had to be here for his dad. There was no escaping that. If he left him to die alone, the guilt would haunt him all his life.

He jumped up, yanked off the strangling tie, put the you-must-dress-like-a-pillock jacket and trousers in the wardrobe, pulled on his jeans and shirt and headed to town. Maybe he'd run into someone. He would need company over the coming months or he'd go mad. The thought brought his mind to his mother. His dad was dying and his mother was on her own. Sylvia had married Barry and was living in Leyland. There would be just the pair of them in the house. He took the stairs two at a time, locked the glass door behind him and ran full pelt to the end of Woodland Grove to feel his legs and lungs, to grasp at something that felt like life in what for the moment appeared close to a living death.

END OF VOLUME SEVEN.